DANGEROUS DESIRE

His lean face was perfectly carved with a wide brow and narrow nose. His cheekbones were angular, hinting at his Slavic origins, and his jaw surprisingly stubborn with just a shadow of stubble from his heavy beard.

He wasn't by any stretch of the imagination "pretty." His features were too hard, too ruthless, for that. But there was something compellingly beautiful about his sheer maleness, and when he offered one of his rare smiles . . . well, there wasn't a female on campus who didn't do a little melting.

He was dark and broody and delectable.

And if she'd caught sight of a menacing glint in the piercing blue eyes that spoke of hidden power and predatory danger, well, she'd convinced herself that it only made him more exciting. . . .

D0150662

Books by Alexandra Ivy

Guardians of Eternity
WHEN DARKNESS COMES
EMBRACE THE DARKNESS
DARKNESS EVERLASTING
DARKNESS REVEALED
DARKNESS UNLEASHED
BEYOND THE DARKNESS
DEVOURED BY DARKNESS
BOUND BY DARKNESS
FEAR THE DARKNESS
DARKNESS AVENGED

Immortal Rogues
MY LORD VAMPIRE
MY LORD ETERNITY
MY LORD IMMORTALITY

Books by Hannah Jayne

UNDER WRAPS
UNDER ATTACK
UNDER SUSPICION
UNDER THE GUN
UNDER A SPELL

Books by Dianne Duvall

DARKNESS DAWNS
NIGHT REIGNS
PHANTOM SHADOWS

Published by Kensington Publishing Corporation

Predatory

ALEXANDRA IVY
NINA BANGS
DIANNE DUVALL
HANNAH JAYNE

ZEBRA BOOKS
KENSINGTON PUBLISHING CORP.

http://www.kensingtonbooks.com

ZEBRA BOOKS are published by

Kensington Publishing Corp.
119 West 40th Street
New York, NY 10018

All Kensington titles, imprints and distributed lines are available at special quantity discounts for bulk purchases for sales promotion, premiums, fund-raising, educational or institutional use.

Special book excerpts or customized printings can also be created to fit specific needs. For details, write or phone the office of the Kensington Special Sales Manager: Kensington Publishing Corp., 119 West 40th Street, New York, NY 10018. Attn. Special Sales Department. Phone: 1-800-221-2647.

Zebra and the Z logo Reg. U.S. Pat. & TM Off.

ISBN-13: 978-1-4201-2512-2
ISBN-10: 1-4201-2512-5

First Printing: May 2013

eISBN-13: 978-1-4201-3095-9
eISBN-10: 1-4201-3095-1

First Electronic Edition: May 2013

10 9 8 7 6 5 4 3 2 1

Printed in the United States of America

Contents

Out of Control

Alexandra Ivy

Prologue

Valhalla was the stuff of myths.

Named for the home of the Norse gods, the sprawling compound was a safe house for those people too "special" to be mainstreamed into society (a nice way of saying an orphanage for the children and adults unwanted by their families). Everyone knew that it was a home for freaks.

Witches, psychics, necromancers, Sentinels, and God only knew what else roamed the grounds protected by a layer of powerful spells. It was a source of fear and fascination for the entire world, but most especially for the citizens of the small, Midwest town who could catch the shimmer of blue reflecting off the protective dome that hid the house from view. And even glimpse the rare sight of the freaks entering and leaving the compound, although people were smart enough to spy on them from a distance.

There were, of course, citizens who called for the entire place to be nuked.

The freaks were dangerous, with powers that none of them truly understood. Who knew what the monsters would do if someone pissed them off?

There were others who said they should be locked away

and studied like lab rats. Perhaps their mutations could be used to help normal people.

Most, however, preferred to ignore Valhalla and the high-bloods—as they preferred to be called—living behind the dome.

Until, of course, they needed them.

Chapter One

The nightclub near the University of Missouri wasn't anything to brag about. Hell, it wasn't much more than a leaking roof held up by four walls and a prayer. In the center was a cramped dance floor surrounded by tables and at the back a long bar ran the length of the wall. Up the narrow staircase you could find pool tables and a few old-time pinball machines, while in the back parking lot the dealers strolled from car to car, searching for shoppers interested in less legal means of intoxication.

A typical college hangout.

Seated in a booth nearly obscured by shadows, Angela Locke watched the crowd of college students bump and grind to a heavy beat that was making her eye twitch.

Not that she wasn't enjoying herself, she sternly chided herself. She might be a few years older than most of the kids in the club, but that didn't mean she was a complete party pooper. Right?

On cue she winced as two girls shrieked with laughter at a nearby table, the aggravating sound some sort of homing signal to the guys who eagerly crowded around their table.

Okay, this wasn't really her scene.

She'd spent the majority of her twenty-six years in musty

libraries or high-tech labs, which meant she was more comfortable with petri dishes and microscopes than the opposite sex.

Her dark thoughts were interrupted as she belatedly realized she was no longer alone.

Glancing up, she met Megan Wagner's exasperated frown. The pretty, pleasantly rounded blonde was one of Angela's few friends at the university. In the process of recovering from a disastrous marriage, the older woman was taking classes to earn her teaching degree.

"Oh, for God's sake," Megan complained. "I didn't bring you here to hide in the corner."

Angela wrinkled her nose. "I'd rather hide in corners than park myself in the spotlight where everyone can see me sitting alone."

Megan folded her arms under her ample bosom, her lush curves displayed in a tight red dress and her blonde curls allowed to fall freely over her shoulders.

"You wouldn't be alone if you didn't put out vibes that you're—"

"A geek? A nerd? A first-class egghead?" Angela offered wryly.

"Unavailable."

"Are you kidding?" Angela shot a glance down at her jade stretchy top that was scooped low enough to reveal the soft curve of her breasts and the too-tight jeans that threatened her circulation. "In this outfit I not only look available, I look like I charge by the hour."

"It's not your clothes. It's your attitude."

Angela blinked. Attitude? She didn't know she had an attitude.

"What do you want me to do?"

Megan placed her hands flat on the table, eying Angela with the same stern expression she used on her students at the local preschool.

"Pay attention to the men who are here, not the one who isn't."

Angela tried to squelch the renegade blush that stole beneath her cheeks.

"I don't know what you mean."

"I mean that it's all fine and dandy to moon over Professor Hottie, but what's it gotten you?" A blonde brow arched. "Unless there's something you're not telling me?"

Angela ducked her head, allowing her finger to trace the beads of moisture that trickled down her untouched drink.

Professor Hottie.

Or, better known as Dr. Nikolo Bartrev.

He'd arrived at the university six weeks before. A tall, dark stranger who'd been invited by the president to review their science curriculum. Angela didn't know precisely what his work entailed, but she did know that one glance into those pale blue eyes and she'd been lost.

Head over heels in lust for the first time in her life.

A damned shame he didn't return her aching need.

"There's nothing to tell," she muttered.

"And that's the point," Megan pressed. "He stops by your lab once a day—"

"Sometimes it's twice."

Megan snorted. "He makes a little chitchat and disappears."

Angela hunched a shoulder. It was true enough.

The first time Dr. Bartrev had strolled into her lab she'd nearly had a heart attack. She'd just finished teaching a freshman biology class and he'd waited for the giggling girls to drag themselves past him before he slowly approached her desk.

She hadn't known what to expect, but after a few minutes of questioning her about her research, he'd turned and left.

Just like that.

Since that day, he'd made a habit of stopping by when she

was in the lab, sometimes discussing her research and other times just randomly discussing her day.

She assumed that he was cleverly extracting information from her to use in his assessment, but she didn't have a clue what he was searching for.

And she didn't care.

His fleeting visits were enough to make her giddy for the rest of the day.

"So?" she muttered.

"Has he ever revealed anything remotely personal about himself?"

Angela grimaced. After six weeks she didn't know a damned thing about the man.

Well, she knew the precise scent of his warm male cologne. And the way his cashmere sweaters stretched over a wide chest and how his pants clung to his tight ass.

But anything about the man beneath the gorgeous exterior? Nothing. *Nada*. *Niente*.

"No."

"Has he ever asked you out, even to lunch?"

"No."

"Has he ever brought you anything? Flowers, candy, a bagel from the cafeteria?"

"No."

"Has he tried to get his hand down your shirt?"

"No."

Megan heaved a sigh. "Honey, that man ain't interested, no matter how much you might want him to be."

Angela lifted her head to meet her friend's sympathetic gaze. "I know."

The blonde grabbed the plastic sword that held a candied cherry from Angela's glass.

"Then drink your gin fizz and give that nice stud muffin by the door a big smile." She pointed the sword toward the delectable blond Neanderthal standing across the dance floor. "And remember—"

"Remember what?"

"You're beautiful."

Angela rolled her eyes. She had a mirror. She might not be the Bride of Frankenstein, but she was a long way from beautiful.

Average brown hair she kept in a ponytail. Average height with average curves. Average features that were pale from the hours she spent in the lab.

The only thing remarkable was the wide brown eyes that were heavily framed with dark lashes, but most of the time they were hidden behind her protective lab glasses.

In summation she was . . . average.

"It's going to take more than one gin fizz to make me believe in fairy tales," she retorted.

"Maybe a kiss will wake you, Sleeping Beauty." Megan waggled her brows. "She was, after all, the first true wall-flower."

Angela gave a choked laugh. Her friend charged through life at full throttle.

"I wish I could be like you, Megan," she said wistfully, thinking of all the nights she sat in her cramped apartment alone.

Always alone.

"Yeah, right," Megan scoffed. "You're a genius who's only weeks away from receiving your PhD in molecular biology and I'm trying to struggle through my undergraduate degree."

Angela shook her head. Because of finances Megan was forced to take night classes while she worked full-time, but there was no doubt her love for children would allow her to achieve her goals.

"You know you're a fabulous teacher, not to mention . . ."

Angela's comforting words dissolved into a silent shock as her heart slammed against her ribs.

Oh hell.

"Hey, that was just getting good," Megan grumbled. Then, noticing that Angela's attention had strayed, she frowned in confusion. "What's wrong? Did Professor Lewis get drunk again and take off his pants?"

Angela reached for her glass to take a deep drink of the gin fizz.

"He's here."

"Who?"

"Niko." She grimaced as the overly sweet drink hit her empty stomach. "I mean, Professor—"

"Hottie?"

"Yep."

Helplessly she watched his determined approach.

Oh . . . crap, but he was gorgeous. From the tip of his glossy dark hair that was threaded with hints of autumn fire and tousled as if he'd just run his hands through the short strands, to the tips of his Italian shoes.

His lean face was perfectly carved with a wide brow and narrow nose. His cheekbones were angular, hinting at his Slavic origins, and his jaw surprisingly stubborn with just a shadow of stubble from his heavy beard.

He wasn't by any stretch of the imagination "pretty." His features were too hard, too ruthless, for that. But there was something compellingly beautiful about his sheer maleness, and when he offered one of his rare smiles . . . well, there wasn't a female on campus who didn't do a little melting.

He was dark and broody and delectable. The sort of man who haunted the fantasies of every repressed virgin.

And if she'd caught sight of a menacing glint in the piercing blue eyes that spoke of hidden power and predatory danger, well, she'd convinced herself that it only made him more exciting.

"Okay, I have to admit he is lickable," Megan grudgingly conceded, glancing over her shoulder. "Like a double-fudge ice cream cone."

"Megan," Angela protested, although she couldn't deny the desire to tug off his blue sweater and gray Chinos to do a bit of tongue therapy.

Megan turned back to stab her with a warning gaze. "He's also gay or married."

Angela's eyes widened. "How do you know?"

"Because he hasn't tried to get you in bed." Megan leaned toward her. "Don't let him ruin your night."

With a tug on Angela's hair, that was for once left to brush her shoulders, Megan was disappearing toward the bar, leaving Angela alone to face the man now towering beside her table.

"Hello, Angela," he greeted, his voice a dark velvet rasp that sent renegade shivers of excitement down her spine.

Oh . . . crap.

She licked her dry lips, trying to squash the embarrassing thrills of excitement.

"Dr. Bartrev," she breathed, her voice barely audible over the music blasting from the overhead speakers.

With a fluid ease, he perched on the edge of the table, his hard thigh brushing her arm.

"I thought we agreed to Niko?"

Yeah. She was so not going down that road.

He was Niko in her fantasies. In real life . . . well, she needed to avoid making an idiot of herself.

"I didn't expect to see you here," she said instead.

"I could say the same." His brooding gaze shifted to the surrounding crowd that was amping up the loud factor with every round of tequila. "This isn't your usual style."

She shrugged. "Megan convinced me this was my last chance to get out and party before everyone leaves for spring break."

"Ah." The piercing blue eyes returned to study her up-turned face. Angela shivered beneath the sheer intensity of that gaze. He had an uncanny habit of appearing completely focused on whatever he was doing. "A girls' night out."

"Something like that." She managed a smile. *Play it cool, Angela. It's not attractive to drool all over the handsome professor.* "What are you doing here?"

"Actually, I was concerned."

She stiffened. "Concerned?"

"Yes."

"Why?" She sucked in a sharp breath, suddenly struck by a terrifying thought. "Is there something wrong with my research?"

"Your work is flawless. As always," he swiftly eased her fear, a strange edge in his voice although she was too relieved to notice. "It's something we'll discuss later."

"Then what is it?"

He hesitated, almost as if considering his words.

"I heard rumors there was a stalker in the area."

"A stalker?" She blinked in surprise. The small Midwest town had its share of petty crime, but violence was extremely rare. "In town or on campus?"

"The person has been seen on campus as well as in the sur-rounding neighborhoods."

"I haven't heard anything. Have the police been notified?"

"Of course." His gaze swept down to her breasts that were on blatant display, and just for a moment she thought she might have seen a flicker of heat in the icy depths. Then, clearly unimpressed, he returned his interest to her flushed face. "You haven't noticed anything unusual, have you?"

She shook her head, telling herself she didn't give a damn. "Not that I can think of."

"There haven't been any strangers lurking around?"

Her lips twisted in a humorless smile. "Most people will tell you that I'm not the most observant person," she said, recalling her mother's resigned complaint that Angela could recite the periodic table when she was barely five, but didn't know the name of one classmate. She hastily squashed the age-old pain before it could fully form. Her mother's death last year meant that the older woman could no longer be disappointed in her only child. "Outside the lab I tend to be distracted."

"What about when you're home?" he demanded. "Have you seen anyone new in the neighborhood?"

"No." She frowned. "Shouldn't the police be asking these questions?"

His smile didn't reach his eyes. "They didn't want to spook the students so I agreed to do a bit of discreet investigating for them."

"Oh." It seemed weird to have a visiting professor investigating a potential stalker, but what did she know? "I'm sorry I can't help."

He reached into his pocket to pull out a pen, scribbling on a piece of napkin.

"Here," he murmured, folding the paper before he lightly pressed it into her unresisting fingers.

Angela's heart slammed against her ribs as pleasure exploded through her. Her head might warn her to stop weaving futile fantasies about this man, but her body hadn't received the memo.

His fingers were hot—shockingly hot—against her skin. A branding heat that sent darts of excitement to the pit of her stomach.

And his scent was wrapping around her like a cloak of invitation.

"What is it?" she husked, becoming lost in the astonishing blue of his eyes.

"My phone number."

"Phone number?"

"I want you to call me."

Her heart gave another stuttering leap. "You do?"

"Yes."

"I . . ." She licked her suddenly dry lips. "When?"

"The very minute you notice anything out of the ordinary."

Shit. She came back to earth with a resounding crash.

The stalker. Right.

She lowered her head, determined he wouldn't guess her flare of humiliation.

"Okay."

"If you notice anything," he insisted. "No matter how small."

"Yeah, I got it."

Without warning his hand was cupping her chin, tilting her face up so he could study her with a faint frown.

"You promise?"

There was another jolt of sensation before she was pulling free of his destructive touch and rising to her feet with a stubborn expression.

"Cross my heart and hope to die."

"Angela—"

"I need to find Megan."

Chapter Two

Standing near the railing of the second floor of the nightclub, Nikolo studied the throng of people that moved below him.

College students jerked and hopped around the dance floor while townies and aging professors lined the bar at the back.

Over and over, his gaze skimmed the swarm of norms before returning to the slender brunette who'd moved to a front table with her friend.

He didn't worry about the aggravating scientist catching sight of him. He couldn't actually make himself invisible, but he could . . . convince people not to notice him.

It was a talent of most Sentinels. Along with heightened senses, predatory instincts, and a cunning patience that would allow him to track his prey from one end of the world to other if necessary.

He also had the ability to sense when a high-blood was near.

Of course, the public was far more accustomed to the Sentinels who performed as guardians to high-bloods. Those Sentinels were raised and trained by monks in mysterious arts that were never spoken of outside the monasteries. They were also heavily tattooed to protect them from being controlled by psychics or attacked with spells.

They were lethal beasts, but they were also ridiculously noticeable in a crowd.

Massive killers tattooed from the top of their bald heads to the tips of their toes tended to attract attention.

Which is why the Sentinels also needed hunters who could travel unnoticed.

Hunters like him. Oh, and the man currently standing a few feet away.

Never allowing his gaze to stray from Angela Locke, he gave a tiny motion of his hand. All high-bloods understood you didn't approach a Sentinel when he was locked on his prey.

Bad, bad things could happen.

"Arel," he murmured, recognizing the scent of the fellow Sentinel.

The younger man stepped forward, the flashing strobe lights shimmering over the honey highlights in his light brown hair and turning his eyes to molten gold.

Most humans dismissed Arel as a charming playboy. A role he performed with consummate skill. But those trained to look beneath the surface could detect the muscles honed to lean perfection beneath his casual T-shirt and faded jeans, and the ruthless determination that simmered deep in the gold eyes.

"Dylan?" Arel murmured softly.

Niko grimaced at the mention of the female high-blood they'd been hunting for the past six weeks.

"Still in the wind."

"Are you positive she'll show up here?"

Niko didn't hesitate. "Yes."

"And you're always right?"

"Always."

Arel snorted. "You know you're an arrogant SOB, don't you, Niko?"

Niko shrugged. Yep, he knew. But his confidence wasn't just conceit.

From the second Dylan had murdered her two guards to escape from Valhalla, he'd dedicated every waking moment to studying his prey.

He knew the day and hour Dylan had been born. He knew that she'd been less than a week old when her parents had left her in the field outside Valhalla. He knew that she nursed a bitter fury at having been abandoned by her family despite her welcome among the high-bloods. Perhaps because she was one of the unfortunate freaks that had been born with a mutation that left her with startling crimson eyes and large black spots on her skin, like a cheetah. Unlike many high-bloods she'd been unable to pass as norm, which only increased her resentment.

Or maybe she'd just been born a psychopath.

Being given special powers didn't mean that a person was automatically a superhero.

High-bloods possessed all the usual failings of norms. Only they could do a hell of a lot more damage if they weren't contained.

Which was where Niko and his fellow Sentinels came in.

He shrugged. "I know what she's going to do before she does," he said.

"And you think because she'd been searching through Calder's files on your scientist that she's coming here?"

"Yes."

Niko had been baffled at first when he'd discovered that Dylan had been sneaking into the Master of Gifts' office. Calder and his order were dedicated to tracking down those high-bloods who either didn't realize they were "special" or were trying to pass as normal. Like a Sentinel they possessed the ability to sense talents, even latent talents, although they used their skills to convince high-bloods to join with their brethren at Valhalla, or in one of the many compounds located around the world. While Niko . . . well, his duties weren't quite so nice.

At last he'd put together the reasons for Dylan's late-night visits to Calder's office.

And it had everything to do with Angela Locke.

"Not that I'm questioning your conclusion, amigo," Arel said in dry tones, "but why is she currently on a killing spree through Texas?"

"She's trying to disguise her true purpose and throw us off her trail."

"For six weeks?"

"She's always been patient."

"True." Arel's features hardened, his charming smile replaced by a cold hatred. Both Niko and Arel had reason to want Dylan tracked down and destroyed. The sooner the better. "She must have planned her escape from Valhalla for months."

"Years," he corrected.

"We can't keep cleaning up her kills, Niko." Arel grimaced. "There have been five more. Plus the losses we suffered—"

"I know how many she's killed," Niko interrupted. He couldn't discuss Fiona's bloody murder.

Not yet.

"Then you'll understand that I was sent by the Tagos to warn you that you have until the end of the month," Arel said, referring to the ultimate leader of the Sentinels. "After that he wants you on the trail in Texas."

Niko shrugged, unperturbed by the warning. "Dylan will be here before then."

Arel snorted. "You're good, but you're no psychic. How can you be so certain?"

"Spring break starts at the end of classes tomorrow," he

said, his gaze narrowing as he watched Angela being led to the edge of the dance floor by a blond jackass who obviously ate steroids like candy. No mere mortal had those kinds of muscles without pharmaceutical help. He didn't like the way the bastard was staring at her overexposed breasts. In fact, he might very well find a way to make Blondie disappear if he laid a hand on the vulnerable female. "It will be the perfect opportunity to make Angela Thorne disappear."

"It's a little late for her to try and be subtle, isn't it?" Arel demanded.

"She wanted to attract attention to draw us south. Now she'll want to fly below the radar. She won't want us knowing that she has the scientist," he pointed out, his tone absent as his attention remained homed in on the female who was moving with a surprising grace. "Besides, it's far more difficult to disappear when you have a hostage."

Easily sensing Niko's distraction, Arel leaned against the railing.

"Is she the real deal?"

"Yeah, she's the real deal." Niko forced himself to shift his attention back to his companion. Until Dylan was dead he couldn't afford to be distracted. Especially not by this particular female. "Calder intended to bring her to the compound after she graduated."

"Why wait?"

"He wanted the female to enjoy being normal for as long as possible."

Arel gave a grunt of laughter. "He's always been too soft-hearted for his own good."

"You won't get an argument from me."

"While you're a coldhearted Sentinel who's willing to use an innocent female as bait for a psycho killer."

Arel's words rasped a raw nerve that Niko didn't even know he possessed until he'd crossed paths with the pretty young scientist who'd slayed him with one shy smile.

Dammit.

Angela Locke was a pawn.

And like any pawn she was supposed to be expendable.

So why had he spent the past six weeks imagining her stretched beneath him as he taught her the true meaning of biology?

He swallowed a low growl. "I get results."

"True enough . . ." Arel's words ended with a low whistle as the frantic music ended and Angela turned to reveal her slender curves so shockingly revealed by those too-tight jeans and the shirt that should be illegal. Damn, Megan. It had to be her influence. "Hellooo. You didn't say anything about her being a beauty."

"Because it has nothing to do with the job," he snapped.

Arel smiled with a slow anticipation. "Hey, if you don't want to bed her, I will."

Niko hissed at his unexpected surge of fury. He was never possessive of women. Not even when they were his lovers.

It had to be this job.

He was . . . on edge. Anxious to find Dylan and make her pay for what she'd done to Fiona.

That had to be it.

Feeling the weight of Arel's all-too-knowing gaze, he sent his fellow Sentinel a scowl.

"Don't you have someplace you have to be?"

A mysterious smile played around the younger man's lips. "Yes, but I don't mind changing assignments."

"Go away, Arel."

Arel chuckled before he placed a hand on Niko's shoulder. "Take care. I've already lost two friends. I won't lose another."

Chapter Three

Usually the small apartment three blocks away from the campus was a place of peace for Angela.

Not that anyone else would share her opinion.

Most people would shudder at the worn furniture that she'd picked up at second-hand stores and garage sales. Not to mention the bedroom that was overflowing with unpacked boxes from her mother's house. Boxes that were filled with painful memories she wasn't prepared to open.

And oh yeah, a kitchen that had become a mini-lab with microscopes, petri dishes, test tubes, and three small fridges that contained her current experiments.

Hardly the palace most women dreamed of.

But for Angela it was far better than a palace.

It was her safe haven.

The moment she closed the door she could forget the day, along with the frustrating challenge of trying to fit in a world that always seemed slightly out of focus.

Today, however, there was no peace as she shut and locked the door.

Pacing across the living room, she peeked through the curtains at the empty street below.

It had started this morning.

She'd spent the entire day with the sensation she was being watched by some unseen lurker.

And she laid full blame on the shoulders of Dr. Nikolo Bartrev.

Not because of his abrupt arrival and equally abrupt departure from the club last night, although the aggravating man had taken away any hope of enjoying the night. Oh, she'd gone through the routine for Megan's sake. She'd danced, she'd sipped her gin fizz, and laughed on cue, but the evening had gone flat.

No, she was used to wishing for things she could never have.

It was his warning of a mysterious stalker that had her jumping at shadows.

Seeing nothing but the usual joggers and occasional car drive past, she gave a shake of her head.

What had she expected?

A stranger wearing a hockey mask and lurking on the sidewalk?

Or maybe a car in the parking lot with a sign that said STALKERS "R" Us?

"This is stupid," she muttered, stepping away from the window and heading into the kitchen.

Spring break had officially started. Classes were out, the majority of the students were even now fleeing town for warmer climes, and she would have a blessed, uninterrupted week to work on her private research.

No doubt Megan would toss her hands up in defeat, but as far as Angela was concerned she'd rather be concentrating on her work than wasting her days on an overcrowded beach.

Okay, maybe if the beach included Professor Hottie she might consider—

Entering the kitchen, Angela came to a halt, a strange sense of alarm tingling down her spine.

Someone had been in here.

She didn't know exactly how she could be so certain. Perhaps the microscope had been shifted ever so slightly. Or maybe there was a lingering scent she didn't quite recognize.

Whatever the cause, her vague unease became full on, adrenaline-charging alarm as she whirled around, intent on fleeing the apartment.

A wise decision that came too late.

She barely managed a step before the door was blocked by a slender figure.

Angela's heart slammed to a halt as she took a swift inventory of the intruder.

The stranger wasn't much taller than her, and was dressed from head to toe in black. Black leather pants. Black turtleneck sweater. Black ski mask.

Good grief. Did stalkers have a uniform code?

She swallowed a hysterical urge to laugh, sternly reminding herself that she was in danger.

Despite the fact the intruder was more or less the same size as herself and clearly female, she wasn't fooled. Beneath the tight clothes she could make out hard, lean muscles that warned the intruder could tie Angela into a painful pretzel.

Or worse.

"Who are you?" she managed to croak, her mind sluggishly trying to shift through her limited options.

No. Not limited.

Nonexistent.

Her cell phone was in her purse that she'd left in the living room. There was no doubt a knife was tucked in her silverware drawer, but it was across the room. And there was nothing close enough at hand to use as a weapon.

For now her options were talking her way out of danger or hoping for a miracle.

Neither seemed likely.

Casually leaning a shoulder against the doorjamb the

intruder revealed she was in far better control of her nerves than Angela.

"Would you believe a friend?"

"No."

A nonchalant shrug. "Then let's say I'm a potential customer."

"Customer?" Angela frowned before she gave a small gasp of understanding. "Oh. I get it."

"Do you?"

"Yes. But I'm afraid you've made a mistake."

The woman adjusted her black glove. Preparing for violence?

"I rarely make mistakes," she drawled. Her voice was oddly beautiful. Almost hypnotic.

Angela licked her lips, flicking a brief glance toward the expensive equipment that was piled on the kitchen table.

"I know it must look like I manufacture drugs, but I'm just a scientist," she said, her palms damp. Had the temperature gone up? Or was it sheer terror that was making her feel as if her sweatshirt and jeans were smothering her? "There's nothing here that will get you high."

"Just a scientist?" The stranger gave a chiding shake of her head. "Now, now, Angela. There's no need for such modesty. You're already considered the brilliant star in the world of genetics."

Angela took a shocked step back. "You know me?"

"Of course. I've been following your career with breathless anticipation."

Okay. The whole encounter had just shifted from scary to terrifyingly creepy.

"Who are you?" she repeated the question that had never been answered.

The intruder straightened, taking a step into the kitchen. "A devoted fan."

Fan? Did scientists have groupies?

Well, beyond Stephen Hawking?

"Look, I'm not sure what's going on, but I'm just a post-graduate student struggling to finish her dissertation," she said, her voice quivering. "If you want to speak with an actual researcher—"

"It's you I want," the woman interrupted.

"For what?"

"A job."

The simple words caught Angela off guard.

Was that why this woman had snuck into her home?

She'd been warned that recruiters could be aggressive when trying to capture the top graduates. Especially recruiters from pharmaceutical companies. But this was beyond ridiculous.

"Actually, I haven't really considered what I plan to do after graduation, but—"

"I'm afraid it's something of a rush job."

With a lift of her hand the stranger yanked off her stocking hat and Angela nearly went to her knees in shock.

"Holy crap," she muttered, trying to make sense of what she was seeing.

The . . . woman (yeah, she was still convinced the intruder was female despite the fact she was completely bald) had eyes that were as red as rubies and a nose that was oddly flat. Like a snake. And worse, her visible skin was patterned with large, dark spots that went way beyond freckles.

The intruder smiled. Not a pleasant smile. More a stretching of her thin lips.

"Yeah, I get that a lot."

"Were you—"

"Born this way?" The woman pulled off her gloves, revealing her hands that were spotted like her face and tipped with claws. "Yes."

Angela tried to clear the mammoth-sized lump from her throat.

"So you're a—"

"Freak."

Everyone knew of high-bloods, or freaks, as most people called them. The special people born with some sort of mutation that made them different from others.

Not that the general population truly knew much about them. There were rumors of witches and psychics and necromancers. And the strange Sentinels. Then there were the whispers that there were true monsters being hidden behind the walls of Valhalla.

As a future geneticist, Angela devoured the bits and pieces of information on the high-bloods. Unfortunately the Mave who ruled the residents of Valhalla and the satellite communities refused to allow her people to be studied. Only scientists who were a part of their community were allowed any research. Even local doctors were forced to contact Valhalla if a freak turned up in the ER. And anyone trying to collect genetic material was subject to punishment by the Mave.

Not something anyone would be willing to risk.

Now, however, she realized that her clinical fascination with high-blood DNA hadn't taken into account the brutal truth of what it meant to be . . . different.

The personal cost was written in the bitter glow of the crimson eyes.

"I'm sorry," Angela whispered before she could halt the impulsive words.

The female snorted. "Not nearly as sorry as I am."

Yeah, Angela got that.

"What do you want from me?"

"Simple. I want you to fix me."

"Fix you?" Angela parroted, her brilliant brain trained to comprehend logical facts, not . . . this. "I'm not a doctor."

"Do I look like a fucking doctor could cure me?"

Angela took another step backward, her ass hitting the edge of the sink.

"What do you expect me to do?"

"Your gift is to alter DNA." The woman pulled off her other glove and tossed it on the ground. Then she ran her fingers over her bald head. "I want you to make me normal."

Through her fog of fear, Angela felt a stab of sympathy. She understood the woman's desperation. She truly did.

But, sympathizing with the stranger didn't mean she could help her.

"That's impossible."

The crimson eyes narrowed. "Nothing in this world is impossible."

"Maybe not, but the technology isn't anywhere near advanced enough. At least not yet."

"Technology?" Something that might have been amusement rippled over the strange, exotic face. "I'm not talking about test tubes and microscopes."

"I don't understand."

The woman waved a hand toward the kitchen table. "Why do you bother with this junk anyway?"

Was this some sort of trick?

"I need it for my research," she said slowly. "Although I admit it can't compare to my lab at the university."

"Come on, Angela," the intruder scoffed. "You don't have to hide the truth from me."

Angela went rigid with a strange sense of wariness.

"I don't know what you're talking about."

The woman gave a sharp laugh. "You haven't figured it out yet?"

"Figured out what?"

"You, Angela Locke, are a freak."

"No." Angela shook her head, squashing the ridiculous urge to slap her hands over her ears. The woman was nuts. A full-blown wackadoodle. "No way."

"How do you think you're able to manipulate cells that no one else can?"

Angela sucked in a ragged breath. Why wasn't she laughing at the woman's outrageous claims?

"The magnetic particles I've developed—"

"No." The woman stepped close enough for Angela to feel the heat she radiated from her skin even through her clothes. Obviously her mutation made her run at a higher temperature. "It's you. It's always been you."

"This is crazy." Angela was trapped, reaching behind her to grasp the edge of the counter. Her knees were threatening to collapse. "I want you out of my apartment."

"If you insist." The creepy smile returned as the woman reached out with terrifying speed to lock her hands around Angela's upper arms, her claws digging through the sweatshirt to puncture the tender skin beneath. "I was going to let you pack a bag, but whatever."

"Stop it," Angela cried, fear and pain hammering through her with equal force. "What are you doing?"

The crimson eyes glowed with an eerie light. "I have a comfy little home all prepared for our arrival. You're not leaving my side until you fix me."

Her grip tightened, but even as Angela braced herself to be dragged from the room kicking and screaming, the stranger was tilting back her head to sniff the air. Like an animal.

Angela shuddered. Oh . . . God. What now?

In answer, the woman whirled toward the door, her hands clenched in tight fists.

"Niko," she hissed, not nearly as dumbfounded as Angela as a tall, stunningly familiar man stepped into the kitchen.

"Dylan," Dr. Nikolo Bartrev drawled, his handsome face carved from granite. "I knew you'd eventually show up here."

* * *

It was rare for Nikolo to be caught flat-footed.

No, it wasn't rare.

It was *never*.

But trailing Angela from the university to her apartment building, he'd taken time to make a sweep of the neighborhood. He was certain Dylan was going to make her move. And make it soon.

He just hadn't expected her to already be in the apartment.

A mistake that might have cost Angela her life.

The realization detonated a strange explosion of fear and fury in the depths of his soul.

A sensation that was as unfamiliar as it was unexpected.

Niko was trained to hone his feelings into a smooth blade of cold, calculating resolve. Becoming emotional only clouded his mind and dulled his instincts.

But silently entering the apartment, he hadn't been worried about his prey. Or even his own life.

His sole focus was reaching Angela before she could be hurt.

Stepping into the kitchen he came to an abrupt halt at the sight of Dylan standing directly in front of Angela. Shit. She was too close to risk an attack.

One swing of her hand and she could crush Angela's skull. Or use her claws to rip out her throat.

He swallowed a growl, ignoring the voice that warned his hesitation might cost him the opportunity to put an end to Dylan's murderous rampage.

He would have his revenge, he grimly assured himself. But not at Angela's expense.

Wiping all expression from his face, he watched Dylan slowly turn, her crimson eyes filled with a mocking amusement that didn't entirely disguise her seething frustration.

"Long time no see," she drawled. "Did you miss me?"

"Like a fucking hole in the head," he retorted, allowing

only a brief glance toward Angela who was studying him with a shocked gaze. "You gave up any claim to loyalty when you killed Adam and Fiona."

"I know you won't believe me, but I wish their deaths hadn't been necessary."

Niko shrugged aside the female's genuine regret. He'd been the one to discover the two Sentinels. Adam had lost his throat when he'd obviously gone into Dylan's room to check on her, while Fiona had been shot in the back of her head while standing guard at the entrance to the psych ward.

Adam had been a longtime friend, while Fiona had been as close as any daughter to him.

He would mourn their deaths for the rest of his life.

"It was a choice, not a necessity."

"Easy for you to say," Dylan countered. "You weren't chained to the walls like an animal."

"For your own safety." Niko made a sound of disgust. "Of course, that was a ruse, wasn't it? You never intended to kill yourself."

The female shrugged. "I needed to distract attention. I knew I was being watched."

Niko narrowed his eyes. It had been one of the clairvoyants who'd picked up on Dylan's growingly dark thoughts, although the Sentinel had the ability to hide her secret plans. It was enough to put a constant surveillance on the unstable female.

"Because you're a psychopath."

"So easy for you to judge when you walk around like a Greek god," Dylan hissed. "How would you feel if you looked like a monster?"

He deliberately allowed his gaze to roam over the spotted skin and too-flat nose before returning to meet the smoldering crimson glare.

"You've never been a monster to your family."

"Family?" Her sharp laugh sliced through the air. "My family tossed me away at birth."

"We were your family," he reminded her. All high-bloods were welcomed at Valhalla and Dylan had been raised by people who loved her. "Your parents gave you to us because they understood the challenges you would face and trusted us to protect you."

She gave a restless shake of her head, her madness refusing to acknowledge she'd been treated with nothing but kindness.

"How did you find me?"

"I'm a Sentinel."

"My trail was in Texas."

"You didn't escape to kill humans."

"So you knew I was coming for the scientist," she murmured, glancing over her shoulder at the white-faced Angela before turning back to Niko with a sudden realization. "Ah, you used her as bait."

"Yes."

There was a raw, pained sound from Angela that pierced Niko's heart. Christ. That was a little tidbit he'd intended to keep to himself.

But even as he ground his teeth at the thought of Angela's sense of betrayal, his gaze never strayed from Dylan.

The bitch was still too close to Angela for him to strike.

"Always so clever, Niko," the Sentinel mocked.

Clever. Yeah, not clever enough to avoid his own trap, he acknowledged wryly, belatedly accepting that Dylan wasn't the only one to have fallen for the bait.

He took a step forward. "It's time to end this."

"Oh no, this isn't the end. The game is just beginning." With the fluid speed of all Sentinels, Dylan turned to Angela, her hand shooting out to grasp her chin with claws that bit into the tender skin. "I'll come for you later, sweet Angela. Niko can't guard you forever."

"Damn."

Niko launched himself forward, but as fast as he was, Dylan was already leaping through the window over the sink and dropping the two stories to the parking lot below.

Without hesitation Niko was in pursuit.

Chapter Four

On some level Angela knew she must be in shock.

Otherwise she'd be curled in the middle of the floor screaming in terror. Or at the very least, calling nine-one-one.

Instead she stumbled toward her bedroom, barely aware of what she was doing as she found a gym bag on the floor of her closet and began stuffing it with clothes.

She had to get away.

Somewhere.

Anywhere.

The destination didn't matter. Just so long as it wasn't here.

Vaguely realizing the bag was full, she zipped it shut and rose to her feet.

It was only when she turned that she realized she wasn't alone.

"Shit." She dropped the bag, reaching behind her back to retrieve the carving knife she'd grabbed on her way out of the kitchen. "Stay back."

In answer Niko took a deliberate step forward, his gaze flicking down to the bag at her feet.

"Good. You've packed."

Her gaze locked on the handsome face that had filled her dreams for six long weeks. God. He looked so . . .

Abruptly her tight knot of fear exploded into sheer rage.

"I told you to stay back," she snarled, waving the knife in warning.

"Please, Angela." He held up his hands. "You need to listen to me."

Her heart squeezed with a crippling sense of betrayal. It didn't matter that she'd known this man for less than two months. Or that he'd never made her any promises.

She'd felt a . . . connection to him.

A tenuous hope that he would be the one man to eventually see the woman beneath the awkward nerd.

God. Could she have been more delusional?

"So I can hear more lies, *Dr. Bartrev?*"

His eyes darkened, as if bothered by the harsh edge of accusation in her voice.

"My name isn't a lie," he said. "I'm Nikolo Bartrev."

"You're not a professor."

"No." He took another step forward and Angela shivered as he dropped his pretense of a harmless professor. It wasn't like he'd snapped his fingers and transformed into another creature. It was more a subtle hardening of his dark, beautiful features. The squaring of his broad shoulders that looked even broader beneath the cream cable sweater. And the swirl of heat that poured through the room, stroking over her in silent warning. "I'm a Sentinel."

She tossed aside the knife. It was worse than useless considering she was more likely to poke it into herself than harm the dangerous predator that watched her with his piercing blue gaze.

And he was a predator.

She could sense it with every fiber of her being.

"I thought Sentinels were marked with tattoos?"

"Those who act as guardians are protected by wards."

"But not you?"

"No. I'm a hunter. I need to . . . blend when necessary."

Her jaw clenched at the painful reminder of his charade. Bastard.

"So what makes you a Sentinel?"

He hesitated, clearly considering his words. Did the high-bloods have a code of silence? She wouldn't doubt it. There was very little information about them in the general population.

"I'm stronger and faster than most people," he at last admitted. "I also have heightened senses."

"And it's your job to track down freaks." She deliberately used the insult.

Beneath her overriding fear she was well and truly pissed. Who could blame her?

Her chin was bleeding from the claws used by the creepy Dylan who intended to kidnap her and force her to play the role of Dr. Frankenstein. And this man—this arrogant jackass—had treated her like she was nothing more than an expendable object.

Something to be used and tossed away.

He gave a dip of his head. "Yes."

"And you always get your man?"

His gaze briefly lowered to the soft curve of her breasts barely visible beneath her sweatshirt.

"Or woman."

Her nipples tightened in instant reaction and she swallowed a curse. The tingling, heart-stopping heat that she'd always savored when near this man was now a brutal reminder of just how humiliatingly naïve she'd been.

"No matter who you have to use?"

He shoved impatient fingers through the short strands of his hair.

"Dylan killed two Sentinels to escape Valhalla, then twelve norms to try and draw us from her true purpose," he rasped. "She has to be stopped."

Angela grimaced. Fourteen people murdered? Okay. Obviously the psycho killer had to be captured.

But that didn't make it any easier to know she'd been used as bait.

"How did you know she would be coming here?"

He shrugged. "You're the only one who has the talent to alter her appearance."

She was shaking her head before he finished speaking.

Dammit. Why were they trying to make her believe she was a freak?

Did they think it would make her more sympathetic to their cause?

"Not. In. The. Mood."

"Fine." Perhaps sensing she was on the verge of a meltdown, he wisely backed off. "We need to go now."

"We?" She made a sound of disbelief. "Are you braindead? I'm not going anywhere with you."

A muscle in his jaw twitched, but he grimly held on to his temper.

"You don't have a choice. Dylan's not going to stop hunting you. Not until she's dead." He deliberately paused. "Or you are."

"I'll take my chances."

"No." He was gripping her upper arms firmly before she even realized he'd moved. Holy shit. He wasn't lying when he said he was faster. "You won't."

She tilted back her head, pretending his touch wasn't searing through her sweatshirt.

The lover of my dreams is now my enemy, she fiercely reminded herself.

"So I'm a prisoner?"

His brows drew together in a scowl. "Dammit, Angela, I'm only trying to protect you."

"A little late for that, don't you think?"

"Late for what?"

She forced herself to meet his ruthless gaze. "If you truly

wanted to protect me you'd have told me the truth from the beginning."

"I couldn't."

"Of course not," she mocked, not bothering to try and pull from his grasp. What was the point? He was clearly ten times stronger than her. Which should have made her wonder why she was pissed instead of terrified. "I'm just the bait, right?"

He heaved a harsh sigh. "I was never going to let you be hurt."

Was he kidding?

She shook her head in disgust. "Well you did."

He hissed, his hands skimming down to her wrists so he could tug her arms up as his gaze inspected her slender body.

"I've seen the scratches on your face. Are you wounded anywhere else?"

She jerked her wrist free and, balling her hand into a fist, she slugged him in the center of his chest.

"*You* hurt me, you bastard," she hissed.

He tensed at her accusation. "That wasn't my intention."

"No?" Ignoring all sanity, she hit him again. "Then why did you pretend to be my friend?"

His beautiful face became wary. "I needed to be close to you."

"Bullshit. You're some magical Sentinel, aren't you?" she demanded. "You could have watched without me ever knowing you were around. Instead you—"

"What?"

She shuddered at the aching sense of betrayal. She was used to being teased, or more often, ignored by the opposite sex. But she'd never been so callously humiliated.

"You let me think you liked me."

"Angela."

"God, I'm such an idiot."

She wrapped her arms around her waist. Hitting him only hurt her hand.

"Don't," he commanded, studying her with a brooding intensity. "You're the most brilliant person I've ever met."

"Am I?" She gave a humorless laugh. "Then why did I spend my nights fantasizing about a man who was willing to offer me up as a sacrifice to a psychopath?"

Something dark and dangerous flared to life in his eyes. Something he'd never allowed her to see before.

But, even as Angela took an instinctive step backward, Niko was reaching to yank her against his unyielding chest.

Danger. Heat. Desire.

She squawked in surprise, her mouth opening to protest his manhandling.

And he kissed her.

Just like that.

His lips were hard, hungry, just as she'd always fantasized, but the brush of his tongue was a gentle caress. He pressed her closer and the feel of his thickening arousal sent a stab of excitement to the pit of her stomach.

She moaned, her hands lifting to his shoulders as fiery heat flowed like lava through her, searing away the world where she was being hunted by a mass murderer and this man was her enemy.

Somewhere in his lust-hazed mind, Niko knew he was behaving badly.

Even for a man who rarely bothered himself with tedious things like good manners or proper behavior, he understood you didn't grab a woman who was furious with you and kiss her like a Neanderthal.

But he'd spent six long weeks denying his rampant desire for this female, pretending that she was just a pawn in his game while he used every excuse to spend time in her company.

Now shockwaves of pleasure jolted through him, making it all blindingly clear.

This woman wasn't a pawn.

She wasn't bait.

She was . . . his.

His hands trailed up the delicate line of her back, his cock already hard and aching for release. He groaned, his tongue dipping between her lips to taste the warm, sweet woman who'd plagued his dreams.

She shivered, but his hunter instincts were easily able to sense it wasn't with fear.

He could hear the rapid beat of her heart, feel the rush of blood beneath her satin skin and catch the scent of her stirring arousal.

She was angry with him, but that didn't halt her response to his touch.

His hand swept beneath the thick curtain of her hair, cupping her nape as he deepened the kiss.

He wanted to toss her on the bed just inches away and devour every satin inch of her. Over and over.

Unfortunately that wasn't going to happen anytime soon.

Not only was Dylan still on the loose, but he suspected that Angela was far more innocent than most females her age.

When he finally had her in his bed he wanted all night to demonstrate why she should remain there.

Reluctantly lifting his head, he gazed down at her upturned face. Over the past weeks he'd memorized every line and curve of her delicate features. Not because of his Sentinel training, but because he'd been fascinated by her quiet beauty. The velvet darkness of her eyes and the lush curve of her mouth.

He'd even learned to recognize the play of emotion over her expressive features.

He knew when she furrowed her brow she was lost in her clever thoughts. And when she chewed her bottom lip she was feeling awkward in a conversation. And when her eyes grew dreamy she was thinking of him.

He stroked a finger over the soft color staining her cheeks.

"You are so beautiful."

She sucked in a shaky breath, her wide eyes dazed. "What are you doing?"

His finger moved to outline her lips. How long had he'd wondered what they would taste like? It seemed an eternity.

Now he knew.

Cherries.

Fresh cherries still warm from the sunshine.

"What I wanted to do from the minute I caught sight of you."

She briefly allowed herself to become lost in his gaze, revealing far more of her vulnerable need than she realized. Then, obviously remembering why he was in her bedroom, oh, and the fact she currently hated him, she gave a sharp shake of her head.

"Liar. This is some new trick to try and—"

He kissed her again.

Okay, maybe he was a Neanderthal. At least where Angela Locke was concerned.

He wanted to brand her. With his touch, his kiss, his passion . . .

He swallowed her choked groan, his hands shifting to tenderly cup her face. Slowly he savored the taste of cherries and delectable woman, his thumbs stroking over the fluttering pulse just below her jaw.

It wasn't until she was arching toward him in silent need that he lifted his head to meet her unfocused gaze.

"You were right," he murmured.

She blinked. "I was?"

"I could have watched you from the shadows."

Another blink. "Then why didn't you?"

He peered deep into her wide eyes. "You know why."

"Niko—"

"We need to leave," he interrupted, forcing himself to drop his hands.

He'd been a Sentinel for a very, very long time. And never had he lost sight of his goal.

OUT OF CONTROL   41

But with this woman . . . dammit.

He was in real danger of allowing himself to be distracted.

Which was a perfect way to get them both killed.

She frowned, struggling to follow his words. "Leave?"

"Dylan hasn't given up her obsession of becoming normal."

"Oh." She pushed back her hair with an unsteady hand. "I don't understand."

"Understand what?"

"Why is she so anxious to become normal? There's a lot of people like you, isn't there?"

"Like *us*," he corrected, knowing at some point she was going to have to accept that she was special. "And yes, there are high-bloods all over the world. But most are able to pass as common norms with a little effort."

She ignored his reminder she wasn't one of the norms. Typical. In the past six weeks he'd realized that Angela was capable of ignoring any number of things. Including her less than "normal" ability to manipulate cells.

"Is her physical appearance all that's different about her?"

"No." He held her gaze. "She's a Sentinel. Like me."

Her expression hardened at the reminder of his position. She might melt at his touch, but she wasn't going to forgive anytime soon.

"A better Sentinel than you?" she taunted.

"No, not better than me."

"Then why didn't you catch her?"

A hell of a question.

When he'd followed Dylan through the window he'd fully intended to hunt her down and put an end to her bloody rampage. A fine plan, but Dylan wasn't without her own skills and she managed to disguise her trail only a few blocks away.

Given time, Niko could have unraveled the various ruses that she'd used to hide her presence. He hadn't been boasting when he assured Angela that he was the better Sentinel.

But even as his duty demanded he carry on his hunt no

matter how long it took, the man in him was urging him back to Angela's apartment.

He'd told himself that it only made sense. Dylan wasn't going to leave without Angela. She was convinced the young scientist was her one hope of living a normal life. But in the depths of his heart he knew that wasn't the reason he'd rushed back to the apartment.

"I couldn't be sure that she wouldn't circle back," he admitted with a reluctant honesty.

"And you were concerned for my safety?" She rolled her eyes, not able to hide her lingering sense of betrayal. "I'm touched."

"Dammit."

He'd royally screwed up. Fine, he got it. But now wasn't the time to soothe ruffled feathers. He could defeat Dylan in a fair battle, but the Sentinel was no longer playing by the rules. Who knew what nasty surprises she might have up her sleeve? Hell, he didn't even know for sure that she was working alone. He needed to get Angela somewhere safe.

With a grimace at the knowledge he was about to give this woman yet another reason to be pissed off, he grabbed her around the waist and with one smooth motion had her tossed over his shoulder.

"Hey," she cried out, swinging her legs in an effort to hit the part of him that was as vulnerable as any man's. "Put me down, you . . . you bully."

Wrapping an arm around her knees, he locked her into place before reaching down to grab her bag from the floor.

Who knew that rescuing a damsel in distress could be such a pain in the ass?

Chapter Five

Angela stewed in silence as Niko headed his battered Jeep north, swiftly taking them away from the outskirts of Columbia to the farmlands that surrounded the town.

It was always a beautiful drive. The manicured fields dissected by meandering streams. The sturdy farmhouses that were dwarfed by red-painted barns, along with sheds and paddocks.

Today it was even more charming with the fading April sunlight offering a hint of spring and the tiny buds beginning to appear on the trees and bushes.

Unfortunately, she was too busy glaring at the stark male profile of Nikolo Bartrev to pay attention to the passing scenery.

He really was indecently handsome, she was forced to acknowledge, even as she considered the pleasure of punching hard enough to break his perfect nose.

He'd lied to her, used her, and now kidnapped her.

Okay, to be completely fair, he'd rescued her from the whacked-out freak. And she wasn't entirely averse to having him near in case Dylan made a repeat appearance. At least until she could find someplace to hide.

But that didn't mean she wasn't still mad as hell.

Or that she wasn't going to try to escape the very second she suspected he was about to serve her up to the wolves. Or in this case—the freaks.

She didn't trust him any farther than she could throw him.

Which wasn't very damned far.

Her dark thoughts were interrupted as the Jeep slowed and Niko halted in front of a heavy gate that blocked the narrow gravel road. Slipping out of the vehicle, he moved to punch a series of numbers onto a computer screen that was set in a small gatehouse before returning to steer the Jeep through the open gates and down the road that was lined with massive oak trees.

She frowned, abruptly conscious of just how isolated they were as he turned yet again and stopped in front of a picturesque log cabin that was nestled among the trees.

The front of the A-frame house was made entirely of glass, giving a hint of the large living room with a silver sectional couch loaded with bright pillows and a spiral staircase in the middle of the planked floor leading to the open loft above.

"What is this place?"

He put the Jeep in park and pocketed the keys. She grimaced, belatedly wishing she'd learned how to hot-wire a car.

Who knew it would come in handy?

"I've been staying here since traveling to Missouri."

She blinked in surprise, her gaze returning to the house that managed to be elegant despite its rustic style.

It looked so . . . normal.

"Here?"

He shoved open the door to the vehicle and stepped out. "Did you think I crawled beneath a rock every night?"

With a shrug, she climbed out to join him on the pathway leading to the wide, wooden terrace.

"It's where most slimy invertebrates slither."

"Slimy?" His lips tugged into a lopsided grin. "Is that a scientific term?"

Her heart skipped a treacherous beat. It was no wonder he so rarely smiled. It was lethal.

"Personal opinion," she managed to mutter.

Grasping her elbow, he led her onto the terrace. Then, reaching the glass door, he paused to flip open a small, metal box and placed his hand against it to be scanned. There was a small beep before the door slid open.

Good grief.

This place had the sort of security she'd only seen in movies.

Perhaps sensing her confusion, he sent her a wry smile as he urged her over the threshold and into the house.

"I borrowed the cabin from a friend," he said, closing the door and pressing a button that reset the lock.

He pressed another button that did something to darken the windows. She assumed it was so they could see out, but no one could see in.

"A Sentinel?" she guessed.

"No, Serra is a psychic."

In spite of the combustible combination of fear and anger that continued to seethe through her rigid body, Angela felt an undeniable stab of curiosity.

Hardly a big shocker.

She was a scientist who'd been obsessed with genetics for as long as she could remember.

"I thought most high-bloods lived together?"

He turned to meet her searching gaze. "Most prefer the comfort, not to mention the safety, of official compounds, but psychics have a need to seek solitude on occasion."

"Oh." She glanced toward the windows that offered a view of the thick woods that encircled the house. The nearest neighbor was no doubt miles away. "I never thought how annoying it must be to hear other people's thoughts."

"This house belonged to Serra's parents before they retired to Florida." His features softened as he spoke of the psychic. "She was fortunate to have parents who remained an important part of her life. They chose this spot to give her a place of peace."

"Is she your lover?"

The words left Angela's lips before she could call them back and her face flushed with heat as he stepped toward her with a wicked smile.

"There's only one female I want in my bed."

A dangerous excitement spiraled through her at his low, husky voice, stealing her breath and making her knees weak.

If only that were true.

If only this intelligent, powerful, drop-dead-gorgeous man had truly been a visiting professor who'd been intrigued by me, the shy young scientist.

Yeah, and if only pigs could fly.

She tilted her chin, trying to pretend as if she couldn't feel the heat of his hard, muscular, perfectly chiseled body searing through her clothes.

"Why did you bring me here?"

His jaw clenched, as if he was frustrated by her refusal to accept that his desire could be genuine.

"The house has a sophisticated alarm system including hidden surveillance. It's also less than an hour from a monastery."

She'd known that the monasteries had a close connection to Valhalla. Not only training the mysterious Sentinels who served as guardians to the high-bloods when they traveled among the regular population, but also offering asylum for any high-blood who felt in danger.

No one was allowed in the monastery without invitation from the monks.

Not the cops, or military, or even the leaders of the country where the monastery was located.

They had the mystical powers to remain impervious to politics.

"You have business with the monks?"

"Using teleportation will be the fastest way to reach Valhalla."

She took a hasty step backward. "No."

"There's no need to be scared."

He studied her as if surprised she would be afraid of being magically transported from one place to another. As he should be. Under normal circumstances she would have been thrilled out of her mind at the opportunity to not only see inside a mysterious monastery, but to travel from portal to portal. It would be . . . amazing. But these weren't normal circumstances and she wasn't going to allow herself to be trapped in a place that she couldn't be sure she could escape from.

"I'm not scared," she said.

"Good." His lips twisted. "Despite all the entertaining tales of people disappearing into outer space or arriving at the destination half-man/half-fish I can promise you that it's perfectly safe."

"I meant that I'm not going to Valhalla."

His brows drew together at her stubborn tone. "Angela, it's the one place Dylan can't reach you."

"Oh yeah? It didn't sound that way to me."

"What didn't?"

"You accused Dylan of killing two Sentinels before managing to escape from this supposedly 'safe haven'," she reminded him, shivering at the memory of the strange female. It wasn't remotely difficult to accept she'd murdered her friends. Dylan was clearly unstable. "Now you want to plant me there like a sitting duck?" Her eyes narrowed. "Or is that the point? Am I still the bait?"

His breath hissed between his teeth, his hand lifting to rake impatient fingers through his hair.

"If you were the bait, I would have left you at the apartment and waited for Dylan to return," he rasped. "Because I can assure you that she would have come for you."

Okay, that was true.

Even if she wasn't in the mood to admit it.

Instead her chin tilted another inch. "You can't force me to go to Valhalla."

The blue eyes darkened with a hint of the predator that waited just below the surface.

Sentinel.

She'd glimpsed the danger that lurked beneath his pretense of civilization. A damned shame she hadn't paid attention to her instincts.

"I think I've already proven I can make you go wherever I want," he reminded her in deceptively soft tones.

"Bastard."

He cupped her chin, his touch unexpectedly gentle. "But, I would rather you go willingly."

"Not. Gonna. Happen," she snapped, hoping he didn't feel her shiver as the heat of his fingers warmed her to the tip of her toes.

And lots of interesting places in between.

His eyes darkened, but this time it was with a stark hunger that made her heart pound.

"What if I say pretty please?" he asked in a low, compelling voice, his thumb brushing over her lower lip.

"Stop that."

His hooded gaze studied her upturned face, something perilously close to possession in his dark expression.

"Ah, if only it was so simple."

Her mouth went dry as her body instinctively arched

toward his solid strength. Dang it. She'd lusted after him for so long. Weaving impossible fantasies in her head.

Now her body didn't seem to understand that she wasn't supposed to be melting beneath his touch.

Traitorous hormones.

"Niko." His name came as a breathy whisper instead of the protest she intended.

He muttered a low curse as his head lowered so he could brush his mouth along the sensitive curve of her neck.

"I like hearing my name on your lips."

Her hands lifted to clutch at the cashmere softness of his sweater as he nuzzled a path upward. Oh . . . crap. It felt soooo good.

The sort of good that made smart women do stupid things.

"I'm mad at you," she managed to mutter.

He found the pulse that thundered just below her jaw, stroking it with the rough rasp of his tongue before giving it a tiny nip.

"I know."

Angela gasped at the primitive stab of pleasure that arrowed through her.

Her limited experience with the opposite sex included a few fumbled kisses, even more fumbled squeezes of her breasts followed by a quickie in her long forgotten boyfriend's dorm room.

Nothing that made her anxious to find a new lover in the past three years.

Not until Niko had prowled into her lab.

Clearly even a female as embarrassingly naïve as she was could sense a man with the ability to please a woman.

She moaned as he outlined her mouth with the tip of his tongue.

"I don't trust you."

"You will," he promised, stealing a deep, drugging kiss.

She briefly savored the taste of warm male desire, her

stomach clenching with anticipation as she felt the hard thrust of his arousal.

This was what she'd sensed the minute he'd walked into the lab.

This smoldering attraction that could burn her to cinders.

Reluctantly she pulled back, her rasping breath the only sound to disturb the silence.

"Just because you can get me into bed?"

"Because I'm going to devote myself to proving I'll never hurt you again," he promised, his gaze locked on her lips that still tingled from his touch. "No matter how long it takes."

She struggled to think.

Who knew it could be such a difficult task?

"Why?"

His finger brushed her heated cheek. "Hmmm?"

"Why are you concerned that I would be hurt now?" she persisted. "It's not like you gave a rat's ass for the past six weeks."

He met her accusing gaze, his expression somber. "The Sentinels—the ones who Dylan murdered—were two of my closest friends." He grimaced. "The pain of their loss blinded me."

She refused to be swayed by the edge of pain in his voice.

"So not all Sentinels are so cold-blooded?"

He gave a short laugh. "Oh, we're cold-blooded, especially when we're tracking prey." His hand gently tucked a loose strand of hair behind her ear. "But a part of our mission is always to protect the innocent."

A tiny part of Niko knew that he was behaving badly.

Again.

The poor female had nearly been kidnapped by a homicidal freak who looked like the definition of a monster. She'd discovered the man she'd come to trust had used her as a pawn. And then forced her against her will to travel to this remote cabin.

And that didn't even include the revelation she was also one of the freaks. Something she'd obviously refused to process.

She was shaken, scared, and mad as hell.

But was he offering her comfort? Giving her the space she needed to come to terms with the upheavals in her life?

No.

He'd barely got her through the door before he had her in his arms, kissing her as if he'd already claimed her as his own.

But while the small shred of decency that had survived his years as a Sentinel urged him to release her, he knew there wasn't a chance in hell of that happening.

He *needed* to touch her. It was a physical ache that he couldn't deny.

"And now?" she asked, her defiant expression doing nothing to hide the vulnerability in her wide, velvet-brown eyes.

His fingers skimmed down the curve of her neck. "Now my first priority is to make certain you're out of harm's way."

A fine tremor shook her body as his fingers continued down to trace the prominent line of her collarbone exposed by the drooping neckline of her sweatshirt.

Not that she was about to admit her ready response to his touch.

Once—before she'd discovered the truth—she would have eagerly shared her desire. It had been obvious in every shy smile and charming blush when he walked into a room.

The fact that he'd driven her to hide her desire was a raw regret that was going to torture him for the rest of his life.

"And then you'll return to the hunt for Dylan?" she pressed.

He shrugged. Just six weeks ago he would have been infuriated by the mere question. Nothing was more important than tracking down the bitch who'd killed his friends.

But his priorities had changed. While he would never be

satisfied until Dylan was brought to justice, his focus was now on ensuring that Angela was protected.

"That will be the decision of the Tagos," he said.

She frowned. "What's a Tagos?"

"The commander of the Sentinels."

"And what will happen to me?"

"One problem at a time, angel," he murmured, forcing himself to step back so he could pull his cell phone from his pocket.

"Wait," she said, grasping his arm, her expression troubled.

"What is it?"

"I haven't agreed to go with you."

He squashed his impulse to inform her that he didn't need her consent. After years of giving commands and having them obeyed, he was going to have to learn the art of negotiation.

A wry smile twisted his lips. He suspected it wouldn't be the first, or the last change he would have to make for this female.

"Fine, but I have to check in and let them know Dylan is still out there," he said.

She regarded him with open suspicion. "No tricks?"

"No tricks." He leaned down to brush his lips over her furrowed brow. "The kitchen is fully stocked. See if there's anything that you'd like for dinner."

She took a hasty step backward, a revealing blush staining her cheeks.

"What about you?"

He swallowed a groan, the sweet taste of her skin clinging to his lips and the scent of her frustrated desire teasing his nose.

Sometimes superior senses weren't always a bonus.

"Me?"

"You eat, don't you?"

His gaze drifted down the length of her slender body before returning to meet her wide gaze.

"What I'm hungry for isn't in the kitchen."

Her lips parted, but perhaps aware he was looking for any excuse to yank her back into his arms and consume her on the spot, she turned to scurry toward the wide doors that led to the back of the cabin.

He breathed deeply of her lingering scent before pressing the number to Valhalla on his cell phone.

Within seconds he was patched through to Wolfe, the current Talos, and all-around badass.

"You have her?" the powerful leader of the Sentinels demanded, not bothering with pleasantries.

"Not Dylan, but I have the scientist."

"You let your prey escape?"

"Yes."

There was a startled silence before Wolfe sucked in an audible breath.

"Talk to me, Niko."

"I've been . . ." It took an effort to say the word he'd never thought he'd utter. "Compromised."

Wolfe muttered a low curse. "Explain."

"I'm no longer impartial," he said, proving the point as he crossed the room so he could keep Angela in sight as she entered the kitchen. "I'm afraid my judgment can't be trusted."

"None of us are impartial," Wolfe said in rough tones, the words thick with self-disgust. As Tagos, Wolfe held himself personally responsible for the death of Adam and Fiona. Not that he wouldn't have even if he wasn't the leader. Calling Wolfe a control freak was like calling a nuclear bomb a small explosive. "Dylan's betrayal has affected us all."

"This is more than my thirst for revenge," Niko confessed without apology. Odd. He should be horrified by the thought that he was about to let a female come between him and his duty. Instead all he wanted was to be done with the conversation so he could head into the kitchen. "I've allowed myself to become personally invested in Angela."

"The scientist?"

"Yes."

"Well, well."

Niko ignored the mocking drawl in his friend's voice. Wolfe was notorious for his belief that Sentinels shouldn't allow distractions in their lives. Lovers were fine as long as they understood they came in a distant second place to the job.

"I need to get her to Valhalla," he said. "But there might be a problem."

He could sense that Wolfe was on instant alert. "Why? It's not that long a drive."

Niko grimaced. "No, but I can't be sure Dylan is working alone. I'd be vulnerable to attack on the road."

"There's something else."

Niko rolled his eyes. All Sentinels were hyperperceptive. It was part of their special ability.

But Wolfe was very close to being a psychic.

Annoying bastard.

"Angela is not entirely pleased by the thought of going to the freak-house," he muttered. "I can't be sure that once we're away from a controlled environment she won't try to escape."

Wolfe's bark of laughter echoed through the phone. "She hasn't become a slave to your charm? There was a time when you only had to smile to get a woman to devote herself to your pleasure. You must be losing your touch, old man."

Niko ignored the insult. He couldn't tease about his feelings for Angela. Or the fact that he'd hurt her so badly he couldn't be sure she would ever forgive him.

"Give me a few hours to convince her that I'm not entirely evil."

"Hmmm. Do you intend to do this convincing in the bedroom?"

"Not your business."

Wolfe gave a short laugh that ended on a weary sigh. "Maybe it's for the best. Things are . . . tense right now."

"Because of Dylan?"

"No. The Mave is convinced we'll be able to clean up that nasty business."

"Then what?"

"I'm not entirely certain, but it has something to do with the necros. Which means their Sentinels refuse to leave their sides. You know how overprotective they are."

Necromancers (or diviners as they preferred to be called) were bonded to a guardian Sentinel while they were still young, never leaving the protection of Valhalla or outlying compounds without one at their side.

"A threat?"

Wolfe made a sound of disgust. "Why would they tell me? I am, after all, only the leader of the Sentinels. It's not like I need to be kept in the damned loop."

Niko grimaced. Politics sucked. Especially for a man who had the tact of a raging bull.

"Arel shouldn't be too far away," he said, eager to change the conversation. "Could you have him join me at the cabin? The sooner he can get on Dylan's trail the better."

Instantly Wolfe was back in commander mode.

"Will he need backup?"

The memory of the hatred blazing in Dylan's crimson eyes made the question easy to answer.

"Yes, but don't tell him I said so."

"You got it, although it will be a few hours before any backup can get there since they have to drive." A pause. "Niko."

"Yeah?"

"Take care of yourself."

"Always."

"Oh, and give that scientist a kiss for me."

Not a chance in hell.

"You should know by now, Wolfe, I don't share," he growled.

Chapter Six

Angela was impressed.

So this was what a kitchen was supposed to look like, she wryly acknowledged.

It was more than the hand-carved cabinets, granite countertops, and stainless steel appliances. It was the heavy oak dining table in the center of the ceramic tiled floor and the matching china cabinet that displayed the prized dishware.

This was a place where families gathered to share meals and laugh away the troubles of the day.

It wasn't a makeshift lab for a distracted scientist. Or a place for a child to sit alone with dinner from the microwave while her mother was flirting with her fellow drunks at the nearest bar.

She squashed the ridiculous pang. She wasn't that lonely ten-year-old girl anymore and she was perfectly happy with her private apartment and her kitchen filled with microscopes.

Pulling a water bottle from the fully loaded fridge, she was debating between a salad and a tuna sandwich when a husky voice whispered in her ear.

"Did you find anything to tempt your appetite?"

With a muffled shriek she turned to glare at the man towering over her.

"Dammit," she muttered, pressing a hand to her racing heart. "You really need to wear a bell."

He flashed his rare, bone-melting grin. "Kinky, but whatever turns you on."

She swallowed a groan as desire blazed through her with stunning force.

Even furious with his betrayal and unnerved by the disruption of her peaceful life, she still wanted him with a raw, aching need that was frightening.

Against her will her gaze drank in the lean, starkly beautiful face and stunning blue eyes that studied her with an unwavering intensity. His hair was even more ruffled than usual and her fingers itched to smooth the dark strands that shimmered like copper in the fading afternoon sunlight.

Then they could travel down to discover if his body was the chiseled perfection she'd always fantasized.

Abruptly realizing his eyes had darkened, as if he could actually sense her disturbing awareness, she shut the fridge door. Instantly she stepped back as his heat wrapped around her.

"How long did you have to practice sneaking up on people?" she breathed, shivering at the prickles that raced over her skin.

"It's a natural talent." He closed the tiny space between them, reaching to pluck the water bottle from her hand and tossed it into the recycle bin. "One of many."

She licked her dry lips. "Is modesty another natural talent?"

"No, but this is."

He leaned down to capture her lips in a kiss of sheer possession.

"Niko," she muttered, the breath squeezed from her lungs

as he wrapped his arms around her, moving slowly, as if to give her ample opportunity to step away.

Or perhaps he was worried his superior powers would frighten her, she realized as he gently tugged her against him.

Tilting back her head she met his smoldering gaze.

"Tell me no and this ends now," he husked.

Her lips parted, but the word was stuck in her throat. "I thought you wanted dinner?" she instead hedged.

His hand shifted to her lower back, pressing her against the thickening length of his arousal.

"You know what I want."

She shivered, her hands lifting to rest against his chest. "Do I?"

His tongue traced the curve of her lower lip. "I can demonstrate if you need clarification."

Oh, she wanted him to demonstrate.

She wanted him to rip off her clothes and take her in a glorious storm of pagan passion. She wanted him to kiss her with a hunger that would drown out the voice of insecurity that whispered in the back of her mind.

"It seems—"

"What?"

"Convenient."

"Convenient?" He made a sound of disbelief. "Trust me, lusting after a female for six weeks is anything but convenient."

"If you were so overwhelmed with lust you hid it well enough. I did everything but spread myself naked on the lab table and you couldn't have shown less interest." She lowered her gaze, her cheeks flushing with embarrassment at the memory of her awkward flirtations and his blatant apathy. He'd only reinforced her opinion she was lacking the mysterious quality that attracted the opposite sex. "Now, when you need my cooperation, you suddenly find me irresistible."

"Angel, look at me," he said, cupping a hand beneath her

chin, urging her face up to meet his eyes that were darkened with regret.

"I'm looking," she muttered.

"It might not have been my intention to hurt you, but I did," he said softly. "You felt betrayed by my charade; can you imagine how much worse it would have been if I'd given in to my desire and taken you to my bed? Not even I am that much a bastard."

The resentment she'd been nursing for the past few hours faltered at his low words.

"So it was for my own good?"

His gaze slid to her mouth. "It certainly wasn't for mine."

He had a point, a tiny voice whispered in the back of her mind. She wasn't sure she'd ever have been able to forgive him if he'd actually taken her as a lover while he'd been lying to her.

Still, that didn't mean this wasn't just another game.

"If you say."

He frowned. "You can't doubt my desire for you?"

"Trust me, you wouldn't be the first man to want to be 'just friends,'" she said dryly.

"Christ, Angela," he breathed. "As much as I want to be your friend, I'm desperate to make you my lover."

Her heart missed a beat as she met his brooding gaze. "Desperate?"

Without warning he grasped her wrist and pressed her hand against the thick length of his erection.

"Tell me, angel, does this feel desperate to you?" he growled.

Her suspicions were seared away as her fingers curled around the impressive bulge. Even through the heavy material of his jeans she could feel the pulsing heat and straining urgency of his need.

It was intoxicating.

Her mouth went dry as her stomach clenched with excitement. She'd never understood why women rushed to the window when the football team jogged past wearing nothing more than gym shorts. The male body was a collection of vital organs surrounded by muscle and bone and hard-wired to a brain that allowed it to function.

It wasn't until this man entered her lab that she got it.

Just being near Niko was like being plunged into an electrical storm. The heat, the sizzle in the air, and the prickles of anticipation that warned she was about to be struck by lightning.

And worse, her brain shut down until all she could think about was wrapping herself so tightly around him he could never escape.

Dangerous, dangerous sensations.

Her fingers slid down his erection, her heart skipping a beat as he seemed to grow even bigger.

"It feels—"

"Yes?" he groaned, his hands gripping her shoulders as if he wasn't convinced his knees would hold him.

Angela felt a strange jolt of . . . what was it? Female power?

He wanted her.

Truly wanted her.

Of all the lies he told her this wasn't one.

"Large," she murmured.

He gave a choked laugh, his face tight with his barely leashed desire.

"Should I be flattered?"

Her awkwardness was forgotten beneath the heady realization that she could affect this man with a mere touch.

"Not really, I don't have much to compare it to," she admitted. "As I said, I've never been the kind of girl that attracts the opposite sex."

"Only because mortal men are blind."

She snorted. "All of them?"

He studied her upturned face with an undisguised hunger that squeezed the air from her lungs.

"If they had the superior senses of a Sentinel they would have seen what I see."

"And what's that?" she managed to ask.

He lifted a hand to tug the scrunchie from the messy remains of her ponytail.

"Thick, sable hair that starts out prim and proper in the mornings, but during the day sexy little tendrils escape to play against your long, utterly kissable neck."

She trembled as his fingers threaded through the loose strands of her hair.

"Oh."

He growled low in his throat as he lifted a fistful of hair to press it to his nose, breathing deeply of the apple shampoo she used.

"Do you know how many hours I devoted to fantasizing about releasing your hair from its bondage so it could spread across my pillows?"

"Bondage?" The word came out as a croak as she all too easily pictured being handcuffed to Niko's bed, her body a willing slave to the promise of paradise.

Keeping one hand tangled in her hair, he used the other to gently trace the sensitive skin of her temple.

"Dark velvet eyes that tempt a man to become lost in their depths," he continued his verbal seduction, his voice smoky.

"Boring brown," she corrected.

He ignored her interruption, his smoldering gaze tracing every line and angle of her upturned face.

"A noble little nose," he murmured. "Did you know you scrunch it up when you're concentrating on your work?"

"I do not."

His fingers drifted down to trace her nose before outlining her trembling lips.

"A mouth that is as ripe and delicious as cherries."

Her lips instinctively parted at his searing touch. "Niko."

"And this skin." The warm fingers continued their path of

destruction down the length of her neck to trace the loose neckline of her sweatshirt. "As smooth as the most expensive silk."

"I'm too pale."

"You're perfect," he growled in response. "Ivory silk. It tempts a man to discover if you're the same porcelain shade all over." Holding her gaze, he lowered his hand to the hem of her shirt. "May I?"

She knew what he was asking. And that if she agreed there would be no turning back.

"Yes," she whispered.

Obviously a man of action, Niko didn't hesitate to pull the sweatshirt up and off her body. It happened so fast that Angela didn't have time to feel embarrassed. Then, catching sight of Niko's harshly appreciative expression, she forgot to worry that she was too skinny, or too pale, or too whatever else her insecurities could imagine.

"Yes," he rasped as his hands reached to dispense with her lacy bra. "Ivory tipped with rosebuds. An irresistible combination."

His fingers cupped the small mounds of her breasts, his thumbs teasing the nipples to tiny points of aching pleasure. She sucked in a startled gasp, her back arching as if to beg for more.

Muttering a low, rough curse, he lowered his head and licked the tip of her breast.

Angela jerked in astonishment, her hands lifting to plunge into the short strands of his hair.

"Dear . . . Lord."

His own hands slid down the curve of her waist, tugging her against his rigid muscles at the same time he sucked her nipple between his lips.

She groaned, as he caught the tip between his teeth. It felt so good. Blissfully, wondrously good.

"I want you," he whispered, kissing a path to her other breast to torment it with the same dizzying skill.

"I want you too," she husked.

And she did.

What had his word been?

Desperately. Yes, that was it.

She wanted him desperately.

This was chemistry at its most basic form.

He made a low sound deep in his throat, planting impatient kisses up the line of her collarbone until he buried his face in the curve of her neck.

"But—"

"No," she snapped.

He pulled back with a frown. "No?"

Dammit. She'd spent six weeks tormenting herself with the fear that this man who filled her every fantasy could never desire her.

Now that she was in his arm, hovering on the edge of paradise, she didn't want it snatched away.

Just once she wanted to say the hell with logic and common sense and give in to temptation.

"Don't give me a reason why we can't do this," she muttered. His hooded gaze skimmed down to her nipples that remained hardened with desire before returning to meet her frustrated gaze.

"It's more a warning."

"A warning? Oh." She wrinkled her nose. "Yeah, I'm not stupid. I know the routine. This is just sex. It means nothing."

"No." The blue eyes flared with a stunning emotion. "It means everything."

If Niko hadn't been battling his caveman urge to strip Angela of her remaining clothes and take her against the fridge, he would have smiled at her baffled expression.

Hell, he didn't blame her for looking at him like he was out of his mind.

Until he'd encountered this woman he would have bet his left nut he would never utter those words.

"What did you say?"

"You heard me." He gently brushed a stray curl from her flushed cheek. "For me this isn't just sex."

"You don't have to pretend, Niko." She unconsciously licked her lips, her expression troubled. "In fact, I would prefer that you didn't."

With a low growl he was scooping her off her feet and heading out of the kitchen.

He didn't know if it was the lip-licking or her refusal to believe that he was sincere that tipped him over the edge, but he knew that one way or another he was going to convince her that this was no longer a matter of duty or revenge or mere lust.

Crossing the living room he carried her up the stairs and into the bedroom loft.

It was a spacious room with an open beamed ceiling and hand-carved furniture scattered across the polished wood floor. At the far end of the room were glass sliding doors that led to a back balcony that offered a view of the pool as the sun slid beyond the horizon.

A beautiful sight, but not nearly as beautiful as the woman in his arms.

Niko moved to gently place Angela on the large brass bed. Then, standing at the edge of the mattress, he simply relished the sight of her stretched across the emerald green comforter.

Man. How many nights had he tortured himself with this precise image?

The dark hair spread in wild abandon. The pale face flushed with need and the midnight eyes smoldering with invitation.

Only this was far better than any fantasy.

A fiercely possessive emotion clutched at his heart as his gaze slid down the delicate curve of her neck and over the soft swell of her naked breasts.

It was raw and primal and shockingly perfect.

With jerky movements that would have made his fellow Sentinels snicker, Niko kicked off his shoes before removing the rest of his clothes. He was acutely aware of Angela's covert survey of his nude body, her breath catching as she caught sight of his fully erect cock.

For once his vanity didn't assume she was impressed by his lean muscles or his wide chest sprinkled with dark hair. Or even the imposing size of his erection.

For all of Angela Locke's impressive intelligence and independent nature, she was still remarkably innocent. Combine that with her mysterious conviction she was somehow undesirable and it was bound to make her skittish.

Moving slow enough it didn't seem like he was pouncing (pouncing could come next time . . . and there would be a next time) Niko stretched out on the mattress beside her so that they were lying face to face. His only touch was the finger he used to trace the line of her jaw.

"No more pretense," he murmured. "The truth. Once I take you I'm never letting you go."

She shivered, her body shifting to press against him even as her eyes held a suspicion she couldn't entirely disguise.

"If this is a ploy to get me in Valhalla . . ."

"I've already given my word I won't force you to go to the compound," he said, his voice thick as his cock jerked in reaction to the brush of her hip.

"Isn't that where you live?"

"For now, but Sentinels aren't vulnerable like many of the high-bloods, so we have the choice of living among norms," he assured her, not bothering to mention that she'd eventually have to spend time at Valhalla. The Mave would want to be certain her growing powers couldn't hurt her or those around her. Yeah, that was a conversation he didn't mind putting off. Indefinitely. "Once Dylan has been captured we can go wherever you want."

"I—"

He smiled wryly as her words disappeared and she stared at him with silent wonder.

"Too much, too soon?" he teased.

With a choked groan she wrapped her arms around his neck. "Kiss me."

He did.

White-hot pleasure seared through Angela as he kissed with a clear intent.

This time there was no teasing, no slow buildup, no tender nibbles.

This was unapologetic hunger that threatened to consume her.

And exactly what she needed.

She didn't want to think of the past, and the future was something to worry about . . . later.

She wanted to become lost in this moment.

As if sensing her need, Niko's kiss became even more demanding, his tongue dipping into her mouth with an intimate sweep. In concert, his hand cupped her breast, his thumb rubbing over the tight peak.

Angela squirmed against him as the electric sensations jolted through her.

"Niko."

He pulled back, studying with a hint of concern.

"Am I frightening you?" he whispered.

Her heart squeezed with a dangerous emotion. God, he was so beautiful. A sexy, lethally beautiful male who had enchanted her the minute he'd strolled into her lab.

But it was his instinctive urge to care and protect her that threatened to destroy the barriers she'd built around her heart.

No one had ever, ever treated her as if she . . . mattered.

As if she was the most important thing in his life.

The knowledge was more erotic than any amount of hard muscles and male beauty.

His brows drew together. "Angel?"

In answer, she plunged her fingers into the heavy thickness of his hair.

"I have wanted you from the moment I saw you in the doorway of my lab," she confessed in soft tones. "I didn't know what hit me."

His soft chuckle brushed over her cheeks, his eyes darkened to indigo.

"Trust me, the feeling was entirely mutual." Holding her gaze he slid his hand down the flat plane of her stomach until he could unfasten her jeans. "I tried to convince myself that you were just a part of the job, but I knew from the beginning I was lying to myself."

Her body felt as if it was on fire as he expertly rid her of her remaining clothes. Then, still holding her gaze, he slid slowly downward. The rub of skin against skin made her shiver with excitement.

His lips touched the base of her throat before moving to her collarbone, tracing the delicate line with the tip of his tongue. Only when she was clutching at his broad shoulders did he allow the teasing kisses to travel down the curve of her breast.

"You're so warm," she whispered.

"All Sentinels run hot." He shifted just enough to capture the tip of her nipple between his lips.

"Oh."

She nearly came off the bed at the avalanche of sensations rushing through her body.

He was good at this.

Really, really good.

While his tongue and even his teeth pleasured her nipple, his hand slid down the curve of her hip. Angela squeezed her eyes shut, allowing herself the pleasure of exploring the broad width of his back, relishing the feel of silken skin over hard muscle.

She was growing lost in the surge of building sensations when his fingers encircled the back of her thigh and tugged her leg over his hip.

Her eyes widened as she felt the hard thrust of his arousal press against her most sensitive spot. She'd expected him to roll her onto her back, not to remain on their sides.

"Like this?"

He smiled at her hint of surprise. "We can do it anyway you want, but I've wanted you for a very long time. This seems . . . safer."

"Safer?"

"If you haven't noticed, I'm several sizes larger than you."

Her own lips twitched. "Yeah, I'd noticed."

His smile faded as he studied her with an oddly somber expression even as his fingers drifted up and down the back of her thigh, the light touch sending shocks of excitement through her.

"I'm also a Sentinel, which means my strength can be hazardous if I'm not careful."

She held his gaze. "I trust you."

His eyes briefly closed, as if her soft words had touched something deep inside him. Then, lifting the indecently long lashes, he met her gaze with a stark need that pierced straight to her heart.

"I've never wanted a woman like I want you, angel," he said, his voice husky. "I can't be entirely certain of my control."

That newly discovered thrill of power flared through her. She didn't know how she'd ever managed to capture the interest of this astonishing, sexy, compelling man. But for once she wasn't going to allow her self-doubts to ruin the moment.

Angela leaned forward, nuzzling the corner of his sensuous lips.

"*I'm* certain." She kissed a path along his knotted jaw and then the strong column of his neck, addicted to his intoxicating taste. "You would never hurt me. Not intentionally."

He sucked in a deep breath.

"No, I would never intentionally hurt you."

She slowly kissed a path back to his lips, her hips rubbing against him in blatant invitation.

"No more talking."

Framing her face in his hands, he claimed her lips in a kiss that she felt to the tips of her toes. Oh . . . yes. She shivered with pleasure, her mouth parting to allow his tongue to tangle with hers.

Drowning in the heat of his devouring kiss, she stroked her hands over the hair-roughened skin of his chest. A delicious excitement curled in the pit of her stomach as he tugged her leg higher on his hip, the tip of his cock sliding through her damp clit.

She hissed in pleasure, her nails digging into his chest.

Easily sensing the growing urgency of her desire, Niko pulled back, his face strained as he struggled to maintain control of his spiraling desire.

"Angel, I can't wait," he rasped. "I need to be inside you."

His rough voice sent a flare of aching desire through her.

"Yes," she breathed, shuddering as his fingers drifted over the curve of her hip.

With infinite care he explored the tender skin of her lower stomach before heading ever lower.

Angela muttered her approval as he covered her lips in a hungry kiss, but even distracted she gave a strangled groan when his seeking fingers stroked through her damp heat.

"God, you feel good," he muttered. "Are you ready for me?"

Ready?

Hell, she'd been ready for weeks.

Another stroke or two of those clever fingers and she'd be reaching paradise alone.

"Please, Niko," she muttered. "Now."

His low hiss filled the air, his erection pressing eagerly against her damp heat.

"Next time," he muttered.

She blinked in confusion. "What?"

He gazed deep into her eyes, a thin layer of sweat coating his face.

"Next time I intend to spend hours pleasuring you."

A sly smile curved her lips. "Or maybe I'll pleasure you."

"Oh, shit."

His control snapped.

Just like that.

Reclaiming her lips, Niko's hands shifted to her lower back and with a forward thrust of his hips he was entering her in one sure stroke.

She gasped, but not from fear.

Exquisite pleasure blazed through her and she pressed her face into the curve of his neck. She'd never done anything but the traditional missionary position. Now she realized that the current arrangement allowed her to feel every slow stroke into her before he was retreating and returning with a slow, insistent thrust.

"Niko," she breathed, feeling overwhelmed.

It was more than the extraordinary bliss of feeling him moving deep inside her. It was the sense of intimate connection with this man that went beyond the physical.

"I knew it would be perfect," he whispered as he continued his measured pace. "I knew *you* would be perfect."

"I never realized."

"Never realized what, my sweet angel?"

"That this could be so—"

"So?"

"Life altering," she breathed, her body moving in perfect rhythm with his.

His low laugh echoed through the air with an unmistakable satisfaction.

"You belong to me now," he vowed.

Belonged?

If she'd been in her right mind, she might have protested the possessive comment.

But instead she arched her back as her body began to tighten with a shimmering anticipation. His steady, unrelenting pace was stoking an inferno deep within her that threatened to combust.

"Angel," he breathed, giving her leg a tug higher as he angled his hips upward.

His slight shift was enough to press him even deeper within her and with a shocking force the tension that coiled between her legs abruptly shattered into a thousand pieces.

She cried out and wrapped her arms around his neck as he gave two more deep thrusts before he was reaching his own climax.

She held on tightly as they both struggled to recover from the explosion of sensations, their ragged breaths the only sound to stir the air.

Chapter Seven

Niko ran a shaky hand down the damp skin of Angela's back, his face buried in her apple-scented hair.

Man, he ached to press her even closer to his trembling body. To hold her so tightly she would never be able to escape. But even now he feared he might accidentally crush her.

She was so fragile. So vulnerable.

The knowledge frightened him on a primal level that threatened to make him do something extremely stupid.

Like lock her in his rooms at Valhalla and never let her out.

Something that this fiercely independent woman would most certainly protest.

"You're quiet," he at last murmured, lifting his head to study her with a searching gaze. She'd never looked more beautiful with her hair tangled around her flushed face and her lips still swollen from his kisses. But he was a Sentinel. He didn't miss the hint of unease behind her air of sleepy satisfaction. "Are you having regrets?"

"No."

She used her finger to draw an aimless pattern over his chest, seemingly unaware that the light caress was enough to kick his libido into overdrive. Of course, just being close to this female was enough to send his libido into overdrive. Or catching her scent. Or seeing her across the room . . .

He swallowed a groan, grimly leashing his insistent desire.

This wasn't a fleeting afternoon of delight.

This was the start of eternity.

Together.

He needed to know what was going on in that clever, always unpredictable brain of hers.

"What is it, angel?"

A brief hesitation. "I was just thinking that we don't really know much about each other."

His hand skimmed beneath the warm silk of her hair, massaging the tense muscles of her nape.

"I know that you're beautiful, frighteningly intelligent, and that you dislike being the center of attention," he promptly informed her. They were beyond him pretending he hadn't spent the past six weeks spying on her like some creepy stalker. "I also know that you rarely allow people close to you, but you're fiercely loyal to the few friends that you trust. And that you're lonely and you've never felt like you belong."

She stiffened, clearly disturbed by the realization of just how much she'd unconsciously revealed.

"You can't know that," she breathed.

"I can because I felt the same."

Her eyes narrowed in disbelief. "You?"

"Sentinels aren't always recognized until they hit puberty," he explained, revealing the sort of information only shared among high-bloods. She would soon be a part of his world. Whether she liked it or not. "When I was a child I went to public school, but even at a very young age I knew that there was something different about me. I could run faster, jump higher, see better, and hear things no one else could."

She frowned. "And that was a bad thing?"

His jaw clenched at the memory of the hateful taunts and brutal ambushes that had dogged his early years.

"Boys can be extremely competitive and no one wants to play with the kid who always wins."

Her expression softened with sympathy. "Ah."

"And that was before my super strength kicked in."

Her fingers spread across his chest. "What happened?"

"I nearly killed a neighborhood boy when he threw a rock and hit me in the head." He grimaced. The memory of the boy lying on the ground with his face beaten bloody was one that had haunted him for years. "That's when my mom called Valhalla."

"Did they come and take you away?"

"Yes."

Her hand lifted to cup his face, her heart far too tender for her own good.

"Were you unhappy?"

"At first," he admitted. "My mother came to visit when she could, but I'd become too wary to make friends." His lips twisted. He'd been a surly, arrogant kid with a chip on his shoulder the size of Mount Rushmore. In no way did he want to admit he was one of the mutants. "Especially when they were all freaks."

Her thumb absently stroked his lower lip, sending a blast of heat through him.

Oh . . . yeah.

He was definitely locking her in his rooms. *Their* rooms. At least for the next month or so.

"What happened?"

"Wolfe, a boy a few years older than me, walked up and punched me so hard he broke my jaw."

"That's terrible," she growled in outrage. "What did you do?"

His lips parted into a wide smile. "Exactly what you'd

expect me to do. I picked myself off the floor and did my best to kill the son of a bitch."

Her frown deepened. "Why are you smiling?"

"Because I discovered that I'd finally encountered someone who could not only match me in strength, but could kick my ass."

"I don't understand."

Of course she didn't.

Only two males could appreciate the nuanced diplomacy of a knock-down-drag-out fight.

"For the first time ever I didn't have to hold back. I didn't have to pretend I was 'less' than what I was." He deliberately caught and held her gaze. "I found the place where I belonged."

"And Wolfe?"

"He's the current leader of the Sentinels and my closest friend."

She lightly ran her fingers up and down the line of his jaw, seemingly fascinated by the feel of his five o'clock shadow.

"You never mentioned your father."

He lifted his hand to press her palm against his cheek. "He died when I was just a baby."

"Oh, I'm sorry."

"What about your parents?"

Her lashes instantly lowered to hide her eyes.

"I was the product of a one-night stand," she said, her voice stripped of emotion. "I never knew my father, not even his name. I doubt he ever knew I existed."

He swallowed a sigh as he felt the barriers rising between them.

One bout of sex, no matter how life-altering, wasn't going to be enough to convince her to lower the barriers surrounding her heart.

"And your mother?" he asked.

"She died a year ago."

He pulled her hand to his lips, planting a kiss in the middle of her palm.

"That must have been tough."

She trembled in response to his caress, but her eyes remained stubbornly hidden behind her lashes. She'd share her body, but not her wounds.

"Yes, but we weren't close." She struggled to swallow, as if she had a lump in her throat. "She never understood my lack of social skills and she was disappointed that I spent more time in the library than with the other kids."

"Disappointed in you?" He didn't have to pretend his angry astonishment. "Impossible."

"She didn't want a valedictorian, she wanted a prom queen." A humorless smile curved her lips. "Or at the very least a cheerleader."

He swore beneath his breath, wishing her mother was still alive so he could teach her just how special her daughter truly was.

And more importantly, what he did to people who would dare to hurt this female.

"Her loss," he rasped.

"I suppose."

He hesitated, wondering if there'd been more to her mother's disapproval than a shallow desire for glitz rather than gold.

"Did she ever sense you were special?"

She tugged her hand from his grasp, pressing it against his chest in instant denial.

"I don't know what you're talking about."

"Angel—"

"No," she muttered. "I won't discuss it."

"Denying your powers won't make them go away."

She gave another shove against his chest. "I'm hungry."

He swallowed a sigh. At some point he was going to have to make her accept the truth of who and what she was.

But not now.

Now he had her naked in his bed, and there were far more pleasurable ways to spend the next few hours.

"Me too," he murmured, pressing his lips to her forehead, his hand trailing up the curve of her waist to halt just below her breast.

Her breath caught and she instinctively arched toward his hardening cock.

"Niko?"

"I swear I'll feed you," he promised, nipping the lobe of her ear as he rolled her flat on her back and covered her with the hard weight of his body. "Anything you want." His hand closed over her breast, his heart coming to a complete halt as he gazed down at her wide, velvet eyes. His. His woman. "Later."

Her hands lifted to wrap around his neck, her eyes smoldering with a matching desire.

"Much later."

It was, in fact, much, much later when Niko at last headed for the shower and Angela made her way down to the kitchen wearing nothing more than an oversized T-shirt.

She'd discovered once she opened her bag that it was never wise to try and pack when in a blind panic. Her hasty lack of attention had made certain she had a plethora of things she didn't need—like mismatched socks and dirty towels—and very little that she did need.

Typical.

Her luck had never been good. And lately it'd been down-right crappy.

Well, except for Niko, she admitted, a precious warmth settled in the center of her heart. He was, hands down, the finest thing that had ever happened to her.

Still, it would have been nice to have her own nightshirt and a toothbrush.

Tossing a handful of dried cranberries into the large salad she'd chopped in a bowl, she was debating whether or not to make a couple of grilled cheese sandwiches when a male voice whispered directly in her ear.

"Ah, so this is where Little Red Riding Hood hides from the big bad wolf."

Nearly leaping out of her skin, Angela whirled around to discover a stranger standing far too close for comfort.

A part of her recognized the intruder was mouthwateringly handsome with pale brown hair that was highlighted with strands of honey and eyes that were a rich gold. But a larger part was far more concerned with the lean, muscular body casually dressed in jeans and a black tee that moved with the same fluid grace as Niko.

This was no harmless trespasser.

"Shit." She pressed a hand to her thumping heart. "Who are you?"

"I'm Arel. A friend of Niko's." The golden gaze skimmed down her slender body. Not so much ogling her barely covered limbs, but searching for potential defects. "He asked me to meet him here."

Yeah. Like she was going to take his word for it.

People who were invited knocked on the front door and waited to be let in. They didn't creep into the kitchen and terrify half-dressed scientists.

Covertly backing toward the counter behind her, Angela sought to distract the intruder.

"How did you get in?"

"Serra gave me the security codes during our short, but highly memorable affair last year." A smile of pure male appreciation curved his lips. "Mmm. I love psychics."

"Yeah." She wrinkled her nose as she put her hand behind her to search for the knob of the drawer. "TMI."

He folded his arms over his chest, watching her with an amused gaze.

"The knife drawer is on the other side of the sink," he informed her. "Of course, I seem to remember there was a rather lethal rolling pin just behind you."

Busted.

With a sigh, Angela gave up her furtive attempt to find a weapon and instead settled for a frustrated glare.

"I suppose you're another Sentinel?"

"I am."

"You people should really learn it's not nice to sneak up on others."

He shrugged. "Old habits die hard and I have to admit I wanted a chance to check you out before we were formally introduced."

Check her out?

That sounded . . . borderline psychotic.

"Do I need to get a restraining order?"

He chuckled at her obvious unease. "You can't blame my fascination," he said.

"I can't?"

"I've known Niko for a very long time and never in all those years has he allowed anything or anyone to interfere with the hunt." His gaze skimmed back to her bare legs. "Not even a woman."

She flinched. Okay, maybe he did know Niko. At least enough to realize that Niko would do anything to catch his prey.

Still, that didn't mean he was there as a friend.

"Don't worry, Niko's record remains intact," she assured him wryly. "I was the bait, not the interference."

The intruder arched a startled brow. "He didn't tell you?"

"Tell me what?"

"I'm here because he called Wolfe to say he was handing

off his hunt for Dylan," he said, a mysterious smile curving his lips. "He wanted me to take his place."

"Why?"

"Isn't that obvious?"

"I've learned that assumptions can be dangerous things," she countered.

"Ah. Fair enough." He studied her with a steady gaze. "He asked me to take over the hunt because he wanted to concentrate on protecting you."

Niko had hinted that he intended to put aside his need for revenge and concentrate on her, but she hadn't truly thought he would allow someone else to take command of the hunt.

"Oh."

"That's it?" the man challenged. "Oh."

She blinked. "I . . . I don't know what to say."

He appeared unimpressed with her reaction. "Did he tell you about the Sentinels that Dylan murdered?"

She licked her dry lips. He was clearly searching for a response from her, but as always she was oblivious to the nuances of his meaning.

"He said they were friends."

"A hell of a lot more than friends," Arel growled. "He practically raised Fiona. She was like a daughter to him."

Angela's heart twisted in sympathy. She was beginning to understand Niko. It wouldn't be enough that he would mourn the loss of his friends. Especially one he'd felt responsible for.

He would blame himself for their deaths.

"What do you want from me?" she demanded in thick tones.

"I want you to understand just what Niko is sacrificing to stay with you."

"That's enough, Arel," Niko warned, leaning against the doorjamb wearing nothing more than a pair of faded jeans and a dangerous scowl.

Chapter Eight

Niko folded his arms over his bare chest, his eyes narrowed.

If he had been in a rational frame of mind, he might have appreciated Arel's loyal attempt to protect him. It was, after all, what friends did. But there was nothing rational in his feelings for Angela, and he wasn't about to allow anyone to threaten her.

No matter how well intentioned.

Easily sensing the tension, Angela cleared her throat then began edging toward the doorway. She didn't need her genius-level intelligence to realize that it was time for a strategic retreat.

"I think I'll go take a shower," she muttered, giving a tiny gasp when he grabbed her by the waist and claimed a possessive kiss before allowing her to scurry away, his gaze never leaving Arel.

With a roll of his eyes, the young Sentinel lifted his hands in defeat.

"You've made your point."

The words were casual, but Niko was well aware that

having accepted Niko's commitment to Angela, Arel would fight to the death to protect her.

It was the way of Sentinels.

"Have you eaten?" he asked, moving to lean against the countertop.

Sentinels burned calories at an accelerated rate, which meant they were always hungry.

"Yeah, I hit a drive-thru before leaving Columbia." Arel's expression hardened. "Tell me about your meeting with Dylan."

Niko grimaced. "She's not going to be convinced to turn herself over to the Mave."

Arel shrugged. "Good."

"She was one of us."

"No. She never allowed herself to accept being different," Arel said. "She was a time bomb just waiting to go off no matter how hard Wolfe tried to diffuse her bitterness."

Niko couldn't argue. Wolfe had done everything in his power to reach the hostile young woman, but she'd never been capable of accepting that she would never be normal.

"A damned shame."

"It will be more of a shame if she gets her hands on your scientist," Arel pointed out.

"That's not happening." His expression held no compromise. He would do whatever necessary to protect Angela.

Arel paced toward the windows overlooking the pool. "Do you think Dylan's still in the area?"

"Yes," Niko responded without hesitation. "She won't leave until I get Angela out of here."

There was a short silence before Arel turned back to study Niko's grim expression.

"Would it be possible?"

"What?"

"Could Angela alter Dylan's DNA?"

"Maybe." Niko hadn't given it a lot of thought. His fascination with Angela had nothing to do with her rare talent.

"According to Calder, her manipulation of cells, or whatever the hell it is she manipulates, is still small and random, but he has hopes that once she fully embraces her talent she'll be able to offer hope to high-bloods who suffer from mutations that are killing them."

"Our very own Dr. Frankenstein."

"Careful," Niko growled.

"It wasn't an insult," Arel hastily assured him. "Just the opposite. Think of the potential benefits of having her work with our scientists. She could save hundreds if not thousands of lives."

Niko shook his head. "It's too early to know how far her skills will develop. Or even if she'll be willing to accept her gifts." He deliberately held his friend's gaze. "It will be her decision. I won't have her bullied into giving more than she's willing to offer."

"Not even if she can help your family?"

"She is my family." Niko straightened, his gaze challenging. "Any argument?"

Arel gave a sudden laugh. "Niko, if I ever find a female who lights up like a neon sign just because I walked into a room I intend to do whatever I have to do to keep her."

Niko stilled, ridiculously pleased by the soft words. "A neon sign? Did she?"

Arel shook his head in disgust. "Wipe that smug smile off your lips. There had to be one woman in the world crazy enough to fall in love with you."

"I only need one."

"Good God. How the mighty are fallen." Arel hissed as the sharp sound of an alarm pierced the air. "What's that?"

Niko was already headed into the living room, moving to stand directly in front of the line of monitors.

"Someone just broke the perimeter."

The men frowned in unison as they studied the thick woods that surrounded the house.

"Nothing," Arel muttered as Niko manipulated the cameras to do a complete scan of the area. "Not even a stray dog."

"It has to be Dylan," Niko ground out.

What the hell was she doing? She had to sense that Arel was in the house. There was no way she could hope to overpower two Sentinels.

Not without help.

"Or a distraction," Arel stated the obvious. "You stay here and I'll try to flush her out."

Niko nodded in agreement. As much as he wanted to be on the hunt, his heart was firmly committed to protecting Angela.

Of course, that didn't mean he wasn't worried about his friend.

"Arel," he called as the younger man opened the door and stepped onto the front porch.

"Yeah, yeah. I'll be careful," Arel called, disappearing into the darkness.

Niko moved to shut the door and reset the alarm, then headed to the back of the house to check the locks. Stepping into the kitchen his instincts were on full alert.

Dylan.

The scent of her filled the air.

On cue, the slender female still dressed in black stepped out of the pantry and offered him a mocking smile.

"About time," she drawled. "I thought Arel would never leave."

"Dylan." He clenched his hands at his side. His weapons were upstairs, but it didn't matter. He could kill as easily with his hands. Or even a well-placed kick. "How did you get past the security system?"

Her eyes glowed with an eerie crimson heat as she strolled forward, one hand held behind her back.

A hidden weapon?

That was the most logical guess, although he couldn't catch the scent of gunpowder or the metallic tang of a blade.

He would no doubt find out soon enough, he conceded with an explosion of frustration.

Goddammit.

Why the hell couldn't this female simply accept that she was made precisely as nature had intended? She was graceful, strong, intensely intelligent and beautiful in an exotic fashion.

Everything most women wanted to be.

"I was watching the property when dear Arel was kind enough to punch in the codes so I didn't have to waste time trying to sneak past the cameras," she confessed.

Fan-fucking-tastic.

"What about the alarm that just went off?"

She shrugged. "I set it off with a delayed explosion."

Ah. Of course.

"Clever, but a waste of your time," he said, his voice steady and his expression carefully devoid of his seething fury.

She strolled forward, a smirk curling her lips. "There's no need for us to be enemies, Niko. Give me the female and I'll walk away. No harm, no foul."

"The female's name is Angela," he said from between clenched teeth. "It's not going to happen."

"Then I'll take her."

He shifted, making sure he was standing between the crazed bitch and the door.

"It won't do any good. She can't help you."

Bitterness flared in the crimson eyes. "Oh, I think you would be surprised what people can accomplish when they're desperate."

"So you've proven," he pointedly reminded her, his acute hearing picking up the sound of the shower being shut off overhead. *Oh. Christ. Don't come down here, Angela.* "You betrayed and murdered your own family. And for what?"

"For a life beyond the prison walls."

His brows snapped together. "Valhalla has never been a prison."

She hissed in anger. "Not to you."

Niko shook his head. He was wasting his breath. Dylan

had convinced herself that her life had been some sort of torture at Valhalla. How else could she excuse the murder of those who'd offered her only kindness?

"And you believe if you can pass as a normal human your life will be filled with endless happiness?" he instead sneered.

Her chin tilted, the slits of her flat nose flaring in anger.

"Endless happiness? No. But fleeting happiness? Maybe," she ground out, taking another step closer. "Why shouldn't I have the opportunity to fall in love? To have children."

He barely listened to her whining. He could smell . . . what? Something he couldn't identify.

Which was worrying the hell out of him.

"If a man loves you he doesn't care about your appearance," he said in absent tones.

"Don't insult me," she snarled. "Would you be bedding your scientist if she looked like a monster?"

Niko didn't even have to consider. "Her looks have nothing to do with my feelings."

"Liar."

Niko narrowed his gaze. "Believe what you want, Dylan, but be very clear on one thing."

"What's that?"

"I'll kill you if you lay a hand on Angela."

A slow smile of anticipation curled Dylan's lips as he widened his stance and squared his shoulders.

"So at last we get to discover who the better Sentinel is."

"Being the superior fighter doesn't make you the better Sentinel," he reminded her, his attention torn between the threat standing in front of him and the nagging fear that Angela would return to the kitchen before he could disable Dylan. The last thing he needed was her leaping into the fray. And she would leap. He didn't have one damned doubt about that. "Or didn't you learn anything in our training?"

"You mean all that shit about loyalty and honor and protecting the weak?" she mocked. "Blah, blah, blah."

"You're lucky Wolfe never heard you call his teaching shit."

"I'm a warrior not a fucking Girl Scout."

Yeah. No argument there.

The mere thought of Dylan as a Girl Scout made him shudder in horror.

"With power comes responsibility." He repeated the words that had been drilled into his head from the minute he'd walked into Valhalla.

Dylan gave a sharp laugh, pulling her hand from behind her back to reveal the small device that was strapped around her forearm.

"And your insistence on clinging to honor will make sure I win."

"Dammit, Dylan," Niko breathed, recognizing the weapon that had been developed as an advanced stun gun only to be banned when it was discovered the electrical charge was enough to stop all but the strongest heart. "Where the hell did you get that?"

"I made it." She lifted her arm toward Niko. "We all have our little talents."

Niko darted to the side, acutely aware that it was a fifty-fifty shot of whether he could survive. If he died, or was even incapacitated, Angela would be at the mercy of the crazed Dylan.

As fast as he was, however, he wasn't fast enough.

Even as he moved he felt the barbs pierce the skin on his back, a massive jolt of electricity blasting through his body.

Shit.

With his last coherent thought, he tried to send a mental message to Arel and warn him of the danger. Then, as his heart threatened to explode, he dropped to the floor, his head banging against the ceramic tiles with enough force to knock him unconscious.

Angela stayed in the shower until the water turned cold and her skin was pruny. She wanted to give Niko and Arel plenty of privacy to talk.

Or argue.

Or have a beer and play lawn darts.

You could never be certain with men.

She blow-dried her hair and then slipped on the one pair of clean jeans she'd managed to stuff into her bag along with a stretchy top.

She was searching for her shoes that had become lost during the heat of Niko's lovemaking when she heard a low grunt of pain.

Had that come from the kitchen?

Had the two men come to blows?

Well, she'd be damned if she would stand aside and allow them to beat each other bloody. Especially if they were fighting about her.

Taking the steps two at a time, Angela jogged into the kitchen, not sure what to expect.

She didn't have enough experience with men to know if they could punch one another and then make up and play nice. Or if she'd have to get between the two and try to make them stop.

Yeah, like she could actually separate two Sentinels.

Her ridiculous imaginings were destroyed by the sight of Niko lying motionless on the floor with Dylan standing next to him.

"Oh my God." Skidding to a halt, she sucked in a horrified breath, her heart forgetting to beat. "What have you done?"

Dylan lifted her head, her crimson eyes shimmering in the overhead light.

"He's alive, at least for now," she purred, her fingers lightly stroking over a strange device strapped to her forearm. "Come with me without a fight and he'll stay that way. Otherwise poor Niko will join his beloved Fiona in the grave."

Angela nearly went to her knees at the tidal wave of relief that flowed through her.

Niko was alive.

That's all that mattered.

"I'll come," she croaked. "Just leave him alone."

Stepping over the unconscious man, Dylan moved toward Angela with a smirk.

"I knew you'd be reasonable once you understood the situation."

A blast of anger shook through Angela. This female had murdered over a dozen innocents, not to mention members of her own family, for her own selfish desires. Now she threatened to kill the man Angela loved—yes, loved—to force Angela to perform a miracle.

If she truly could alter cells, she'd turn the bitch into a newt.

"I understand that you're a psycho," she muttered.

"Careful, scientist," Dylan hissed. "My temper isn't always stable and I might break your neck before I remember that I need you."

It wasn't an empty threat. Angela could see the barely leashed desire for violence shimmering in the crimson eyes.

With a shudder, she struggled to form a coherent thought through the fog of anger and sheer terror.

Niko was unconscious, but where was Arel? Had he already left? Or was he lurking close enough he could come to the rescue?

Licking her dry lips, Angela glanced down at her bare feet. "I need to get my shoes before we leave. Oh, and my purse. They're upstairs—"

"Don't bother trying to stall," Dylan interrupted with sharp impatience. "Arel is still searching the woods for me. We'll be long gone before he realizes he's been outmaneuvered." Her lips twisted with smug amusement. "Poor schmuck." She gave a jerk of her head toward the door. "Let's go."

Her heart sank. It seemed she was on her own.

"What about Niko?" Angela glanced toward Niko's face, which was unnaturally pale. What the hell had this woman done to him? "We can't just leave him here. He needs a doctor."

Dylan shrugged. "He should wake in an hour or two."

"Should?"

Dylan ran a loving finger over the strange contraption on her forearm.

It was obviously a weapon, although Angela had never seen anything like it.

"This is more or less a prototype. I can't be sure of the lingering effects," Dylan revealed, her glance deliberately shifting toward Niko. "Now walk or I'll shoot him again."

"Bitch," Angela breathed too low to be heard, grudgingly turning to walk out the back door.

At least Arel was near, she tried to reassure herself. He would make sure that Niko was given the medical attention he needed.

And as for her . . . well, what was destined to happen would happen.

As the resigned thought flared through her mind, Dylan moved to her side, grabbing her upper arm in a ruthless grip. Then, with an obvious lack of concern for the fact that Angela was incapable of seeing in the dark, the Sentinel hauled her away from the manicured lawn to the surrounding trees.

Stumbling forward, Angela was kept upright by the silent female who prowled through the thick underbrush with an eerie grace.

Not that she appreciated the assistance. The rough jerks on her arm sent jagged bursts of pain through her shoulder and her bare feet were being shredded by the fast pace over the small rocks and thorn bushes.

At last they reached a small lake nestled among the trees that no doubt looked picturesque during the daylight, but at night reminded Angela of something out of a *Friday the 13th* movie.

An image that was only reinforced when they reached a car that was hidden among the shrubs and Dylan shoved her into the backseat.

"Give me your hands," she commanded.

Angela hesitated, then held out her hands. Why bother fighting the inevitable?

Reaching behind her back, Dylan pulled out a pair of zip cuffs and bound Angela's wrists together.

"Ow," Angela protested as the plastic cut into her skin. "Do they have to be so tight?"

Dylan hissed in annoyance, twisting so she could reach into the front seat.

"I didn't want to have to do this."

Angela pressed herself back into the cushion as Dylan turned back with a roll of duct tape.

Christ, did the woman always drive around with all the tools necessary for a successful kidnapping?

"No. Please," Angela pleaded. "I swear I'll be quiet."

"Yes." The Sentinel ripped off a piece of the tape and slapped it across Angela's mouth. "You will."

Obviously satisfied that Angela was properly cowed, Dylan slammed shut the door and rounded the car to climb behind the steering wheel. She started the engine and set the car in motion, darting through the trees with a speed that would have made Angela screech in terror if she hadn't had so many other things on her list of worries.

Somehow in the whole scheme of her current life, being smashed into a tree at this point didn't seem so bad.

Eventually they hit a narrow dirt road and crashing through the gate that marked the edge of the property, Dylan shoved the gas pedal to the floor and sent them hurtling down the road with bone-jarring speed.

Angela struggled to stay upright, more than once hitting her head against the window as Dylan took a corner or hit a pothole. She lost track of time, but she sensed they were traveling east of Columbia.

Not that it mattered . . .

This time no one was going to be making a perfectly timed appearance to save her from the crazy freak. What difference did it make where she was killed and her body dumped?

Drowning in her dark thoughts, Angela barely noticed when the car came to a halt. It wasn't until the car door was opened and Dylan was hauling her out of the backseat that she came back to her senses.

And immediately wished that she hadn't.

Not only was her entire body one big cramp, but there was a stench of garbage and something that she couldn't quite identify wafting in the air.

Meth?

With casual indifference to the pain she might cause, Dylan ripped the duct tape off Angela's mouth, her expression hard with warning.

"You can scream if you want," she said, gesturing toward the filthy trailer park that was filled with a half dozen shabby trailers. "No one around here gives a shit."

Angela believed her.

The very air reeked of a grinding poverty that would steal the soul of anyone unfortunate enough to be stuck in the barely habitable structures. They were far too busy trying to survive in a world that threatened to crush them to worry about anyone else.

"I don't know why you brought me here," she muttered as Dylan forced her up the stairs of the nearest trailer. "I told you, I can't do what you want."

"Of course you can." Dylan efficiently dealt with the complicated lock before swinging the door open and shoving Angela inside. "It's all about focus."

"But . . ." Angela's protest died on her lips as she tripped over the threshold to discover a small living room that had been scrubbed clean and stripped of most of its furniture except for a table that was nearly hidden beneath a stack of scientific equipment. "Are those mine?" she demanded in shock.

Dylan shoved her forward so she could enter the room and shut the door behind them.

"You've convinced yourself you need technology to work your magic, so here it is."

Angela scowled at the persistent implication she was a fellow freak.

"It's not magic. And this equipment is only for my personal use. I would have to be in a fully functioning lab to try and complete my research."

"You'll do it here." Removing her gloves, Dylan used a claw to slice through the cuffs that were shutting off the blood supply to Angela's hands and pushed her toward the table. "And you'll do it now."

Managing to stay upright, Angela rubbed her sore wrists and pretended to study the equipment.

You couldn't argue with a crazy person.

Besides, it gave her the opportunity to covertly survey her surroundings.

To the right was an open kitchen with the standard stove, fridge, and microwave framed by cheap cabinets. There was a window over the sink, but it was too small for her to wriggle through.

To her left a doorway led to the back of the trailer, but the lights were out and it was too dark for her to make out more than a narrow hallway.

Directly opposite her was a pair of windows, covered by hideous paisley curtains. They had potential as an escape route, she decided. Always assuming she could somehow distract her dangerous captor long enough to attempt an escape.

Sensing Dylan's growing impatience, Angela sucked in a deep breath and turned her head to meet the crimson gaze.

"Fine. I'll need to start with a blood sample."

The Sentinel strolled forward, offering Angela a sneer as she reached for one of the unused slides. "Not that I don't trust you, but I'll do it." Using her claw, she poked the end of her finger and smeared the drop of blood on the slide. "Here."

Angela took the slide and grudgingly headed for the table.

It was ironic, really.

There wasn't a scientist alive who wouldn't sell their soul for a glimpse at this rare blood. Some would even be willingly kidnapped (okay, that was an oxymoron) for the privilege.

But Angela would have traded the opportunity in a heartbeat if it meant being safely tucked in Niko's arms.

Turning on the microscope, she settled on the lone stool in the room and adjusted the settings, unnervingly aware of Dylan's impatient stare.

On the wall a clock ticked and more distantly a dog barked, but what felt like a threatening silence was wrapping around Angela, making it almost impossible to concentrate.

At last she had to do something, anything to slice through the thick air.

"How did you learn about me?" She glanced up to see a puzzled expression on Dylan's exotic face. "I mean, none of my work has been published yet."

"Oh." Dylan shrugged. "Your professor contacted Calder when it became obvious you were more than just another grad student."

Angela froze, not certain what part of the explanation bothered her the most.

"Which professor?" she finally managed to croak.

"I think his name was Appold."

The fact that the woman knew the name of the professor who'd taken Angela under his wing and had become a trusted mentor shook Angela more than she cared to admit.

Could it be true?

God almighty.

Was her growing skill at manipulating cells actually a result of some mutation?

The thought was almost too overwhelming to even contemplate.

Not because she was prejudiced against high-bloods. Or even horrified at the thought of becoming one of them.

It was quite simply impossible to spend twenty-six years of her life believing herself to be one thing, and then in the space of one day being forced to accept she was another.

She was a logical, pedantic type of gal.

She needed time to process the data.

Clearing the lump lodged in her throat, she wiped her damp hands on her jeans.

"Who is Calder?" she asked.

"The Master of Gifts," Dylan readily explained. "His order is in charge of seeking out high-bloods who either don't know they're special or those who are trying to blend in among the norms."

"And he knows my professor?"

"Yes, he's one of Calder's order who keeps his eyes open for high-bloods in this area."

She briefly wondered why Appold hadn't told her of his suspicions from the beginning. Had he intended to spring the good news on her along with her diploma?

"Here's your doctorate, Angela, oh, and by the way, you're a freak. . . ."

She thrust away the futile thought.

She was more interested in the future. Hey, there was a minuscule chance that she might survive the night. She needed to be prepared.

"Do they force all high-bloods to Valhalla?"

Dylan's humorless laugh echoed through the empty trailer. "Let's just say that they strongly encourage people to travel to the mother ship."

"Why?"

"They need to know if you are going to be a danger to yourself or others."

"Oh." Angela slowly nodded. "I suppose that makes sense."

"Fantastic," her companion mocked. "Now that we've shared our little heart-to-heart, will you get to work?"

She heaved a sigh, knowing she'd put off the inevitable for as long as possible.

"Fine, but I'm warning you . . ."

Her words came to a stuttering halt as she glanced into the microscope and actually concentrated on the blood sample.

"Good . . . Lord."

Dylan moved to stand at her side. "What?"

"I've never seen cells like this," she muttered, distracted in spite of herself. "Fascinating."

"I don't want to be fascinating," Dylan snapped. "I want to be normal."

Angela lifted her head to watch Dylan's expression harden with bitter self-hatred.

"You know that none of us are normal?" She tried to squash the woman's expectations. Every woman wanted to look like Megan Fox, but the reality was that fate was rarely that kind. "There are differences in all of us, some are just greater than others."

The crimson eyes flared with fury. "I don't need a lesson in biology, I need a cure."

"But—"

A claw pressed to her throat, bringing her words to a sharp halt.

"Let me make this simple, scientist," she snarled in lethally soft tones. "Do it or die."

Chapter Nine

This wasn't the first time that Niko had stared death in the face.

Years before he'd fought off a group of morons who were in the process of lynching a young female psychic who'd been trying to make a living as a traveling gypsy.

Another time he was tracking a witch who was convinced she was destined to trigger doomsday and got caught in her lethal spell.

But he'd never teetered so close to the edge.

And certainly he'd never debated whether it would be preferable to battle through the pain so he could live. Or simply slip into the waiting darkness.

It was the image of dark, serious eyes and a lush, feminine mouth that had driven him to madness only hours before that gave him the grim determination to crawl back from the abyss. And, of course, the persistent sound of his name being shouted in his ear.

Scowling in annoyance, he forced open his heavy lids, not at all surprised to discover his fellow Sentinel crouched beside him with a worried expression.

"Arel?" he managed to croak.

Fierce relief flared through the golden eyes. "Welcome back, Sleeping Beauty."

Pressing a hand to his aching head, Niko struggled to a sitting position. Shit. He was as weak as a kitten.

"Why the hell am I lying on the floor?"

"A good question." Arel's gaze was watchful, no doubt assessing whether he needed to call for a healer. "I'm assuming it has something to do with Dylan."

"Dylan." The memory of the crimson-eyed bitch who'd tried to crispy-fry him seared through his mind. "She was here."

"Yeah, I got that," Arel growled, his fury barely leashed. "What did she do to you?"

Even though his mind was fuzzy, Niko had a vivid recollection of the pain that had halted his heart.

"She shot me with a shockwave."

Arel frowned. "I thought they'd all been confiscated?"

"She claims that she built her own."

"Of course she did." Arel curled his lips in disgust. They'd all known Dylan spent her free time tinkering with her inventions. A pity they hadn't kept a closer eye on just what she was building. "Bitch."

Slowly gathering his wits, Niko glanced around the empty kitchen, his abused heart slamming against his ribs.

"Angela?"

Arel grimaced. "Gone."

"Goddammit."

Niko surged to his feet only to lurch forward as his legs refused to cooperate. Thankfully, Arel was swiftly rising to catch him before he could do a face-plant.

"Before you have a meltdown, I can track them," Arel hastily assured him.

"I don't doubt your skill, amigo, but—"

"No, it's not about skill," Arel interrupted, making sure

that Niko could stand on his own before he stepped back and pulled a phone from his pocket. "Look."

Niko blinked to clear his bleary gaze, then focused on the road map that was visible on the phone screen. Leaning closer, he noticed the tiny light that was blinking.

GPS.

And if he knew Arel, then the blinking red dot was Dylan.

"You tagged her?" he demanded, afraid to hope.

Arel smiled with grim satisfaction. "I set a trigger on the back porch before I came in. As soon as Dylan opened the door it attached itself to her shoe."

Niko released a shaky sigh despite the cold chill that inched down his spine at the realization of how easy it would have been for Dylan to disappear with Angela while he was unconscious.

"What if she hadn't come through the back door?"

"I might have set a few others," Arel admitted. "You know me. Better safe than sorry."

"You?" Niko snorted. "Safe?"

Arel gave a casual lift of his shoulder. "Okay, call it overkill."

Overkill. Yeah. That was definitely more Arel's style.

"How long have I been out?"

"At least half an hour."

Niko growled in frustration. Dylan might need Angela alive and relatively unharmed if she was to get what she so desperately wanted, but that was no guarantee of her safety. The female Sentinel was as volatile as she was unstable.

A lethal combination.

"We have to go."

Arel moved to block his stumbling path toward the door. "Dammit, Niko, you can barely stand."

Niko glared at his friend. "Don't even start."

"Be sensible. I could travel faster without you."

Niko was shaking his head before Arel finished. "This is an argument you're not going to win, so give it up."

"Stubborn bastard."

Moving like a drunken sailor, Niko sidestepped Arel and continued across the room and out the back door. He'd made it past the pool when Arel caught up with him. Offering Niko a frustrated scowl, the younger Sentinel led him to the garage where he'd hidden his vehicle.

Niko lurched into the garage, giving a lift of his brows at the sight of the large four-wheel drive pickup with massive tires that looked like they should have been on a tank.

"Christ," he muttered, struggling to lift his foot high enough to reach the running board. "Overcompensating for anything, amigo?"

"I just like power," Arel said, giving Niko a shove in the ass to get him up and in the passenger seat.

Slamming shut the door, Niko waited for his companion to swing behind the driver's wheel and start the engine.

"If you say so," he mocked at the throaty roar that filled the air.

Arel shot him a jaundiced glare, pausing to attach his phone to a mount on the dashboard before backing out of the garage.

"You're not in any condition to question my manhood."

"Which is the only reason I'm questioning it now," Niko confessed, leaning his throbbing head against the seat. "You can't kick my ass when I'm hurt."

"Don't count on it." With an evil grin, Arel shoved the truck in gear and took off like a bat out of hell. "Hold on."

"Shit." Niko braced his hands against the glove compartment, clenching his teeth as the truck swerved around a corner and bounced across a shallow ditch to head straight across an empty field. "Is there something wrong with the road?"

"Shut up," Arel muttered, his gaze shifting between the dark field and the map on his phone.

Niko bit his tongue, closing his eyes so he could try and

concentrate on recuperating his strength. Dylan had clearly gone over the edge. There was no reasoning, no hope of compromise with the female.

This was going to be a fight to the death.

He managed to maintain his silence until Arel rammed through a fence at a hundred miles an hour and nearly sent them into the lake.

No one was more anxious than he was to get to Angela. No one. But he was just beginning to shake off the effects of the shockwave. He couldn't afford to be injured before he even reached Dylan.

"I could drive," he rasped.

Arel slowed as they neared the signal still blinking on the GPS.

"Has anyone told you that you have control issues?"

Always.

"Never," he lied as Arel pulled the truck to a halt just outside a trailer park.

"Dylan's close," Arel murmured, his nose wrinkling at the stench of garbage and human misery. "Damn. Why here?"

Niko allowed his gaze to search the heavy shadows that shrouded the park, briefly puzzled by the tug of awareness that flowed through him.

Was this a new trick of Dylan's?

Then, as the sensation settled deep in his heart, he realized this was no trick.

And it had nothing to do with Dylan.

"Niko?"

Belatedly realizing that Arel was studying him with a worried gaze, Niko returned his attention to their grim surroundings.

"If she intended to have a hostage she would want to be isolated from nosy neighbors."

"True." Arel pointed across the narrow parking lot. "There's her car. Stay here and I'll find out which trailer she's in."

"No need." Niko nodded toward the trailer set a short distance from the others. "It's that one."

Arel turned to frown at him. "How can you be sure?"

Niko pressed a hand to the center of his chest. "I can feel Angela."

Arel's golden eyes widened in shock.

On very rare occasions a high-blood could be so deeply connected to another that they formed a bond that could be felt on a physical level.

Niko had always pitied the poor schmucks who allowed themselves to be melded. Why would anyone want to be leashed for their entire lives?

It was . . . abnormal.

Now, he accepted he hadn't known a damned thing.

This wasn't a leash, and it certainly wasn't abnormal.

It was as perfect and natural as breathing.

Angela completed him.

Yeah, yeah. It was sappy. But that's exactly how he felt.

"It's gone that far?" Arel growled, not nearly as pleased as Niko by the unexpected gift.

Niko smiled, shoving open the door of the truck so he could jump out to stand on the dirt path.

"So it would seem."

Arel cursed, hurriedly moving to stand at Niko's side. "You still need to stay here while I scout out the best way to stage an attack."

"There's no strategy." His gaze searched the trailer for any hidden traps. "I'll go in the front door and while Dylan is distracted you'll go in from the back and rescue Angela."

In less than a heartbeat Arel was standing directly in front of him, his hands planted on his hips and his expression set in stubborn lines.

"No."

Niko narrowed his gaze. "I don't want to pull rank, but I will."

"You're no longer in charge of this mission," Arel reminded him in sharp tones. "I am."

"I'm taking back command."

"Goddammit, Niko. You're not thinking clearly."

Niko refused to back down. "I'm thinking clearly enough to know I'm going to kill that bitch."

"How?" Arel snapped. "There's no way in hell you could survive another hit from her weapon."

Niko couldn't deny the blunt truth. It'd been a miracle that his heart had restarted after the first shock. The chance it could endure another blast . . . it was pretty much zero to none.

But it didn't change a damned thing.

He was going to do whatever it took to get Angela out of that trailer safe and sound.

Whatever it took.

"I'm prepared this time," he tried to reassure his companion. "She won't have a chance to shoot me."

"Niko—"

Growingly anxious to reach Angela, Niko didn't wait to hear Arel's arguments. He understood his friend's concerns. Hell, he even agreed with them.

He was emotionally compromised and physically weakened. But none of that mattered.

Not now.

"Let's do this thing," he said, heading directly toward the trailer.

Dylan would sense his approach before he could reach the door. There was no point in being subtle.

Besides, he wanted the bitch focused on him. That was the only way Arel would be able to slip in unnoticed.

"Goddammit." Arel moved to walk beside him. "If you get yourself killed I swear I'll drag your sorry ass back from the grave."

Niko grimaced. "Not even a necro can perform that miracle."

Necromancers—or diviners—couldn't actually manipulate

the dead, although they were capable of entering the recently deceased's minds to view their last thoughts.

"I'll travel to hell myself if I have to," Arel muttered.

Niko turned to meet his friend's worried gaze. "Just promise me that you'll make sure Angela is safe, no matter what happens."

The lean face tightened, as if Arel was struggling against the urge to continue his futile argument. Then, heaving a sigh of resignation, he clapped Niko on his shoulder.

"You know you don't even have to ask, amigo. I've always considered you my brother. How could I treat your woman as anything less than my sister?"

It was exactly what he'd expected, but he needed to hear the words spoken out loud.

"Thank you." He returned his attention to the trailer. "Now go."

Waiting until Arel had jogged to the back of the lot, Niko stepped onto the pavement that marked the edge of the park, a humorless smile curling his lips as the door to the trailer was thrown open and Dylan confronted him with an infuriated scowl.

"How the hell did you find me?" she snarled.

Niko hid his shudder of relief as he caught Angela's scent. He could smell her terror. It spiced the air. But on the plus side her heart was still beating and there was no hint of blood.

Thank the gods.

"Ah, Dylan." He forced a mocking smile to his lips. "Long time, no see."

Her eyes glowed like pits of hell in the moonlight. "I asked you a question."

He halted several feet away, but Dylan remained firmly lodged in the doorway. Dammit. He needed to lure her away from the trailer. Something easier said than done.

"How many times do I have to tell you that I'm the better Sentinel?" He deliberately prodded her pride. "It doesn't matter where you go or how hard you try to hide, I will always find you."

She stroked her fingers over the weapon still strapped around her forearm.

"Not if you're dead."

"Fool me once, shame on you." He curled his forefinger in invitation. "Aren't you going to come out and play?"

She leaned against the doorjamb. "No, I don't think I will."

"Afraid?"

"Too well trained to fall for such an obvious trap." She sniffed the air. "Where is Arel? Trying to sneak in the back door?"

Niko's smile never faltered despite his stab of fear. The bitch was supposed to be attacking him, not remaining lodged in the trailer like a rabid guard dog.

So how did he convince her that she had no choice but to fight?

By proving that the risk of leaving Arel and me alive is too great . . .

The thought seared through his mind at the same time he was struck by inspiration.

There was only one thing that Dylan feared.

And that was losing her one chance to be made normal.

She had to believe her dreams were about to be shattered.

Niko folded his arms across his chest, trying to look nonchalant.

"I wanted to make sure you didn't slip away before we could finish this."

"I'm not afraid of you." Dylan flared her flat nose in what he assumed was disdain. "Or your devoted sycophant."

"Arel isn't going to be happy to be called a sycophant," he drawled. "And I don't give a shit if you're scared or not. All I need to do is keep you cornered until the cavalry rides to the rescue."

She pretended indifference, but Niko didn't miss the sudden tension that gripped her body.

"What do you mean?"

"Arel contacted Wolfe when he found me unconscious," he smoothly lied, betting on the fact this female wouldn't have any inside connections left at Valhalla. One phone call and his fib would blow up in his face. "The Tagos wasn't pleased to discover you're carrying around an illegal weapon, let alone kidnapping a scientist who they hope will be the salvation of those high-bloods who can't survive their mutations."

Her laugh was strained. "I suppose you want me to believe he's sending a hundred—oh wait, maybe it's a thousand—warriors to capture me?"

"I don't have a clue, but since the guardians can only transport two or three at a time, you won't have to worry about a thousand arriving on your doorstep." He waved a languid hand toward the empty road. "At least not in the next hour or so."

Dylan frowned, proving she hadn't had word that the guardians were refusing to leave their necros, and that there was no possibility of *any* backup arriving in time.

"No," she hissed. "You won't ruin this for me. Not now."

He smiled in open challenge. "There's no escape."

The crimson eyes at last smoldered with the panic he'd been hoping for.

Even a Sentinel made stupid decisions when driven by fear.

"I can go through you," she rasped.

He held out his arms in mocking invitation. "You can't kill two of us."

"Watch me."

Lifting her arm she released a blast from her shockwave. Already anticipating the shot, Niko lunged to the side, allowing the electrical charge to slam into the tree behind him.

"Is that all you got?" he taunted, brushing off the bits of bark and shattered wood that clung to his jeans.

"And the healers told me that I was the one with the death wish," Dylan snarled, leaping off the front steps of the trailer even as she was sending another invisible bolt of power in his direction.

He felt his hair rise as the electricity filled the air, his gaze trained on the female launching a kick at his head.

Distantly he was aware of the wary humans peeking out their windows and a few braver souls who stepped out of their shabby homes, but he didn't worry they would interfere.

Life was difficult enough for these norms. They didn't willingly place themselves in danger.

He was far more concerned by the barely audible sound of Arel's soft murmur as he spoke to Angela. No doubt he was trying to convince her to slip through the back door rather than charging into the fray. His scientist might be brilliant, but she could be as stubborn as hell.

Reassured by the sudden fading of her scent, Niko grasped Dylan's foot and twisted it to the side. The well-trained Sentinel flowed through the air, easily landing on her feet as she let off another shot.

Niko hissed as the bolt went just above his ducked head, close enough to make his ears ring.

Christ. He had to disable the shockwave. Sooner or later he was going to run out of luck. And then . . .

Bad, bad things were going to happen.

Avoiding a punch aimed at his chin, he charged forward, ramming his larger form into Dylan's slender body. Together they hit the ground with enough impact to rattle Niko's teeth and knock the air from his lungs.

She jerked her head backward, making him see stars as she connected with his chin. Then, when he maintained his grim hold, she turned her head to sink her sharp teeth into his forearm.

"Shit, Dylan," he growled.

"Let me go," she demanded.

He ignored the pain of his torn flesh. "Not a chance in hell."

"Then we'll both die."

"You're in no position to threaten—" He forgot what he was going to say as she twisted to the side, managing to lift her arm far enough to press a button on her homemade weapon. A clock appeared on a digital panel, the numbers counting backward. "What have you done?"

"Every evil villain has a way to self-destruct," she jeered. "Unless you release me then we both go boom."

He believed her.

Dylan might be crazy as a hatter, but she didn't bluff.

If she said the thing was going to self-destruct, then that's exactly what it was going to do.

The question was whether he held on or risked letting her go so she could disarm the weapon. He wasn't a martyr. Not by a long shot, but he knew if he let go of Dylan there was no guarantee that she wouldn't escape. Or even manage to kill him with her stun-gun-from-hell.

Hearing the sound of his name, he lifted his head to see Arel standing at the back of the trailer with a struggling Angela in his arms.

She was clearly trying to break free so she could get to him, even knowing she was no match for a Sentinel.

And in that moment his decision was made.

The fragile, precious female would never be safe so long as Dylan lived.

And if that meant he had to sacrifice himself in the bargain . . . then it was a price he would pay without regret.

"Then we both die," he said, his gaze glued on Angela as time ran out.

Angela hadn't wanted to sneak out the back door with Arel. Not when she heard Niko baiting the deranged female Sentinel.

The aggravating man was risking his own life so she could be rescued.

But Arel hadn't given her much choice as he'd simply grabbed her by the waist and hauled her down the narrow hall and out the door. It wasn't until they rounded the trailer to see Niko on the ground with Dylan that Arel came to an abrupt halt, as transfixed as Angela by the sight of the two warriors lying so still.

Something was happening.

Something . . . terrible.

Futilely trying to squirm out of Arel's ruthless grasp, she turned her head to glare at her captor in frustration.

"Dammit, what are you doing? We have to help him."

Arel's handsome features looked as if they'd been carved from granite. "He made me swear to keep you safe."

"I don't care, I—"

She was still turned toward Arel when an explosion sent them both tumbling to the ground.

"Shit," Arel rasped, already on his feet and racing across the pavement before Angela managed to regain her senses.

Holy crap.

With her ears ringing and her skin raw from being peppered by the barrage of small stones and shattered glass that had been caught in the blast, she lurched upright, her blurry gaze immediately searching for Niko.

He was still on the ground, but Dylan—or at least what was left of the female Sentinel—had been blown several feet away. Arel was standing over her, his face twisted with an odd combination of fury and sorrow as he bent to pick up the weapon that lay beside her ruined body.

That bit of twisted metal had to have been the source of the explosion, but Angela didn't give a shit about the how or even the why.

She just needed to know that Niko was okay.

Falling to her knees at his side, she reached to brush her hand over his cheek.

"Niko," she breathed, a savage pain clawing at her heart as she felt the heat rapidly draining from his skin.

Arel crossed to kneel next to her, the force of his anger a tangible sizzle in the air as he gently turned Niko onto his back to reveal the gaping wound that marred his chest.

"Goddamn that bitch."

Angela's fingers frantically moved to Niko's throat. She was unable to look at his bloody, torn flesh.

"I can't find a pulse," she said on a soft sob. "What can we do?"

There was a long, agonizing hesitation before Arel awkwardly rose to his feet and pulled a phone from his pocket.

"I'll call for a healer."

"They'll never get here in time."

"Just—" Arel gave a helpless shake of his head. "Stay here."

Angela watched the younger Sentinel walk away with the phone pressed to his ear before she turned back to the terrifyingly motionless man lying at her knees.

"Oh, Niko. Don't you dare leave me," she quietly murmured, her hands running a path along the gruesome injury as she willed his shredded heart to beat. "Not after you forced me out of my laboratory. And made me discover who I am." Her teardrops trailed down her cheek and dropped into Niko's tousled hair, shimmering in the copper highlights. Oh . . . God. He couldn't die. She wouldn't let him. "And then you went and made me fall in love with you, you irritating man." There were more tears, and a strange heat that seemed to flow from her palms. She ignored both as she continued to pour out her raw, mindless grief. "I can't do this alone. I need you." She lowered her head until her face was buried in his throat, drowning in his familiar scent. "Please, Niko, please."

She wasn't sure how long she knelt there, rubbing her hands over Niko's chest, but it was at last the feel of fingers lightly touching her shoulder that brought her back to her surroundings.

"Angela," Arel murmured softly.

"No, I can't bear it."

"Angela, look."

Reluctantly she straightened, assuming that Arel was warning someone was approaching.

"What?" she demanded when she realized the lot was empty.

With a bemused expression, he pointed toward her hands, which remained on Niko's chest.

"That."

It took a minute to see through the tears, then slowly she focused on the torn flesh that had started to knit back together.

"Oh my God," she breathed in shock. "He's healing."

"You're healing him," Arel insisted.

She froze at his astonishing claim. "Me?"

"He has a heartbeat." Arel's fingers tightened on her shoulder, his urgent tone sending a flare of hope through her heavy anguish. "Don't stop."

"Niko." Her hand resumed its soft strokes, her gaze glued to his face. Did he have more color than before? And was that a breath she heard? "Niko, can you hear me?"

There was nothing for long, agonizing minutes. Then, when she was beginning to fear that her grief was making her imagination run wild, there was a flutter of his lashes.

"Angela?" he croaked in husky tones.

She gave a choked cry, overwhelmed with relief. "It's a miracle."

Arel released a joyous laugh, his fingers giving her shoulder a squeeze.

"You're the miracle."

"Finally, you got something right, amigo," Niko whispered, his gaze trained on Angela's flushed face. "She is a miracle. *My* miracle."

She shook her head. "I can't believe it. I mean . . . I've been able to alter cells on a small scale, but this—"

"Gifts often reveal themselves under stress," Arel said. "Although not usually with such spectacular results."

"I'm not sure I could ever do it again," she admitted, still shaken by the thought of how close she'd come to losing the man she loved.

"Your powers are yours, angel. No one will ever force you to offer more than you're comfortable giving." Niko lifted a hand to brush away her tears. "Now can we go home?"

"Home?" She studied his beloved features, knowing he wasn't referring to her empty apartment. "You mean Valhalla?"

"Yes." He managed a weak smile, his thumb tracing her lower lip. "You're one of us now."

Her eyes shifted to the wound that was continuing to heal before returning to meet his steady gaze.

She was one of them.

A freak.

A high-blood.

A Sentinel's lover.

And nothing had ever made her happier.

"You're right," she murmured, bending down to gently kiss the man who offered her a future she never dreamed possible. "It's time to go home."

Hello Readers!

I hope you enjoyed Angela and Niko's story. This is a short introduction to my new series, *The Sentinels*. This series will revolve around people who are "gifted" with special abilities and the warriors who protect them. Next up is Duncan O'Conner's story. He's a hard-nosed police detective who requests the services of Callie Brown, a high-blood necromancer, when a young woman is found murdered in her kitchen. Callie's skill allows her to view the last memories of the dead before the soul leaves the body. Most cops consider it a gruesome talent, but Duncan isn't so squeamish. Callie has managed to solve a dozen murders over the past five years. Besides, he can't deny a fascination with the beautiful high-blood. She stirs a passion in him that threatens to consume them both.

Coming in June 2013 will be *Darkness Avenged*, Santiago and Nefri's story. Can you believe this is the tenth book in the Guardians of Eternity series? I never imagined when I first came up with the idea of a clan of vampires in Chicago that it would grow and expand to include such a wide variety of creatures. Weres, witches, Sylvermyst, and of course, one naughty gargoyle. And it's all because of you!

So thank you dear readers, and happy reading!

Alexandra Ivy

TIES THAT BIND

NINA BANGS

Chapter One

A ticking clock.

The creaks and groans of an old building settling.

A print of Edvard Munch's *The Scream* hanging on a pale green wall.

They didn't mean much individually. But as Cassie sat alone in the office of Eternal Rest Funeral Home listening to the tick tocks, the creaks and groans, and staring at the print . . . She took a deep breath and prayed for human contact before she did her own interpretation of *The Scream*.

Those creaks and groans? Definitely sounds of the dead rising, shuffling across the floor in the basement, coming for her. The ticking clock counted down the minutes before the walking dead crashed through the office door and tore her into bite-size bits.

Cassie shivered. Why had she agreed to sub for Felicity for even three minutes let alone three hours? She hated funeral parlors, hated the concept of putting dead bodies on display, *hated dead bodies.* For twenty-seven years she'd avoided going to a viewing—as a child with tantrums and as an adult with polite refusals.

Now, because her best friend had plied her with sobs and a giant guilt trip, she was here, by herself—not one other freaking person in the building except for dead guys—in the office of Eternal Rest. And it was getting dark outside.

She should have stood firm against Felicity's begging. No one needed her here. She'd only answered the phone once in the last two hours. Fifteen minutes ago a woman had called to ask about her husband's funeral. The woman had hung up with a huff of irritation when Cassie couldn't help her.

Cassie's heart did a giant *ker-thump* at the shrill sound of the doorbell. *Get a grip.* Zombies didn't ring the bell.

The back entrance, the one with the very large doors that opened to allow very large things—definitely *not* thinking about what those were—to be carried in and out. She took gulping breaths and tried to calm her primal fears. But that was the problem with primal fears—they weren't rational, and she couldn't control them.

Cassie pushed to her feet and hurried toward—thank God—human interaction. As she yanked the doors open, and flipped on the outside light, she thought about shoving aside the man standing there and running like hell. *Breathe, breathe.* Fact: she could leave whenever she wanted. But then Mr. Garrity would fire Felicity. Fact: a live person stood not three feet from her. Her panic subsided.

"Can I help you?" She smiled as she took inventory. He looked around forty with thinning hair and an ordinary face. Cassie felt the rest of her fear slide away.

"Where's Felicity?"

He didn't sound too surprised that she was gone. Did her friend make a habit of skipping out on her job? "She had an emergency. She'll be back in"—Cassie glanced at her watch—"an hour." That's all Cassie had to last. Sixty more minutes.

Felicity owed her big-time for this. No explanation, just a frantic call. Panic had ridden her voice as she'd begged Cassie to fill in for her. And no matter what, Mr. Garrity couldn't find out that she was gone. She'd promised to leave the back door unlocked and then hung up.

Cassie had sat staring at the phone. What kind of emergency? It must've been serious from the sound of her friend's voice. Her conscience pointed out that Felicity was allowing her to sleep in her spare room while Cassie searched for work. This small favor was the least she could do in return. Cassie wished her conscience would mind its own business. After about a half hour of mental hand-wringing, though, she'd temporarily beaten her fears into submission and headed out to spend a few hours in her personal nightmare.

"Does Mr. Garrity know you're here?" He speared her with a hard stare.

Cassie had to protect Felicity's job. She pasted on her most sincere expression. "Of course." On the shades-of-gray scale, this lie was almost white. Her conscience subsided with a grumble.

The man nodded. "I do special jobs for Mr. Garrity. When a client wants a picture hand-etched onto a headstone, I'm the one who does it. Felicity probably told you that."

"Uh, sure." Felicity had told her nothing.

"I delivered one here this morning, but I have to make some minor changes."

He held up a few pointy tools she hadn't noticed at first. She frowned. Why would he deliver the headstone here and not to the cemetery? "So you do custom work?" That was her, the queen of obvious.

He smiled for the first time. "Every headstone is one of a kind. Why don't you get the keys to the basement rooms and meet me down there?"

"Keys?" She'd seen the elevator doors in the hallway right behind her, but Cassie had tried not to think about what lay beneath her feet. Not too successfully if she was imagining zombie attacks.

He'd stopped smiling. "The keys are in Felicity's desk."

"Right. Desk." Something didn't feel right. Cassie glanced past him to where he'd parked his small, unmarked delivery truck. Another man was climbing from the passenger side of the truck. Now this guy was scary, and big, but he was human and alive. Both points in his favor. She dismissed her feelings. This whole place spooked her.

The first man nodded toward his friend. "Forgot to introduce myself. I'm Tony and the big guy is Len. Takes size to handle the stones."

"Hi." Cassie smiled at both men. No way was she giving her name. If the funeral director got cranky because Felicity had called in random secretarial help while he was gone, Cassie didn't want to be in the line of fire. "About those keys. Why don't you wait here for a moment? I'll find them and bring them right back." She did *not* want to take that elevator anywhere.

"Can't waste time waiting for you. I have someplace to be in twenty minutes. Besides, I might need your help." Tony held her gaze. "Oh, and make sure you press the bottom button."

Help? For what? Musical accompaniment? He could hack away at his tombstone in time with her chattering teeth. But she couldn't think of an excuse that wouldn't make her look like the giant wuss she really was.

The two men walked past her, heading for the elevator.

"Oh, um, do you know where Mr. Garrity is?" In fact, where *anybody* was? There hadn't been one person in the place when she'd arrived. She refused to think about the non-living that probably populated the basement.

Len answered her. "Mr. Garrity was also called away on an . . . emergency." He seemed to think that was funny, because he smiled.

Cassie thought he had a sinister smile. Okay, maybe not. Her imagination was a terrible thing. Proof? Nonexistent zombies shambling down the hallway. To stop herself from babbling something that would get Felicity in trouble, she turned and walked back to the office.

On the way there, it occurred to her that the men wouldn't save any time by making her bring the keys downstairs because they'd still have to wait for her to unlock the door. She shrugged the thought away.

Keys, keys . . . She found them in the top drawer of the desk. That part had been easy. Now for the tough part. She had to go back to the elevator, walk inside, and hit the down button.

By the time she reached the elevator, she'd almost made herself believe that this whole experience was a character-building event. She'd be stronger for having spent time at Eternal Rest. *You are such a liar.*

Inside the car, she had a choice of three unlabeled buttons. The funeral home was only one story, so that meant ground level and two levels below ground. Weird. She hit the bottom one. All the way down she tried to convince her heart it didn't need to pump gallons of extra blood so she could handle a few minutes among the dead. Her heart didn't believe her. It redoubled its efforts.

The elevator doors slid open, and Cassie stepped out. She was in a long wide hallway with closed doors lining both sides. Was this usual for a funeral home? The lights were a little too dim, the shadows a little too deep. Relieved, she saw Tony and Len waiting for her at the end of the hall in front of the door on the right.

Please, no bodies, no bodies, no bodies. Her legs felt rubbery by the time she reached the men. They moved aside so she could open the door. She was proud that her hand didn't shake as she slipped the key labeled with the number eight into the lock and turned it. Cassie pushed the door open and then started to step aside.

After that, things happened too fast for her to react. Tony reached into the room and flipped on a light at the same time someone gave her a hard shove. She stumbled into the room, tripped over something on the floor, and went down hard on her hands and knees. She heard the door slam shut behind her.

She opened her mouth to scream. Then she looked down. The scream froze in her throat.

She was kneeling in a pool of blood—

And staring into Felicity's sightless eyes.

Dead. Felicity was *dead*.

Cassie couldn't move, couldn't breathe, couldn't *think*.

She didn't see her best friend sprawled on that floor, didn't see the girl she'd shared notes with in school, the woman who'd comforted her when she'd lost her job. Cassie only saw—

A dead body. She was kneeling next to a *dead body*. Whimpering, she scooted backward, still on her hands and knees. The blood smeared, sticky on her hands, soaking into her jeans.

Never get it out, never get it out. Panicked, she knelt up and tried to wipe her hands on her top.

"Gee, looks like your friend had more of an emergency than she expected." Tony's voice.

His soft laughter jerked her back to some level of sanity. Scrambling to her feet, she whirled to face the two men standing in front of the only door.

She still couldn't force any sound from her locked throat muscles, clenched teeth. But she didn't need to, because Tony had plenty to say.

"Mr. Garrity got a call on his cell phone from a Mrs. Hodges. She was really upset that you couldn't help her when she called. Said the regular woman was a lot more efficient." He took a step toward her.

Cassie backed up a step, her eyes riveted on what he held in his hand. The long pointed tool now looked exactly like what it was—a weapon.

"This really upset Mr. Garrity. See, no one should've been

here to answer any phones. And since he was tied up with his . . . emergency, he asked us to take care of the problem. Lucky that we live close by."

She was going to die. Just like Felicity. She'd be lying in a pool of her own blood staring at the ceiling. Funny, the thought of dying didn't paralyze her with fear. It was just the bodies. It had always been the bodies.

"Why?" She forced the one word past lips that felt numb. Not much, but it was at least a start. *Don't look at the body, don't look, don't look, don't look.*

Tony shrugged. "No need to know all the details. Besides, I was telling the truth about that appointment. Let's just say your friend found something she wasn't supposed to find and was running off to give it to someone we didn't want to have it. So we stopped her." He smiled. "Now we're going to stop you."

She saw the intention in his eyes as he started toward her. *Survive.* That's all that mattered. *Weapon.* There had to be something. Panicked, she bumped into a table beside her. An empty glass sitting near the edge fell to the floor and shattered. Without thinking, she crouched and picked up the largest shard.

Len chuckled. "Looks like the little girl thinks she can defend herself."

Tony wasn't laughing. He launched himself at her, ready to bury the tool's point in her heart. *Then she'd be just a body, a body, a . . .*

No! Cassie reacted. Lessons learned from years of modern dance kicked in. She might not have the talent to be a professional dancer, but she knew the moves.

Leaping into the air, she spun away from Tony's charge. At the same time she slashed at him with her glass shard. She was too terrified to aim. But she'd hurt him. She'd felt the resistance of the glass digging into his flesh.

Sobbing, she whirled to fend off another charge. A charge that didn't come.

Silence filled the room. Then she heard Len cursing. Glancing down, she saw Tony sprawled on the floor. Saw the moment he died, his throat sliced open. Saw the blood pouring from the wound. *The body.* She dropped the bloodstained shard.

Nothing to protect yourself with now. The thought floated around in her mind, for the moment overwhelmed by the coppery scent of blood and the memory of the glass cutting, ripping, ending a life.

She supposed she was lucky then that Len didn't attack her right away. Forcing herself to think instead of just feel, she looked at him.

But he wasn't watching her. He was staring past her at . . . She turned.

The horrors never ended. A transparent coffin rested on another table. A man's body lay inside. He was naked, and his pale skin gleamed under the ceiling light. Someone had set a headstone beside the table. Only two things about the stone registered.

A sick mind had created that image. It was an etching of the man in his coffin with thick chains wrapped around almost every inch of his body. A huge padlock trapped the man inside. The etched lock almost seemed to glow.

And a name. Ethan.

"You stupid bitch! You killed the binder."

Cassie had never heard that much fear in any person's voice. A binder? What was a—

The man in the coffin turned his head. He opened his eyes and stared at her. Eyes with no pupils, no white, just solid black.

She stopped breathing.

Len screamed, a high keening sound filled with unspeakable terror. He threw himself toward the closed door.

The coffin shattered.

Chapter Two

Cassie flung her hand in front of her eyes and turned her head away to protect herself from flying glass. At the same time, she bent to retrieve her own glass shard. Because beneath her gibbering fear, she still wanted to live. Then she straightened.

Who to face? But her subconscious recognized the real danger. She looked at where the coffin had rested. . . .

At the man crouched among the shattered remains, all smooth bare skin and hard muscle. Cuts from the broken glass dripped blood that trailed over his chest and stomach. His tangled dark hair framed a face that spoke of violence in shadowed planes and sharp edges. He stared at her, his black eyes alive with rage and something so predatory that she stepped back. Len seemed safe compared to this . . . She wasn't sure anymore. The word "man" suggested human. Too tame a category for what glared back at her. Male. Definitely male.

As she stared with unblinking horror, he curled back his upper lip, exposing long sharp fangs.

She gripped her small glass shard so tightly it dug into her palm. Blood trickled between her fingers. The pain kept things real, because on some level she still wanted to believe she'd wandered into a dark nightmare alley. But this was no dream. And she didn't have any illusions that her puny weapon would stop him.

Then she realized he wasn't looking at her any longer. His gaze swept past her to focus on Len, who was throwing himself against the door in a vain effort to break it down. The force of his desperation shook the room.

The fanged . . . male laughed, a soft sound that terrified her more than an angry roar ever would. She edged over to the wall and pressed herself flat against it, wished she could sink into it and disappear, and prayed to a God she hadn't spoken to since she was ten.

"Leaving so soon?"

His voice was dark and deep, filled with such menace that she had to force herself not to join Len in flinging herself against the door. Instinct whispered, "You're prey. Don't move. Don't breathe. Don't call attention to yourself."

"I'm sorry that I don't have more time to discuss things with you—life, death, and how payback is a bitch." He didn't move closer to Len.

Len finally turned away from the door. All color had drained from his face, his eyes were wide and staring. "No. Don't. Tony did the binding." He sounded almost incoherent.

"But Tony is dead. That only leaves you." He sounded regretful that Tony was beyond his reach. Then he smiled.

Cassie shuddered. She felt what was coming, sensed death filling the room, the air thick with fear and finality. She told herself to close her eyes.

She watched.

Suddenly, Len's head jerked sharply to the left, farther than any human neck should be able to twist. If there was an accompanying sound, Cassie couldn't hear it past the roaring in her head. Len dropped to the floor. Cassie recognized death in his loose-limbed sprawl and empty eyes. *And no one had touched him.*

She stared at Len's killer. Was she imagining the slight

change in his face—the more predatory shape of his eyes, a
more dangerous slant to his mouth? Cassie blinked. Of course
she was. No way could she trust any of her senses right now.

It was too much, *too much.* She slowly slid down the wall
until she was sitting. She opened her hand and released the
bloody piece of glass. Cassie couldn't even blink as she stared
past Felicity, Tony, and Len. She'd finally found something
that frightened her more than dead bodies.

He ignored her as he methodically stripped Len of his
clothes. He pulled on the dead man's pants and shrugged into
his shirt. He glanced at the shoes. "Too damn big." But he put
them on anyway. Finally, he turned his attention to her.

"What's your name?" He moved closer.

Cassie should be a shaking, drooling puddle of terror,
but she felt strangely calm. Her heart still pounded way too
fast, and she knew her breathing wasn't normal, but she felt
detached from what was going on around her. He would kill
her now. He didn't need to know her name to do that. But
she couldn't work up enough emotion to care. "Cassie."

He crouched in front of her. "Well, Cassie, we need to get
the hell out of here. Now." He reached for her.

She started to cringe away from him but then stopped. *Get
out of here?* He wasn't going to kill her? Why not? Cassie's
thoughts felt as though they were slogging through knee-deep
mud, each word coming loose with a sucking sound.

His black gaze pierced her. "Here's the deal. If you stay in
this room, Roland Garrity will take care of the job that Tony
and Len botched. Even if you run home, you'll die. You can't
hide from him." He grabbed her hand and hauled her to
her feet.

She flinched at the sharp pain in her cut palm.

He didn't miss her reaction. Loosening his grip, he examined her bloody palm. "Nasty cut." He glanced up at her from
under thick dark lashes. "It's not wise to tempt me." Without
warning, he bent his head and slid his tongue across her palm.

The stroke felt warm, and weird, and something . . . more. What should have been a shudder turned into a shiver. But she stopped wondering about her strange reaction as she stared at her palm. The cut was closing. And within a few heartbeats, she couldn't see where it had been. "What . . . ? How . . . ?" She knew her eyes must be wide and staring.

He didn't bother answering. "We're wasting time. Let's go."

"What if I don't want to go with you?" She realized she was in shock, but even knowing that, she couldn't shake the inertia holding her in its grip.

"Did I say you had a choice?"

He led her to the door, and she didn't fight him. Even through the shattered reality messing with her mind right now, she recognized the futility of trying to escape.

"I need to call the police." She glanced back at Felicity. Her friend was *dead*. Soon the horror of what had happened would crash over her, and she'd drown in her what-ifs and should-haves. But not now. Now her mind was still wrapped in a cotton wool world.

"No police." He barely touched the door and it swung open. "Tony would've had instructions to call in as soon as you were dead. He hasn't called, so Garrity will know that something went wrong. Right now all of his people will be on their way. We don't want to be here when they arrive." He pulled her into the elevator and hit the top button.

"But the police . . ."

He hissed at her. "By the time the police get here, the bodies will be gone. Where's your purse?"

"How can they get rid of the bodies so fast?" She winced. When had Felicity become just a body?

Cassie was starting to think again. She needed her cell phone and her car keys. Once out of the elevator, she ran down the hall with him right behind her. She grabbed her jacket and purse before following him out the back door. Night had fallen while people died in the funeral home's basement. She was selfish enough to be thankful she hadn't been one of them.

"They have . . . resources. Where did you park your car?"

"Out front." She hadn't wanted her car sitting in the funeral home's parking lot. Stupid. As if death would stick to her tires if she parked it there.

They were almost to the street when he suddenly grew still—not moving, not even breathing. Cassie looked away. His complete stillness creeped her out. She scanned the street. Quiet. A mixture of homes and businesses. For the first time, she really thought about running.

"Don't. I'd catch you. Besides, we don't have time for that crap. I can feel them. Any minute now they'll turn the corner and see us." He'd emerged from his suspended animation thing and herded her toward the street.

How had he known . . . ? No, she'd think about that later.

When they reached her car, he took her keys from her and slid into the driver's seat. She didn't argue. Her mind was starting to function, and depending on his answers to her questions, she might decide to bail at a stoplight along the way. Then she remembered. He could kill without touching his victim.

"Won't need to kill you. All the doors are locked. Relax and enjoy the ride." He pulled away from the curb and merged into Philly traffic.

Cassie sucked in her breath. Okay, she couldn't ignore it this time. Her fear had receded a little, but now it came flooding back. "You were in my mind." *Breathe, breathe.* "Look at me."

He glanced at her and smiled. The smile didn't reach his eyes.

Blue eyes. Straight, even teeth. She folded her hands in her lap to stop their shaking. Had she hallucinated the black eyes and fangs? Had seeing Felicity's corpse pushed her over the edge? She closed her eyes for a moment, and once again saw his body lying in that glass coffin with the headstone beside it. She opened her eyes.

"Is your name Ethan?"

"Yes." He didn't elaborate.

"Where're we going?"

"To check on some friends."

Ask him. The sensation of the world she thought she knew flipping upside down made her want to throw up. *Ask him.* Cassie had never thought she was a coward except for her horror of dead bodies. But at least there was a good reason for that particular phobia. The fear she'd felt in that room, though, proved she'd never make anyone's top ten fearless women list. To make up for her total shutdown back there, she had to ask him.

"What are you?" *Please, please don't say it.*

"I'm vampire." He never took his eyes from traffic. "But you knew that already, didn't you?"

"There are no such things as—"

"There are. I'm one. Get over it. We don't have time for you to have hysterics." His voice was cold, devoid of any sympathy, any understanding.

"Bastard." She didn't know how he'd react to name-calling, but for just this moment she didn't care. Surprised, she realized that some of her fear *had* faded. No matter what he was, or *said* he was, he hadn't killed her yet. Maybe a person could only sustain mind-numbing terror for so long.

"Technically, no. If you're making a judgment of my character, though, then you've nailed it. Give me your phone."

Cassie pulled her cell phone from her purse and handed it to him, then watched as he tapped in a number while weaving in and out of traffic.

"That's dangerous."

He took his attention from the road to stare at her. "I can't die."

"I can." Did anyone really have eyes that blue? Pale skin,

blue eyes, dark hair. She'd guess at an Irish ancestry. But then what did she know about vampires? They all had pale skin, didn't they?

Vampire. She flinched as she thought the word. Even after everything she'd seen, she wasn't doing a great job of wrapping her mind around the realness of him.

She waited quietly as he tried to make his call, then another and another. No one answered. He didn't leave any messages. And he didn't return her phone.

"Something's wrong." He sped up.

"You think?" She was substituting snark for courage.

A short time later, he parked on a street lined with row houses. Cassie didn't have a clue what part of the city this was. She'd moved to Philly a month ago to search for a job. The city was still strange to her, and getting stranger every minute.

They got out and he led her down a side street before turning into an alley that ran behind the houses. "We'll be going in the back way."

Cassie didn't care which entrance they used. She was still fixated on the vampire thing. "If you're a vampire, couldn't you just dematerialize and pop up wherever you wanted? Avoid traffic?" *Avoid women who won't shut up?* She closed her mouth.

"Not one of my powers. But I can move so fast humans think that I've vanished. Can't move that quickly right now, though. Energy's low. I was in that damn coffin for days. And killing Len drained whatever I had left. I need to feed." He glanced at her. "Want to volunteer?"

She widened her eyes. He was joking, right? "Umm, no."

He looked away and picked up his pace. He was walking so fast now that she almost had to run to keep up.

"Too bad." He didn't sound as though he was joking.

She could see him studying a man who was outside emptying his trash. *Don't even think about it.* She wouldn't

survive watching him chug down a human energy drink.
Cassie rushed into speech. "Where're we going?"

"To my house. Three of my friends are staying there with
me." His eyes narrowed. "None of them answered when I
tried to call."

Please, no more life-or-death moments today. Sudden
weariness washed over her. Her adrenaline supply must be
running low. "Won't Garrity check there first?"

"He didn't capture me there, so he might not know about
it." His smile was a mere baring of teeth. "And if he does,
he'll think I'm too smart to go home. He vastly overestimates
my intelligence."

"But what if he has people watching the place?"

"I'll kill them."

His answer would've horrified Cassie this morning. Now?
It made perfect sense.

He finally slowed down and moved into the shadows.
Silently, he pointed at a brick row house with a green rocker
on the back porch. She covered her mouth to keep from
giggling at the image of a vampire rocking on his porch.
Or maybe the urge to giggle was the first stage of hysteria.

Sliding along fences and gliding around trash cans—*he*
slid and glided, she shuffled and tripped—they drew close to
the house. Then he raised his hand to stop her. He grew still
again, and she held her breath. She wanted the house to be
empty so they could leave for somewhere safe.

"There's one person in there." He sounded grim.

She didn't question how he knew. "Anyone you know?"

"Yes." With no other explanation, he guided her to the
back door. He did his magic door-opening thing again and
slipped into a darkened kitchen. He beckoned her inside.

Cassie was beyond thought, beyond feeling, beyond everything. Right now he was the only real thing in her life. So she
followed him.

He moved quietly into what must be the living room. She

couldn't hear his footsteps. Behind him, she was an elephant tramping through a field of bubble wrap, announcing her presence with every step she took.

For the first time, she noticed the smell. It was coppery and too familiar.

He stopped so suddenly that she almost slammed into his back.

"Hello, Ethan." The male voice came from whoever was sitting in an overstuffed chair she could see silhouetted in the darkness.

"Dan. What're you doing here?"

Ethan's voice might sound neutral, but she sensed tension, and something else.

"Trying to figure out who the hell to call." The man's, or maybe vampire's, voice sounded terrified. "I couldn't reach you on your cell. Then I came here. I used the key you gave me. No one was here, but . . ." His voice trailed off.

Cassie moved up beside Ethan. Her eyes had adjusted to the dark and there was a tiny bit of light filtering in through the slats of the blinds. She could now see that the room was trashed—furniture overturned and pictures knocked from the wall. There were dark stains on the walls and carpet. "Is that . . . ?" *Blood.*

The other man said it for her. "There's freaking blood everywhere. *Fresh* blood. What's going on, Ethan?"

That explained the coppery scent. The rising panic in his voice mirrored her own emotions. She wished someone would turn on a light so she could see both of them. Then she thought of Roland Garrity hunting them and decided the darkness was just fine.

"I'll explain later. Do you have your car?"

Cassie didn't have to be particularly sensitive to feel Ethan's rage. It didn't seem aimed at the man in the chair. She thought that Roland Garrity should be very afraid.

"No. There was nowhere to park, so June just dropped me

off. I told her I didn't know how long I was staying, and I'd call her when I was ready to leave."

Cassie had kept silent as long as she could. "Who is this, Ethan?" Using his name sort of moved him a little out of the mythic-monster column into the almost-human one.

Ethan turned to look at her. In the darkness, his face became a stranger's again, all sharp planes and dangerous shadows. She'd been wrong. He wasn't even close to the human column.

"This is Dan. My brother."

Chapter Three

Why the hell had he brought her with him, and what was he supposed to do with her? Ethan wasn't impulsive, so his unexplained need to keep her out of Roland Garrity's hands didn't make any kind of sense. He should've just sent her on her way with a warning not to go home.

Whatever his reason, he had to park her in a safe place soon because he could feel his Second One beginning to rise. And if she thought he was terrifying now, did he have a surprise for her in a few hours.

"He's your brother?"

Her expression said everything her words hadn't—monsters didn't have mothers, fathers, brothers. Definitely should've ditched her.

"You have a problem with that?"

"No, I was just wondering—"

"You can wonder later. I'll grab a few clothes and then we have to get out of here." *I was just wondering how many throats you've torn out, how often the bloodlust drives you to murder, if you have a conscience, a soul.* Not as many as you'd think, never, sometimes, and probably not. He'd keep his answers to himself, though.

He didn't give her a chance to comment as he strode to his

bedroom, crammed some clothes and shoes into a bag, and
then handed the bag to his brother. Quickly, he herded everyone out the back door, through the tiny yard, and into the
alley. If Garrity had someone keeping an eye on the place,
they must be out front because he didn't sense watchers
nearby.

Then he paused. His place had looked as though a bomb
had gone off inside it. There must've been lots of noise. The
row houses were connected. Mrs. Kimsky didn't get around
much anymore. She would've been home. And what about
George and Janice on his other side? They only went out on
Friday nights. This was Wednesday. If any of them had heard
a fight in his house, they would've called the police. They
hadn't.

*Keep going. Being vampire means checking your emo-
tions at the door.* Yeah, that was why Cassie was standing in
this alley with him. Because he was so good at not feeling
anything. No use fighting it, he was going to check on his
neighbors.

"I have to do something before we leave. Stay close and
don't make any noise." He speared Cassie with a glare intended
to keep her quiet for a few minutes.

Dan didn't say anything. He knew what his brother was,
and he understood the need for caution.

Ethan went through the back gate and across the small
yard. Mrs. Kimsky's door was unlocked. Not a good sign.
"Step in and shut the door. Stay here and let me do the
checking."

He didn't have far to go. What was left of his neighbor
lay on the living room floor. In pieces. Blood was soaking
into the carpet. The TV was still on.

"Oh, my God!" Horror filled Cassie's hoarse whisper
behind him.

He glanced back. "I told you to let me . . ."

Cassie stared at the body, her eyes wide, unblinking. There was so much fear. She shook with it. Bracing herself against the doorjamb, she covered her mouth with her hand. To hold back a scream or to keep from throwing up? Maybe both.

Ethan could hear Dan puking into the kitchen sink. "Next time listen to me." He sounded hard. Good. He *wanted* them to believe he was a cold-blooded son of a bitch. Because he was— he closed his eyes for a moment—most of the time. "Open the door and get some air. Both of you. I have to find something." He didn't look to see if they followed his directions.

Trying to make sure he didn't step in any blood, he went into the bathroom. He pulled a large bath towel out of the linen closet and began his hunt. A few minutes later he joined the other two at the door with a spitting, hissing bundle of pissed off cat safely wrapped in the towel. He watched Cassie's eyes widen when she saw the bloody claw marks on his hands and arms.

He scowled at her. "What?"

She didn't get a chance to say anything because Dan spoke. "You're taking the old lady's cat with you?"

Ethan didn't have time for explanations. "Out. I have to check the people on the other side of my place."

Everyone was silent as they walked to the second house. Ethan knew what he'd find. The hunters must've left the door open because he could smell blood and death long before they climbed the steps.

Dan stopped on the porch. He put the bag of clothes down. "This is as far as I'm going."

Ethan didn't blame him.

"Here. Hold the cat." He shoved the animal at his brother before stepping into the house.

Cassie walked in behind him.

He paused in the kitchen. "This will be just as bad. Wait with Dan."

"No. I *need* to see it." She met his gaze. "I've been afraid of the dead all my life. But my best friend is one of those dead now. This is more important than my fear. I have to see what they did so I'll never forget, so I'll know exactly what I'm destroying when I take these animals down."

Ethan raised one brow. Wow, where had that come from? Beneath all her fear, something fierce lived. He looked away. He didn't want to find her interesting in any way. "You couldn't even imagine what things did this."

Cassie looked puzzled. "Roland Garrity's people, right?" Then she shook her head. "No. I can't believe humans would do that to an old woman."

You'd be surprised what humans would do. He walked toward the dining room. "They didn't do the actual killing, but they held the remote." She wouldn't understand. He hoped she'd never have to.

They found George and Janice on the stairs. They must've tried to flee to the second floor. It hadn't worked. Body parts littered the steps and blood dripped over the side onto the floor below.

Cassie didn't last this time. She ran for the downstairs bathroom and slammed the door behind her. He waited until her retching stopped. When she finally opened the door and joined him, she was pale but steady. He said nothing, only returned to the back door. He waited until she was outside before closing it carefully behind him.

But even closed, he could still smell the blood. The Second One screamed, clawing at his soul, demanding that he feed, *kill.* He clamped down on his hunger. But it wasn't the hunger for blood that would grip him soon. He hoped Cassie was gone by then.

Dan took one look at the stark horror in Cassie's eyes and didn't ask any questions.

Ethan talked to his brother on the way to Cassie's car. "You're still living at June's place?"

Dan nodded. "Things haven't been too great between us lately, though. I'm thinking about moving back to my own condo."

"Don't. At least not until things are safer." The ones who'd found him might not know about his brother, or where he lived. But Ethan didn't want to take a chance. Dan would be safer staying with his girlfriend for now.

"Are you going to tell me what's going on?" Frustration roughened Dan's voice.

"Yes." They'd reached the car. "Once I figure it out myself."

Ethan slid into the driver's side and headed back out into traffic. He'd made sure that Cassie was beside him. She'd be easier to control in the front seat. At least she hadn't blurted anything about what had happened at the funeral home. In fact, she hadn't said anything for too long. Probably in shock from the last few hours.

The only one who had anything to say on the drive was the cat, and she kept up a constant stream of yowling complaints. Finally, Ethan pulled over a few blocks from June's apartment.

"I'll let you out here. No one followed us, but I still don't want to take the chance that someone might see you going into June's building."

Dan didn't comment as he handed the cat over to Cassie, got out, and slammed the door. Ethan watched him walk into a store that was still open. Then he pulled away from the curb. And just when he was wondering if Cassie would ever talk again, the floodgates broke.

"We need to call the police. You can't leave those poor people alone like that in their houses."

"I'll take care of it when we stop."

"Where're you taking me?" She didn't do a great job of covering the quaver in her voice.

"Somewhere safe for now."

"When are you going to explain what the hell is going on?"

"Later."

"Wow, way to ease my fears with your detailed explanations."

"Look, it's been a long night. Let's save all the questions until we can relax and get something to eat." The word "eat" drove his hunger into a frothing frenzy. It didn't help that he could hear her heartbeat, sense the blood coursing through her veins, and knew that all he had to do was stop the car and . . . *No.* He stomped the hunger into submission.

He concentrated instead on the slight shifts he could feel in his facial muscles, the tingling in his fingertips, and the tightening of Len's borrowed shirt across his shoulders. Not enough change for her to notice yet. But soon, very soon, she'd see.

There was a long simmering pause.

"Why did you bring the cat?"

"To eat. *You* wouldn't volunteer, so . . ." He shrugged.

She gasped and tightened her grip on the cat. The cat rewarded her with an annoyed hiss.

If the last few days hadn't sucked so badly, he would've laughed. Or maybe not. The idea that she might actually believe he ate small animals bothered him. Not comforting. Nothing she said or did should be able to touch him.

"Relax. I don't eat cats." He knew he sounded angry. But it seemed that everything about her made him mad. *Those big brown eyes and all that blond hair don't make you mad. Neither does the rest of her body.* Okay, so maybe it was all about sex deprivation. He could live with that explanation.

She nodded and some of the tension left her. "How old is your brother?"

"Twenty-seven."

She frowned. "Then that means you can't be ancient." The fact that he wasn't seemed to bother her.

"I'm thirty-two, but I was turned when I was twenty-eight. So I'll pretty much look that age forever."

"But I saw you kill Len without touching him. Doesn't a vampire have to be old and powerful to do that?"

He made an impatient sound. "Power doesn't come with age. Wisdom does. And a smart vampire will live a long happy life." He thought about that. "Or unlife. If that's not a word, it should be."

Her questions stopped for a short time while he bought cat food and litter box stuff. Once back in the car, he hoped she'd run out of things to ask.

"Why did you save me?"

There it was. The one question he'd hoped she'd keep for later. "I don't know." An honest answer.

She didn't look satisfied. Too bad. Relieved, he pulled in beside Zareb's warehouse.

Cassie seemed to finally realize they'd stopped. She looked around. "Where are we?"

"A warehouse. That's the Delaware." He pointed to where she could just see the river flowing dark and cold past the back of the building. "This isn't a residential part of Philly. Once the warehouses shut down for the night, the area pretty much empties of traffic and people. We'll be safe."

They climbed out of the car. It was so quiet their footsteps rang loud in the darkness. Even the cat had shut up. Nothing moved. She tugged her jacket more tightly around her. The night must've turned cold. He felt nothing. For a moment, he considered pulling her against him, but offering warmth or comfort would only lead to other temptations. He led her toward a door hidden in the shadows.

He pressed a small button next to the door and waited. She shivered beside him, and with a frustrated curse he gave in and wrapped his arm around her. When she moved closer, he wasn't sure if it was an attempt to get warm or a lesser-of-two-evils thing. Even a human had to pick up on the scary vibes surrounding this place.

After what seemed forever, the door creaked slowly open. No light came from inside. No one stood in the opening. If anything, the blackness seemed deeper, more silent than the night. Ethan felt Cassie cringe away from the open door.

"You're safe." Maybe.

He pulled her inside. The door closed behind them.

"Come." The voice was a deep rumble. Disembodied. Terrifying.

Even knowing who spoke, Ethan couldn't control an instinctive shudder. He led Cassie further into the darkness.

Suddenly, a candle flickered on, quickly followed by more and more until the room was ablaze with their glimmering lights. With a quiet whoosh, flames leaped in the fireplace.

A figure glided from the shadows. Tall and muscular, he moved with that strange flowing motion only very old vampires achieved, those who no longer remembered they'd once been human.

Ethan knew by Cassie's frightened gasp when she finally got a good look at their host. And if Ethan hadn't been determined not to make an ass of himself, he would've gasped too.

"Hello, Ethan." The vampire shifted his gaze to Cassie. "You come bearing gifts. A beautiful woman and . . ."

Screeching and hissing, the cat leaped from Cassie's arms.

"A bad-tempered cat." He smiled. "We'll dine well tonight."

Ethan grabbed her hand before she could make a dash back to the door.

"Cassie, meet Zareb." He took a deep breath he no longer needed. "My maker."

Chapter Four

Cassie didn't think there was room inside her for more fear. She was wrong. Zareb had an overwhelming presence. His movements were too fast, too smooth, too predatory. He'd pulled his long black hair back and fastened it with a leather thong that had a silver medallion on it. His sharp cheekbones and exotic darkness drew attention to his eyes. He had terrifying eyes. They were slightly tilted and glowed yellow. *Glowed. Yellow.* No white showed, and he had vertical slits for pupils. Cat eyes.

The yellow glow should have been the scariest part of him. It wasn't. There was something else. . . .

He captured her with his eerie stare, and suddenly she couldn't understand why she had ever thought his eyes were strange. His gaze drew her, filled her with a yearning that was almost pain. It reached down, down to a place never touched before.

She couldn't blink, couldn't look away, couldn't control the erratic beating of her heart, and couldn't seem to breathe. Cassie gasped for air even as she sank into the alien beauty of those eyes. And if her heartbeat felt as though it was stalling, threatening to stop altogether, she couldn't muster the energy to worry about it while the yearning grew and grew.

Cassie jerked as Ethan commanded, "Stop it." She didn't think he was talking to her.

Startled, she closed her eyes. She concentrated on breathing and felt her heartbeat kick back into a normal rhythm. What had just happened? *You couldn't breathe, your heart was stopping.* She'd almost *died.*

When she opened her eyes, Zareb had turned his attention to Ethan.

"And here I thought you'd brought her as a gift to atone for abandoning your loving father."

Ethan simply stared at him from the shadows.

Zareb smiled. "I suppose the loving father reference was a bit overdone. But you do owe me some recompense for my anger, and yes, there were a few moments—very few, I'll admit—of heartfelt sorrow."

Ethan made a dismissive sound. "I brought you a pet that will suit your 'loving' personality."

The cat poked her head from beneath the couch and hissed her general discontent with everyone in the room.

Zareb's smile widened. "So you have."

Cassie's whole body thrummed with her need to run to the door, rip it open, and race screaming into the night. Her instinct had it right, but her mind insisted she listen to reason.

Even if she *could* escape, even if she *could* go home, even if she *could* be safe there . . . Okay, so none of those "even ifs" were viable options. And it wasn't just about her anymore. If she tried to run to family, to friends, she'd put them in danger too. The police? They'd question her and then release her. Back to square one.

Besides, wherever she went, her nightmares would follow. She still saw Felicity's body and those other people when she closed her eyes. If Cassie didn't do something to help stop the ones who had murdered her friend, she might never sleep again.

At this moment, Ethan offered her a lifeline, even if it was frayed and liable to dump her into the deep without warning.

She blinked hard. No tears. Not yet. She would do the sobbing and wailing thing in private, if they ever allowed her to be alone again. *If she lived long enough.* Until then, Cassie would stuff the huge empty place inside her with answers to her questions. She took a deep breath and met Zareb's gaze. "What did you just do to me?"

"Women." Zareb's sigh was filled with drama and sly amusement. "They can never just accept things. They always want explanations."

Thank heaven he didn't try to meet her gaze.

"I was merely playing. I rarely allow myself recreation time. You wouldn't have died." He cast a quick glance her way. "I'm very careful not to kill unless it's unavoidable. I've killed often over the centuries, and the Second One is too close, too powerful now."

What did that even mean? Since he didn't offer to explain, she launched another question. "Did you make Ethan vampire because he was dying and that was the only way you could save him?"

He looked surprised in the same way he would if the cat had spoken to him. "No. I was bored that night, and I hadn't made any children in a long time." He shrugged powerful shoulders. "It was simply a need to procreate. So I made Ethan vampire." His full lips twitched in the tiniest of smiles. "He was angry with me for a very long time. In fact, this is the first time he's visited me of his own free will. I'm ecstatic."

Well, Cassie could get rid of any heart-of-gold hopes she had regarding him.

Zareb looked at Ethan. "I assume there's some pressing reason for your presence here."

"We have a situation."

Ethan still stood in the shadows. Cassie frowned. She couldn't see his features clearly, but she would swear there was something different about him, something changing. She pushed the thought away. Too much had happened today, and her mind was probably a little unreliable right now.

Zareb glanced at the cat hiding under his couch and at Cassie. "Yes, we do." He motioned toward the couch. "Since you've already interrupted my busy night, you may as well sit down."

Cassie walked to the couch and sat on the edge. The cat seemed to think that underneath it was a better place to be. The cat was probably right. Ethan didn't leave the shadows.

Zareb stood beside the couch staring at Ethan. "You killed tonight."

"How did you know?" The question just popped out of Cassie. And when Zareb turned his yellow gaze on her, she felt her courage shrivel and crawl down her throat. He was just that scary.

"The Second One is rising."

Zareb evidently thought his explanation was sufficient because he turned back to Ethan. "You have about two hours. The woman must eat and you must feed. I was about to make a dinner run when you arrived, and since the woman doesn't seem to be on the menu, I'll pick up something for you on the way back." His eyes narrowed, yellow cat eyes filled with darkness. "Do I need to bring the others with me?"

"Yes."

Cassie's heartbeat picked up its pace. Ethan's voice . . . It was different—deeper, smoother, *more threatening*. And for one mad moment she wanted to ask Zareb to take her with him. Then she thought about his eyes. Maybe not. He moved toward the door.

"Wait." Cassie couldn't do much for the dead, but this one thing she *could* do. "The police. They need to know about the dead people in those houses." She didn't know why that was so important to her. The dead sure didn't care. But *she* cared.

Zareb raised one brow. "Dead people?" He looked at Ethan.

"The dead are in the houses next to mine. I didn't kill them. Explanations when you come back."

Zareb nodded. "I'll make an anonymous call."

"You know where I live?" Ethan sounded surprised, and not too happy.

"Of course." Zareb sounded amused. "I made you. You can never hide from me." And then he was gone.

Silence settled over the room, the shadows seemed to thicken, and Cassie's fear expanded exponentially. She took a deep breath. "You may as well come out where I can see you. Not knowing what's going on is scaring me more than if you've morphed into something gross."

Ethan's cold laughter scraped along her nerves, frightening enough for her to rethink her come-out-of-the-shadows request. Some things were better not seen.

Too late. He moved so quickly that she didn't even have time to gasp, to run into the bathroom and hope the door had a lock. He was simply there beside her on the couch.

Cassie stared at him and swallowed hard. *Don't scream.* Prey screamed. Prey ran. Prey *died.*

He leaned close and smiled. "It will get worse before it gets better."

She couldn't look away, a bird caught by a raptor's stare. He looked bigger, harder. He'd split Len's shirt, exposing a broad expanse of muscled chest and abs. Cassie was tempted to continue staring at his chest, because the rest of him was . . .

"Look at me."

The voice in her head was warm and rough and an absolute compulsion. Slowly, reluctantly, she lifted her gaze to his face.

Cassie now knew the true meaning of terrifying beauty. His hair had become a silken fall so black that it shone with blue highlights. And his face . . . What was happening to his face? His eyes seemed larger, and they now had the same tilt as Zareb's eyes. They were green with no white showing and vertical slits for pupils. Cat eyes.

She pushed words past lips that felt frozen. "Will they be yellow like Zareb's?"

He nodded. "Blue and yellow make green. In two hours they'll be pure yellow."

His voice was darkness, leading to places she feared but would explore if he beckoned. *No.* She wouldn't explore anywhere with him. His eyes probably had the same power that Zareb's had. Even as she pummeled herself for her momentary weakness, she reached out to run her fingers lightly along his jaw and watched it clench.

"Is this the Second One you've been talking about?" If so, he was the most beautiful thing she'd ever seen. Words couldn't describe him, so she didn't try. Cassie only knew his beauty hurt, a deep hungry hurt that made her yearn. . . .

Cassie yanked her hand away from his face. She knew her eyes were wide. "You're doing the same thing that Zareb was doing."

He didn't look away. "Not yet. Even Zareb wasn't showing you the full power of the Second One."

"Explain." She was tired of not knowing, not understanding. Cassie had been lost since the moment she'd walked into Eternal Rest Funeral Home.

Ethan finally moved. He stood and then paced over to the fireplace. "The ones who wrote the vampire legends were wrong." He stood with his back to the flames. "It was never about bloodlust. We can feed whenever we want. We're no more ruled by our hunger than you are." He turned his back to the fire and stared at her. "It was always about the kill."

"Zareb said he knew you'd killed because the Second One was rising. Who or what is the Second One?" Fascinated, she watched his face changing in small increments even as they talked—lower lip growing fuller, lashes lengthening, each change making him more breathtaking. Then she looked away. Beauty that hurt to look at couldn't be good.

"The First One is our humanity. Even as vampire it's dominant unless we kill. The act of killing wakens the Second One."

"You make it sound as though the Second One is a separate entity." Trying to keep from staring at him became harder with every passing moment.

"It is. The Second One is an elemental consciousness passed on in the blood my maker used to create me. It lies dormant until it senses a kill. It doesn't care about conscience or human emotions. Its primal drive is to destroy."

"After what I saw today, I don't think you need any help in the killing department." Fear coated Cassie's thoughts, making it tough for her to concentrate. *He's turning into this thing. I'm alone with him, alone with him, alone with*— She shook her head to clear it.

"What I did today is my particular vampire talent, not attached to the Second One. I have control of when and how I use it."

"Meaning you *don't* have control of the Second One." She stared down at her hands. *Blood.* Her hands were covered with dried blood. So were the rest of her clothes, even her shoes. How had she not noticed before this? His voice dragged her back.

"I can't stop the change. It's not that it makes me lose control, it's . . ." For the first time he seemed lost for words.

"Yes?" No matter what he said, it wouldn't matter, because Cassie had reached her limit for shocking disclosures. Her mind was beginning to shut down, refusing to react emotionally, trying to protect itself. *A little too late.*

"Scientists are finding out more things about the brain every day."

She blinked. What the hell did that have to do with anything?

"Some believe that beauty stimulates primal brain circuits.

It's not a response anyone can control any more than they can control their reaction to cocaine." He shrugged. "And if the beauty is extreme, it acts as an overdose and—"

"People die." She remembered the feeling of her heart slowing, faltering, almost stopping. "I can't believe it." But she did.

"The beauty of the Second One's face attracts its victims, its eyes hold them captive while it kills." He turned to face the fireplace, his back straight, tension radiating from him. "In two hours you won't be able to look at me. If you try, the Second One will kill you. I'll be Medusa in reverse."

She swallowed her fear as she stood. "Then I won't look at you." *Even though I want to so badly it hurts.* "I . . . I have to take a shower, change clothes." She raked her fingers through her tangled hair. She couldn't think. Clothes. She didn't have any, and she couldn't see herself returning to Felicity's condo anytime soon.

"The bathroom is down the hall to the right. There's a lock on the door."

Left unsaid was that a lock probably wouldn't stop a determined vampire. But Cassie was too desperate to shed her bloody clothes, to scrub the blood from her body to care. "Clothes?"

"The closet across from the bathroom. Zareb . . . entertains a lot. You should find something to fit you."

Cassie nodded even though he still faced the fireplace. She grabbed her purse and scurried down the hallway. From the closet she grabbed a top, pants, and a pair of shoes that looked as though they'd fit, then locked herself in the bathroom.

A little of her tension eased away as the hot water sluiced over her body. Cassie scrubbed until her skin felt raw, until not a speck of blood remained. And she thought about Ethan.

What she'd felt when she looked at him, the yearning, wasn't the same as what she'd felt for Zareb. Yes, she understood that in both cases she was reacting to the Second One in them, but still, it had felt different with Ethan—more personal, more . . . something.

Once out of the shower, she used the dryer lying on the counter for her hair and then pulled her makeup bag from her purse. The makeup, the hair, they were important. They gave her confidence, and confidence along with a few weapons would be all she'd have tonight. *And Ethan.* A vampire. Funny, just when she'd thought she had life figured out, it had given her a swift kick in the behind.

Cassie was still thinking about her reaction to Ethan as she dressed in her borrowed clothes and then returned to the living room. Head down, lost in thought, she had almost reached the couch before the complete silence hit her—no greeting from Ethan, no hisses from the cat, not even the crackling of the fire. She looked up.

Vampires, lots of them, stood in the shadows at the edges of the room. Motionless, silent, they watched her from gleaming eyes, *hungry* eyes. Except for one. He wore sunglasses and had a hoodie that hid most of his face. Which was scarier, what she could or couldn't see? Her breath caught in her throat.

Zareb broke the silence. "Ethan told me what happened to both of you." He pointed to a bag he'd set on the coffee table. "I stopped at McDonald's. Ethan already ate." He didn't offer to explain.

A vampire stopping at McDonald's. That should make her laugh, but all Cassie could do was shudder at the thought of all those silent killers listening as the water ran—imagining, hungering.

"My children and I will be paying a visit to Eternal Rest as soon as Ethan's change is complete." The predator lived in Zareb's voice, his gaze. "You'll stay here with the cat."

Cassie opened her mouth and said what was probably the most stupid thing she'd ever uttered.

"No."

Chapter Five

"Did she just defy you, Zareb?" Darren's voice was quietly mocking.

Ethan frowned. Darren wasn't one of his favorite vampire brothers. He'd killed too often with too much enjoyment, and now the Second One was close to claiming him permanently. It made him eager for violence wherever he could find it. At least he'd had the sense to wear his sunglasses and hoodie.

"Can you allow that to go unpunished?" Darren injected a fake note of concern into his voice.

Ethan ground his teeth. He'd gladly separate Darren's useless head from his shoulders. The jerk wanted to see Zareb hurt Cassie. He lived for causing pain.

One glance at Cassie assured Ethan that she recognized the danger too. He crouched. When had his mind made the decision to defend her against his maker?

Zareb didn't even glance at Darren. "Your need to see blood flow is much too obvious. Do you really think you can manipulate me, Darren?"

"Of course not." Darren sounded nervous as he moved farther into the shadows.

Zareb's smile never reached his eyes. "I didn't think so."

He looked at Cassie. "And why do you think you should come with us?" His expression gave away nothing.

She fixed her gaze on the middle of his chest. "If someone found Ethan's home and attacked his friends, then who's to say they don't have a list of where all of you live? I don't think Cat and I would do a great job of defending the old homestead."

"I'm certain that Cat is a ferocious warrior." Zareb's lips tipped up in a brief smile.

Ethan relaxed a little.

"Besides, they killed my friend. I want . . ." She took a deep breath. "I *need* to be there to see that they're punished."

Zareb nodded. "I understand the hunger for vengeance."

She corrected him. "Justice."

He shrugged. "Call it what you will. You deserve to see them punished."

"You're letting her come?" Ethan narrowed his eyes. Amazing. His maker didn't do crap like this. Stupid. Who took a human into battle anyway?

Zareb moved toward the door. "Yes."

Ethan didn't even try to explain away his need to protect her. "She'll die."

"It's her choice." Zareb's expression said the decision was made.

Ethan glared as he watched his maker head for the door. "Do you still keep your weapons in the same place?"

Zareb paused. "Yes. You're going to arm her? Excellent idea. I've learned that the least capable among us often perform extraordinary feats given the right incentives." Then he left. The other vampires disappeared after him.

"And sometimes the 'least capable' have skills that could put your butt in the ground." Her mumbled response was almost lost in the slamming of the door.

Ethan would have smiled, but he was too pissed to find anything funny right now. "You'd be a lot safer here."

Her gaze challenged him. "I'll be a lot 'safer' if I operate under the assumption that hiding isn't an option until these animals are stopped. Because from what you've told me, they're very good at finding people, and a false sense of security could kill me."

Cassie was wrong. She hadn't seen what they'd be facing.

He reached for another argument. "What do you fear the most, Cassie?" Whatever it was, he'd use it to convince her to stay away from Eternal Rest.

"Having to cook dinner for my whole family? World's worst cook here." Her smile was small and tight, but at least it reached her eyes.

"Right. Won't have to cook Garrity dinner." He searched his mind for a clue to her real fears.

Then he remembered her words when she'd seen the bodies of his neighbors: *"I've been afraid of the dead all my life."*

"Death. You're afraid to die." He knew he sounded triumphant. "If you go with us, there's a good chance it could happen."

She ignored him.

Frustrated, he watched her pull on a borrowed jacket. If she was determined to go, he'd have to give her a weapon, for all the good it would do. Ethan turned to head down the hallway. He pulled open the door to the smallest bedroom, strode to the walk-in closet, and took the key from the hook beside the door.

"Wait." Her voice was right behind him. "Did you just get that key off the wall? I didn't see a key there."

"You weren't *supposed* to see it. A cloaking spell. Zareb wears many hats. Sorcerer is one of them." He hoped he sounded as angry as he felt.

He could sense her rolling this latest bit of weirdness around in her mind. He yanked open the door and turned on the closet light.

"Wow." Her hushed exclamation said it all.

"Wow, indeed." He stepped inside the huge walk-in closet

and studied the hundreds of weapons lining its walls. "Can you shoot a gun?" As he spoke he lifted a small handgun from the wall.

"Yes." She reached past him and chose a different one.

He frowned. "Why not the one I picked?"

"I've practiced with this one."

He watched as she chose ammunition and deftly loaded the gun. She shoved it into her purse.

Ethan studied her. "You're different from when I first met you."

She didn't answer, just lifted a knife from the wall, chose a sheath, and strapped it to her thigh.

"That's a big-ass knife."

"That's why I like it." She started to turn away.

"This is the real you, isn't it? So who was that person back in the funeral home?"

Her eyes looked flat, expressionless. "I killed the binder, didn't I? Oh, and I still don't know what a binder is."

"You got lucky. Who taught you how to use a gun and knife?"

"My grandfather."

He picked up on the slight hesitation before she said "grandfather."

Ethan had a gut feeling. "Does your grandfather have anything to do with your fear of death?" Maybe she'd seen him die. That could be traumatic for a kid.

He needed to know, and he was prepared to stand here until she told him. Ethan didn't have a clue why knowing was so important to him. This whole not-having-a-clue thing was getting old fast.

She met his gaze, and for a moment he thought she'd refuse to explain. But then she sighed and looked past him. "I'm not afraid of death. I'm afraid of dead bodies."

"Why?"

Cassie hesitated, and he could almost hear her inner battle. "I'd like to know." He tried to soften his voice, but he hadn't done soft in a lot of years. His "soft" probably sounded like an angry growl.

He told himself that she knew his secrets so it was only fair that he know hers. But that wasn't the reason at all.

"My grandparents lived on a farm. Once a year my parents would leave me with them for a week. I loved the animals and all that space to play. My grandmother spoiled me the whole time I was there. My grandfather was a scary man once my parents had gone, though. He never touched me, but I saw how he treated his animals, how he treated Grandma. Even though she was afraid of him, she begged me not to tell my parents, because if he got mad he'd have one of his 'spells.' She swore he was a good man, just crotchety in his old age. I was young, so I believed her." She still wouldn't look at him. "When I was ten years old, my grandmother died. She'd been sick, and one afternoon my grandfather came in from working in the fields to find her dead in her bed. He told me to go into the room and say my last good-byes to her. I was frightened. I refused."

Ethan watched her raise a shaking hand to push back a strand of hair.

"He'd always been about staying strong and controlling situations. When his dogs didn't obey him, he tied them to a tree. When Grandma didn't obey him . . ." She shook her head. "I don't really know because she never told me, but I suspect it must've been bad for her to fear him that much. He'd taught me to hunt, to know my way around most weapons by the time I was eight. He saw my refusal to go into that room as weakness. His cure was to chain me to my grandmother's bed, close the bedroom door, and leave me alone with her corpse for two days."

Ethan couldn't believe his explosion of fury. He hoped the man was still alive so he could kill him. The Second One murmured its approval.

"He released me on the third day. The first thing I did was

to run all the way to the next farm and call my parents. They came and took me away. I never saw the old man again. I refused to talk about him, but a few months later Mom told me that he'd been committed and that he would never hurt me again." She laughed softly. "It was too late, though. That particular horse had already left the barn." Cassie finally looked directly at him. "But after what happened in the funeral home, after what they did to Felicity, you can count on me to do my part tonight."

"Is he still alive?"

"No." Then she walked away. "Let's get going before your maker sends someone to see what's keeping you." She didn't glance back as she walked into the living room. She stopped at the door. "Did you feed the cat?"

He almost smiled. Almost. Such an ordinary question in the midst of extraordinary events. "Yes. And Zareb took care of the litter box." Something he'd never thought to see his maker doing. He would've taken a picture and loaded it onto YouTube if he hadn't thought that Zareb would kill him.

Ethan had stopped to pull a hoodie from the closet. His change was almost complete. From this moment until the Second One retreated, Cassie couldn't see his face. He pulled the hood far enough forward so he was hidden in shadow. On the way out, he picked up his sunglasses.

She frowned. "The Second One?"

He nodded.

Then they left. Cassie didn't say anything until they were in her car. "No one waited for us."

"We'll meet up near Eternal Rest. They'll all come in their own cars. They'll park a few blocks away and wait for Zareb to give instructions."

"Cars?" She smiled. "I'm disappointed. I thought vampires would have a sexier way of getting around than that. I know you don't do the dematerializing thing, but how about flying? Do vampires fly?"

"No." Ethan knew she was trying to sound calm, but he could hear her quickened heartbeat, sense her tension. "If we could do all the things myths say we can do, we'd have conquered the world centuries ago. We have preternatural speed and strength, enhanced senses, and our own specific gifts. And if you belong to my bloodline, you have the Second One."

She remained silent for a few minutes, and Ethan was hopeful that she'd run out of questions. She hadn't.

"I was in the shower when you explained things to Zareb. So how did you end up in that glass coffin? And please tell me what a binder is?"

He kept his attention on the road. He didn't want to repeat the story, but she had a right to know. "I was in Jersey when they caught me." He wouldn't go into details about the chase, about how the hell they even found him. "They shot me up with something to keep me weak until they got back to Eternal Rest. Then they took my clothes and dumped me into the coffin. I was still too weak to do anything when the binder came in with his freaking headstone." Where had they found someone like him?

"They? Who are 'they'?"

"I don't know. Some kind of hunters." Human, but not human. And they'd brought beasts with them. His mind skittered away from thoughts of the beasts.

"So explain 'binder.'"

Ethan could feel her gaze on him, but he didn't turn to glance at her. He couldn't take the chance that she'd see his face. "A binding spell bends someone to your will, makes them do what you want them to do." He shook his head. "But I've never seen or felt anything like this. Tony brought in his headstone, set it next to me, and suddenly I couldn't move a muscle. I was like that for days." He'd fought, tried to at least twitch. Nothing. He was a mind trapped in a useless body. He'd never admit how terrified he was. "I don't know where Garrity found someone that powerful."

Cassie nodded. "The etching on the tombstone showed

you wrapped in chains and a lock on the coffin. So he made you feel exactly what his drawing depicted."

"I don't know why they wanted me, or why they put me in a glass coffin. I need answers." He hoped he would get those answers tonight.

Even though Ethan suspected that Cassie had more questions, she stayed silent for the rest of the drive. He parked her car three blocks from the funeral home. His car was still in Jersey. At least he hoped it was.

Once out of the car, Ethan moved close to her. Her emotions touched him—fear, sorrow, anger, determination. He'd tried to stay clear of the feelings of others in the past. Nothing good came from allowing yourself to be sucked into the maelstrom of human emotions. Involvement made you careless, vulnerable.

He recognized the risks. But this time he couldn't resist. Ethan wrapped his arm around her waist and pulled her close. "Whatever goes down when we get there, Zareb will want me to go in first because I have the big guns tonight. He'll follow me in. He'll choose a few others to go in with us. The rest will stay outside to deal with guards or anyone trying to flee."

"What about me?" Her expression said that if they planned to tuck her safely behind some tree, they could just forget about it.

"I want you between Zareb and me. It'll be the safest place. You know what I can do. And Zareb is old enough to remember the pharaohs. Hell, he might've been one. He has crazy survival skills."

She nodded, her whole body tense.

He couldn't help himself, Ethan reached over with his free hand and slid his fingers along her clenched jaw. "I'm here." Stupid words. They'd mean nothing to her.

She drew a deep shuddering breath and relaxed into him. "Thanks."

And that one word made him feel . . . good. No matter what they'd find when they reached Garrity's, or how much the Second One's need for violence pushed at him, right now, with her human warmth pressed against his side, he was content. Not a word anyone would use to describe him.

Ethan stilled as he felt the familiar touch in his mind. Zareb could get into his brain without Ethan even knowing he was there, but his maker always announced his presence as a courtesy.

Ethan listened to Zareb's message and then spoke to Cassie. He made sure he didn't look at her as he talked. "Zareb just did some mental messaging. He's already at Eternal Rest. Armed guards are scattered around the place. People are moving things out in a hurry. Guess they figure they might get company. He's not going for sneaky. As soon as we get there, we'll go in."

"Good. I don't think I'd survive a long wait." She paused. "Can all vampires read minds?"

He slowed down a little as they got closer to the funeral home, his senses alive to any enemy who might be nearby. "Most can read human minds, but nonhuman minds are tougher. A maker is always able to access the minds of those he created."

She smiled. "Well, at least you didn't shatter all of my illusions about the children of the night." Cassie stared into the darkness. "We must be close."

He nodded.

She opened her purse and rested her hand on the gun inside.

Ethan leaned down until he could whisper in her ear. "I'll keep you safe tonight. Trust me?" Stupid question. He was a vampire.

"Yes."

He released her and beckoned her deeper into the shadows. He put his finger to his lips. They crept from building to building until they finally worked their way around to the back of Eternal Rest.

Zareb glided from the darkness. Ethan could see the silhouettes of the four other vampires who would go inside with them. He only hoped crazy Darren wasn't one of them.

Zareb's whisper was brief. "Ethan, Cassie, and I will go in the back door. The rest of you will go around to the front. If everyone else did their jobs, the outside guards should be gone by now." Zareb watched the other vampires fade into the night. He avoided meeting Ethan's gaze as he nodded at him. "Let's go." He didn't even glance at Cassie. "Oh, and the door's locked."

Ethan turned his head away as he spoke to her. "Don't hesitate to kill." He took his place in front of her and faced the back door. "And whatever you do, don't look at my face."

He pulled the hoodie from his head, took off his glasses and shoved them into a pocket, then lifted his foot and kicked in the door.

Chapter Six

No plan? Just kick down the door and wing it? Where was the damn plan? Cassie's heart was beating so fast she thought it might explode from her chest. That would pretty much put a kink in their covert action. Covert? Hah.

She gripped her gun as she wondered how Zareb would even know if his outside vampires had gotten rid of all the guards. No sounds of a struggle, no screams, no grunts or triumphant whoops. Cassie didn't want to think about fanged shadows moving silently through the night.

Then she remembered what Ethan had said about a vampire's power to read thoughts. Zareb would be connected mentally to all of his children. He was probably in her mind right now too.

A soft chuckle from behind Cassie shivered up her spine.

"Why would I not be there? Your mind is a delight, Cassie." Zareb's whisper seemed way too close. "If it makes you feel any better, I'm in everyone else's mind as well, even the enemy's. My only limit is distance."

She forced herself not to respond. Instead, she stared at Ethan's back as he strode down the hallway. He was all power and smooth deadly grace. And even in the midst of her panic attack, his presence did weird things to her nervous system.

Zareb spoke softly. "If I'm not mistaken, four of them are heading our way right now, and they're extremely pissed off."

The sound of running footsteps snapped her attention back to the hallway. Four men rushed toward them, guns in one hand and swords in the other. Swords? Really? They looked human to her—no fangs when they snarled—but they moved faster than a human would. What were they?

The need for action was almost a relief. Cassie pulled her gun from her purse. But she needn't have bothered.

Ethan waited. The men facing him slid to a stop and then just stared. They dropped their weapons. Their expressions slowly shifted from fury to something so creepy that it made Cassie shiver. They looked as though they were in some sort of ecstatic trance—eyes half closed, mouths twisted in grotesque travesties of smiles. They stayed frozen like that while she held her breath. Then they simply collapsed. She exhaled. She recognized death in their loose-limbed sprawl.

Don't shake, don't shake. Whatever those men had seen in their last moments had killed them. For the first time, the Second One became real.

"But they died happy. How many of us will be able to say that?" Zareb's voice in her head sounded mildly amused.

Cassie tried to control her horror. She'd seen enough violent death today to fill several lifetimes. Zareb's attitude shouldn't shock her. But it did.

"When you live thousands of years, Cassie, death becomes an old friend." Zareb spoke aloud as he watched the vampires he'd sent around to the front entrance coming toward them.

Ethan pulled his hoodie over his head again. He hadn't spoken or looked at them since they'd entered Eternal Rest.

Cassie couldn't stop the questions flooding her mind. If the Second One was in control, did it recognize her? Did it care about any of them? The thought of a cold emotionless entity crouching inside Ethan's body not only terrified her but also made her incredibly sad. She forced her gaze from him.

Zareb didn't ask the others if they'd cleared the front of the building. The fact that they were standing here proved they had.

Cassie tried not to stare at the bodies. "Those were humans, weren't they? Then how were they able to move like vampires?"

Zareb looked thoughtful. "I don't know, but I intend to find out." He walked to Ethan's side. "What do you think about getting into the basement?"

Ethan kept his head turned away. "If anyone is down there, they can nail us as we get off the elevator. Let's look outside. They wouldn't want to get trapped with just one exit. I'm betting on a trapdoor and stairs."

"Wait." Cassie held up her hand. "When I used the elevator, there were three buttons. The top one was ground level. I hit the bottom one and it took me to where Ethan was being kept. But there was a second button in between the other two."

Zareb nodded. "The place probably has a sub-basement." He looked at the vampires who'd entered by the front door. "Two of you stay here to stop anyone coming up on the elevator. The other two check out the second button. When I call for you, come down to the bottom floor." Then he waved for Ethan and her to follow him.

Once outside, Cassie stayed close to Ethan's back. The darkness closed around her. The brave words she'd spouted to Ethan were all lies. Fear was a scalding acid eating its way through her. Her legs shook, but she forced herself to keep going. She owed this to Felicity.

Ethan worked his way around the house, his gaze fixed on the ground. She couldn't see anything but grass in the darkness. Finally, he stopped. He bent down and lifted a large square of what must be fake lawn. It looked exactly like the rest of the lawn to Cassie.

Then everything happened almost too fast for her to follow. Zareb stepped around her and carefully raised the trapdoor hidden beneath the grass. It didn't make a sound. Light spilled from the opening, revealing stairs. He stood aside so Ethan could descend first.

Once again Zareb was in her mind. *"Stay out of the way. I've called the others down. We have to do this fast and get out of here. Reinforcements will be on the way."* Then he leaped down the steps in a blur of motion.

No way would Cassie be left standing by herself in the dark. She took a deep breath. Oh, what the hell. She pulled the knife from its sheath and the gun from her purse. With a weapon in each hand, she admitted that her grandfather had done one thing right. He'd taught her to be comfortable fighting with either hand.

Cautiously, she followed the two vampires. There was no need for quiet, because as soon as Ethan and Zareb hit the basement floor, shouts and gunshots exploded.

Just as she took the last step down, silence fell. Cassie suspected what she'd find when she looked around.

Six humans—at least she assumed they were human— were caught in the Second One's deadly web.

Zareb was busy in the corner of the room where three glass coffins rested on gurneys. A naked man lay inside each of the coffins. She shuddered. Déjà vu. There were no signs of any headstones. She'd bet that the six men had been getting ready to move the coffins out of Eternal Rest.

Cassie turned her attention to Ethan. She didn't hear the man silently descending the stairs behind her until he shoved her to the floor. She fell to one knee and lost her grip on the gun. It slid under a nearby cabinet.

Cassie looked up in time to see the man step behind Ethan. He raised the sword he carried over his head.

Ethan's attention was focused on the men in front of him. Even as she watched, the men started to collapse. Zareb was turned toward the coffins.

With no conscious thought, just the lessons drilled into her

by the man she'd called Grandfather, Cassie raised her knife
in one smooth motion and threw it. If her target was human,
he was dead, because the knife was buried to the hilt in the
left side of his back.

He fell and his sword clattered to the floor.

She might never have wanted to see or think about her
grandfather again, but right now she was glad she hadn't
stopped practicing with weapons. Cassie had promised
herself that she'd never be a victim again.

She stood up, unable to look away from the body of the man
she'd killed. *Bodies, so many damn bodies.* She tried to close
her eyes, but she couldn't blink, couldn't turn from the man.

Luckily, others were capable of movement. Ethan put on
his sunglasses and yanked his hoodie over his head before
turning around. He took in the situation at a glance. He didn't
get a chance to say anything because at that moment, the four
vampires that Zareb had left above burst from the elevator.

Ethan didn't rush over to help the others get the men out
of their coffins. He moved to Cassie's side, still keeping his
face turned from her. He didn't speak.

She needed him now—his strength, his solid presence
standing between her and the body of the one who would
always be *her* dead man, between her and the six bodies
sprawled in the middle of the room. She knew she was sway-
ing. But she didn't move toward him, didn't know how to
relate to the Second One, wasn't sure she even could.

And just when she thought she'd turn and run screaming
up the stairs, Ethan moved. He simply took her hand and
pulled her against him.

His words were almost a whisper. "Thank you."

That's all. But that's all she needed. Those had been
Ethan's words. And if she was wrong, then she'd just hold on
to her illusions.

Zareb moved quickly toward them along with the rest of
his vampires, who were holding up the three semiconscious

men they'd rescued. "We have to get out of here. I sense others coming. This isn't the time for a stand."

Ethan didn't argue as he scooped her into his arms and then moved with preternatural speed. They were a blur as they all rushed up the stairs and into the darkness. Once hidden by the night, Ethan set her down.

Zareb allowed the others to scatter, but put up his hand to signal that Ethan and Cassie should wait. "I'll destroy Eternal Rest before I leave. You head home."

Before his words could even sink in, the funeral home exploded in flames. Cassie only had a moment to be thankful that no other buildings were close by, and then Ethan dragged her away.

Zareb disappeared in the opposite direction.

Cassie remained silent as Ethan drove. She was tired all the way to her soul, but she knew sleep would be tough tonight. If she'd thought that seeing lots of bodies would desensitize her, she was wrong. She'd killed two men today. They would follow her into her dreams and beyond.

Ethan spoke just before they reached Zareb's place. "Those three vampires are the friends who were staying with me." He allowed the silence to build. "I'm thankful that we reached them before Garrity's new binder did."

"If the binder had already put the headstones by them, would destroying the headstones have broken the binding?" Nightmares or not, she needed sleep so that she could think clearly. Right now everything was just a tangled web of confusion.

"You didn't get a good look at me when I was in that coffin. If you had, you would've noticed the same scene that was on my headstone burned into my chest."

"That's just sick." She frowned. "Wait, I saw you right after you escaped from the coffin, and all you had were cuts from the glass."

He nodded. "No one burned that into me. It just appeared

at the same time the binder put the headstone next to my coffin. At the moment he died, the image disappeared from my chest. I think that even if someone had destroyed the headstone, as long as the binder was still alive, the image would have stayed on my body." He seemed to think for a moment. "And the binding would have held."

Cassie didn't have time to comment on that because they'd reached Zareb's warehouse. She climbed from the car and headed for the door. Ethan put his hand on her arm to stop her.

"I wanted to tell you how amazing you were back there. I'd have gone to my final death tonight if you hadn't thrown that knife."

She couldn't see his face, but she sensed his smile.

"Zareb has a talent for reading what's inside a person, knowing how to get the most from them. I know why he let you come with us. I think he knew that you were capable of performing 'extraordinary feats.'"

Cassie didn't want to be pleased. Killing a person shouldn't make anyone feel proud. But it wasn't the killing that brought her a sense of wonder. It was the fact that subconsciously she'd known that she couldn't allow this man to die.

"Thank you." She took a deep breath and asked the question that had nagged at her all night. "You sound normal. Why aren't you all primitive rage and savagery with the Second One in control?"

She could *feel* his gaze—hot, *disturbing*.

"Exactly because the Second One *is* a primitive force. It only has one focus—violence. When it doesn't have a target, it subsides." He paused. "But it's still there, waiting for the moment it senses anger or any emotion it can hook its claws into. I have to be careful until it fades. Oh, and my face will still kill."

"How long until it's gone?"

He shrugged. "Not for a while now. I killed again tonight."

Cassie swallowed hard. She should leave now, walk into the building, because his closeness was making her forget things she needed to remember—he was a vampire, he had killed ten men tonight, he was a *vampire*.

But her feet didn't move. Everything that had happened today, every moment of emotional turmoil was breaking like waves against the dam she'd erected in her mind. And the dam had sprung leaks. Lots of them.

Even as she took the step toward him that she knew would change everything, the dam collapsed and her emotions swept her away.

If she thought he'd be the one to wield some common sense, she was wrong. With a guttural groan, he pulled her to him.

"You shouldn't do this to me when the Second One is around. It doesn't understand limits."

Cassie closed her eyes as she reached up to trace his jaw with shaking fingers. "Bring it on. It seems I'm into expanding my limits today. I'm willing to live dangerously for a little while longer."

And with a muffled curse, he covered her mouth with his.

Chapter Seven

There were moments when people did things they never thought they'd do. This was one of them. She would kiss a vampire.

It was her in-between time—after Felicity's death, after she'd killed two men, but before the dreaded instant when she'd have to finally accept that everything she'd experienced today was real. And definitely before she lay alone in her bed and slept, only to live it all again in her dreams.

This was her moment to forget—no before, no after, just now. And what a now it was. Ethan wouldn't kiss her gently. Not with the Second One lurking so close to the surface. But that was okay, because she didn't want kind and understanding right now. She wanted a kiss that would obliterate her memories of the day.

He pulled her to him, and she savored the anticipation. He was sexy, masculine, and warm. Who knew a vampire could feel warm? His lips moved over hers—no attempt at seduction, just all hard demand. And she opened to him.

Let the sensations begin. Or not. Because something strange was happening. She'd prepared herself to absorb the scent, the feel, the taste of him. That's what you did when you kissed someone. But instead, she fell straight through the hole that must've been in the bottom of her box of sensations and hurtled into . . .

What the . . . ? Darkness, heat, and emotions so strong that they shook her. No up, no down, just feelings—stomach-churning desire and a need that clawed her bloody inside. She was moving too fast, gasping for breath as everything gathering inside her expanded, threatening to fill her universe.

Every once in a while she'd catch a glimpse of reality in a flash of light seen out of the corner of her mind's eye—his tongue stroking and tasting, his lips sensual and tempting. But then it would be gone.

Emotions. So many of them. All struggling to be acknowledged, to be *felt.* Finally she couldn't stand it anymore. It was too much, too unexpected, too frightening. What the hell was happening? She opened her eyes.

For one terrifying second she stared into the reflection of herself in his glasses—wide-eyed, confused, *scared.* And then he turned his head away.

"Don't look at me when the Second One is near. Not even if I'm wearing the glasses." His voice was a raspy warning. "Unless you have a death wish." He released her and stepped back.

Cassie swayed, not sure if she was about to humiliate herself by falling flat on her face. Taking a deep breath, she locked her knees and stood tall. It had just been a kiss. *Right. Way to lie to yourself.*

"I don't understand." *Any of it.* Not what he was or why one kiss felt as though he'd changed her on a molecular level.

"I explained before. You stare at my face and the Second One notices. It wants me to chuck the glasses so that it can reach you through my eyes. It wants to *kill* you." He shrugged. "If it catches me at a weak moment, I'll take them off."

He'd misunderstood her, but that was okay. Her reaction to his kiss was too raw, and examining it would hurt.

"We need to go." He sounded angry.

What did *he* have to be mad about? She was the one who

had just discovered a whole new weird world inside her. Since Cassie didn't trust herself to speak rationally, she simply nodded and followed him.

Zareb waited for them in his living room along with the three rescued vampires. He sat in a leather recliner, and the cat lay in his lap purring as Zareb idly stroked it. He speared Ethan with a hard stare.

"It took you long enough to get in here." Zareb's expression said he knew exactly why they'd made him wait. "Your friends will be staying here along with you and Cassie until we find our favorite undertaker and fit him for one of his own coffins. The bastards won't get through *my* defenses."

Left unsaid was that Ethan had been woefully negligent in not erecting a twenty-foot impenetrable wall around his house. Cassie noticed that Ethan didn't argue about their staying with Zareb, so this place must be safe. And Cassie was all about staying safe right now.

"How much do we know?" Even as he spoke, Ethan stepped into a shadowed corner.

Cassie had to sit down before she fell down. The memory of what forever after would be known as The Kiss, along with everything else that had happened today, was finally taking its toll on her.

The three rescued vampires sat on the couch. They still looked groggy. After removing the knife sheath and dropping it to the floor beside her, she collapsed onto the only chair left. Cassie still clutched her purse with the gun inside. She never wanted to be without a weapon again.

"We still know almost nothing. Perhaps when their heads clear we'll learn more." Zareb glanced at the vampires on the couch as though he could force them into coherency by his will alone.

After being around him for a while, Cassie was almost willing to believe he could. "How were they captured?"

"They've been mumbling something about humans that

moved too fast and creatures like nothing they'd ever seen before." Zareb glanced at Ethan and Cassie. "Anything to add?"

Cassie nodded. "The humans that ran at us in the hallway moved like vampires."

"The creatures they brought with them to capture me looked like someone had taken parts from different animals and glued them together." Ethan spoke from the shadows.

One of the vampires on the couch continued in a monotone. "Big hairy bodies. Claws like some prehistoric raptor. Fangs of a freaking saber-toothed tiger and . . ." He paused before going on. "And the eyes of a vampire."

Zareb frowned. "Disturbing."

Another vampire joined in. "The creatures didn't maul us much, just helped to subdue us so the human bastards could shoot us up with something that knocked us out." He peered at Ethan and then at Cassie. He offered her a lopsided grin and a wink. "You look too good for Ethan. I'm Stark. When you dump his ass, look me up."

Cassie swallowed her laughter. Now wasn't the time.

The last vampire on the couch finally spoke up. "I heard one of the humans promise to reward the creatures when they visited the neighbors."

Cassie remembered the torn bodies and shuddered.

"How did they get to Ethan's house? I doubt they could parade their furry friends through the streets without anyone noticing." Zareb stopped stroking the cat. It hissed its displeasure but didn't leave his lap.

"A truck? They could've parked behind the house and gotten them inside without anyone noticing once it got dark." Ethan sounded as though he was ready for the conversation to be over.

"Why are they capturing vampires and putting them in glass coffins? And what did my friend Felicity know that got her killed?" Cassie's lids kept sliding shut.

They all thought about her questions in silence for a few minutes. None of them offered answers.

Zareb finally stood. He set the cat gently on the floor before facing his guests. "I have one thing to add. I was in the minds of the humans down in the basement before Ethan short-circuited their brains. One of them was thinking about someone called the Collector. I got the impression that this Collector was the boss, and that he *wasn't* Garrity." He motioned for the three vampires on the couch to follow him. "I'll show you your rooms."

She thought about mentioning that no one had introduced her to the other two vampires, but she was too tired to care. "Where will Ethan and I sleep?" Cassie didn't want to think about the nightmares waiting for her tonight, but she couldn't stay awake much longer.

Zareb paused. "I only have one guestroom left. It's the one Ethan used when I first turned him. You can share it with him." His smile said he knew his choice would upset her, but he didn't give a damn.

Cassie narrowed her eyes and pressed her lips together to keep from shouting at Zareb. He'd enjoy it too much. Instead she turned to Ethan. "I'll sleep on the couch."

Zareb didn't even turn. He threw back over his shoulder, "Can't. It's a sofa bed and I'm sleeping on it. I wouldn't usually give up my own bed to guests, but I want to be the one closest to the door if trouble comes calling. My three friends here are still a little loopy and Ethan's Second One would overreact. You? You're only a human. Sorry."

He wasn't sorry. She watched the cat leap onto the couch. It lay down and watched her from half-closed eyes. Cassie recognized the self-satisfied feline smirk it wore. The damn cat would get to sleep on the couch while she'd be sleeping . . . She glanced at the floor. Maybe with a few blankets and a comfy pillow it wouldn't be—

"No." Ethan emerged from the shadows, his hoodie and glasses still in place. "We can share my bed. It's not far from dawn, so you don't have to worry about me staying awake looking for my chance to pounce on you." He strode past her, headed for the hallway.

And because she was so exhausted that her brain felt scrambled, she followed him.

He opened the door at the end of the hallway and stepped aside for her to enter. She had a vague impression of a large space, a massive four-poster bed, and furniture scattered around the room that looked as though it belonged in some ancient castle. No windows.

"This was originally Zareb's room. He wanted to re-create the special feel of that last great castle he conquered." Ethan laughed softly. "The one with the throne and the willing widow. My maker can be a nostalgic bastard."

Cassie stared at him stupidly. "Huh?"

"But then Zareb decided he had to move into the modern era. His present room is metal and glass along with a big-screen TV that takes up a whole wall."

She didn't give a damn about Zareb. "Shower."

Cassie didn't really need a shower. Her last adventure at Eternal Rest had been a bloodless one. Ethan's kills were terrifyingly tidy and her knife had produced no splatter. She could skip the shower. But even though there was no physical evidence of death, she still needed to wash the feel of it from her body. Yes, it was all in her mind, but right now her mind was running the show.

While she stood in the middle of his room and tried to keep her eyes open, he disappeared, only to appear a few seconds later with a nightgown and robe. Where had he . . . ? Then she remembered. The hall closet with all the extra clothes. When she turned to go back out the door to reach the hall bathroom, he stopped her.

"The room has its own bathroom." He pointed to a door in the far wall.

A few minutes later, Cassie stepped into Zareb's glorious shower. It could hold a small army. She made the spray hot enough to peel the skin from her body and then scrubbed and scrubbed. When she finished, she turned off the water and sank onto the stone ledge for a short rest. Yes, she was putting off the moment when she'd have to go back into the bedroom and face Ethan. She closed her eyes. It would only be for . . .

When she opened her eyes again, she was lying in bed staring at the clock on the nightstand next to her. Almost noon. She turned her head. *Their* bed.

Ethan lay on his back next to her. Asleep.

How . . . ? The last thing she remembered was sitting on the ledge in the shower. Ohmigod, she'd conked out. He must have gotten her out of the shower, dried her, and pulled on her night-gown. Then he would have had to carry her to the bed. How had she slept through all of that? The wet and naked part made her feel a little warm. Memories of the The Kiss tugged at her.

He wore a sleep mask, but no hoodie. She dared to look. After all, if *he* slept, then the Second One probably did too.

Ethan's face left her breathless. Even without being able to see his eyes, she felt the inexorable pull that the Second One's victims must feel. But at least she was able—with super-human strength—to drag her gaze from that full lower lip, the lines and planes of a face that would bring humans to their knees in the streets if he chose to mingle.

She shifted her gaze lower. He'd pushed the covers down to his waist, exposing sculpted arms and a muscular torso that made her swallow hard. Sure, she'd seen it all before in Garrity's basement, but this was the first time she'd had time to appreciate it. Cassie bit her lip, focusing on the pain to stop herself from reaching out to touch, to smooth, to rip the damn covers off to see if he slept naked.

Taking a deep calming breath, she wondered how she'd survive another night sharing his bed. Because only total exhaustion had kept her from lying awake thinking about him next to her.

But then she remembered Felicity. She hadn't dreamed

about her friend last night. She must have been too tired to dream. But the nightmares would come. And she didn't want to be sleeping in this bed when she woke screaming.

She climbed from the bed. No need to tiptoe around. Ethan was deep in his day sleep. And if legends were to be believed, the place could collapse around him and he wouldn't wake. Throwing on her robe, she went in search of coffee.

Cassie was lost in thought about Felicity as she walked into Zareb's kitchen. What would her friend's family think when they found out that she'd just disappeared? Felicity had never talked much about her family, and Cassie had never met them.

Her frustration grew. She couldn't contact them, couldn't tell them the truth. And what about her own family? When she finally called them, she'd have to pretend that everything was fine. She hated lying.

All thoughts came to a sudden halt, though, when Cassie looked up and saw two massive men standing by the sink. She couldn't control a startled yelp.

They didn't smile. Jeez, they both had to be at least six feet five with muscular everything. They must be brothers— same size, same hard features, same orangey hair and strange amber eyes.

She froze. Who were they? If they were the enemy, then she was screwed because a houseful of sleeping vampires wouldn't be much protection.

Her weapon. She'd left her gun in her purse. The purse was still in the bedroom. *Memo to self: gun goes everywhere, even to the bathroom.*

No one spoke, so she finally broke the silence. "And you are?"

The one on the right answered. "I'm Ben and this is my brother Todd. Zareb hired us to guard the place during the day. You're the human." He still didn't smile.

You're the human. That must mean that he wasn't. "What are you?"

The other man, Todd, finally smiled. "We're the ones strong enough to keep you safe, little girl. Maybe you'd better hope you never have to find out what we are."

Well, that solved that. Little girl? Jerk. At least they'd cooked breakfast. "Do you mind if I steal something to eat and some coffee?"

Todd shrugged and picked up the conversation with his brother that she must have interrupted. Sports.

She tuned them out. No way did she want to spend any quality time around these two. Cassie piled bacon, scrambled eggs, and a piece of toast on a plate, then poured a cup of coffee. She carried all of her food back to the bedroom. A sleeping Ethan made a better companion than they did.

She set her food and coffee on a small table tucked into the corner of the room and sat down to eat. Then she noticed that the cat had slunk in behind her. She'd leaped onto the bed and promptly curled up at the foot of it.

Cassie smiled. "We agree on something, cat."

She stopped smiling as she slid her gaze the length of as much of Ethan's body as she could see. Then she looked at that breathtaking face. Not too long at one time. Just a glance here and a glance there.

Finally she accepted the truth. She couldn't sleep next to Ethan for another night. The attraction was too strong, her sensual thoughts too potent, and her willpower almost non-existent. If she was lucky, they'd locate Garrity tonight and she could find somewhere else to stay.

Cassie forced herself to turn her back on Ethan and stare at the wall. She thought about the horrors of yesterday, grounded herself in what was important, and tried to ignore the vampire in her bed.

No, she definitely wasn't spending another night sleeping next to him.

Chapter Eight

The sixth night.

For five nights she'd lain alone in their bed with her eyes closed so he wouldn't know that she was still awake when he finally returned. Forget sleep. She couldn't relax until she was sure Ethan had gotten home safely before dawn.

For five mornings she'd lain awake gazing at his face—and when the sheet gods smiled on her, his body—before falling into an uneasy and nightmare-ridden sleep herself.

At least she could stare her fill, because the Second One had faded almost completely. It was the almost that bothered her. She could see the tiny changes the Second One had left behind, the ones that were part of him now—his slightly fuller lower lip, eyes that seemed a little larger, a little more beautiful than before. Cassie tried not to dwell on the consequences if he continued to kill.

For five days she'd gotten up and dressed right before dusk and then waited for him to awaken.

That had been the best time of the day because he'd had time to talk with her. A lot. He'd explained how they were making a systematic search of the city. Until Garrity was eliminated, she had to stay hidden. She'd reminded him that she was the one who had saved his vampire butt at Eternal

Rest. He was grateful, but no, she couldn't hunt with them. Arguments ensued. She'd enjoyed them a little too much.

And they'd spoken about other stuff. About his human life as a horse trainer and how he sometimes still went for night rides. About her life as a consultant, a life that seemed to grow more distant and unreal as the week progressed.

Cassie had also unburdened herself about emotions she normally would've felt hesitant to share—her memories of Felicity, feelings about her grandfather she'd bottled up inside for a very long time, and her attacks of conscience over the men she'd killed.

But most important of all were the things they didn't talk about. How she came alive when he was near. How the need to touch him became a driving obsession as the days passed. How she knew if he disappeared from her life tonight she'd mourn his loss for a long time. And how sometimes she caught him staring at her with an intensity that made her catch her breath, made her weak with need.

Tonight was the sixth night. Tonight would be different.

She heard the door open. Cassie didn't hear him enter. She never did. He moved so silently that she didn't know he was in the shower until she heard the water running.

She pushed aside her usual fantasy, the one where she watched the warm water sluice over his powerful back, thighs, and perfect tight butt. The one where she moved up behind him and molded her bare body to all that heat and smooth wet flesh.

Tonight would be different. She opened her eyes.

After what seemed an eternity, Cassie saw the bathroom door open. She watched him move quietly across the room, his face in shadow. When he reached the bed, she saw that he wore his sunglasses.

He'd killed. She almost closed her eyes. Almost. But she wouldn't allow the Second One to destroy her hopes tonight.

She felt him slide into bed. He was naked.

Ethan broke the silence. "You're awake."

She smiled. "I've been awake every night."

"I know."

Okay, that shocked her. "How?"

"Your heartbeat. It was too fast for normal sleep." He rolled onto his side facing her. "I stayed awake listening to it every night until the day sleep took me."

She glanced at his face from the corner of her eye and then away. "I never knew." Now that the moment was here, Cassie fumbled for words. "I watched you sleep. In the morning." Fine. Now he'd think she was some kind of creepy voyeur.

"And what did you think about while you watched me, Cassie?"

His voice was deep dark chocolate coating all of the desires she'd kept carefully hidden for the past five nights. Now was the time for truth.

"I thought about making love with you." She held her breath. Only desperation would drive her to say those words. What if he didn't feel the same way? After all, he'd had five nights to make his move if he was interested. What if—

His soft laughter wrapped her in warmth. "Good. I wouldn't have made a seventh night."

"Why didn't you say something?" *Do* something? She turned on her side to face him, careful not to focus on his face for too long.

He reached out to touch her then, just a slide of his fingers along her jaw. But that simple touch amplified her needs, sent them crawling along her nerve endings, awakened her in ways she'd never imagined. Something exciting and new opened its eyes for the first time and blinked in the bright light of her anticipation.

"You kept your eyes closed. No matter what you thought you wanted, Cassie, you weren't ready to see me yet." He leaned closer. "The *real* me. Acceptance comes from in here." He tapped one finger over her heart.

That tap felt like the boom of a kettledrum and her heart leaped in response. "Are we finished with the deep stuff yet?" Her breaths were coming faster. When had she grown into an impatient bitch? *About six nights ago.*

His smile was a flash of white in the darkness. Without answering, he pushed himself to his knees and leaned over her. "Sit up."

Now that she'd exhausted her supply of bravado for the night, she simply obeyed. Raising her arms, she allowed him to slip her nightgown over her head while she focused on his throat and the pulse that beat there.

Cassie looked up to find him staring at her, and she swore she could see his eyes gleaming behind the dark lenses.

"You're beautiful. I thought that from the first moment I saw you." He lowered his head to kiss a path starting at the sensitive skin beneath her ear and continuing down her neck.

Cassie closed her eyes and murmured her pleasure.

She felt him pause at the hollow of her throat, his lips all heat and pressure. Cassie swallowed hard and knew he'd feel it. "From the first moment? I don't think so. Your eyes were black and you were flashing fangs."

He didn't answer for a moment as he slid his tongue along her collarbone, then kissed the swell of her breast. "I compart-mentalize my emotions well. My rage was completely sepa-rate from my appreciation of you."

She was finding it hard to concentrate. To ground herself, she smoothed her fingers over his broad shoulders and along his biceps. His muscles tensed beneath her touch.

This time the sensations came. His scent—clean, male, and filled with memories of the night. His skin, smooth and warm. His taste? She'd find out.

But as she leaned in to kiss him, he put his hands on her shoulders and took her down to the bed with him. Then he rolled her onto her back and straddled her hips. "There. That's better."

Cassie forgot not to look. She opened her eyes and glared up at him. "Excuse me? Where's the equal access? You can reach everything. I can only reach . . . some things." She took a deep breath and dropped her gaze.

"Ah, but they're the important things."

He tangled his fingers in her hair and leaned down to cover her mouth with his. Cassie explored the taste of him fully as the long drugging kiss threatened to spiral out of control. She closed her eyes again as she traced each fang with the tip of her tongue. So different from her, but so right for him.

He finally broke the kiss in favor of focusing his attention on her breasts. And as he circled her nipple with the tip of his tongue and then covered it with his lips, she encouraged him with breathy moans.

The heat of his mouth, the way he flicked each nipple with his tongue before nipping gently, and the pleasure/pain as he drew on it made her gasp.

Pleasure drove her. Cassie arched her back as he licked a path over her stomach. Then she spread her legs when he moved lower to trail the tip of his tongue up her inner thigh.

But when he slid his hands under her bottom, lifted her to meet his mouth, and then used that same tongue tip to tease the sensitive nub that was control central for what seemed to be every nerve ending in her body, she took a dive into the same place she'd visited the first time they'd kissed.

"Please, please, please." Her breaths came in tortured gasps as she pleaded with him. *Please hold me so close that you absorb every cell in my body. Please fill me so the emotions won't hurt so much. Please let me touch you.* Cassie didn't think she meant his body with that last "please." But then she wasn't doing much thinking at all right now.

Raw emotions and sensations that threatened to wash her away shook her until she gripped the bottom sheet as an anchor. She whimpered as he slipped his tongue in and out, in and out.

Cassie clenched her muscles around the indescribable pleasure—trying to slow it down, hang on to it. Finally her emotions overflowed the dam she hadn't done much to shore up.

Need, want so intense that it hurt, and an unnamed emotion that tugged and tugged at her heart until she expected it to explode from her chest battered her. With a growl she didn't even recognize as coming from her, she raised herself enough to tangle her fingers in his hair and yank.

He didn't fight her. She sensed that his eyes would be black behind his glasses, and she would've sworn his hands shook as he grasped her arms and flopped onto his back, dragging her on top of him.

Cassie wasn't sure who the vampire was here, because she wanted to eat him alive, drain him of every drop of whatever magic he was feeding her. She whimpered as she rose to straddle him the same way he had her. Strands of thoughts mixed with the sensations and emotions, driving her into a feverish frenzy to . . .

She knew if she didn't put her mouth, her hands, on his body, there'd be nothing but an empty husk of a woman left when this was over. The heat of her hunger would burn her to gray ash and then the ash would blow away on the wind of her frustrated need.

Cassie memorized every line, every curve of him as she slid her fingers over his smooth sleek body. Her fingers trembled as she spent quality time running one fingernail lightly over the hard length of his erection. Before she knew it, her mouth had replaced her hands.

She'd never get enough of him. She glided her tongue over his cock—all velvety soft skin and hard male need—and slipped her lips over the head. As she mimicked the rhythm of love, she soaked up his deep groans.

It wasn't enough, it would never be enough. Her feelings

fought the tangle of physical sensations, trying to tell her something, something important.

But all coherent thought fled on the surge of what had to be her own Second One, and it was shouting, "Now, now, now."

It must've been loud enough for Ethan to hear because he put his hands on her hips and effortlessly lifted her onto his erection.

Slow. She wanted to make it last. Forever. But her body didn't agree. Cassie felt the head of his cock pressing, pressing and . . . She. Couldn't. Stand. It.

She lowered herself slowly, with exquisite care, with deep breaths each time she felt him spread her apart and push in a little farther. Slowly, focusing on the moment, the sensation, the *feeling.*

Then he *moved.* With a hard thrust, he drove into her and she lost it.

She met his thrust with her own, joining them completely, and nothing she'd ever experienced felt like the sensation of him completely filling her—pressing, pressing.

She cried out as the deep dark emotional place she'd found before swallowed her. Want so powerful, so primal that she felt tears streaming down her face. She wanted, no *needed* his body, his soul, his everything. This couldn't be love, because love wasn't this savage. And right now she could've stepped right out of the primordial ooze.

Then she stopped thinking.

The friction. The rise and then the plunge to meet his thrusts. The hammering of her heart. The harsh rasps of her breath. The sensation of his body hard between her thighs. The friction, friction, and oh my God!

Her orgasm caught her and shook her with so much power that she couldn't even scream. She hung there while spasm after spasm shattered her past and rebuilt her future expectations. Never would she feel this way again.

And as the spasms slowly grew weaker, she mourned their loss. She was thinking again. Had he gotten his release? He hadn't . . . "You didn't bite me." She weakly climbed off him and lay on her back beside him.

He picked up her hand and placed it over his heart.

Surprised, she could feel his heartbeat. "It isn't racing."

"Believe me, for a vampire, that's a racing heart. Any more excitement and I would've been the first vampire to die of a heart attack."

She laughed, but then grew silent. Something was wrong. Cassie didn't know how she knew, but she felt the tension in him. Was it her? "Is everything okay?" Did she sound pitiful or what? *Tell me I didn't take the most incredible trip of my life alone.*

"What we just had . . ." He didn't turn his head to look at her.

Lost for words? Not something she expected from Ethan.

"It changed everything, Cassie."

What the hell did he mean by that?

"But something's wrong. I feel it." Strange how she was so sure she could sense the feelings of a man she'd known for such a short time. It was what it was, though.

Ethan finally looked at her, but his glasses hid his emotions.

"You felt what happened between us." He held up his hand to stop her response. "Just know that I *will* keep you safe." His lips softened into a smile. "Because I can't imagine ever finding someone like you again in a thousand lifetimes."

Chapter Nine

Cassie's surge of joy came first. It was all emotion. No thoughts involved. She would have been happy to stay in that state forever.

But her mind couldn't keep from messing with her happiness. The doubts began. He hadn't mentioned love. Vampire or not, he was male. Was this only about mind-blowing sex? And he'd mentioned a thousand lifetimes. She'd be able to share only one with him. He'd have to trudge through the other nine hundred ninety-nine alone.

Since she didn't particularly want to start a dialogue on any of those topics, she chose to discuss something impersonal, nonthreatening. "Is there a reason you think you might *not* be able to keep me safe?"

Only when she saw the flash of disappointment in his expression did she realize her mistake. He'd opened to her, told her his feelings, and she'd ignored him. Regret weighed her down, but it was too late to go back. She'd chosen to retreat from emotions that were too scary, that opened her up to hurt, and that had happened way too fast.

His expression smoothed out and he turned his head away. "We lost Darren tonight."

Shock punched her hard enough to drag a gasp from her.

"How?" She hadn't really known Darren, and he'd been a jerk the one time they'd met, but she hadn't wanted him dead.

Ethan laid his arm across his eyes as though the dim glow from the nightlight was still too much. "We've been splitting into small groups searching for Garrity and his men. Tonight it was just Darren, Zareb, and me. We found a gang of Garrity's enhanced humans—or whatever they are—and their beasts. Lots of them. They were trying to capture a lone vampire."

Cassie realized how totally selfish she was. All she felt was terror at knowing the danger he'd faced, *was* facing every night. She didn't have any fear left over for Zareb or the others.

"There were too many of them. We knew if we tried to fight them, there was a good chance they'd get one of us. Vampire numbers are down in the city, so we couldn't afford to lose anyone. We decided to follow them instead and see if they led us to Garrity."

He paused and she sensed he was back in the darkness watching the enemy, wanting to destroy them, but knowing he couldn't do a damn thing.

"But Darren had always been a killing machine. He was too close to the edge. His Second One took control. It didn't have a lot of survival instincts, just a lust for slaughter. He attacked Garrity's men before we could stop him."

She wanted to say something comforting, but her mind was blank to everything except the horror.

"He caught a lot of them by surprise, and they looked at him. The ones that did died. The rest were smarter and didn't stare directly at his face. Once Darren betrayed our presence, we had to fight too."

He turned his head enough for her to see the bitter twist of his lips.

"Zareb went into kickass sorcerer mode, I was picking the humans off without getting my hands dirty, and Darren was berserk. We made a great team." He paused and allowed the silence to gather. "We'd killed most of the humans and a lot of the beasts, but we were tiring. We decided to leave."

He took his arm from his eyes. "We turned to run but Darren stayed. I saw one of the beasts rip his head from his body." Rage filled his voice. "I stayed long enough to destroy the beast, and then I followed Zareb."

Ohmigod, Ethan had almost died tonight. The realization froze her.

Ethan snorted. "The vampire we saved escaped while we fought Garrity's men. Gratitude isn't a vampire characteristic."

"I'm sorry about Darren." She had no other words.

"This is why I worry. Garrity could take Zareb or me some night and then he'd come for you. I have to find a way to keep you safe." He was silent for a moment. "Your family doesn't live here?"

"No." She knew what he was about to suggest. "Forget it. My family might live in a different state, but I still wouldn't take the chance of leading those monsters to their doorstep."

He simply nodded before climbing from the bed. She couldn't help appreciating the play of muscles across his back and the motion of his tight butt cheeks as he walked across the room and reached into the closet. He came back to bed with his sleep mask and hoodie.

He took off his glasses, and she quickly looked away.

"I like to see the woman I'm making love with."

She smiled absently while he slipped on the sleep mask and pulled the hoodie over his head.

"Would someone who was with you a lot ever become immune to the Second One?" Dumb question. She would only be with him until Garrity was dead. That should make her happy, right? It didn't.

He remained silent so long that she thought he wouldn't answer. "Eventually you'd be able to look at my face without being affected as long as my eyes were covered. There's no immunity to the face and eyes together."

She felt his stare.

"You'll wake before I do. Dress and get out of the bedroom before me."

She could only nod. There was nothing left that either of them was willing to talk about. Cassie glanced at him. He'd tugged the sheet completely over his head. Evidently breathing wasn't an issue.

They both lay still until the clock told her that dawn had arrived. She didn't need to see Ethan to know that the day sleep had taken him.

Closing her eyes, she forced everything from her mind. Allowing her thoughts to run in circles would drive her crazy. She could only help Ethan if she stayed sane. And somewhere during her attempt to think of nothing, she slept.

Cassie sat on Zareb's couch with the cat curled up beside her and watched them leave. After finding out what had happened last night, she was terrified to see them go.

Ethan paused to look back at her right before he walked out. He had his glasses on and was holding his hoodie closed over the lower half of his face.

For a moment hope flared that he'd come back to kiss her good-bye.

He shook his head. "Can't. Not when I'm like this."

She didn't bother yelling at him for being in her mind. "You did the first time."

"That was different." He didn't explain how it was different. "Stay safe."

"Right back at you. . . . What the heck *is* your last name?" She was doing her best to sound perky, but Cassie had the feeling that even though her "per" might be fine, her "ky" was drooping badly.

"Russo. For now."

His voice had that deeper, more dangerous tone she associated with the Second One.

"Well, right back at you, Russo."

She kept her smile pasted on her face until they'd left. Then she sighed and looked down at the cat. "Anything you want to see on TV?"

The cat yawned to express her complete disinterest.

"Me either." Cassie glanced over at the two men who stood by the door looking bored.

Colin and Dylan. They were almost carbon copies of their brothers, Ben and Todd—big, muscular, with shaggy orangey hair and amber eyes. They were her bodyguards for the night.

"The TV is all yours, guys." She'd go into her room and read a book.

She wandered into the bedroom, grabbed her book from the nightstand, and flopped onto the bed.

A half hour later she was still on the same page. She put the book down. Cassie hated waiting here for Ethan to come home. She felt useless. But she'd learned a lot during the last week. Not the least of which was that she had no place in the middle of a battle involving vampires. She'd been lucky to survive that first day. Even loaded down with weapons, she was a liability. Ethan might try to protect her instead of watching his own back.

Just when she was about to give up on the book and try the TV again, someone tapped on the bedroom door. She climbed off the bed to answer it. Colin, or maybe it was Dylan, stood waiting.

"Zareb just sent us a text message. They're in a battle and pretty much outnumbered. They need us now." He looked torn. "I sent for someone to take over for us. He'll be here in about twenty minutes. We don't like leaving you alone, but Zareb wouldn't ask for us if he wasn't in a bad situation."

Cassie didn't hesitate. "Go. I'll be fine."

Colin nodded and ran back down the hall. A few minutes later, she heard the front door close. She was alone with her panic.

What had happened? Were they all still okay? Why

couldn't Zareb call in some of his other children who were scattered throughout the city? *Was Ethan safe?*

She was pacing the living room with her phone in her hand when the knock came. Cassie frowned. That was fast. The new guard must have been closer than Colin had thought.

Cassie hurried into the bedroom and got the gun from her purse. If she had to open the door, she'd do it with a weapon in her hand. She shoved her phone into her pocket.

Before opening the door, she tried looking through the peephole. Damn it, the outside light had burned out. "Who is it?"

"New guard." The man's voice was gruff but sounded normal.

Taking a deep breath, she opened the door.

Cassie glanced past him to make sure no one was lurking in the shadows. "Did you see anyone—?"

She didn't get any farther because someone grabbed her arm and yanked her outside. Before she could raise her gun to shoot, something massive hit her with enough force to flatten her. The gun fell from her hand. Dazed, she stared up into gleaming feral eyes.

The animal, because it *was* an animal, curled its lips back to reveal fangs at least six inches long. Terror froze her in place.

A man leaned over her. "Don't move, lady. Oh, and I wouldn't scream. Loud noises make Henry here excited. I'd hate to deliver you with puncture wounds."

It only took seconds for Cassie to put together the steps of her stupidity. She hadn't asked Colin for the name of the new guard, and she hadn't asked this man for any proof of identity. He worked for Garrity. And she was having an up-close-and-personal introduction to one of his beasts because she'd been naïve enough to think she could shoot faster than the animal could move. She wasn't suicidal, so she remained motionless.

"Very good." The man sounded almost fatherly. "Cooperation makes things a lot less messy. Now I'm going to call off

Henry, and you're going to get up and walk quietly to that big van. Understand?"

She nodded, never taking her attention from the beast's lethal fangs.

Her heart pounded, pounded, pounded as she took short gasping breaths in an attempt to control her fear. *Think.* Panic wouldn't save her ass.

As she climbed to her feet, she noted that her captor had picked up her gun and shoved it into a jacket pocket. He held the end of a long leash that was attached to the beast's collar. The leash looked way too flimsy to contain all that animal power, so she assumed there was more involved in controlling it.

Cassie didn't move as the man took her phone from her pocket.

"Love cell phones." He chuckled. "They store so much great info on them. For example, that bloodsucker we offed last night had the phone numbers of the guards that I just sent on a trip to an empty lot on the other side of Philly. Guess they'll be pissed." He handcuffed her hands behind her and nudged her toward the van. "We need to move fast. Bet they called in a new guard to watch you. I don't want to be around when he gets here."

Cassie bit her lip to keep from screaming. She wanted to fight. But her common sense kicked in. The beast hadn't killed her, so they must want her alive for some reason. Fighting wouldn't free her, and there was no one around to hear her scream. Besides, alive was a lot better than dead.

She stared at the van's open doors. *To hell with common sense.* She fought. Cassie kicked the man in the leg at the same time she screamed. When he tried to grab her arm, she bit him. She had to keep him from putting her in that van until the new guard arrived.

But as she stumbled away, he moved with a speed no human should have. She had no way to defend herself as he

reached her. He punched her in the stomach. At the same
time, she felt a searing pain in her arm. Cassie fell.

With a curse, the man dragged her to her feet and toward
the van. "See, that was just dumb. You upset Henry, and he got
your arm with a claw. The boss'll be mad because you have a
mark on you. That doesn't make me happy, and you want to
keep me happy, lady."

He shoved her into the van and pushed her down onto the
bench. Then he locked her cuffs to a short chain attached to
the side of the van. The beast crammed its massive body into
the back with her. It crouched a few feet away, its unblinking
stare fixed on her. Cassie swallowed hard. She would *not*
throw up.

The man closed and locked the back of the van before
climbing into the driver's seat. He started the van and pulled
away from the warehouse.

"How did you know I was alone?" *Don't panic, don't panic.*

"I watched. Two guards went in. The same two came out."

"Where're you taking me?" Her stomach ached and she
could feel blood trickling down her arm.

"To hell, lady. And if you try any more tricks, you'll get
there sooner than you expected."

Asshole. Cassie didn't ask anything else.

Instead, she tried to get her terror under control by staring at the beast. *Face your fears.* The man had called him
Henry. Who would give an animal this frightening such an
ordinary human name? Someone sick, that's who.

He's only an animal. Calm down. Right. That was like calling a tornado only a breeze. She took a close look at him.
Huge furred body. A grizzly came to mind. Three clawed toes
on each foot. The talons were at least five or six inches long.
And the middle talon on each foot was longer and more
curved than the others, good for ripping out stomachs and
throats. *Breathe, just breathe.* They looked like the talons

she'd seen in pictures of the Velociraptors from *Jurassic Park*. And those fangs. Definitely saber-toothed tiger–sized.

Finally, she lifted her gaze to the beast's eyes. She caught her breath. The beast stared back at her. *Those eyes.* Cassie recognized them—haunting, compelling, savage.

They were the yellow eyes of the Second One.

Chapter Ten

Cassie quickly shifted her gaze while she tried to control her shaking. "His eyes . . ." She bit her lip to keep from screaming when the animal edged a little closer, as though he knew she was talking about him.

The man sneered as he glanced at her in the rearview mirror. "Recognize them, do you? Go ahead, stare at him. You won't die. He has the Second One's eyes, so he can draw you in, but he doesn't have the pretty face to go with them. That means he can't kill you that way. Doesn't matter, though, because he has lots of other ways to end your life."

Questions whirled in her mind until she felt dizzy. What *were* the beasts? Where was this guy taking her? What would happen when they got there?

Then she thought of Ethan. Would he search for her? She had to believe he would. Cassie prayed that Garrity wasn't going to use her as bait. Not that she'd have to live with any guilt if she was the instrument of Ethan's death, because she had no doubt Garrity intended to kill her once her usefulness ended.

And just when she didn't think she could stand one more minute of feeling Henry's stare on her, his *hunger,* the van pulled up behind what looked like a large abandoned building. She didn't see any lights inside.

The man got out and came around to open the van's back doors. Henry jumped out and waited as his handler snapped his leash onto his collar. Then the man climbed in to release Cassie from the van. He didn't take off the cuffs.

He gave her a little shove toward a door hidden in the shadows. "We've kept Mr. Garrity waiting long enough."

Inside, the darkness was complete. Henry's hungry whining urged her to go faster. Panic made her clumsy, and she tripped on what felt like a raised board. Unable to break her fall, Cassie fell to her knees hard and for a moment the pain took the place of terror. Something sharp had torn her pants and cut into her knee. But then the man was there yanking her to her feet and pushing her forward.

While she stumbled along, Cassie sensed others in the darkness. They didn't speak, didn't move. Guards?

Finally, she reached another door. He pulled it open and light flooded out. Cassie saw a stairway leading down. Anxious to stay a few steps ahead of Henry, she didn't hesitate.

Once the man joined her at the bottom, he led her to the end of a hallway and then knocked on the door there. With an electronic hum, the door slid open.

He pushed her inside. "This is as far as I go." The door slid closed, leaving her alone with . . .

The smell of disinfectant made her wrinkle her nose. She glanced around the large room. It looked terrifyingly familiar. Lab equipment, sinks, and containers with God knew what in them. Gurneys, some of which had empty glass coffins on them. A man and woman stood by one of the gurneys watching her with unblinking intensity. Human? She thought so. At least the woman was. The man had that complete stillness she associated with vampires.

Cassie's gaze finally settled on the far corner of the room. A desk with a man sitting behind it.

"Garrity, I presume." Cassie hoped she sounded at least semi in control. She clenched her cuffed hands into fists so they wouldn't shake.

"Cassie, I've looked forward to this moment." He smiled, but it didn't reach his eyes. "Come. Sit." He pointed to one of the two chairs facing his desk.

Just to make sure, she reached back awkwardly with her cuffed hands to try the door handle. Locked. Taking a deep calming breath, she walked to the chair he'd indicated and sat. Then she took stock of Roland Garrity.

Cassie had pictured someone who would look the part of a human monster. He disappointed her. Standing, he'd be of average height and build. Thinning, light brown hair. Faded blue eyes. A weak chin. She would pass him on the street and never notice him.

Right now, she didn't have control of her physical situation, but her mouth was still her own. "Why did you bring me here? If you try to use me as bait, Ethan won't be stupid enough to walk into a trap."

Garrity raised one brow. "Bait? I'm afraid you overestimate your importance to the vampires. They won't bother searching for you." He leaned forward to rest his elbows on his desk. He steepled his hands and studied her. "No, I only went to the trouble of sending Caleb to take you for two reasons—vengeance and to make sure Felicity's family doesn't discover that I was involved in her disappearance. Families can be tenacious and meddlesome."

Vengeance. Cassie repressed a shudder. She didn't trust herself to speak, so she simply stared at him.

He went on as though he hadn't expected her to comment. "You are directly responsible for the loss of Eternal Rest. Now I'll have to deal with insurance and a police investigation besides having to find a new place of business. I believe you owe me for all the trouble you've caused."

"What're you going to do?" No matter how horrible, she wanted to know his plans.

"First I'll explain all this"—he swept his hands wide to encompass the room—"because no one should have their human life terminated without knowing why it happened. And then I'll change you from a pain in the ass into a useful commodity."

Human life terminated. There it was. She was going to die. There was a kind of sick relief in knowing the worst. Cassie didn't say anything, because if she tried to speak she knew her voice would shake. She wouldn't give him the opportunity to gloat over her terror.

"I and all my employees are part of a larger organization run by a brilliant man. He's never shared his name with us, but I understand his desire for anonymity. We simply call him the Collector." He paused.

"And he collects what?" She was proud that her voice sounded clear and steady. He would never know how much effort she'd put into those four words.

"Nonhumans with extraordinary powers and humans with potential." He leaned back in his seat again, his expression filled with admiration for the Collector. "He's an amazing scientist, and he's found a way to transfer power from nonhumans to very rich humans willing to pay for it. The nonhumans are kept alive while their power is slowly leached from them. Our clients have a lifetime supply as long as they don't get greedy."

Cassie knew her horror was written all over her face. She couldn't put together words to describe her disgust. So it was lucky that Garrity wasn't expecting a comment.

"Those we choose to sell must be physically beautiful as well as powerful. We package our products in attractive clear glass coffins so that our clients can not only enjoy their new power but also have something aesthetically pleasing to admire." He raised one brow. "Any questions so far?"

Can I throw up on your desk? She forced words past the boulder lodged in her throat. "Fine, so I understand why you collect beautiful vampires. But why humans?" Other questions pushed and shoved to be next in line.

He looked surprised that she'd ask that question. "Every

human has latent power. When the human becomes vampire, that power is freed. Of course, we can't charge as much for humans we've just changed because they don't have a proven gift yet." He smiled. "You can think of them as sort of grab bags. The buyer has no guarantee, but sometimes he gets a pleasant surprise."

Cassie felt as though her eyes were glued open. She couldn't blink, couldn't breathe, and her heart was pounding so hard that she wondered if every vampire in the city could hear it. No, he couldn't be going where she thought he was going.

Garrity's smile was twisted and evil and *happy.*

"Will *your* buyer get a pleasant surprise, Cassie?"

Whatever had been holding her in her seat snapped. She was out of it and running for the door even though she knew it was locked. Reason didn't enter into the blind terror she felt. She kicked at the door and screamed. And when the human who wasn't a human grabbed her, she bit and kicked and cursed.

Somewhere deep inside where her reasoning self hid, she wasn't surprised when she felt the prick of a needle. Cassie fought to stay awake, because to close her eyes was to lose her humanity. The man picked her up and placed her on one of the empty gurneys. He took the cuffs off her and then immobilized her with leather restraints. As her vision began to dim, she was aware of Garrity leaning over her.

"This is your binder, Cassie." He beckoned the woman closer. "She's a member of a powerful binder family that works exclusively for the Collector. Fortunately, he's loaned her to me until I replace Tony." He frowned. "You'll have to bring a good price to make up for killing him.

"Once we've drained you and replaced your blood with nice fresh vampire blood, we'll tuck you into your shiny new coffin, bind you there, and then bury you in one of the cemeteries I own until someone purchases you." His smile returned. "Did I mention that the Collector is brilliant? We can hide our merchandise in ordinary graves where no one would think to look." He started to turn away, but then glanced back. "I do hope you're not claustrophobic."

Cassie couldn't keep her eyes open any longer. Her lids drifted shut, and surprisingly, the last thing she thought about was Ethan. Now she'd be able to stay with him for the rest of his nine hundred ninety-nine lifetimes. As blackness descended, she screamed and screamed and screamed inside her head.

Chapter Eleven

No one would look at his face. Ethan didn't blame them. The Second One was strong tonight.

He'd hunted for Cassie alone last night. And when he'd tracked down a group of six of Garrity's men, he hadn't hesitated. He'd killed them all along with their two beasts, one at a time, while he hid in the shadows. The last man he'd kept alive long enough to get the information he wanted.

He put on his sunglasses and pulled his hood forward to hide his face.

Zareb paced his living room restlessly. The other vampires stood motionless around the room's edges, unwilling to come closer to him or Zareb.

"You returned home almost at dawn this morning. Tell me anything you didn't have time to tell me before the day sleep took you." Zareb paused in his pacing.

Ethan almost growled. Cassie had been gone for three days. The hell with talking, he wanted to get moving. They'd finally figured out where Garrity had Cassie, and Ethan wanted to be there *now*. He'd kill every one of the bastards. And if they'd hurt her—he wouldn't even consider the possibility that she was dead—he'd kill them slowly. No Second One for them. Too easy. The Second One rumbled its thoughts on that.

But Zareb wouldn't get his ass moving until he got an answer to his question. "The Collector is a scientist and a fucking entrepreneur according to what the guy said last night. I told you about the coffins and the binders. This Collector rewards those who work for him by feeding them small doses of energy from captive vampires. That's why his men move so fast."

"And?" Zareb glanced at his watch.

"The Collector created the beasts. He's a stem cell research genius. The beasts really are made from a bunch of other animals." He stopped and closed his eyes. This was the hardest part to tell. "He searches particularly for vampires from our bloodline who're lost to the Second One. I don't know how the hell he does it, but he uses their brain cells to create the beasts' brains. They have our intelligence, hunting ability, and the Second One's mindless lust for killing. The one difference is that the Collector has programmed their brains so that he or his people can control them." He turned away. "I'm sure he was pissed off that one of his beasts killed Darren and that Garrity didn't get a chance to harvest his brain."

The gathered vampires moved restlessly. Their hate, their need to kill battered at Ethan.

"After we take care of Garrity, this Collector is fucking finished." Death lived in Zareb's eyes. "Let's go."

Ethan was oblivious to the dark streets, to the others in the car. He reached out with his thoughts, searching, searching. Damn it, why couldn't he sense her? He finally grew aware that the car had stopped. He climbed out and waited while other cars parked nearby.

Zareb had pulled out all the stops. Twenty of his children surrounded him. The four brothers who guarded his home stood a little apart from them.

One of the brothers spoke. "We left her alone, so we're here to help get her back."

Zareb nodded. "We're a mile from the building where we

think Garrity is headquartered. He's grown careless and arrogant. He doesn't know how many children I have or how powerful we are when united." He stared into the darkness. "Run, my children. And then kill."

And so they ran, shadows gliding silently around buildings and through streets. Ethan was the first to reach the abandoned building. The rest spread out around it, looking for other ways in. He wanted to tear the door off with his bare hands, but Zareb moved in front of him.

"You're too lost to your anger. We don't need any noise to announce our visit. Let me." Zareb touched the door and it simply dissolved.

Ethan stepped inside and then froze. He knelt and touched his finger to the floor. Her blood, her scent. He looked back. "She's here."

They flowed silently into the building.

Cassie lay in her glass coffin. She could see everything as long as she didn't have to turn her head. Her mind was alive, a maelstrom of panicked thoughts and emotions. Where was Ethan? Had Garrity caught him? And how could she exist like this—her eyes the only thing she could move—for a lifetime?

No, no, no! Horror broke over her in waves of terror and despair. She was a vampire. She could live for *many* lifetimes. *Like this.*

She couldn't even twitch, but her senses were so sharp they almost hurt. Cassie could hear sounds from outside the coffin—whispers, laughter, and a discussion about when the best time to bury her would be. Her heartbeat raced, and she would've screamed if she could make a sound. Her mind spun images of looking up from the bottom of her grave as clods of earth landed on top of her coffin over and over until she was imprisoned in darkness. Since she couldn't pray for death, she'd pray for insanity.

Objects within her range of vision looked vibrant, almost unreal. Every detail, no matter how tiny, was distinct. Right now she could see her binder working on another victim's headstone. His name was Jon. Cassie never knew that hate could devour. She didn't need a Second One urging her to kill the binder bitch. She'd put her shiny new fangs to good use if she ever got free.

No smells seeped into the sealed coffin, but if fear had an odor, she was suffocating in it.

At least they weren't starving her. Out of the corner of her eye she could see a stand with a bag of blood hanging from it. The blood was draining down a narrow tube that had been inserted through a small opening in the coffin. Since her arms were at her sides, she couldn't see it flowing into her body.

Cassie closed her eyes, the only physical power she still controlled. She would survive on blood until . . . Would some merciful person eventually remove the tube? Did she want to die from starvation? *Would* she die? A question she hadn't asked. Maybe even starvation wouldn't kill her, just torture her forever.

What about her family? She'd never see them again. They'd grow old wondering what had happened to her, imagining her lying dead somewhere, never knowing that her fate was much worse than that.

And when she thought she couldn't bear the parade of horrendous possibilities one more second, she thought of Ethan.

Ethan who had dragged her from that nightmare basement in Eternal Rest. Ethan who loved his brother, cared about the death of his neighbors, and who rescued a bad-tempered cat that no one else would have wanted.

Ethan. The man she wanted to sleep beside for the rest of her lifetimes and now never would. The realization that she loved him came too late, much too late. A tear slipped down her face and she couldn't even freaking wipe it away. How pathetic was that?

The sounds of raised voices yanked her from her pity party. Damn, she wished she could turn her head. Everyone was yelling at once. She could just see Garrity.

"What do you mean they killed all the guards? There were two dozen of you up there. How did they get past the fucking beasts?" Garrity was shouting into his cell phone.

The binder crouched, whimpering beside Jon's headstone.

Cassie pictured herself bringing the stone down on top of her murderous head. And then she forgot about the woman. Was the place under attack? Finally, she dared to think the impossible.

Had Ethan found her?

Garrity cursed as he shoved the phone into his pocket. He ran toward the other side of the room, but Cassie couldn't see what he was doing. Then she heard the sound of a door opening.

"Cut the crying crap and get over here. I always have an escape route. This tunnel will bring us out one street over. Once I close this door behind me it'll lock. I won't wait for you even for the Collector." Fear lived in Garrity's voice.

"Then maybe you'll wait for *us.*"

Cassie would've laughed if she could. She recognized the voice of Ethan's friend. Stark.

"We figured you'd have a secret hole to crawl into, so we looked for it."

Garrity came back into view as he scuttled away from the door. He grabbed the screaming binder and yanked her in front of him. Then he dragged her back toward his desk. Cassie could hear him pulling a drawer open.

Frustrated, Cassie lost sight of him again.

"I won't need a sword. This gun will splatter your skulls all over the room. No regenerating a new head." Garrity's voice shook. "And I have her in front of me. I'm walking out of here and you're not going to stop me."

Stark's laughter rang with wicked anticipation. "Oh, I'm

not going to kill you. Someone else wants that pleasure. But forget about walking out of here because . . ."

Cassie rolled her eyes to the left in time to see the hall door implode.

"My buddy's here to send you to hell." Stark's voice ended in a snarl.

Whatever Garrity saw in the hallway, it sent him stumbling over to put her coffin between himself and the door.

Cassie was still thinking about that snarl. That sound couldn't have come from Stark's throat. Cassie mentally cursed as she made a desperate attempt to see. She needn't have bothered. Suddenly, a tiger leaped into view. It faced Garrity across the width of her coffin. It rose onto its hind legs and put its freaking front paws on the coffin and growled at him.

"Look at me."

The new voice came from the doorway. Cassie knew that voice. *Ethan.*

"Don't look." Garrity sounded as though he were in full panic mode as he warned the binder.

Too late. The binder had looked. Cassie watched her die. And as much as Cassie wanted to feel sorrow at another death, she could only remember what they'd planned for her.

The binder's death freed her. Cassie pounded on the coffin and shouted for someone to let her out. She watched in horror, unable to help, as Garrity's finger tightened on the gun's trigger.

Then he was yanked from her view. She twisted her head in an attempt to see what was happening at the same time she heard one blood-chilling scream. Then silence.

Zareb loomed over the coffin and lifted the lid. "Ethan really should have made it last a little longer. But the Second One was impatient. It doesn't understand the beauty and satisfaction that come from a lengthy vengeance."

Ethan shoved Zareb aside and lifted her from the coffin.

He'd remembered to put his glasses back on and he'd pulled
his hood as far forward as he could.

"Are you okay? Did they hurt you?" He grabbed a sheet
from the nearest gurney and wrapped it around her.

Then he gathered her close to his body and she could hear
the rapid beat of his heart against her cheek.

How to tell him—what she was, and how she felt about
him. But she didn't have to bother with one of those disclosures. He lifted her chin and stared at her.

"You're vampire."

She nodded. Would that make a difference?

"I'm sorry." His voice was soft with his regret.

What should she say? It's no big deal? Hey, I was ready for
a lifestyle change anyway? There was no good response, so
she simply nodded.

Cassie felt dazed as she looked around her. A bunch of
vampires and four tigers were crowded into the room. Some
of the vampires were smashing coffins and equipment while
others searched through file cabinets and Garrity's desk for
information. The tigers just lay there looking bored.

"Tigers?" The word came out as a squeak.

Ethan laughed. "Those are our four guards. They're
shifters. They wanted in on the takedown."

She swallowed hard. Vampires and shape-shifters were
real. What other myths and legends were real? "Can we find
somewhere to talk alone?"

"Let's go home. They don't need us here. I came in Zareb's
car. I'll borrow it and he can get a ride with one of the others."

She waited while he retrieved the key and then followed
him back to the car. As if by mutual agreement, neither of
them spoke during the drive. Once back in Zareb's home, he
heated some bagged blood for her and drank some himself.
Then, still silently, he led her to their bedroom.

Cassie really wanted to just jump into bed with him and
make love forever. But that would be impulsive. This was one

of the most important decisions of her life, and she had to take her time. She took a shower first and then waited while he took one.

He came to the bed naked except for his dark glasses. It wasn't hard to keep her gaze from his face. She had other interesting places to look, scenic views to enjoy.

Ethan slid into bed and drew her to him. She hadn't bothered with a nightgown so it was skin against skin. She couldn't help it, she rubbed her hands over his back, his buttocks, and then she closed her eyes as she tangled her fingers in his hair and he covered her mouth with his in a long drugging kiss. The sensory overload almost blew her vampire circuits.

When she finally drew back, she knew she'd stalled long enough. "I had lots of time to think while I was in that coffin." She couldn't do this with her eyes closed, so she drew in a deep breath of courage, and stared at his face. And discovered something amazing. Yes, she could still feel the pull, the compulsion, but she could resist, *she didn't have to look away.*

"Uh-huh."

He smoothed her hair from her face and then kissed her forehead, her cheek, her throat.

Just say it. This had all seemed a lot easier in theory. She took a deep breath. "I . . ."

"You love me?" His breath was warm on her neck.

"Yes." She absorbed the wonder of him.

"I know."

"How?"

He smiled and she had to rethink her earlier confidence that she could resist him.

"Okay, maybe I didn't know. But I had hope. Lots of hope. Besides, I've just spent three nights practicing how to say 'I love you' in a way that would convince you that I could make you happy for life." His tone suggested he hadn't quite believed he could do any convincing at all.

Fine, so she was crying. She swiped at her tears with her fingers. She glanced at them. "Oh, yuck. I'm really crying bloody tears. Gross."

His soft laughter sent chills wherever chills could go.

"Then I'll have to make sure you don't cry anymore."

She wrapped her arms around him and squeezed. "I love you. And you don't have to worry about making me happy for just one lifetime. Now we have a thousand lifetimes to work on it."

He used his thumb to dry any remaining tears. "And once we reach a thousand lifetimes, we can start all over again."

IN STILL DARKNESS

DIANNE DUVALL

Chapter One

Like the last survivor in a postapocalyptic world, Richart d'Alençon strode down the deserted North Carolinian street. Buildings long since abandoned for the night stared out at him with vacant eyes. Quiet enfolded him, both comforting and disconcerting.

A new enemy had risen among the vampire ranks. A self-proclaimed vampire king, who had ordered his followers to transform their victims instead of just feeding from them. Most nights Richart fought and defeated two or three vamps at a time. A couple of the older immortals had been encountering groups of six, seven, and eight. But tonight . . .

Richart had not encountered a single vampire, and soon dawn would break.

A woman cried out in the distance, snagging his attention.

"H-how did you do that?" she asked shakily.

"He's a vampire, bitch," a young man taunted.

Darting between businesses, Richart plunged into the trees beyond, traveling so swiftly most humans wouldn't see him. Those who did would see but a blur.

"Look into my eyes," a second man said, artificially deepening his voice and speaking with a laughable B-movie version of a Transylvanian accent. "Look into my eyes and know me for who I am."

Richart burst from the trees and raced through the oil-stained parking lot in front of a big-ass 24-hour superstore, letting the ridiculous conversation be his guide.

"I am Dracula," the second vamp continued dramatically.

"Look," the female captive countered, "just take the money. Here's my purse. Take it."

Richart almost laughed. She may not know what the hell was going on, but she wasn't buying that the kid in front of her was the legendary horror figure Dracula.

"I don't want your money," Dracula said petulantly, losing the accent.

"Dude, just bite her," a third vamp urged. "I've got shit to do."

Richart zipped past two employees taking a smoking break. Busy chatting and texting, they would assume the breeze that ruffled their hair was caused by a gust of wind, not an immortal warrior seeking prey.

Circling around to the back of the sprawling concrete structure, he found three vampires. All appeared to be in their early twenties and huddled in the shadows between two Dumpsters, out of range of the cameras mounted on the corners of the building. Between their lanky forms, Richart glimpsed a small, slender figure shoved up against the wall and held there by a fourth vamp, the one who called himself Dracula.

"Shut up!" Dracula snarled at the others, then went B-movie Transylvanian again. "I am Dracula. I am . . . vampire." He peeled his lips back and revealed gleaming fangs.

The woman's eyes widened. "Oh, shit."

Richart could do nothing to free her until the vampire released her. If he struck now, the vamp could break her neck.

So he simply cleared his throat.

The vampires all looked in his direction.

"Where the hell did you come from?" one spouted and shifted, giving Richart a clearer view of the captive.

The woman turned her head to meet Richart's gaze.

And the oddest little tingle danced through his chest.

She was pretty, with fiery red hair that fell just beneath her shoulders, pale freckled skin, and wide hazel eyes that met and held his, full of both hope and fear.

Dracula drew his lips farther back from his fangs and hissed like a cat.

Crossing his arms over his chest, Richart leaned against the building. "Yes—yes. I have a very nice pair of those myself." He smiled, revealing the tips of his own fangs.

Hope fled her features as the woman turned back to Dracula.

"This one's ours," Dracula said, "so fuck off. You know the king doesn't want us to fight."

These guys must be new. They didn't even realize he was an immortal, not a vampire.

The woman surreptitiously stuck her hand in her purse, then yanked it out and sprayed Dracula in the eyes and mouth with pepper spray. With his heightened sense of smell and taste, it would've felt like she had just held a blowtorch to his face.

Dracula stumbled back, howling and scrubbing at his eyes.

Richart drew two daggers and shot forward, burying one to the hilt in Dracula's chest and driving him away from the woman.

"Immortal Guardian!" the first vampire blurted.

Quick as lightning, Richart sliced Dracula's carotid and brachial arteries, then turned to fight the remaining three.

The woman took off running. Two vamps converged on Richart with bowies as long as his forearm. Faster and stronger than the vampires, Richart fended off almost every blow and scored plenty of his own, stabbing and slicing until the vamps began to bleed out faster than the virus that infected them could repair the damage.

As the two sank to their knees, clasping their throats, Richart approached the last vampire.

He had caught the woman a few Dumpsters down, shoved her up against the wall, and sunk his teeth into her neck.

Richart swept over to the vampire's side. The tip of his dagger pricked the skin above the vamp's carotid artery.

The vampire froze, eyes darting toward Richart.

"Release her and back away," Richart advised quietly.

The vampire tightened his arm around her torso and slid one hand up to grasp her chin. Fangs receding, he murmured, "Draw another drop of my blood and I'll break her neck."

As Richart watched, the boy backed away with the woman. One step. Two.

Richart remained still, biding his time.

Three more steps. The vampire shoved the woman at Richart with a touch of preternatural strength and took off, his form blurring as he fled into the night.

Richart stumbled backward and wrapped his arms around the woman to keep her from falling.

Clinging to the front of his shirt, she buried her face in his chest. "Is he gone?"

"Yes," he responded, surprised she was so coherent. When vampires and immortals turned, glands formed above the retractable fangs they grew that released a chemical much like GHB under the pressure of a bite. So she should be slurring her words.

Hell, he was surprised she still stood.

"What about the others?"

"They're gone," he assured her. Or they would be soon. A quick glance confirmed that they were shriveling up like mummies as the virus, unable to heal their wounds fast enough to keep them from dying, devoured them from the inside out in a desperate bid to live. By the time it finished, nothing would remain of them save the clothing and jewelry they wore.

Weaving on her feet, the woman straightened and looked up at him. She couldn't be much more than five feet tall and he was six foot one. "Y-your eyes are glowing."

Her pupils were dilated, blocking out almost all of the pale green, leaving only a few flakes of brown.

Richart retracted his fangs. "Yes. I know it looks bad, but—"

She shook her head. "I think they're beautiful."

Was that the drug talking? Or did she really think so?

"You saved me," she said, awe and gratitude in her melodic voice. Loosening her death grip on his shirt, she cupped his face in both hands.

His heart skipped.

When was the last time a woman had touched his face so tenderly?

When was the last time a woman had touched him at all? Other than his sister punching him in the shoulder, doing her damnedest to kick his ass when they sparred, or doling out a hug here or there, he honestly couldn't remember.

"Thank you," the woman whispered. Rising onto her toes, she drew his head down and brushed her lips against his.

The contact hit him like an electrical shock. His heart began to pound as she tilted her head and increased the pressure, brushing, stroking. She combed her fingers through his short, black hair, sending shivers through him.

He parted his lips, met her tongue with his when she boldly thrust hers forward.

Pure heat.

She leaned into him, clutched him tighter.

His body hardened. His breath shortened. His arms tightened around her.

Her knees went limp. Her lips tore away from his as her

head fell back. Her eyes closed. Her mouth hung open, lips pink from kissing him.

Richart stared down at her as his pulse pounded in his ears.

Yeah. She was out.

Damn it. That had been the best kiss he'd had in at least a century.

And damn *him* for enjoying it. She was drugged, out of her senses. She wouldn't even remember any of this when she woke up.

Sighing, he examined her neck to make sure she wasn't bleeding from the vampire's bite, which would soon heal and fade. He checked her pulse to ensure she hadn't lost too much blood, then gently folded her over his shoulder.

Since he was finished hunting for the night, he would see if he couldn't clean up this mess himself instead of calling in the human network that aided Immortal Guardians.

Opening the purse she had dropped, he drew out her keys and wallet. Her driver's license yielded a name and address. He smiled. Jenna McBride. With her red hair and freckles, it suited her.

Thirty-seven years old.

Really? He would've guessed mid-to-late twenties.

Tucking the wallet away, he studied the keys. There weren't many. Just a generic car key with no alarm to guide him to the right car in the parking lot, two door keys, and a worn Shrinky Dinks keychain that looked as if it had been fashioned by a child.

Was she married?

No. There had been no ring on her finger when she had clasped his face. And the vampires hadn't stolen it. The only things they had desired were her blood and fear.

It doesn't matter if she's single. She's human. You're immortal.

No shopping bags littered the ground. The two employees taking a smoking break outside the superstore had worn the same color shirt and pants the woman did, so she must work there.

"Let's get you home," he murmured and raced around to the front of the building. So swift the surveillance cameras would only catch hazy movement that would likely be mistaken for a dust devil, Richart sped up and down the rows of vehicles until he came to an '80s economy car that bore Jenna's scent on the door handle.

Getting an unconscious woman into the passenger seat of such a small vehicle at preternatural speeds was awkward as hell, but he managed to do it. He slid behind the wheel, his knees practically impaling his chest. A quick seat adjustment and he started the car.

Minutes later, Richart pulled into the parking lot of a nearby apartment complex and brought the car to a halt beneath a second-floor door that bore the number on her license. Exiting, he readjusted the seat in hopes Jenna would think she had driven herself home and just been so tired she couldn't remember it. He experienced a moment of unease when he opened the apartment door and immediately scented a male. Pausing just inside, he listened carefully.

Down the hall, someone slept. A lover, perhaps?

Richart carried Jenna, cradled peacefully in his arms, down the hallway and paused outside the first door.

Not a lover. Most likely a son. Though the bedroom door was closed, a male's scent dominated the room. Jenna's delightful scent, on the other hand, led him past a small bathroom to a bedroom at the end of the hallway.

He placed her on the unmade bed and gently removed her shoes. Drawing the covers up to her shoulders, he stared down at her.

He had done this so many times over the years, seeing vampire victims safely to their homes. But, for once, he found himself oddly reluctant to leave.

Listening to the soothing thump of her heartbeat, he

glanced around the room. A full-sized bed. A less-than-stable-looking desk supporting an outdated computer. A closet with not many clothes. And a battered dresser upon which rested a small TV and a handful of photos.

Four of the pictures depicted a boy ranging in age from infancy to high school graduation. A fifth showed a very young Jenna holding a baby while a grinning teenaged boy stood with his arms around them both.

Richart's gaze returned to Jenna.

And still his feet refused to move.

His cell phone vibrated in his pocket. Removing it, he glanced down at the text sent by Sheldon, his Second or human guard:

Sunrise in 15. Where the hell R U?

Richart tucked away the phone. Leaning down, he brushed the hair back from Jenna's face and pressed a kiss to her forehead. "Have a nice life," he whispered.

He straightened. The world around him went black as a familiar feeling of weightlessness claimed him. A split second later he stood in the living room of his home.

Richart let out a piercing whistle.

A thud sounded in the study. "Ow!" a male voice complained. "Damn it! Don't do that! You scared the crap out of me!"

Though such usually sparked a smile, this morning Richart felt only . . .

He frowned. What *was* it he felt? Regret? Sadness?

Yes, as though he had just lost something.

Sheldon entered the room. "You cut it kinda close tonight. What happened?"

Richart shook his head, baffled by the uncharacteristic emotions buffeting him. "Nothing out of the norm." Determined to shake it off, he strode toward his young Second. "What's the news on the vampire king?"

* * *

"You should try to eat something."

Jenna's stomach turned over at just the *thought* of putting food in it. "No way."

"Come on. You said you didn't eat before you came in tonight."

"That's because everything I ate this afternoon came right back up."

Debbie grimaced. "Food poisoning sucks."

"Yes, it does." Jenna smiled at a customer who walked past, then followed as Debbie wheeled her cart to the end of the aisle and continued to restock the makeup shelves.

The store was fairly quiet, though somewhere in the distance a child threw what sounded like a doozy of a temper tantrum.

Leaning into the basket, Jenna opened a box, drew out a handful of lipsticks, and started arranging them on the display.

"You're the manager. You don't have to do that anymore," Debbie pointed out. "Why don't you take it easy tonight? No one will fault you for it."

She shook her head. "I get antsy when I'm idle."

Debbie's eyes suddenly widened. Her face lit up with a wide smile. "Don't look now, but . . . guess who just entered!"

Jenna felt a sinking sensation in her stomach that had nothing to do with the chicken sandwich that had made her so sick. "Who?"

"Prince Charming!" Debbie blurted, looking over Jenna's shoulder toward the store's only entrance open at four o'clock in the morning. "Mr. Tall, Dark, and Yyyyyyyyyyyummy!" The last was said in a growl that reminded Jenna of the Cookie Monster. "And he's headed this way!"

She groaned. "Please tell me you're joking."

The Prince Charming currently making Debbie drool was

an incredibly handsome Frenchman who had been frequenting the store for the past month or so. Every time he came in, he made a point of seeking out Jenna wherever she might be and speaking to her. First it had been to ask where he might find Krazy Glue. Then it had been to ask if she knew what houseplants fared well in low light. Then it had become friendly chatting with a hint of flirtation.

And this man didn't need to flirt to get a woman's attention. He was gorgeous. At least six feet tall. Broad shouldered and leanly muscled like an NBA player with short black hair and expressive light brown eyes. Always dressed in black with a dark coat that Debbie referred to as his *Blade* outfit, hold the leather.

Debbie frowned. "That's weird. He was all smiles a second ago and now he's frowning. If I didn't know better, I'd think he heard you."

"He's sixty yards away. He can't hear us. Trust me."

"True. So what's the deal? Why don't you want to see him? I thought you liked him."

"I *do* like him," Jenna said as she grabbed some nail polish and slipped into the next aisle, out of Richart's sight. She really did. They had had coffee together a few times on her breaks, and she couldn't remember the last time a man had captivated her so much or made her laugh so often. "It's just . . ." She set the containers down in a pile on the bottom shelf and motioned to herself. "Look at me."

"Yeah. You do sorta look like death warmed over."

"Exactly. I don't want him to see me like this."

Debbie's eyes darted to Richart. "He's smiling again. Are you sure he can't hear us?"

"Debbie! Focus!"

"All right—all right. Here." Leaning in, she pinched Jenna's cheeks.

"Ouch!"

"Oh quit complaining, you need a little color. And smooth your hair back. It's all straggly."

Jenna hastily smoothed back the hair that had escaped her ponytail and made sure her shirt was neatly tucked in. "How do I look?"

"About as good as you feel."

"Great."

"The circles under your eyes have a lovely purplish hue."

"You're not helping."

"Shh-shh. Here he comes." Debbie leaned over the cart and pretended to search the various boxes.

Jenna grabbed the discarded nail polish and started distributing them to their proper places on the shelves.

"I don't see it," Debbie said. "Nancy may have forgotten to order it. You want me to go check?" Convinced that Richart had a thing for Jenna, Debbie always found an excuse to leave the two alone.

Or as alone as they could be in a massive superstore.

"Good evening, ladies," Richart greeted them, stopping beside Debbie's cart and giving them both a smile. His eyes met and held Jenna's.

Her heart, as usual, began to slam against her ribs with all of the enthusiasm of a crushing teenager's. And her stomach filled with butterflies that really didn't mingle well with the nausea plaguing her.

"Hi," she said. The moment she had first seen Richart, a sense of familiarity had overwhelmed her. But she was certain she had never met him before. She would have remembered his good looks, his warm, friendly demeanor, and that smooth French accent. It was a puzzle.

"Hi," Debbie chirped. "How's it goin'?"

Still smiling, he drew the sides of his coat back a bit and tucked his hands in his pants pockets. "It's been a quiet night."

"For us, too," Debbie replied, then looked at Jenna. "I'm

gonna go see if it's in the other basket. If it isn't there, I'll check the back."

"Okay. Thanks."

Debbie gave Richart a little wave.

He bowed slightly, watched her leave, then turned a discerning gaze on Jenna.

"So." She mentally told the butterflies to simmer the hell down so she wouldn't start dry heaving in front of the first man to interest her in years. "I assume in the private security business a quiet night is a good night?"

He nodded. "Very much so."

Though young (a good seven or eight years younger than she was by her guess), he was a partner in what sounded like a very successful and very elite private security company.

"Never a dull moment?" she asked with a smile.

"Rarely," he admitted. His brow furrowed. "Are you feeling all right tonight?"

She winced. "I look that bad, huh?"

"You're as beautiful as ever, just a bit peaked."

Seriously, who wouldn't like this man?

"I ate some bad fast food earlier and am paying for it big-time."

"Why aren't you home in bed?"

Because I have a son on his way to medical school and need every penny of every paycheck to supplement his scholarship and keep the student loan debt he racks up to a minimum.

She shrugged. "For food poisoning? Nah. I'll be fine."

Richart wasn't so sure about that, but didn't press it. Her pale, freckled skin, which usually held a faint hint of pink, had acquired a yellowish cast. Her pretty eyes, more brown than green tonight, were shadowed.

If she had looked this pallid after being bitten by the vampire from whom he had rescued her, Richart would have been worried that she might be transforming, but that had taken place weeks ago. And he had kept an eye on her ever since, watching to ensure the vampire who had fled would not return to harm her.

Of course, keeping an eye on her had only enhanced his interest. He couldn't forget that kiss. Or the feel of her slender body pressed against his. He liked her smile. He liked her laugh. The camaraderie she shared with Debbie.

His Second had caught on—Richart still didn't know how, because Sheldon wasn't the sharpest knife in the drawer—and had told him to stop stalking her.

Dude, just talk to her already. It's getting kinda creepy.

Richart had only been looking for an excuse, so . . . he had followed Sheldon's advice and asked her where to find the Krazy Glue. Soon they had worked up to chatting like old friends and having coffee together whenever he managed to time his visits with her breaks.

"How's John?" he asked.

As expected, her face lit with pride at the mention of her son. "He just aced another exam."

"Excellent."

She clearly adored John, whom she had borne when she was a mere seventeen years old.

An employee walked past and waved. "I'm out, Jenna."

"'Night, Tracy."

"Enjoy your night off tomorrow," Tracy called over her shoulder.

Richart turned back to Jenna and arched a brow. "You have tomorrow night off?"

She nodded. "I'm glad it wasn't tonight. Being sick on my night off would have really sucked."

Don't do it. Don't do it. Just tell her to have fun and get some rest. Keep it casual. "Would it be too presumptuous of me to ask if I might cook dinner for you tomorrow night? Something mild that won't upset your stomach further?" *Imbécile.*

She blinked. "Really?"

"Yes. I could pick up the ingredients and cook them at your place so, if you still aren't feeling well, you won't have to go out or dress up and can lounge around in . . ." Hell. What did women wear when they were just hanging around the house? His sister always sported combat gear and weapons.

"Yoga pants and a tank top?" she suggested.

He had no idea what yoga pants were, but had to struggle to keep his body from responding to the mental image of Jenna in a tank top. "Perfect."

She bit her lip.

"Not perfect?"

"There's just one thing," she broached with reluctance. "John works until nine tomorrow night and I don't think he's planning to meet with his study group, so he'll probably be home by ten. I'm not sure what you have in mind, but I wouldn't feel comfortable . . . pursuing anything"—her cheeks filled with a pretty pink—"amorous with him home or ex-pected home any minute."

He smiled. "I assure you such was not my intention."

"Oh." The pink deepened. "Embarrassing. I'm sorry. *I* was the one being presumptuous. I didn't—"

He touched her shoulder. "I meant such was not my inten-tion while you feel unwell."

"Oh," she repeated, then sent him a shy smile.

"I have a confession to make, Jenna," he said, defying caution. "Normally, I rarely patronize this store."

"You've been in here at least every other night for the past month."

He nodded. "Yes. Because, once I met you, I couldn't stop thinking about you."

She smiled, all awkwardness falling away. "Really?"

"Yes."

"Me, too," she admitted. "It's funny. The first night you came in, I had the strangest feeling that I knew you."

Chier. Somewhere in her subconscious she must remember the night he had rescued her. But that time should be nothing but a black void. She should have no memory of it at all, not even enough to make her think she had seen him before.

"You did?" he asked as casually as he could.

She nodded. "I wanted to ask you if we'd met, but was afraid you might think it was a pickup line or something."

"Ah." *Smooth.*

"Have we met?" she persisted, face curious. "The feeling was so strong."

"I'm sure I would remember if we had." Not a lie, but misleading.

She nodded, brow faintly furrowed. "Yeah, me too."

Richart's phone vibrated in his pocket. Drawing it out, he glanced down to note the caller: Chris Reordon, the mortal in charge of the East Coast division of the human network that aided Immortal Guardians.

Richart gave Jenna's shoulder another light touch. "I'm sorry. I have to take this."

She nodded.

"Yes?" Richart answered.

"I just received a call from a woman in distress," Chris said without preamble. "All she had time to do is say, 'Oh, crap' and drop the phone before vampires attacked and gunshots sounded."

"Could you tell how many there were?"

"No. But, judging by the sounds of it, a hell of a lot. Étienne is at UNC Chapel Hill near Kenan Stadium. I need you to teleport to him and be ready to go as soon as I track down where she is."

Richart walked a couple of paces away. "Could it be Tracy?" Tracy was his sister Lisette's Second, and 9mms were her weapons of choice.

"It isn't Tracy. I would have recognized her voice."

Relief rushed through him.

"We're tracing the call now," Chris continued, "and should

have a location by the time you rendezvous with Étienne. If it's a place you know, teleport directly to the location and join the fight. If it isn't, Étienne has his car with him and will get the two of you there as fast as he can."

"I'm on my way." Tucking his phone away, Richart turned back to Jenna. "Looks like I spoke too soon. It won't be a quiet night after all. A problem has arisen that requires my immediate attention."

"Okay."

"May I have your phone number so I may call you tomorrow to obtain your address?" He didn't wish to frighten her by admitting he already knew it.

She recited it quickly. "Be careful," she added as he bowed and backed away.

Warmth filled him. "Feel better," he replied, earning another smile.

It took Chris longer than anticipated to trace the call, which came from way out in the boonies. Étienne violated just about every traffic law to get the two of them there as quickly as possible. When the car flew over a hill and Richart spied the battlefield ahead, he teleported himself the remaining distance and drew his swords.

Gaping, he took in what must be three dozen shriveling-up vampire corpses scattered across a blood-soaked field. *"Merde!"*

The threat, it would seem, had been annihilated. All the vampires had been taken out by . . .

His gaze strayed to a battered-all-to-hell black Prius upon which sat a small female figure, nearly hidden behind the irate, eight-hundred-plus-year-old British immortal who stood protectively in front of her, eyes blazing amber fire.

"Really?" Marcus bellowed. "You show up *now?*"

"The call didn't come from your phone," Richart explained.

"So Chris didn't know you were the one who needed help or where to send us until the GPS identified your location."

"I dialed the number," the woman murmured, voice pained, "but the vampires attacked before I could say anything."

Marcus nodded, the eyes he trained on Richart still furious. "It took this long for him to track our location? I thought that shit worked faster than that."

"No, it took this long for us to get here. You *are* way out in the sticks, you know." Richart eyed the two of them curiously.

Marcus continued to stand protectively in front of the woman, one hand tucked behind him, resting on her legs.

Interesting.

Marcus's scowl deepened. "Why didn't you just—"

"I'm not as powerful as Seth. I can only teleport to places I'm familiar with, and I'm new to the area."

The hem of Richart's long coat fluttered as his brother's car skidded to a halt inches away.

The driver's door flew open and Étienne leaped out, weapons at the ready. "*Merde!* How many were there?" he asked with astonishment.

Richart turned in a circle, taking in the rapidly decomposing remains of the vampires the duo had defeated. "Thirty-four by my count."

Étienne gaped at Marcus. "And you took them all out by yourself?"

Marcus shook his head. "*We* took them all out."

As one, Richart and his brother shifted so they could better see the injured woman, who seemed to want to lose herself behind Marcus.

"Two defeated thirty-four?" Richart said with a shake of his head. It was an unheard of feat. Richart would have thought only Seth—the eldest and most powerful immortal and leader of the Immortal Guardians—would have been capable of such. "Incredible."

Étienne nodded, his gaze pinned to the woman.

Small, attractive, and blood-splattered, she boasted red hair that must have been dyed. All immortals had black hair.

Well, all but a couple who had brown hair.

"I didn't know Seth had called in another immortal," Étienne said, drawing the same conclusion Richart had. "Pleasure to meet you. I am Étienne d'Alençon, and this is my brother Richart."

Was that jealousy Richart saw flare in Marcus's eyes?

"Ami isn't an immortal. She's my Second."

Richart felt his jaw drop. "She's *human?*" he asked incredulously.

How had one immortal and one human stood against so many vampires?

Once again, he took in the multitude of corpses littering the field.

Vampires had not even attacked in these numbers when Bastien, an immortal who had thought himself a vampire for two centuries, had raised an army and waged war with the Immortal Guardians a couple of years ago.

What the hell was going on?

Chapter Two

Jenna was beset by nerves all day as she anticipated her date with Richart.

It hadn't taken her long to tidy the apartment. Once done, she rearranged the kitchen cabinets and drawers, placing the nicest of her mismatched dishes and glasses in the front and on top.

She couldn't remember a time when money hadn't been tight. Her parents had kicked her out when she had turned up pregnant at sixteen. Her boyfriend's parents had declared their child-rearing days over and done little more than give Jenna and Bobby, John's father, first and last month's rent on their first apartment. The two had married and worked their asses off, but—unable to afford health insurance—had accrued thousands of dollars in debt thanks to the medical bills pregnancy and giving birth had generated. Debt they had still been struggling to pay off when Bobby had been killed in a car accident three years later.

So nice dishes and pretty glasses had been beyond her budget.

Hell, the only furniture she had owned for years—other than baby furniture—had been throwaway pieces other tenants had left out by the Dumpster and an inflatable mattress.

But eventually, she had paid off the debt and managed to put away a little extra here and there until she had acquired enough to furnish the apartment with something that wouldn't embarrass John when he invited friends over.

Or her. Richart had said he wouldn't pursue anything amorous tonight, but she was nevertheless glad she had an actual bed in case something developed between them later.

Butterflies flocked to her stomach. She hadn't had a date in . . .

Hmm. She drew a blank on that one.

Debbie had set her up on a blind date a couple of years ago that had gone rather well, Jenna thought, until she had mentioned having a son who planned to go to medical school. Her date had apparently mentally jumped ahead to marrying her and having to shell out a couple hundred thousand dollars in educational fees for a son who wasn't his and had run, not walked, in the opposite direction.

Dating wasn't easy for single moms.

The phone rang.

Jenna jumped. Shaking her head at herself, she answered. "Hello?"

"Hello."

Her heart began to pound at the sound of Richart's deep, silky voice. "Hi."

"How are you feeling?"

"Much better, thank you." Well . . . a little better, anyway. Though her stomach remained unsettled, she felt somewhat confident that she would be able to eat whatever meal he prepared without projectile vomiting it on him afterward.

"I'm glad to hear it. I thought I would run some dinner ideas by you and see what you think would be the most gentle on your stomach."

So thoughtful. "Okay. What did you have in mind?"

Richart began to list entrées he could prepare for her. Clearly the man could cook.

Jenna didn't know how half of the dishes he mentioned were prepared or if she even had the pots and pans needed to do it, so she went with the safest option. "How about the light salad and fettuccine Alfredo?"

"As you wish," he responded cheerfully. "I shall see you tonight."

When Jenna opened her door shortly after sunset, Richart smiled and decided that he *loved* yoga pants and tank tops. The soft gray pants hugged full hips and slender thighs before falling in straight lines to a pair of sneakers. A white tank top clung to a narrow ribcage, minuscule waist, and breasts he thought would fit perfectly in the palms of his hands, which tightened around the handles of the shopping bags he carried.

"I took you at your word and stayed in my comfy clothes," she said with a hesitant smile, stepping back and motioning for him to enter.

"I like your comfy clothes," he professed, inhaling her sweet scent as he strode past into the small living room. Jenna plus a hint of the chocolate-raspberry soap she used. A delectable combination.

She had even worn her hair down. At work she usually pulled it back with clasps or ties or put it up in a ponytail. Tonight it fell freely in shining waves as red as the sky at sunset, tumbling across her shoulders and tempting him to comb his fingers through it.

No touching, he admonished himself. *At least, no touching that might lead to* more *touching. She's ill and you're immortal and haven't told her. Nor do you plan to tell her. So, what the hell are you actually doing here?*

Giving in to weakness.

He hadn't felt this drawn to a woman since before his transformation. She made him forget the dark violence that was such a large part of his existence and made everything somehow less tedious, so he actually looked forward to rising each day, eager to see her again.

"How are you feeling?" Richart asked as she closed the door.

"Both hungry and nauseated at the same time. I haven't eaten anything all day because my stomach still isn't right. But I think the Alfredo is mild enough to stay down." She grimaced.

"What?"

She gave him a self-deprecating smile and led him into the kitchen. "Nothing. It's just . . . I've never talked about vomiting on a first date before. Real romantic, right?"

He grinned. "More romantic certainly than not mentioning it was a possibility, then spewing your dinner all over your companion as he leans in for a kiss."

She laughed. "Thank you for being such a good sport about it."

"Thank *you* for letting me cook you dinner." He set his bags down on the counter and started removing the ingredients he'd purchased on the way there. "I should probably warn you that I haven't been on a date in quite a while, so I'm a little rusty."

Her eyebrows flew up as she transferred the cold foods to her refrigerator. "How long has it been?"

"Longer than I care to admit. My job and odd hours tend to make dating difficult."

She nodded. "Being a single mom and working the night shift does, too. I haven't dated in a while either."

"Excellent. Then, if neither of us remembers the rules, we don't have to follow them."

"Sounds good to me." She closed the refrigerator door and leaned her hip against it, crossing her arms just beneath her breasts. "Listen, I'm sort of a get-the-truth-out-there-so-when-it-comes-up-later-it-won't-be-an-issue kind of gal, so there's something I wanted to mention."

This couldn't be good.

She hesitated. "You know I'm older than you, right?"

Richart stared down at her and forced himself not to laugh at the irony. He may be over two hundred years old, but he looked as if he were in his late twenties, thirty at the most. And Jenna was worried that her being thirty-seven would be a problem?

"Honestly, I could not care less how old you are, Jenna," he assured her, all the while calling himself a bastard for not taking the opening she had provided and broaching the topic of who and what he was. She valued truth. If he continued to keep it from her . . .

A hint of insecurity entered her features. "I don't mean to press this, but . . . I dated a guy once—very briefly—who said the same thing until his friends found out and started to razz him about it. I'm thirty-seven. Are you sure that isn't a problem?"

"I don't know why his friends would tease him about dating you unless they were envious. You look like you're in your twenties, Jenna. Not much older than your son, in fact. And, if you looked like you were in your forties, guess what. I would be just as interested."

She smiled and closed the distance between them. "And if I looked like I were in my fifties?"

"Still interested."

"Sixties?"

"I happen to think laugh lines are hot."

She laughed. "Good, because I have a feeling you're going to give me a few."

"I should hope so," he said, telling himself not to think about the fact that he would still look and feel as he did now when she was in her sixties, seventies, and eighties and all of the problems that would generate.

You're getting ahead of yourself, old man. This is your first damned date. Not your engagement party.

"You don't mind that I'm older than you. You don't mind that I'm a single mom, putting a son through college." She shook her head and smiled up at him, expression soft. "You're a rare breed, Richart d'Alençon."

She didn't know the half of it.

Unable to resist, he dipped his head and touched his lips to hers in a gentle caress.

Her breath caught.

Lightning struck.

Both their hearts began to beat faster.

Resting a hand on her waist, Richart tilted his head and explored those smooth pink lips that had drawn his gaze so often, then drew back before his emotions could take over and make his eyes begin to glow.

"Wow," Jenna breathed, staring up at him.

"I am so smitten with you," he admitted softly.

"I love the way you talk."

"My accent?"

"That, too, but . . . I love the way you phrase things. Like the heroes from the historical romance novels I read."

He cringed. Apparently, he was showing his age.

She smiled. "Don't look like that. I meant it in a good way."

"If you say so."

Her stomach chose that moment to rumble and growl. Both laughed as she covered her flat belly with one hand. "Sorry about that."

He shook his head. "Let's get started so we can get some food in you."

Hands down, it was the best date Jenna ever had. Richart was charming and funny and so sexy he took her breath away. Just as that kiss had. She couldn't stop thinking about it.

And the man was an excellent cook. She had never been a big fan of salads, had always found them pretty bland, but he concocted some kind of homemade salad dressing that was absolutely delicious.

"How's your stomach?" he asked, taking her empty salad plate and replacing it with one heaped high with fettuccine Alfredo.

"Doing good," she responded with relief. The first taste of his creamy Alfredo sauce elicited a moan. "This is delicious. Where did you learn to cook?"

"I taught myself." He shrugged. "No reason not to really. I don't know why some men balk at it. I love food and saw no better way to ensure I would always have a tasty meal at my disposal."

"Smart man. I like that."

He winked.

Her pulse jumped.

The front doorknob rattled as a key slipped in and unlocked it.

Aaaaaaand the moment's over, she thought as her son opened the door and entered.

Jenna watched Richart with some trepidation. Saying he had no problem with her being a single mom was one thing. Not minding her son intruding on their romantic dinner was another.

John hesitated before removing his key from the lock and closing the door behind him.

Awkward.

Jenna smiled at him. "Hi, honey. How was school?"

"Same old same old," he said with a shrug and a tentative smile.

Richart rose and, setting his napkin on the table, took a step forward and offered his hand. "You must be John."

John set the tall pile of books he carried on the sofa. He often went straight from school to work. "And you must be Richart." He shook Richart's hand. "Am I pronouncing that correctly?" he asked, making sure *Reeshart* was correct.

"Yes. Richart d'Alençon. It's a pleasure to meet you."

"Likewise."

Jenna couldn't gauge her son's thoughts and had no clue how he felt about his mom dating. Such had rarely happened.

Richart motioned to the table. "Won't you join us?"

"Oh." Clearly surprised, John eyed the food with longing, glanced at Jenna, then looked at Richart. "Nnnno. No, thanks. I have some studying to do and wouldn't want to intrude."

"I made more than enough," Richart tempted. "Please, sit and join us. Jenna has told me so much about you. It would be nice to get to know you better."

Jenna stared, knowing with absolute certainty that Richart wasn't simply mouthing platitudes to score points with her. He actually meant it.

Again, John looked to Jenna.

She nodded and smiled.

"Okay." He started for the kitchen.

Richart followed. "Jenna tells me you attend UNC Chapel Hill."

"Yes." John pulled down a plate and turned toward the stove, where Richart waited.

Richart motioned him closer and began filling his plate.

John met Jenna's gaze and raised his eyebrows.

She grinned.

John was almost as tall as Richart and still seemed to be growing at age twenty. His shoulders weren't quite as broad and his physique was leaner, but his brown hair was cropped short like Richart's.

"A friend of mine used to teach at UNC," Richart mentioned.

"What department?"

"Music."

"Oh, yeah? A guy in my study group is minoring in music. What's his name? Maybe they took some classes with him."

Richart smiled as the two returned to the table. Richart retook his seat at Jenna's elbow while John took the chair across from him. "Dr. Sarah Bingham."

John's eyebrows flew up again. "You know Dr. Bingham? Carl said she was really something." Something awesome, his tone declared.

Richart picked up his fork. "She is."

Jealousy stirred as Jenna watched Richart smile with what could only be affection.

John tucked into the food. "Man, this is good."

"Thank you."

"Whatever happened to Dr. Bingham? She only taught there for a year, then disappeared."

"She married a friend of mine and now works in the same business I do."

John's eyes widened. "Dr. Bingham works in private security? Doing what? She's like five feet tall and weighs less than my mom."

Richart pointed his fork at John. "But she's a fierce fighter and could take you down in seconds."

"No shit?" He darted Jenna a look. "Sorry, Mom. No kidding?" John was usually careful not to curse in front of Jenna. He thought doing so was disrespectful, and he would probably pass out if he ever heard some of the language she used when she was stuck in traffic.

"No kidding," Richart insisted.

"Wow. You can't judge a book by its cover, can you?"

Richart gave his plate a wry smile. "No, you can't."

Silence fell.

"So," John began slowly, "is this weird? My being here?" He glanced back and forth between them.

It seemed weird as hell to Jenna.

Richart shook his head. "I don't want it to be weird. I'm very taken with your mother. If I haven't bungled tonight too badly"—he sent Jenna a flirtatious smile—"I hope to see her again."

"I'd like that." Had she said that too quickly?

Richart reached out and took her hand, giving it a squeeze,

then returned his attention to John. "Which means I'll be seeing you again, too, so I want us to be comfortable around each other."

John eyed their clasped hands. "Sounds good. But it still feels weird."

Jenna laughed and was relieved when Richart did, too.

"We'll figure it out eventually," Richart promised. "What courses are you taking?"

While John gave Richart a quick rundown on the classes he was taking, Richart leaned back in his chair. He stroked Jenna's hand with his thumb, sending little sparks of electricity dancing through her, as he nodded and commented here and there.

John finished his meal and pushed back his chair. "Speaking of which, I need to go ahead and hit the books. Finals are coming up and I don't want to wait until the last minute to cram." He offered his hand to Richart, who stood and shook it. "Thanks for dinner."

"Thank you for joining us. I enjoyed meeting you."

"Me, too." John put his plate in the sink, then gathered his books. Offering a final wave, he went to his bedroom and closed the door.

Smiling, Richart met Jenna's gaze as he retook his seat. "I like him. He's everything you said he is. And I see a lot of *you* in him."

"You do?" John looked so much like his father. It warmed her to know there was a little bit of her in there, too.

He leaned in closer. "I meant what I said, you know."

How could a man who didn't wear cologne smell so good?

He caught her hand and brought it to his lips. "You have totally captivated me and I would love to see you again."

"I'd like that, too."

"Would tomorrow night be too soon?"

She smiled. "No, but I work tomorrow night."

"How about an early dinner?"

"Sounds good."

He nodded and glanced at the clock hanging in the kitchen. "I hate to leave, but . . ."

"Work?"

He nodded and rose, collecting their dishes.

"Don't worry about those. I'll take care of it."

He frowned and shook his head. "You still aren't feeling well."

"I'm feeling much better." She didn't know if it was his company or the fettuccine, but she really did. "I'll do it."

"If you're sure . . ."

"I'm sure," she insisted, took the plates, and carried them to the sink. When she turned around, she found Richart donning his long black coat in the living room.

He was so handsome.

She walked him to the door. "This was nice."

He nodded. "I was just thinking the same thing. I haven't smiled so much since . . ." He tilted his head to one side. "Actually, I'm not sure. It's been a long time."

"Then I'll endeavor to make you smile more often."

"An easy task to accomplish. Just keep being you." Leaning one shoulder against the door, he cupped her face in one large hand and studied her, his smile softening. "You're so beautiful, Jenna."

In that moment, staring up at him, she could almost believe it.

Lowering his head, he captured her lips.

This kiss was nothing like the one they had shared in the kitchen. It was no first tentative exploration. This kiss was explosive and intense, his velvety warm mouth sending her up in flames.

He slipped his tongue inside to duel with hers, tempting and teasing. One strong arm locked around her waist and drew her into his tall muscled form, pressing her breasts to his hard chest and washboard abs, her hips to the arousal that sprang to life behind his zipper.

Holy crap. Her pulse turned to molten lava. Her knees weakened even as she rose onto her toes and wrapped her arms around his neck, burrowing her fingers through his short silken hair.

He ended the kiss and pressed his forehead to hers, eyes closed, his breathing as harsh as hers. "I wish I didn't have to work," he murmured.

She nodded. Sliding her hands down to tangle in the soft material of his shirt, Jenna lowered her heels to the floor. "And I wish my son weren't in the next room."

He muttered something in French. "I forgot about that."

Gradually their breathing calmed.

He sighed. "I keep telling myself to go, but I don't seem to be moving."

"I can live with that."

Chuckling, he raised his head. "All right." He stole another quick kiss and opened the door. "I'm out."

With great reluctance, Jenna stepped back. "Okay."

"I'll see you tomorrow," he said softly as he stepped out into the night. "Feel better."

"I already do."

For the next week Richart lived a dual life. He began each evening by having dinner with Jenna. Sometimes he took her out. Sometimes he cooked for her at her place. Then they parted ways. She went to work, and he left to hunt and fight bloody battles with vampires.

He thought about her all the time. Her laugh. Her smile. Her wit. Her delectable body pressed to his. He was falling in love with her and thought—hoped—she might be falling in love with him. Her face lit up when she saw him, as did his own, he was sure. They never ran out of things to talk about when they were together. And the passion building between them . . .

Richart was having a hard time concealing his nature from her.

Whenever immortals experienced strong emotion, their eyes glowed. That was damned difficult to hide when the slightest touch of her hand enflamed him. Hell, just looking at her made him want to rip her work clothes off and lick every inch of her body.

But he resisted the urge and, though he knew it frustrated her, was glad either work or her son frequently intruded and kept them from doing more than the most basic of passionate explorations. He just didn't feel right about making love with her without first revealing who and what he was.

"Earth to Richart."

Richart blinked and realized his Second stood in front of him, holding out two daggers. "Oh. Thanks."

Sheldon shook his head and crossed his arms over his chest as he watched Richart tuck the blades into the sheaths on his thighs. He was young for a Second, only twenty years old. Inexperienced. And not the quickest learner. But Richart liked him and appreciated the boy's humor and teasing nature.

"When are you going to tell her?" Sheldon asked. He alone knew Richart was seeing someone.

"That I can't see her tonight?"

"No, genius. That you're two hundred years old. Don't you think she should know she's sleeping with Methuselah?"

"First, thank you for that," Richart offered dryly as he grabbed a couple more daggers. "Second, we haven't slept together yet. And third . . ."

"What?"

"It isn't the easiest topic to broach. And telling her could put her in danger."

Sheldon frowned. "You mean Reordon? He wouldn't harm her, would he?"

Chris Reordon took his job protecting Immortal Guardians very seriously. "At the very least, he would interrogate and threaten her to ensure her silence. And if she didn't react well and told someone else . . ."

Sheldon scowled. "No wonder Roland kept Reordon away from Sarah. But Jenna wouldn't blab, right? I mean, you know her."

"And Roland knew his fiancée several centuries ago when he told *her*. Did she accept him? No. She betrayed his trust, and he awoke the next morning to a mob wielding fire, wooden stakes, and pitchforks."

"Wow. No wonder he's such an untrusting bastard." Sheldon glanced at the clock. "Almost time for the meeting."

Richart took out his cell phone. "I really hate to do this. It's her night off, and I didn't get to see her yesterday." But when Seth called a meeting, one didn't balk at attending.

Disappointed, Richart dialed her number.

Chapter Three

A biting winter wind ruffled Richart's hair. Barren limbs of deciduous trees clacked together overhead while the leaves of evergreens fluttered and swished.

What's going on with you? a female voice with an accent identical to his own asked in his head.

Richart glanced over at his sister and brother, who examined him much like they would a previously undiscovered insect.

Stay out of my head, he warned them. Both were telepathic. Richart lacked that gift and had often bemoaned the fact as a child until he had learned he could teleport and they couldn't. They could still read his thoughts or send him their own, though.

We know when you block your thoughts and have respected your desire for privacy, Lisette said and shared a look with Étienne. *But we don't have to read your mind to know something is up.*

Richart frowned at the dark forest that surrounded them.

A vampire, claiming he desired the Immortal Guardians' help, had arranged a rendezvous with Marcus, Ami, and Roland (the last of whom the vampires believed was Bastien) in a clearing that had once been the site of Bastien's lair. Seth had ordered Richart, his siblings, and Roland's wife, Sarah, to follow and linger downwind in case it was a trap.

Sarah likely had no notion the French immortals were communicating silently and stood off to the side, staring intently into the trees as if she could see her husband waiting on the other side.

In lieu of answering, Richart decided to change the subject. *Did anyone else notice the way Marcus looks at his Second?*

Étienne smirked. *As if he wishes to devour her? No, I didn't notice at all.*

Richart smiled.

Rustling sounds, a mile or two distant, reached their ears. The vampires' scents—four instead of only the one who had arranged the meeting—followed.

Étienne drew his katanas.

Richart palmed two daggers as Lisette drew a pair of shoto swords.

"I thought this was supposed to be a private meeting," they heard Marcus drawl.

"Insurance," a vampire responded arrogantly. "Can't blame me for being careful, can you? Besides, if he's who you say he is, then maybe he can help all three of us."

Richart caught Lisette's gaze and raised an eyebrow.

It's a trap, she confirmed with a frown. *Three face our brethren while a fourth lingers in the trees, but . . .* She shook her head. *Their thoughts are all so loud and jumbled, I can't discern what the trap entails.*

Richart looked to Étienne, keeping an ear tuned to the conversation that continued in the clearing.

Étienne wagged his head back and forth. *The madness has taken them. Their thoughts are impossible to separate, as if all are shouting at once. There are only four of them, but . . . So many voices. It's as though they suffer from multiple personality disorder. I can't discern their plan.*

Richart nodded.

"So be it," the vampire addressing Marcus said with satisfaction.

Boom!

Pain pierced Richart's ears as an explosion shook the ground beneath his feet. The scent of multiple vampires abruptly tainted the air as gunshots sounded and the clang of metal striking metal disrupted the night.

A shrill whistle followed as Marcus signaled for them to join the fight.

Sarah darted forward so fast she seemed to vanish.

Richart teleported to the clearing. His eyes widened.

So many!

He swiftly thrust a dagger into the heart of one of the *dozens* of vampires surging toward Marcus, Ami, and Roland.

Those three stood back to back to back, Ami firing her Glocks, Marcus wielding his short swords, and Roland cutting through the vampires with his sais.

As the vamp Richart impaled sank to the ground, Richart teleported again, appearing several yards away, arms extended, daggers held tightly in his palms. His blades slit the throats of two vampires racing toward Marcus and severed their carotid arteries. As they dropped to the ground, Richart teleported again and again and again, taking out vampires every time, spawning utter chaos as the vampires began to divide their attention between fighting Marcus and the others and looking around wildly for *him*.

Richart smiled darkly. He loved his gift. Loved the fear it inspired in his opponents.

He teleported over to his brother and took out two of the many vampires clamoring to kill him.

Étienne laughed, never ceasing his swings.

Grinning, Richart teleported over to the mob that continued to assault the trio in the center of the clearing. As soon as he appeared, sinking his blade into yet another vamp, a bullet struck him in the shoulder.

Ami gasped, her guns falling silent.

Richart couldn't fault her for shooting him. He had teleported between her and her target. He waved it off and teleported again as she resumed fire.

The battle waged on.

For every vampire the immortals and Ami killed, two or three seemed to take their place. Richart couldn't believe their numbers. Even Bastien had not commanded an army this large.

And where the hell were they all coming from?

The gunshots ended as Ami ran out of ammo and exchanged her firearms for katanas.

Richart kept one eye on her as he continued to fight, knowing her strength could not match that of the insane vampires slathering around her like rabid dogs.

Sure enough, a vamp ducked one of her swings and hit Ami hard in the head.

Richart teleported behind her and caught her as she reeled dizzily. Wrapping one arm around her waist to steady her, he hurled throwing stars with the other until she regained her feet.

"Thanks," she rasped over her shoulder.

"I'm taking you to safety," he announced, grabbing one of her katanas and fending off the onslaught.

"No!"

It didn't matter if she protested. She was injured and vulnerable. The vampires were targeting her as an easy kill.

"No!" she repeated and shoved him away. "I'm fine! Just give me my damned sword back!"

She didn't wait, just yanked it out of his hand.

Richart felt something prick the skin beneath one ear.

As he reached up to see what it was (it felt like a bee

sting), Marcus whipped around and yanked what looked like a tranquilizer dart from Richart's neck.

A similar dart hit Marcus in the shoulder.

Richart frowned. Drugs didn't affect immortals. Didn't the vamps . . . know . . . that?

Weakness engulfed him. Richart stumbled and grunted as a vampire took advantage and stabbed him in the side. Lashing out, Richart searched the blood-painted mass of fighting, snarling bodies around him and saw his sister drop to her knees. "Lisette."

"Richart!" Ami shouted.

Vision fuzzy, he turned and found her propping up a barely conscious Marcus, who now sported several of the darts.

"Get them out of here!" she shouted, her pretty, crimson-splashed face panicked. "Now!"

Richart teleported to his sister's side, touched her shoulder, and took her to David's home.

David was the second eldest and second most powerful immortal in existence and maintained an open door policy for all immortals, Seconds, and members of the human network. With the drug coursing through his system, slowing his movements, and clouding his thoughts, Richart could think of no safer place.

In David's spacious living room, David's Second Darnell, Lisette's Second Tracy, and Sheldon sat side by side on one of the sofas, their gazes glued to Darnell's laptop.

As soon as Richart and Lisette appeared, they leapt to their feet.

Richart staggered.

"What happened?" Sheldon asked, eyes wide.

Tracy and Darnell hurried over to catch Lisette as she lost consciousness.

"Drugs," was all Richart could manage.

"Dr. Lipton!" Darnell bellowed over his shoulder moments before Richart teleported away.

As soon as he appeared back at the battle, another dart struck him.

Swearing, he yanked it out, sped over to his brother's side, and touched his shoulder.

The world around them blurred as he took them to David's.

Sheldon and Cameron, Étienne's Second, waited anxiously in the living room. Darnell, Tracy, and Lisette were gone.

Cam lunged forward and caught Étienne as he slumped toward the floor. Sheldon stepped forward and held up an M16. "Take me back with you."

Richart clasped Sheldon's shoulder. The room around them dimmed, but they didn't teleport. He tried again and only managed to teleport them to the front door.

Swearing, he grabbed the M16 and shoved Sheldon away. His surroundings went black. He made it back to the clearing this time. Sarah and Ami were trying to hold off the many remaining vampires while supporting Marcus and Roland.

Everything was . . . out of focus. Confusing. Richart couldn't think straight. He needed to be able to think straight so he could teleport the others to safety.

Sarah and Ami spoke urgently beside him.

He looked around, past the glowing eyes of the vampires who circled them like jackals.

Where was Lisette? Had he teleported her already? What about . . .

Where was Sheldon? Hadn't Sheldon been with him just now?

Sarah folded her husband over one shoulder, then leaned forward so Ami could fold Marcus over the other one. If she intended to flee, the heavy men's weight would significantly slow her retreat.

Richart glanced down and discovered he held an M16. He thrust it into Ami's small hands. His own seemed uncooperative.

Another dart hit him.

Sarah would never be able to outrun the vampires if Ami slowed her down, too.

Even as the thought flitted through his mind, he heard Ami convince Sarah to leave without her.

Good. At least Sarah, Roland, and Marcus would get away.

Richart and Ami would be left to fight the two dozen or more vampires who remained. Ami was mortal and no match for their speed or strength. And he was so weak he could barely lift his arms. If he couldn't teleport the two of them out of there, their fates would be sealed. Both would die this night.

Odd that he would think of Jenna in that moment, lamenting that he would never see her again.

He needed to try to teleport Ami away.

As he reached for her shoulder, his vision dimmed and went black.

The apartment was quiet, save the faint clicking sounds the flatware made against their plates as Jenna and John ate a late dinner.

"I'm sorry Richart had to cancel tonight," John said, his gaze far too discerning.

Jenna had been disappointed as hell when Richart had called and said he couldn't make it. Apparently some problem had arisen at work that required his attention.

She sighed. Or had it?

Had it just been an excuse? Had he grown tired of either work or her son's presence constantly impeding their desire to become more intimately involved?

At a loss, she decided to seek John's advice. Her son was popular with the girls and had dated far more than *she* had in her lifetime, so . . . why not? "Should I read anything into it that he canceled two nights in a row?"

If he thought it odd that his mother wanted his opinion on

her love life, John hid it well. "I don't think so, considering the line of work he's in."

"But? I hear a *but* in there."

"But I *do* think it's odd that he always comes over *here* and hasn't taken you to *his* place yet. I mean, you have dinner together every night. I would think he would be getting tired of me being a third wheel on the nights he doesn't take you out."

"He said his nephew lives with him. So it wouldn't be any different at his place."

"Are you sure?" he asked. "I mean, maybe you should suggest it . . . just to make sure he isn't one of those guys who cheats on his wife and doesn't tell his mistress that he's married."

Her heart sank.

"Don't look like that," John said quickly. "I'm probably just being paranoid. You're my mom. I'm suspicious of *every* man you date."

"Like there have been that many," she muttered.

"Come on," he cajoled. "It's probably what you said. Or maybe he's a slob and doesn't want you to see."

That made her smile. "He isn't a slob." Richart was always meticulously groomed and dressed. She couldn't imagine his home being less so.

"Hey, you never know. A friend of mine—"

A large dark figure suddenly loomed in Jenna's peripheral vision.

Letting out a surprised shriek, she jumped up, bumping the table and knocking over her glass of tea.

John grabbed his steak knife and leaped up to confront . . . "Oh, shit!"

Jenna's eyes widened. Her breath stopped. Shock immobilized her.

Richart stood in the middle of their living room, having appeared out of thin air.

She swallowed, mouth dry.

His eyes glowed a brilliant amber. They *glowed.* His breath was labored, soughing in and out of parted lips that exposed gleaming fangs. His hair was windblown, his face splattered with—

"Is that blood?" John asked shakily, moving over to stand protectively close to Jenna.

She nodded. Nearly all of Richart's dark clothing glistened with the ruby liquid and sported numerous cuts and tears. There even appeared to be a bullet hole in one shoulder.

Richart said nothing, just swayed where he stood.

"Richart?" she asked, voice and body trembling as tea slithered over the table's edge and hit the floor with a *tap tap tap.*

He turned toward her, but didn't seem to see her.

"Richart?" she repeated and took a step toward him.

John grabbed her arm. "Stay back."

Jenna shook him off and slowly forced her feet to carry her forward.

Swearing, John stuck close to her side, his steak knife at the ready.

"Richart," she called again when she stood only a few feet away.

The glow in his eyes began to fade, returning them to the warm brown of which she had become so fond. The fangs receded, disappearing into his gums as if they had never been.

He mumbled something in French.

Jenna consulted her son. "Do you know what he said?"

He shook his head. "I've forgotten most of the French I learned in high school."

Richart blinked and dipped his chin. He seemed to be having a hard time focusing. "Jenna?"

"Yes."

Panic danced across his face as he lunged forward and grabbed her upper arms.

"Whoa-whoa-whoa!" John tried to intervene, or at least to break the bruising grip, but couldn't.

"What are you doing here?" Richart demanded, his accent so thick and his words so slurred she had difficulty understanding him. "It's too dangerous. You must go."

Jenna gently clasped his arms. "Richart, we're in my apartment. Do you understand me? We're in my apartment." She spoke slowly and deliberately, heart pounding in her chest.

His brows drew down in a deep V. "Your . . . ?" He glanced around. Releasing one of her arms, he rubbed his eyes and looked around again.

She could feel him trembling. The hand that gripped her shook violently. And he began to slowly press downward as if he had to use her to prop himself up.

Jenna watched him take in the sofa, the stained coffee table, John, and their abandoned dinner.

Relief softened his features as he swayed. "We made it out? I got us out?"

Before she or John could ask out of what, Richart looked around again. "Where is Ami?"

Jenna felt the sharp glance John sent her. "Who is Ami?" she asked.

His frown returned, as did the alarm. "What?"

"I don't know who Ami is, Richart. You just . . . appeared . . . out of nowhere. Alone."

"She wasn't with me? I left her there?"

John stepped forward. "Left her where? Who's Ami? What the hell is going on?"

Richart began to mumble in French again.

Jenna gave him a little shake. "Richart!"

"I must go back," he said, face stricken. He released his hold on Jenna and, breaking her own, staggered away two steps.

When he listed to one side, Jenna hurried forward to steady him.

He pushed her away. "Don't touch me," he wheezed. "I'll take you with me."

"What?"

John grabbed her by the shoulders and drew her back.

Richart reached beneath his coat and drew out two very lethal looking daggers.

John swore.

Richart squeezed his eyes closed, so wobbly on his feet the faintest breath of wind would have knocked him on his ass.

As Jenna stared at him, his form began to fade, becoming translucent. Her breath caught. She could actually see the other side of the room through him.

"What the . . . ?" John whispered.

Then Richart became solid again. He opened his eyes, saw them, and growled with frustration. Stumbling a couple of steps to the left, he thrust out an arm and pressed a bloody fist against the wall until he could regain his balance, then straightened. He squeezed his eyes shut, brow crinkling with concentration. Again his form began to fade, becoming phantomlike.

"Mom . . ." John said. "Are you seeing this?"

Jenna didn't have to look up at him to know he was as freaked out as she was. "Yes."

Once more, Richart's form solidified. He opened his eyes, spoke vehemently in French, then lurched forward. His knees buckled. Losing his battle with gravity, he crashed through her coffee table, reducing it to large splinters as he hit the floor hard.

Her heart now lodged in her throat, Jenna jerked away from John and knelt at Richart's side. "Richart?"

Rolling onto his back, he stared up at her with unfocused eyes. "I left . . . her there," he whispered, those eyes—dilated she could see now—filling with moisture.

"It's okay," she murmured, combing his damp hair back from his face.

He shook his head. "I left her. They'll . . . kill her." A tear slid down his temple. His weapons *thunk*ed to the floor as his hands went limp. "They'll"—his eyes closed—"tear her . . . apart."

As Jenna watched in horror, he sighed. Then his chest rose no more. "Richart?"

Nothing.

Burying her hands in his bloody shirt, she shook him. "Richart?"

No response.

"Richart!"

John knelt by her side. "Mom . . ."

Unable to speak past the lump in her throat, she shoved her fingers against Richart's throat above his carotid artery. Seconds ticked by, passing as slowly as hours. Her vision wavered as tears filled her eyes and spilled over her lashes. "I can't feel a pulse." Her breath hitched. "I can't feel a pulse!"

John shoved her hand away and pressed two fingers against Richart's neck.

She gripped Richart's arm. "There's nothing."

"Shh." He lowered his ear to Richart's chest.

"He's—"

"Shh!"

This wasn't happening.

Whatever the hell this was, it wasn't happening. It couldn't be!

"John—"

"Quiet!" her son ordered harshly.

Jenna stared at Richart's face. How could he have come to mean so much to her in such a short time? The thought of losing him . . .

More tears welled.

"I've got a pulse," John blurted, face pinched as he sat up.

"What?"

"He's alive."

Jenna rose onto her knees, hope a frightening force that lent her strength despite her trembling. "Are you sure?"

"Yeah. It's slow as hell, but it's there."

Elation filled her, rendering her weak again. "We have to call nine-one-one."

He caught her wrist and stopped her before she could rise and lunge for the phone. "And tell them what? That your vampire boyfriend needs medical attention?"

And there it was. The V-word she had been trying her damnedest to avoid.

"There are no such things as vampires."

"Proof of their existence is currently passed out on our living room floor."

"He isn't a vampire," she denied.

"His eyes glowed and he had fangs."

"But he doesn't now!"

"Exactly. Fake fangs don't retract into your gums. Glowing contact lenses don't have an on/off switch."

She stared at her son, wanting to cling to denial a little longer.

"And humans don't have pulses so slow as to be virtually undetectable," he pronounced.

"But he ate food."

"Maybe vampires can eat food in real life."

"Do you realize—"

"Yes! I realize how ludicrous that sounds, Mom, but . . . !" He drew in a deep breath. "Look, I don't know what the hell he is, but I do know what he isn't: human. And since the news hasn't been filled with vampire reports, I'm guessing he's been keeping it a secret."

He had certainly been keeping it a secret from her.

"Well, we can't just leave him here," she said. He was wounded, badly, judging by all of the blood. He needed help.

"If you're asking me what we should do . . ." He shook

his head. "As your son, my first instinct is to protect you by waiting for the sun to rise and shoving his ass out the door."

"John!"

"Don't worry. My second inclination—again because you're my mom and I know you care about him—is to do what I can to help him. Let's put him to bed and see if we can do anything about his wounds."

Jenna gave John a quick hug. "I love you."

He hugged her back. "I love you, too. I just hope we aren't making a huge mistake."

They stood. John kicked the daggers away from Richart's hands.

"Put him in my room," Jenna instructed.

Offering no protest, John bent down, hoisted Richart over his shoulder in a fireman's carry, and straightened. "Holy crap he's heavy." He staggered toward the hallway.

Jenna ducked past them and hurried into her bedroom.

Grabbing the old, timeworn blanket at the foot of the bed, she threw it over the covers to protect them a bit from the blood. She stared as John deposited Richart's limp form on the bed.

Had Richart not canceled, she likely would have spent tonight making love with a vampire.

"Mom?"

Get it together. "Right." Moving forward, she tugged off Richart's boots.

John removed the long coat, then Jenna started on the buttons that ran down the front of Richart's black shirt. When she reached the last one and parted the material, both she and John gasped.

Richart's torso was a sticky red. His shoulder did indeed sport a bullet hole. The rest of him . . .

Puncture wounds, deep cuts, and gashes that must have been carved by blades as sharp as Richart's daggers marred much of his form.

"We don't even have what we need to *bandage* those, let alone close them," John said.

"Whatever we need, go buy it," Jenna told him.

"I don't want to leave you here alone with him."

Jenna met his gaze. "We've been alone together nearly every night this week and he hasn't harmed me. Do it. I'll be fine."

"What if he wakes up, wanting blood? *You* go. I'll—"

"John." Her tone offered no compromise.

He nodded, Adam's apple bobbing up and down, and left the room.

A couple of minutes later, he returned, wearing a fresh sweatshirt, jacket, and jeans. He handed her a canister of pepper spray and one of Richart's daggers. "If he threatens you, hit him with the pepper spray, then carve him up."

Lovely.

Jenna took the weapons and kissed John on the cheek. "Hurry."

Nodding, he left the room. A moment later, the front door closed.

And Jenna was left alone with the vampire she loved.

Jenna glanced at the clock for the hundredth time since John had left.

Richart had not roused once. Not when she had finished undressing him. Not when she had sponge-bathed the blood from him. Not when she had attempted to clean his sticky, bloody hair. And not when she had worked a pair of John's boxers up Richart's long, muscled legs and over his . . .

Her gaze darted to his lap, covered now with a clean blanket.

She hadn't seen a naked man up close and personal in years. She had hoped to see Richart naked when the day had begun, but not like this.

She rested her hand on his bare chest.

Warm. Weren't vampires supposed to be cold to the touch?

His chest rose slightly, then fell still once more.

The front door opened and closed. "I'm home," John called. Moments later he entered the room, jacket zipped up tight against the cold, a shopping bag dangling from each hand.

"Did you get everything you need?" she asked.

Setting the bags down, he unzipped his jacket and tugged it off.

"Yes, but I didn't get everything *he* needs."

"What do you mean?"

"If he's a vampire—"

"Please stop calling him that. It's just too weird."

"I know. But, if he *is* one, he probably needs blood more than anything else."

Jenna eyed Richart with dread. Did he really drink blood?

"Has he moved at all?" John asked.

"No. But he still has that slow, faint pulse."

He spilled bandages, tubes, and bottles onto the bed. "I'm gonna go wash up, then we can get started."

Chapter Four

Yawning, Jenna focused gritty eyes on the clock again. It would be noon soon.

John slept in his bedroom. He had a final exam tomorrow and Jenna had insisted he get some rest.

Richart's chest rose and fell in another barely detectable breath.

He still hadn't stirred. Nor had his wounds miraculously healed as they often did in movies.

Was John right? Did Richart need blood?

She thought of all the films and TV shows she'd seen in which a human had slashed his or her wrist and held it over a vampire's mouth until he latched on and began to drink.

She was so not going to do that.

Not yet, an inner voice murmured.

Not ever, she insisted, but wondered if she would feel the same way if Richart still hadn't awakened by . . .

By when? Tomorrow? How long could they wait without trying something else?

Thump. Thump. Thump.

Jenna jumped at the loud pounding on the front door.

Frowning, she rose and headed for the living room.

John shuffled out of his bedroom, sweatpants and T-shirt rumpled, hair sticking up on one side. "Is he awake?"

"Not yet."

"Was that—?"

Thump. Thump. Thump.

She nodded and continued into the living room and over to the door. Rising onto her toes, she peeked through the peephole.

A tall red-haired young man who looked to be her son's age stood there, shifting anxiously from foot to foot.

"Yes?" she called.

He straightened, eyes fastening on the peephole. "Hi. I'm looking for Jenna?"

"And you are?"

"Sheldon Shepherd, ma'am."

Who the hell was that?

"Do you know him?" John whispered.

"No."

"What do you want?" John demanded in a deep, hostile voice.

Jenna peeked through the peephole again.

Sheldon went still. "I . . . ah . . . I'd just like to talk with you for a moment, ma'am, if that's all right. We . . . ah . . . we have a mutual friend who . . . with whom I've lost contact and . . ." He glanced around, frustration written all over his face.

Jenna lowered her heels to the floor. "He must be a friend of Richart's," she whispered and reached for the lock.

John caught her hand. "Or he could be one of the people who hurt him."

"If he's a friend, maybe he can help him."

"And if he's not?"

"Hello?" Sheldon called.

"Just a minute," Jenna called back.

"Hang on," John said and hurried from the room. When he

returned, he carried one of Richart's daggers. "Just in case. No way am I going to let whoever cut *him* up cut *you* up."

He casually slid his arm a little behind his back so the blade wasn't visible.

Nerves jangling, Jenna opened the door.

Sheldon looked down at her. "Hi. Jenna?"

"Yes."

He offered his hand. "I'm Sheldon. Nice to meet you."

Jenna shook his hand, not getting any kind of danger vibes from him, but still on guard.

"I'm sorry to bother you, ma'am, but"—he looked to John, then met Jenna's gaze again—"may I speak with you privately for a moment?"

"No," John said before she could answer.

Jenna shot John a warning glare. "What is this about, Sheldon?"

He looked from side to side and down to see if anyone was outside who might overhear them. Leaning forward a bit, he murmured, "It's about Richart. I don't want you to worry, but . . . something happened last night and I've lost contact with him. I—"

"What is your relationship with Richart?"

"Oh. I'm sorry. I'm his nephew."

Relief rushed through her. Richart had mentioned his nephew several times, but she didn't remember him ever calling him by name. "Come in." She stepped back so Sheldon could enter and closed the door behind him. "This is my son, John."

Sheldon offered his hand to John, who shook it with reserve.

"What's going on with Richart?" she asked.

"I'm not at liberty to go into detail. It's highest level clearance only. In fact, I shouldn't even be here, but . . . Richart was . . . out on assignment last night and some problems arose. The situation deteriorated quickly. There was a lot of confusion and . . . I've lost contact with him. I hoped you might have heard from him." He glanced around the room, his words slowing as he noticed the splintered coffee table, the bloody fistprint on the wall. "I really need to talk to him."

"He's here," she announced, hoping her instincts were correct when they insisted he was friend and not foe.

Relief blanketed his features, though some wariness remained. "Is he okay?"

She shook her head and motioned for him to follow her back to her bedroom. "He collapsed shortly after he . . . appeared."

"Do you mean arrived?" he asked carefully.

"No, I mean he just appeared. Out of thin air."

"Oh, shit. Okay. There's an explanation for that."

"Of course there is," John drawled, bringing up the rear. "He's a vampire."

"He isn't a vampire!" Sheldon denied. "Wait. You guys believe in vampires?"

"We sure as hell do now," John answered.

Jenna nodded as they entered the bedroom. "It's hard not to after seeing Richart's glowing eyes and fangs."

Again he swore. "Yyyyyyeah. There's an explanation for that, too."

They surrounded Jenna's bed.

"Has he regained consciousness?" Sheldon asked as he leaned down and drew the covers back. Bandages and butterfly closures decorated most of Richart's torso.

"No," Jenna answered.

"Are his wounds still bleeding?"

"No." Had she not seen Richart's fangs and eyes, she would have puzzled over that. She had not even needed to apply pressure to them. The bleeding had just . . . stopped.

Sheldon peeled back one of the bandages. The wound beneath was a few inches long with ragged edges held together by butterfly closures. A dark, ugly bruise surrounded it. "Is this how it looked when you cleaned it?"

She nodded. "Should it have healed by now?"

He replaced the bandage and straightened. A full minute passed while he stared down at Richart. "You know what?" he said finally. "Screw protocol. Screw the rules." He met Jenna's gaze. "Yes, it should have healed by now. *All* of them should have at least *partially* healed by now, especially if you . . . I mean if he . . ."

She raised her eyebrows. "Drank my blood?"

Heavy pause. "Yes."

"He didn't."

Sheldon spun on his heel and left the room. "I'll be back in a minute," he called over his shoulder. A moment later the front door opened and closed.

John brought the dagger out from behind his back and slipped it in the bedside table's drawer. "This just keeps getting more and more surreal."

Jenna nodded and sat on the bed. "It was weird hearing him confirm it."

"Actually he said Richart *wasn't* a vampire."

"Then he asked me if Richart drank my blood and said his wounds should have healed by now."

"Yeah. I don't get it either."

Sheldon returned in short order. Rapping his knuckles on the front door, he let himself in, then strode into the bedroom carrying a cooler and a duffle bag.

Jenna's stomach sank when he opened the cooler and drew out two bags of blood.

"You've got to be kidding me," John muttered. "He's going to drink that?"

"No."

While Jenna watched in silence, Sheldon set up an IV and began siphoning blood into Richart's vein.

"Why don't you just . . . use his fangs?" she asked.

Sheldon gently peeled back Richart's upper lip enough to show her that he no longer sported fangs. "Can't use them if they aren't there."

A frown creased John's face as Sheldon exchanged the already empty bag with a full one. "Shouldn't it take longer for those bags to empty?"

"Honestly?" Sheldon put the empty bag back in the cooler. "I've never done this before, so I don't know."

Jenna stared at Richart, willing him to open his eyes and let them know this was helping. "Has this never happened before?"

"The injuries or the not waking up thing?"

"Both."

Sheldon sat in the chair John had carried in earlier from the breakfast nook. "He's been injured like this, but . . ."

"He didn't lose consciousness?"

"No."

"What's different this time?"

Sheldon sighed and dragged a hand down over his face. "I shouldn't be telling you any of this."

"No," she agreed. "Richart should. But he can't. So I need you to do it for him."

"We think he may have been drugged."

"Who's we?"

"That one would take too long to explain."

John's frown deepened. "Vampires can be drugged?"

"He isn't—" Sheldon broke off, muttered something under his breath. "Until tonight, no drugs affected him. At all. Period. If he drank five gallons of vodka and swallowed four bottles of sleeping pills, nothing would happen. He wouldn't get drunk. He wouldn't get loopy. He wouldn't get sleepy. And he sure as hell wouldn't die. He would feel exactly the same afterward as he did before. He would just need a little blood to replace what he lost while his body repaired the damage. But tonight . . ." He shook his head. "He was hit with several darts carrying an unknown substance. The others hit with the same drug—"

"There are others?" Jenna asked, not knowing why that surprised her.

"Yes. They were transfused hours ago, right after it happened, and should have awoken immediately, but . . ."

"What?" she asked.

"They haven't stirred. This drug is something we've never encountered before. We don't know if it was a tranquilizer, a poison, or what. We don't know why it affects them when nothing else does. And . . . we don't know how to help them."

Jenna swallowed hard. "Are you saying you don't know if Richart is going to wake up?"

"He will," Sheldon said, voice filled with determination. "He has to." He replaced the second empty blood bag with another full one.

"Are you really his nephew?" she asked. Richart had withheld a lot of information from her. Had he lied outright, too?

"No, though I may as well be. He treats me like family because I'm a descendent of his first Second. Damien was my great-great-I-don't-know-how-many-greats grandfather and was like a brother to him."

Holy crap. "How old *is* Richart?"

He grimaced. "Old enough and mellow enough I hope to forgive me for not knowing how to keep my damned mouth shut. I'll let *him* tell you his age."

No wonder Richart hadn't cared about the age difference. He must have inwardly laughed his ass off when she had asked him if it bothered him that she was older than him.

Sheldon peeled back the bandage he had peered under earlier. The wound it covered shrank as they watched, dwindling to nothing as the bruise around it faded.

John moved closer. "That's amazing."

Nodding, Sheldon systematically removed all of the other bandages.

Had Jenna not seen the wounds with her own eyes, she would have never known Richart had been injured.

Sheldon retook his seat and caught Jenna's eye. "I hope you'll cut him some slack over keeping this part of his life from you."

John snorted.

Jenna . . . didn't know what to think. She felt numbed by the shock of it all. "He knew how much I value honesty and chose to keep this from me."

"It isn't an easy secret to share." When she remained silent, he said, "He didn't cheat on you. He doesn't have a wife tucked away somewhere. He's just . . ."

"What?"

"Different. In a way that, when revealed, usually sparks violent reactions in others."

"So—what—he thought if he told me I'd come after him with a torch-bearing mob and try to stake him?"

"You wouldn't be the first to do so."

That was unsetting. "People who found out what he is have tried to kill him?"

"Richart and others of his kind, yes." He nodded at his *uncle*. "Who do you think developed the drug he was hit with tonight?"

Jenna stared down at Richart, her hip pressed to his.

His chest rose and fell more often. Not as often as a human's, but more than it had before.

"Look," Sheldon said, drawing her gaze, "I know all this must have been a hell of a shock to you. I know you must be pissed, finding out that Richart isn't quite who you thought he was. But he's an honorable man, Jenna. If he weren't, I wouldn't have practically begged him to let me serve as his Second."

"You used that term before," John said. "What's a Second? Is that like his Renfield?"

Jenna's head began to pound. Dracula had always had a human assistant, a *Renfield* as fans of the fictional figure had come to call him.

But Richart wasn't like Dracula. He wasn't.

"Yeah. I guess you could say that."

Crap.

"And now, if you'll excuse me for a moment, I need to make a call. A lot of people are worried about Richart. I should let them know he's safe and tell them his condition." He rose. "I didn't ask this earlier . . ." He hesitated, as if he really didn't want to ask whatever it was.

Could things actually get worse?

"Did Richart speak before he passed out?" he finally queried.

"Yes. A little bit. Most of it was in French—"

"Did he mention someone named Ami?"

"Yes. He said he left her behind."

Sheldon gripped the back of the chair with a fist. A muscle in his jaw jumped.

Jenna remembered the torment in Richart's eyes, in his voice. *They'll kill her. They'll tear her apart.* "He tried to go back for her, but couldn't."

Sheldon lowered his head, raised a hand to rub his eyes.

"He said they'd kill her," she continued softly.

Head still down, Sheldon nodded. "Yeah." Turning away, he headed out of the room. "Excuse me."

Jenna saw her own concern reflected in her son's face. She glanced at the clock. "When are you supposed to meet with your study group?"

"I don't think I should go. I think I should stay here."

"No." He'd worked his ass off all semester, balancing work and school. And the exam he'd take tomorrow counted for sixty percent of his final grade. The partial scholarship that covered half his tuition was contingent upon his maintaining a high GPA. "Go. Study. I'll be fine."

Sheldon spoke softly in the living room. "Cam? It's Sheldon. I found him."

John looked toward the living room. "It isn't safe."

"That isn't for you to decide," Jenna reminded him.

Again Sheldon spoke. "I need you to keep this from Reordon if you can. Richart didn't want him to know. He's been seeing someone. I think the drug got his wires all crossed and he accidentally teleported to her place. . . . No. She cleaned him up and has been watching over him. . . . No . . . I'm sure. She hasn't told anyone. Nor will she. She cares about him as much as he cares for her."

"John," Jenna said firmly, "go. I don't know what I've gotten myself into, but I'm not going to let it threaten your future." He opened his mouth to protest. "Go!" she insisted.

Sighing, he pointed to the drawer in which he'd placed the dagger. "If you need it . . ."

She nodded.

He padded down the hallway to his bedroom, went inside, and closed the door.

"I'll stay with him," Sheldon said. "No, he's safe. No one else can track him here. Besides, you can't do anything for him *there* that we haven't already done for him here. . . . No way . . . I don't give a damn. Richart doesn't want Reordon anywhere near her. Why the hell do you think I'm using a prepaid, untraceable cell phone? Richart would kick my ass from here to Antibes if I let any harm come to her."

Was Reordon Richart's enemy? Sheldon seemed to think she needed protection from him, whoever he was.

"Have Étienne and Lisette regained consciousness?" He swore. "What about Roland and Marcus?"

Jenna combed her fingers through Richart's hair. Étienne and Lisette were his brother and sister. He had spoken of them with great affection. She hated to hear that they, too, had been harmed.

"Listen, there's something else," Sheldon said, voice

somber. "I think Ami may be dead. Apparently Richart tried to teleport her with him, but the drug was fucking with him too much and she didn't make it here. . . . What? . . . He did? . . . Uh-huh. . . . No, I didn't bring my cell with me. I didn't want Reordon to be able to locate me. I'll just call every hour to check in."

John returned to Jenna's bedroom, clothed in jeans and a heavy sweater with a book bag looped over his shoulder. "Are you sure you're okay with this? I don't feel right about leaving. I'd rather risk losing my scholarship than risk losing you. You're more important."

Jenna crossed to him and leaned up to kiss his cheek. "I'm fine. Sheldon will be here with me."

"Mom, we don't know Sheldon from Adam. For all we know, he's—"

"I trust him," she said. "If you're worried, just call me in a while to see how things are going."

He groaned. "Fine. But if you don't answer, I'm hauling ass back here with reinforcements."

"That's fine, honey. Study hard."

Rolling his eyes, he left the room. "If anything happens to her," she heard him tell Sheldon as he passed him in the hallway, "I'll hunt you motherfuckers down and laugh while I feed you your own entrails."

Jenna leaned into the hallway and stared at her son's back with wide eyes. She had never heard him sound so menacing.

"Dude," Sheldon responded, "vampires threaten to feed me my own entrails all the time. You're going to have to come up with something better than that."

"Fine. I'll cut off your balls, shove them down your throat, and watch you choke on them."

"That'll do." Sheldon shuddered. "Okay, I see we're going to have to have a little talk, John. Here's the thing. Since Richart is planning to explore the Kama Sutra with your mom, *if* she forgives him . . ."

"Really?" John said. "You're going to put *that* image in my head?"

". . . you and I are going to be running into each other a lot, so you need to understand something," he said earnestly. "You can't threaten a man's balls, dude. A man's balls are off limits. Even *vampires* don't fuck with a man's balls. That's just . . . mean."

John glanced at Jenna.

She raised an eyebrow. "Still think I'm in danger?"

"Hell, no."

"Good. Go study."

Shaking his head, John left.

Sheldon met Jenna in the doorway. "I know you're probably just as concerned as he is, but I won't let any harm come to you, Jenna. And I promise I'm not here to harm you myself. If I let you get so much as a paper cut, Richart would hang my ass out to dry."

"You seem very loyal to him."

"I'd give my life to protect him. And, since he cares for you, that means I'd give my life to protect you, too." His voice rang with sincerity.

Jenna nodded. "So what do we do now?"

He sighed. "Now . . . we wait."

Richart bit back a groan. Some asshole was mowing his lawn or trimming his hedges or juggling fucking chainsaws in rhythmic intervals. On. Off. On. Off. On. Off. The noise assaulted his ears in perfect accompaniment to the pounding that made his head feel like someone was hitting him repeatedly in the forehead with a snow shovel.

What the hell?

He tried to open his eyes and found his lids too heavy to lift.

"Wake up, Richart," Jenna whispered in his ear. Her delicate fingers delivered soothing strokes to one of his hands.

Had he fallen asleep at Jenna's?

"Wake up, Richart," she repeated in those same warm tones.

The buzz sawing grew louder. The pain in his head intensified.

"Wake up, Richart," she said once more, amusement creeping in. "Because, if you don't, I might have to smother Sheldon to get him to stop snoring."

Had he the strength, he would have laughed.

Then her words sank in. Sheldon was here? What was Sheldon doing here?

Where was *here?* His mind was all foggy.

Had he and Jenna spent her night off at *his* place? All of the things he had planned to do to that lovely body of hers and he had fallen asleep? Sheldon must have laughed his ass off when he had gotten home.

"Wake up, Richart. I need to know you're okay."

That didn't sound like he'd fallen asleep.

He tried again to force his eyelids open.

Her hand tightened on his as she combed her fingers through his hair.

"That's it. Open your eyes for me."

At last, he succeeded and tried to bring his surroundings into focus.

What was wrong with his eyes?

What was wrong with *him?* Why couldn't he think straight or hold on to a thought for more than a fleeting second?

As his vision cleared, he realized he lay in Jenna's bed, a blanket drawn up to his waist, leaving his chest bare. His Second was sprawled in a chair across the room, legs straight, feet splayed, arms dangling over the chair's arms, head back, mouth gaping as he emitted periodic snores.

At least I've located the damned chainsaw.

Daylight framed the closed blinds on the only window the room boasted. A discarded IV stand sporting an empty bag of blood stood sentinel beside the bed.

"Richart?" Jenna sat beside him, her hip a gentle pressure against his. Faint signs of fatigue lined her pretty face.

He curled his fingers around hers, still trying to find his voice.

"How do you feel?" she asked.

It took a couple of attempts to coax sound to emerge. "Like I have the worst hangover ever. What happened?"

She shook her head. "Sheldon wouldn't tell me what happened before you got here, just that you were out on assignment and something went terribly wrong. John and I were having dinner here last night when you suddenly . . ." She closed her eyes for a moment. "It feels so weird to say this."

"What?"

"You . . . teleported into the living room."

Alarm surged through him.

"Sporting fangs."

He clamped his lips shut.

"Drenched in blood."

Holy hell.

"With glowing eyes."

Every curse word he knew in every language he had ever learned paraded through his mind.

She knew. At least part of it anyway. "You called Sheldon?" he asked, avoiding her gaze.

"No. Your cell phone was shattered in whatever fight left you so torn up. He came looking for you around noon."

She *knew*.

John knew.

She'd never forgive him.

Fear-induced adrenaline surged through him, finally resurrecting a few memories.

The ambush. The vampire king. The darts.

Grabbing the pillow from behind his head, he threw it at his somnolent Second's slack face.

Feet flying up, Sheldon snorted and jackknifed into a

seated position. "I didn't do it!" His eyes sought and found Richart. "Oh, shit. You're awake. *Man,* you had me worried." He crossed to the bed.

Richart squeezed Jenna's hand and pulled himself up into a seated position. The room tilted. Dark clouds invaded his vision and swirled around before clearing as the dizziness ebbed. "Étienne and Lisette?"

Jenna moved to sit at his side and wrapped an arm around him for support.

A tiny spark of hope flared. She wouldn't do that if she hated or feared him, would she?

"As of half an hour ago, they still haven't regained consciousness," Sheldon said, "but their wounds have healed like yours."

"Roland and Marcus?"

"They're awake, but not at full strength."

"Ami?"

The younger man's gaze darted to Jenna and back. He raised his eyebrows in question, silently asking if he should speak freely.

"Just say it. I'm going to tell her everything as soon as you leave anyway."

"The vampire king or one of his followers captured her."

Dread flooded Richart's stomach like acid.

"Bastien tracked their scents to Carrboro and lost them," Sheldon continued, "but Marcus went after her as soon as he woke up and found her."

"She's alive?"

Sheldon nodded.

"In what condition?"

"I don't know. Last I heard Darnell was heading over to Marcus's place to check on her. I'm sure Seth has been called in by now to heal her."

Richart dropped his legs over the side of the bed and braced his bare feet on the carpet. Leaning forward, he propped his elbows on his knees and dropped his head into his hands.

"It wasn't your fault," Sheldon told him.

Richart shook his head. "I should have stayed. I shouldn't have teleported that last time. I thought I could take her away from there."

"If you had stayed, you would have died."

And Ami still would have wound up in the vampires' hands. The vampire-hunting profession was very good at producing no-win situations. "Go home and get some rest."

"I don't think I should leave you. You aren't at full strength."

"Go home," Richart insisted, his tone offering Sheldon no wiggle room. "I'll be along in a while."

"What if you can't teleport?"

"I'll call you and you can drag your ass back and give me a ride. Or, if the sun has set, I'll walk."

Nodding, Sheldon grabbed a piece of paper and pen from the bedside table and scribbled something down. Once finished, he handed the scrap to Jenna. "Here's a number where you can reach me. If he needs anything, call me."

"Okay." Jenna took his Second's hand. "Thank you, Sheldon."

Bobbing his head, Sheldon gave her hand a squeeze, scrutinized Richart one last time, then backed out of the room. The front door opened and closed, then they were alone.

Chapter Five

Silence descended upon the room, heavy with things unsaid.

"It belatedly occurs to me," Richart began rustily, "that I should have asked you if you wished me to leave."

"No." She added nothing more. Nor did she move away, sitting close behind him on the bed.

Richart found himself at a loss. He didn't know how to do this. How to reveal all of his secrets. How to coax a human into accepting him without fear or loathing. A human whose scorn he couldn't bear to face.

"Why won't you look at me?" she asked.

Richart rubbed his eyes and pinched the bridge of his nose, hoping it would help clear his head and ease the pain it housed. "I've never done this before."

"Done what?"

"Tried to find a way to tell the woman I love that I'm not human."

She drew in a sharp breath.

"Tried to find the right words to convince her not to fear me or revile me after letting her see me at my worst, covered in blood, with my damned eyes glowing and my fangs bared.

What you must think of me . . ." Rising shakily, he braced a hand on the wall.

"Are you okay?"

He winced. "My head is fucking killing me." He cupped his throbbing forehead in a palm. "Forgive me. I didn't mean to speak so crudely."

"I've said worse, stuck in traffic."

His lips twitched. Only Jenna could make him smile when things looked so damned grim. It was one of the reasons he loved her despite all of the monumental obstacles littering their path. "You know what the ironic thing is?"

"What?"

"If this battle had not taken place, I would have told you everything last night."

The bedding rustled as Jenna rose on the other side of the bed.

"I know it sounds like I'm just saying that to cover my ass, but it was your night off. If we couldn't be alone here, I was going to boot Sheldon out of my place and . . ." He shook his head. "I wanted so badly to make love to you, but didn't feel right doing so without first telling you the truth."

Jenna circled the bed and stood no more than a foot away from him. "Is that why you held back whenever we . . . ?"

"Kissed?" He studied her beautiful face, following the lovely line of her neck down to her full breasts. "Touched?" Despite the lethargy that plagued him, Richart felt his pulse leap and his body harden as memories of slipping his hands beneath her shirt, unfastening her bra, and filling his palms with that soft, silky flesh flitted through his mind. Dragging the cloth up and closing his lips over the tights buds. Hearing her moan and feeling her clutch him tightly in response.

Squeezing his eyes closed, he turned his head aside.

"Richart? What's wrong? Is it your head?"

He shook his head. "It's my eyes."

"Are they hurting?"

This was so not the time for his nature to assert itself. "No, it's . . ." A huff of frustration escaped him. "They glow when I'm in the grips of strong emotion and—trust me when I say I realize now is not the time for this—but just the thought of making love with you . . ."

He jumped when her small, cool fingers touched his jaw and turned his face back toward her.

"Let me see," she coaxed.

He did as bidden.

Her hazel eyes brightened, illuminated by the amber glow emanating from his own.

She raised her other hand, cupped his face in both, and studied him with such painful intensity that he forgot to breathe. "They're beautiful," she whispered.

A lump rose in his throat. "Don't fear me, Jenna."

Amusement lit her features. "It's kind of hard to be afraid of a vampire who apologizes for using harsh language in front of a lady."

Could he really be so lucky? "I'm not a vampire."

"And I'm not a lady." She motioned to the bed. "Stop worrying about how I'll react, sit down before you fall down, and explain all of this to me." She started to step back, then paused. "Wait. Scratch that. I need to do something first." Slipping her arms around his waist, she pressed her face to his chest and hugged him close.

Heart pounding, Richart wrapped his arms around her.

"There was a moment last night," she murmured, "when I thought you were dead. You lost consciousness and your chest stopped rising. I couldn't find a pulse." Her hold tightened. "I've only felt that overwhelming despair and helplessness once in my life, when police showed up at my door and told me John's father had been killed in a car accident." She burrowed closer, her breath warm on his chest. "I don't ever want to feel that way again."

Richart buried his face in her hair. "I'm sorry."

Many long moments passed while they clung to each other.

Sighing, Jenna loosened her hold and looked up at him. "Feelings that deep aren't going to dissolve overnight because I found out your eyes are prettier and your teeth are sharper than I thought they were."

Richart dipped his head and captured her lips with his own, pouring everything he felt into the contact until both were breathless.

When she placed a hand on his chest and applied gentle pressure, he reluctantly withdrew.

"I need you to explain everything to me before we get too distracted."

Nodding, he sank onto the bed, stretched his legs out, and leaned back against the headboard, then pulled her down beside him, catching and holding her hand.

"Now they're even brighter," she said, her eyes locking on his with fascination.

"You do that to me," he admitted. "I've had a hell of a time hiding it from you."

Swiveling to face him, she sat with her legs crossed and toyed with his fingers. "So . . . how old are you?"

He grimaced. "Two hundred and thirty."

She shook her head. "I feel so stupid for making such a big deal out of being older than you."

"Please don't. I was the one who feared you would reject me if you knew my true age."

She offered him a small smile. "I won't lie. If you actually looked your age, I wouldn't have given you a second glance."

He laughed. "I don't blame you."

"How can you be so . . . ?"

"Old and young at the same time?"

She nodded. "And not be a vampire? I mean, the fangs . . ."

"I'm infected with a virus. A very *rare* symbiotic virus that behaves like no other on the planet. We don't know where it originated. We know only that it first conquers, then replaces the immune system, lending those infected with it far greater strength, speed, and regenerative capabilities. It heightens our senses, causes extreme photosensitivity, and . . . we don't age. Essentially, we are immortal, and call ourselves such."

Jenna stared at him, her thoughts reeling. "A virus."

"Yes, one that can only be transmitted through a bite."

"Do you drink blood?"

"I do require frequent infusions of blood. The virus depletes my body's supply as it repairs damage. But I don't drink it. During my transformation, I grew a pair of retractable fangs that function like IV needles. When I bite into a blood bag, my fangs siphon the blood directly into my veins."

"Do you ever bite people?"

"We all did before we were able to collect and store blood donations in our own blood banks. But we never frightened or killed the donors." He grimaced. "Well, not unless they were fiends who preyed upon the innocent."

"So you're an immortal, not a vampire."

"Yes."

"But Sheldon mentioned a vampire king, so vampires do exist."

"Yes. I was different from other humans even before I was infected, as were my brother and sister and all of our immortal brethren. We called ourselves *gifted ones*. We didn't know it then and still don't know why, but our DNA is more advanced—a great deal more advanced—than that of ordinary humans." He shrugged. "It's why I can teleport."

"That isn't a result of the virus?"

"No. I could teleport as a child. My brother and sister are both telepathic. Some can heal with their hands. Others can move things with their minds. The eldest of us can do far more." He toyed with her hand. "As you said, vampires *do* exist. They are ordinary humans who have been infected with the same virus. They lack our special abilities and, without the protection our advanced DNA affords us, suffer progressive brain damage that causes a rapid descent into madness. They prey upon humans, inflicting upon their victims every monstrous impulse."

"How have I never heard of this?" she asked in disbelief. "How have *none* of us ever heard of this?"

"Immortals hunt vampires and destroy them. It's what we do, every night, to eradicate the threat and to prevent the public from learning of our existence and theirs."

"But, why don't the vampires' victims report it?"

"They have no memory of the attacks."

"You erase their memories?"

"No. Small glands above our fangs—and the fangs of vampires—release a chemical that behaves much like GHB under the pressure of a bite. If the victim lives, he or she will have no memory of what happened."

"I'm sorry. I'm just having a hard time believing that."

He looked away. "Do you remember the first night we met, Jenna?"

"Yes. You came into the store and asked me where to find Krazy Glue."

When next he met her gaze, his eyes had returned to their usual brown. "That wasn't the first night we met."

"What do you mean?"

"A few weeks before that, I was hunting in the area—"

"Hunting vampires."

"Yes. And found . . . you. You must have just come off your shift. Four vampires had swept you behind the building and cornered you."

Her blood went cold. "What?"

"You fought and pepper-sprayed one, but were bitten by another before I could wrest you from him."

Horror filled her. Somehow this revelation was worse than anything that had come before it. She had been attacked? By vampires? And had no memory of it? "That isn't possible."

"There was a night, was there not, a few weeks before we

met in which you couldn't remember leaving work the night before, driving home, or putting yourself to bed?"

Oh, crap. There *had* been. She had awoken in her bed, still wearing her work clothes, and hadn't been able to remember how she had gotten there. It had all been a blank. She had ultimately chalked it up to exhaustion.

"I was attacked by vampires?"

"Yes."

"Why didn't you tell me?" How could he keep something like that from her?

"Jenna—"

"I was attacked, Richart! You should have told me!"

"How?" he asked helplessly.

"Easy. You should have said, *Jenna, I know this is going to sound strange, but you were attacked by vampires and I rescued*—okay, I see your point. I would have thought you were off your rocker." She rubbed a shaking hand over her face. "I can't believe this. Did they . . . ? What did they do to me?"

"Other than the bite, you were unharmed. They must have just taken you when I came upon you."

"Am I infected?" If all Richart had said was true, she would turn into a psychotic vampire if she transformed. She didn't have the special DNA needed to make her immortal. She couldn't read minds or teleport or see the future or whatever else they could do.

"No. A single brief bite won't turn you. You would either have to be bitten fairly often over a stretch of time or have your blood drained until you were on the brink of death, then be infused wholly with infected blood."

And the vampire had only bitten her the once. Briefly.

Richart covered the hand she had braced on the mattress with one of his. "Are you all right?"

She met his concerned gaze. "I'm freaked out over being attacked and having no memory of it. That's really scary."

"I know."

"So you—what—killed them *Blade*-style?"

He smiled. "All but one, who got away, yes."

"One got away?" Panic shrieked through her. "What if he came back? What if he bit me again and I just can't remember it?"

"He didn't."

"How do you know?"

"Have you experienced missing time again? Have there been any blank spots you couldn't recall?"

She thought hard, trying to think of *any* other instances. "I don't think so. But how can I be sure?"

"I've been guarding you," he admitted, seeming almost ashamed.

"Guarding me?"

"I used speed and stealth to obtain your work schedule and have been at the store every night when you arrived and departed in case he returned and tried to harm you."

She stared at him. "Every night?"

"Yes."

"Is he likely to return?"

"No. He would have done so before now."

"Yet you continued to watch over me."

He shrugged. "At least you said *watched*. Sheldon kept accusing me of stalking you."

She supposed some *would* see that as stalking. To Jenna, it seemed sweet. He had been protecting her all this time. "So . . . that's everything then?"

He lowered his eyes.

"Damn it! What else could there be? You're immortal. I was attacked by vampires. Vampires nearly killed you last night. You can teleport. What are you going to tell me now? That Sheldon is a werewolf?"

"Sheldon isn't a werewolf, no."

"Then, what?" She wondered how many times she would feel this gut-churning dread before the day ended. "Did you ask me out because you were trying to lure the vampire out of hiding?"

His head snapped up. "No! Of course not. I asked you out because the night I rescued you you kissed me."

What? "I kissed you?"

"Yes. You were grateful that I saved you. You were drugged by the vampire's bite, so your inhibitions were lowered and . . . you kissed me." His eyes began to glow again.

Why did that make her heart pound? "Please tell me it wasn't a sloppy, drunken kiss."

"It was not a sloppy, drunken kiss. It was sweet and erotic all at once and I was captivated. I couldn't stop thinking about you afterward. Days went by. Then weeks. I watched over you. Watched you come and go. Listened to you chat with your colleagues. And, when I couldn't keep my distance any longer, I gave in to temptation and . . ."

"Asked me where to find the Krazy Glue?"

"Yes."

"Your eyes are glowing again."

"I can't help it. Even with my ears filled with cotton and a sledgehammer assaulting my head, I want you."

And she wanted him. Despite everything. Or because of everything. She would decide which later.

Richart watched Jenna, waiting for condemnation, acceptance, a *Can we talk about this later? I need time to think.* Anything that would give him a clue to her thoughts.

She rose onto her knees and scooted closer. Slinging a leg across his own, she straddled his lap.

Lust slammed through him as she settled upon the erection barely concealed by his boxers. Clarity came with it, finally erasing the fuzz the drug had induced.

Clamping his hands on her tempting ass, deliciously clad in tight yoga pants, he leaned forward and ravaged her lips with his own. She responded with all of the heat and urgency that seized him, parting her lips and inviting him within. Richart thrust his tongue forward, teasing and tasting hers as his heart slammed against his ribs.

"I hated keeping secrets from you," he whispered.

"I understand why you did."

He grabbed the hem of her sweatshirt and drew it over her head.

Her hair crackled with static electricity and clung to him as he wrapped his arms around her mostly bare form. So soft and warm and *his*.

He reached behind her and unfastened her bra. "Have I mentioned I haven't done this in a while?"

"Me either. It's been years for me."

"For me it's been decades."

Her eyebrows flew up. "Decades? But . . . you're so gorgeous."

He laughed. "As are you." Drawing the lacy material down, he revealed pale breasts with hard pink tips. "Human males are idiots."

Her laugh turned into a gasp as he leaned forward and drew a taut bud into his mouth, sucking, nipping, and stroking it with his tongue.

Jenna tunneled her fingers through his hair as fire invaded her. "Are you sure you're up for this?" she forced herself to ask between gasps. The man had almost died, after all.

"I think you can feel that I am."

She certainly could and rocked against him, thigh muscles bunching as pleasure darted through her. "I meant . . ." She moaned as he slid one hand up to cup her other breast and knead it before his fingers went to work on the sensitive tip. "I meant . . . your head . . ."

"My head aches," he muttered, "but I couldn't care less. I've been wanting to do this for weeks."

He abandoned her breast and reclaimed her lips. Falling backward on the bed, he rolled her beneath him. Jenna gasped as he inserted a knee between her legs and began to apply rhythmic pressure.

She loved the feel of him above her, his weight pressing down on her, his heat surrounding her. She loved *him*.

He trailed kisses down her neck, her chest, stroking one breast, then the other as he rose onto his knees. His tongue found her belly button the same time his fingers clasped the elastic waistband of her pants. "I love yoga pants," he murmured.

Jenna laughed and shifted her hips as he drew them down, taking her panties with them, and tossed them on the floor.

"Now you," she insisted.

His boxers landed on the dresser.

He had the hottest body. All muscle and sinew. Strong and perfect.

She felt a moment of insecurity. While she had managed to keep her weight down over the years, having a baby, then lacking both the time and energy to exercise hadn't exactly left her with the tightest, most fit physique.

"You're so beautiful, Jenna," he murmured, those large warm hands exploring every inch of her as he raised eyes that glowed with desire to meet hers.

"*You're* beautiful," she said.

Growling, he slid farther down the bed, slid his arms beneath her knees and lowered his head to take her with his mouth.

Jenna threw back her head and gripped the sheets as pleasure scalded her, heating her blood. Moaning, she reached down and clutched his hair with desperate hands. His mouth was so warm, his tongue doing things she didn't even know a tongue could do until ecstasy exploded within her.

Crying out, she rode the wave as Richart continued to play, prolonging her orgasm, then sending her off into another.

Panting, she collapsed against the sheets.

Richart rose above her, his expression fierce and triumphant and full of longing.

Jenna planted a hand on his chest and gave him a little push.

He fell back, watching her with those hypnotic amber eyes as she rose and straddled his knees.

"My turn," she said, then grasped his heavy erection and engaged in a little play of her own, stroking, squeezing, reveling in every groan she elicited.

"Jenna."

Smiling, she lowered her head and closed her mouth around the warm soft tip. He moaned and muttered something in French.

She hadn't done this in a very long time, but any concern she felt that she might not be doing it well fled when he tunneled his fingers through her hair and urged her on.

"So good," he murmured.

His pleasure sparked a return of hers. She loved the way he tasted, the way he reacted to every long draw, every stroke of her tongue. And she loved the ecstasy that swept his handsome features as he came hard, calling her name.

Easing up to lie beside him, she watched the rapid rise and fall of his chest.

He turned his head, met her gaze. "That was incredible." Rolling onto his side, he smiled. "My headache is gone."

Jenna laughed. "Good."

He leaned in, brushed her lips with his. "*Very* good. Because I'm not finished with you."

Her breath caught as he fondled her breast. "You aren't?"

He shook his head, a mischievous gleam entering his glowing eyes as he slid his hand down her stomach to the heart of her and teased the sensitive nub hidden there.

She wouldn't have thought she would be able to orgasm again, but the need that rapidly rose told her otherwise.

"You're so wet," he whispered, rising up to settle between her thighs. "I want to be inside you the next time you come."

She wrapped her arms around him. "And I want you there."

Richart stared down at Jenna's pretty face, flushed with pleasure. Positioning his cock at her entrance, he slid inside.

She was warm and tight and delightfully eager.

She slid her hands down to grip his ass.

Richart lowered his head to take her lips once more, kneaded her breast as he withdrew, then drove home again. And again. And again. The pleasure once more rising. Even better this time with her body clutching his.

He had known it would be like this. All those nights he had imagined being right here, moving inside Jenna, his feet hanging off the too-short bed, he had known it would be better than anything he had ever experienced before. And, when she threw back her head and cried out as another orgasm claimed her, her inner muscles tightening convulsively around him and driving him into his own, he knew he was lost. There would never be another for him.

Jenna was it. She was the one.

Rolling to his side, Richart held her close.

And tried not to think what the future would hold for them.

The weeks that followed were perhaps the most blissful of Jenna's life. She and Richart were inseparable. When they weren't working, they were together. When he was working and she was at home, they talked on the phone or texted, pausing only long enough for him to slay vampires, which was bizarre.

She learned something new about him every day. None of it frightened her, though, despite his concern that each revelation would be too much, that this or that would be the thing that was just too weird for her.

One night Richart hefted her effortlessly onto his back and raced through the countryside at preternatural speeds. It was scary and exhilarating and *so* much fun. Richart could outrun cars. And did so just to impress her, his eyes sparkling with boyish pleasure as she laughed.

He made her feel like a teenager again. Carefree and young, despite the fatigue that pulled at her. Working all night and playing with Richart nearly all day was taking its toll. But it was totally worth it.

They never spoke of the future. Never discussed what might happen to their relationship long-term. What would happen when she began to age and he stayed young.

He had mentioned once that, if she wished, she could have her DNA tested to see if she could be transformed without turning vampire. Jenna suspected he hadn't mentioned it again because he feared what the test may reveal and wanted to hold on to hope for just a little longer.

The fact that she was actually a brunette seemed to please him. Jenna had been dyeing her hair off and on ever since she had begun to go gray prematurely at the age of twenty. An overwhelming majority of *gifted ones* apparently had black hair. He did know of two, however, who had brown hair.

He hadn't asked her if she *wanted* to be transformed, probably because it wasn't as easy a decision to make as one might think. If she were transformed, Jenna would outlive her son, the grandchildren he would give her in the future, and their grandchildren, too.

Shaking off the somber thoughts, Jenna finished washing the breakfast dishes and dried her hands on the towel hanging beside the sink.

"What time is Richart coming over?" John asked, still poring over one of his textbooks at the table. He wouldn't have to leave for his first class for another hour.

"I don't know. He said it might be a late night and didn't want to talk because his sister and another immortal were with him and would overhear."

"Ahh."

In the next breath, Richart appeared in the living room.

He wore his usual vampire hunting togs: black shirt, black pants, long black coat, daggers and throwing stars in every loop and pocket and sheath. Smudges of blood adorned his upper lip and chin, as if someone had punched him hard enough to break his nose. His eyes glowed a vibrant amber. His features, when he caught and held her gaze, bore an intensity that sucked the breath from her lungs.

"What happened?" Jenna asked, closing the distance between them.

Looping an arm around her waist, he yanked her to him and claimed her lips in a long, passionate kiss.

Jenna forgot everything as fire burned through her and every nerve ending sprang to life. Forgot the blood on his chin. Forgot the weapons weighing him down and poking her as he pressed her against him. Forgot her son.

By the time Richart raised his head, she was as breathless as though she had just run the 400-meter relay.

Richart looked over her shoulder and nodded abruptly. "John."

"Hey," John said, sounding stunned.

"Excuse us, please." As soon as Richart finished the husky proclamation, he whisked them to his bedroom in his home.

Jenna had no time to ask him what was wrong. He went to work, removing their clothing at preternatural speeds. His kiss was fierce, his hands aggressive in their exploration of her, turning her body to liquid fire.

Richart said nothing, the need to touch Jenna, to feel her against him, overwhelming. He was so desperate for her. He worried he might be hurting her until she wrapped her legs around him and begged for more.

Tossing her onto the bed, he dove after her. There was little foreplay this time. He needed her too much. As soon as he felt how wet she was for him, he sank inside, taking her fast and hard with strong, powerful strokes.

Jenna clutched Richart closer, panting, pleasure rising. His touch contained a hint of desperation, a roughness that had never been there before and excited her above and beyond. She cried out as ecstasy consumed her, reveled in hearing her name on Richart's lips as he came soon after.

Her muscles went limp.

Richart sank down on her, forearms braced on the bed to keep the bulk of his weight off of her. "Did I hurt you?" he murmured.

"No. It was fantastic."

He nodded, face buried in the crook of her neck, and rolled them to their sides, still joined.

Jenna waited for her heartbeat to slow its frantic pace. Richart never loosened his hold on her, cradling her close.

"Did something happen at work today?" she asked tentatively.

A moment passed. "We lost some good people tonight."

"Oh, no." She rubbed his back in soothing strokes. "I'm so sorry."

"It was bad. Like nothing I've ever seen. We had *no* warning." He loosened his hold and relaxed a little, resting his head beside hers on the pillow so their noses almost touched. "You know the immortal I always complain about having to hunt with?"

"Bastien?"

"Yes. He's in love with a mortal and almost lost her today. I was with him while he sat there, agonizing and blaming himself, waiting to hear if . . ." He shook his head. "I just kept thinking . . . what if it were me? What if it were us? What if you had been harmed?" He stroked her face with gentle fingers. "I love you, Jenna."

Her throat thickened.

"I know it may seem too soon," he continued.

It didn't. Not for her.

"But I love you. I do."

Jenna pressed a hand to his jaw and smoothed her thumb across his stubbled cheek. "I love you, too."

He closed his eyes, turned his face into her touch. "The thought of losing you was too much. I needed to hold you. To lose myself in you." He urged her closer. "I just needed to be with you."

She could live with that.

Quiet enfolded them.

The corners of his lips twitched.

"What?" she asked.

"I think we may have shocked John."

She laughed. "Somehow I think this won't be the last time."

He smiled. "I think you may be right."

"So. You spending the day with Jenna?" Sheldon asked as Richart donned his coat.

He nodded.

"What's wrong? You guys have a fight or something?"

"I feel guilty," Richart confessed. "She works long hours all night, then I keep her up most of the day. It's wearing on her."

"Mentally or physically?"

"Physically. She tries to hide it, but she's exhausted. There are circles under her eyes. She keeps getting headaches. And she's so run down she's caught that flu that's going around."

"That sucks. Try to get her to go to sleep earlier."

Richart smiled wryly. "I always intend to, but . . ."

Sheldon smiled. "I hear ya. Hey, do you want me to make her some chicken soup?"

"No. I've tasted your chicken soup. I want her to feel *better* not *worse*."

"Smart ass."

Richart teleported to Jenna's living room and found John waiting for him.

John raised a finger to his lips, then motioned for Richart to accompany him outside.

Puzzled, Richart followed him out onto the landing and waited while he closed the door behind them.

"Something's wrong," John said without preamble.

Richart frowned. "What?"

"You need to talk Mom into seeing that doctor you mentioned."

"Dr. Lipton? I already tried once. Jenna said doctors can't do anything for the flu unless they catch it in the first twenty-four to forty-eight hours, that it just needs to run its course."

"This isn't the flu. It's been two weeks."

Richart nodded. "Dr. Lipton mentioned that some of her colleagues who came down with it took a couple of weeks to recover, that it was quite a nasty strain." Richart hadn't been sick in over two centuries, so he relied on Dr. Lipton and Jenna to apprise him of how these things usually went.

"I'm telling you," John insisted, "this isn't the flu. It's something else."

"How can you be so sure?" Jenna seemed sure.

"Because Mom doesn't get the flu."

"She's never had it before?" Wasn't the flu fairly common among humans?

"I'm saying she doesn't get sick. Period."

Alarm bells sounded. "Ever?"

"Ever. She's never even had a cold. Not that I can remember."

Jenna sure as hell hadn't told him that. "She had food poisoning a month ago."

"I'm not convinced that's what that was." John looked away, jaw clenching and unclenching. "Look, I like you, Richart, and I don't want there to be any tension between us for Mom's sake, but I have to ask. . . . Have you been biting her?"

"No." *Hell,* no. She had already been bitten once by the

vampire who had attacked her that first night. Any more bites and she would have become more susceptible to . . .

Merde.

"I'm just asking because I know you said vampirism is caused by a virus and that frequent exposure . . ." He stared at Richart. "What? What is it? Your eyes are glowing."

Was it possible? Could she have been bitten again without him realizing it?

When? He was always there when she reached and left work. And any shopping she needed to do she did during daylight hours.

"Have any of your mother's friends or work colleagues dropped by after dark?"

"No."

"Have you brought any friends home?"

"My study group takes turns meeting at each other's places. They've been over here a few times."

"At night? After Jenna got home from work, while I was still out hunting?"

"Yeah. Why?"

Cursing, Richart practically tore the door off its hinges in his hurry to get inside.

Clad in a T-shirt and striped pajama bottoms, Jenna looked up, pallid face brightening, when he burst into her bedroom. "Hi." Her smile faded as he sat beside her on the bed. "What's wrong?"

"Just give me a moment." Leaning in close, Richart buried his face in her neck just above her carotid artery. He drew in a deep breath. Held it. Found her scent. But not the scent he feared most.

"Richart?" Concern crept into her voice.

As John entered the room, Richart leaned back and palmed one of his daggers. "I need you to trust me, sweetheart."

"Okay," she answered, winning his heart all over again.

Taking her hand, he pressed the tip of the dagger to her palm and applied just enough pressure to produce a tiny nick. A single bead of blood welled.

Richart raised her hand until it almost touched his nose, again drawing in a deep breath.

And there it was. The virus.

A growl rumbled deep in his throat.

She frowned. "Richart?"

"You're infected."

John took a step forward.

Jenna stared up at Richart, fever blazing in her eyes. "Infected with what?"

"The vampiric virus."

"No. I told you. It's the flu."

"I can smell it, Jenna. You're infected."

Her face grew paler. "That's not possible. You've never bitten me. I haven't blacked out. And you've been watching over me at the store."

He would figure it out later, after he took her to the network doctors. If she was this sick already . . .

He swallowed. It may be too late to prevent a transformation.

Rising, he wrapped the blankets around her and scooped her up into his arms.

John stepped forward. "Wherever you're going, I'm going with you."

Though teleporting two at a time would sap his energy, Richart didn't argue. "Grab my shoulder."

A second later they stood in Dr. Lipton's office.

Weakness struck. He staggered to the right, bumping into John.

John tightened his grip and helped Richart remain upright. "You okay, man?"

Leaning over her desk, Dr. Melanie Lipton jumped and spun around. "Richart. Hi. What—?"

"Jenna's infected."

Melanie paled. "What?"

"He *thinks* I'm infected," Jenna corrected. "I think it's the flu."

Melanie met Richart's grim gaze and motioned for them to follow her. "Let's go to the infirmary."

Chapter Six

Jenna did everything she could to convince herself that Richart was wrong, that it was just a bad case of the flu. Hadn't Debbie even come down with it? And Jed in Lawn and Garden? Harry in Automotive?

But it was hard to ignore the looks Richart and Dr. Lipton kept exchanging. Looks that said Jenna was screwed.

"It's such a pleasure to meet you, Jenna," Dr. Lipton said as Richart lowered her to an exam table. "Richart talks about you all the time."

"Nice to meet you, too. This is my son, John."

"Good to meet you, John."

"Nice to meet you," he murmured.

"Richart," Dr. Lipton said, "you and John go wait out in the hallway so your hovering won't distract me." She winked at Jenna. "Plus, if Richart isn't in the room, I can share all kinds of embarrassing stories about him with you."

Richart narrowed his eyes in warning, then kissed Jenna. "We'll be right outside if you need us."

Jenna smiled and nodded.

As soon as the door closed behind them, Dr. Lipton shook her head. "That man is so in love with you."

"I love him, too."

Dr. Lipton's gaze sharpened as she donned a pair of latex gloves. "Enough to transform for him?"

"I thought I couldn't do that safely."

"If he's right and you've been infected, you may not have a choice. How many times has he bitten you?" There was no mistaking her disapproval.

"That's just it. He hasn't."

Her brow furrowed. "Ever?"

"Ever. A vampire bit me once a couple of months ago. He caught me leaving my job and Richart stopped him. But Richart has been there every night since and made sure the vampire didn't return. I can't be transformed by just one bite, right?"

"Not unless he drained you almost to the point of death, then infused you with his own blood."

"Richart said he didn't do that; so it must be the flu."

Dr. Lipton didn't seem convinced. "Let's start with your symptoms."

Jenna rattled them off and answered questions about severity, onset, and the like as Dr. Lipton took her temperature and engaged in various and assorted poking and prodding.

She was pretty in a girl-next-door kind of way with brown hair, brown eyes, and a trim figure encased in jeans, a T-shirt, and a lab coat.

"I'm going to level with you, Jenna," she said finally. "I think Richart's right. I'll run a blood test to be sure, but I already know what it's going to tell me."

Jenna broke out in a cold sweat as fear rippled through her. "I'm becoming a vampire?"

"Yes."

She would suffer progressive brain damage and go insane.

"I'm sorry," Dr. Lipton offered with genuine remorse. "There really isn't any sugarcoating this. I can't even give you hope that you might be a *gifted one*. Nearly all *gifted ones* have black hair and brown eyes. A few, like me, have brown hair. But never red."

"I'm a brunette. I dye my hair."

Dr. Lipton studied her. "Have you noticed any special gifts or abilities? Know the phone is going to ring before it does?"

"No."

"Know what someone else is feeling? Hear their thoughts?"

"No. I don't have any special abilities, Dr. Lipton."

"Melanie."

"I'm screwed, aren't I, Melanie?"

She sighed. "Yes. As I said, I'll run some tests to be sure. See how far the infection has progressed. Take a look at your DNA and see if it bears the extra memo groups that would identify you as a *gifted one* and protect you from the brain damage. But I'm not very hopeful."

"I can't believe this." Her mind raced as nightmare images unfolded before her. John having to watch his mother descend into madness. Jenna having to leave to ensure she wouldn't harm him. Richart watching and waiting for her to reach the point of no return, then taking her life.

What would it do to him to watch her turn into one of the monsters he hunted? Would she have to leave him, too?

Richart paced back and forth in front of the door to the infirmary.

John stood nearby, looking up and down the hallway, taking in the multitude of guards armed with automatic weapons. Half a dozen stood sentinel near two doors a little farther down.

Dragging his eyes away, John turned to Richart. "What's in there? What are they protecting?"

"They aren't protecting what's in there. They're protecting everyone out here. Those doors lead to vampires' apartments."

John's eyes widened. "Vampires live here?"

"A couple do, yes. They surrendered instead of following the example of their brethren and fighting to the death. They've been working with Dr. Lipton and the other doctors in hopes of finding a cure for the virus or some treatment that might prevent the brain damage it causes in humans."

"How's that going?"

Richart shook his head and lied. "I don't know." They had been searching for a cure for thousands of years with no success.

John swallowed. "If Mom becomes a vampire, is she going to go crazy and want to hurt people?"

Richart nodded, throat too thick to speak.

Face grim, John resumed his perusal of the hallway. "What is this place?"

"Network headquarters, the hub of the East Coast division of the human network that aids us."

"Why are there no windows?"

"Because we're five stories underground."

Minutes passed.

"I don't understand how Mom could be infected if you didn't bite her."

"I've been thinking on that." Fulminating over it more like. "It has to be a member of your study group."

John's head whipped around. "What?"

"It can't be anyone at her job. When bitten, she would've blacked out and not made it home. She would've woken up on the floor in the store's back room or her car or somewhere she shouldn't be and realized she'd lost time, that she couldn't remember how she had gotten there."

"Wouldn't the same be true if one of my study partners had bitten her?"

"Not if he did it while she was sleeping. If he came over on a night I wasn't there and she went to bed early or napped until I finished hunting, he could've asked to use your bathroom, snuck into her bedroom, and fed from her without her ever knowing she had been bitten."

"Shit!"

"I'm guessing you had a study session right before she contracted food poisoning? She always bears your study partners' scents from brushing shoulders with them and the like. The punctures heal swiftly and the effects of the GHB-like chemical she would've been exposed to don't last long, so I wouldn't have noticed anything amiss."

"We thought it was the fast food the group ordered in. . . . *Shit!* This is *my* fault?"

"It's the vampire's fault. Not yours."

"How do we figure out who it is?"

"We'll take care of that after your mother is . . . better."

After she finished turning. After she became a vampire.

There wasn't going to *be* a better for her—not long-term—and Richart felt a part of himself die at the knowledge.

The elevator at the end of the hallway pinged. A moment later, the doors slid apart and a blond male about five foot eleven exited. The guards all greeted him with respect as he strolled toward Richart.

Richart didn't even try to hide the hostility he felt toward him.

"I hear we have a visitor," Chris Reordon said.

Richart took a menacing step forward. "Stay the hell away from her, Reordon."

"What *is* it with you immortals?" he demanded with a scowl. "You keep trying to hide your mortal girlfriends from me even though you *know* I'm just trying to protect you. It's my job."

"And we all know how ruthless you can be in carrying out your job. I won't have you strong-arming and intimidating her. And don't ask Dr. Lipton her name because if you issue a single threat I'll cast aside concerns about Seth's wrath and—"

"I don't have to ask her name. I already know it."

"What?"

"Jenna McBride. Thirty-seven years old. Widowed mother of John."

"How do you know that?"

"After you outed yourself, teleporting to her *living room*— and I can't tell you what a brilliant move that was—I tagged you with a tracking device and followed you to her apartment. After that, the rest was easy."

"If you give her even one moment of unease—"

"Ask me why it was so easy."

Richart frowned. "What?"

"Ask me why the rest was easy."

"I don't have to. Everyone knows you're good at what you do. It's why you're the highest ranking mortal on the East Coast."

Chris smiled. "I am good, aren't I?"

Richart grunted.

"But I didn't even have to try with this one, because we already had Jenna on file. She's a *gifted one*."

The world went still.

"She came to our attention during her pregnancy," Chris went on. "Her boyfriend's parents insisted on a paternity test to prove John's father really was his father before the two married. DNA samples were taken from both Jenna and Bobby."

"And hers was different," Richart murmured. "More advanced."

"Much more advanced. Call-in-the-media-it's-a-fucking-miracle advanced. Just like yours. We had to run damage control, alter medical records and quite a few memories. We've been keeping tabs on her ever since."

"But she doesn't have any special abilities."

"She doesn't get sick," John said.

Chris nodded. "Exactly. You're a *gifted one,* too, you know."

John's eyebrows flew up. "I am?"

Chris nodded. "You guessed something was wrong with your mother before Richart did, didn't you?"

"Yes."

"There's a *gifted one* in Virginia who is uniquely accurate at diagnosing patients without running any tests. Considering how well you're doing in school, I'm guessing you'll be the same. You and your mother are probably descended from healers."

"How do you know I'm doing well in school?"

"As I said, we keep tabs on all *gifted ones* who come to our attention, often orchestrating things to keep them close in case another incident should arise." He looked at Richart. "Don't tell the other immortals that. If they knew just how many *gifted ones* we've guided to this area, they'd try to turn the network into a dating service. And I can't do my job with that kind of drama surrounding me."

Richart's heart began to pound. Elation flooded him, along with relief so great it practically lifted his feet off the floor. Spinning around, he burst through the door to the infirmary.

Still seated on the exam table, Jenna jumped.

Dr. Lipton smiled. "I heard. Congratulations."

"Congratulations on what?" Jenna asked, fear and despair battling for dominance in her eyes. Dr. Lipton hadn't softened her prognosis, and Jenna was clearly doing her damnedest to hold it together.

"You're a *gifted one.*" Richart closed the distance between them and swept her into his arms.

She wrapped her arms around him and held him close. "No, I'm not. I can't be. I don't have any special abilities."

"John said you never get sick."

"I got food poisoning last month."

"That wasn't food poisoning. That was the virus beginning to go to work on you."

"But—"

"Sweetheart"—Richart leaned back and grinned down at her—"you're a *gifted one.* This is *good* news."

"I just don't see not-getting-sick as an ability. It isn't something I *do.* Not willfully."

"You're likely descended from healers," Richart explained. "Healers have remarkable regenerative capabilities. Remember how swiftly my wounds healed after Sheldon transfused me?"

"Yes."

"Healers can do that even before their transformation. It's what enables them to heal others. But the more their DNA has been diluted with ordinary human DNA over the millennia, the weaker their abilities. Were you born a hundred or even fifty years ago, you might have been able to heal with your hands. Instead, your body can fight off any illness to which you're exposed, save the vampiric virus, and probably recovers from injuries abnormally fast."

She was quiet for a moment. "I did recover from childbirth quickly. But . . . you're sure about this? How do you know I'm not just really healthy? Dr. Lipton hasn't done any blood tests yet."

He told her about the revelations that had arisen from the paternity test years ago.

Her lips began to tilt up. "So I'm not going to go insane?"

"No."

She threw her arms around him and squeezed him tight, then leaned back. "But I *am* transforming."

He glanced at Dr. Lipton.

"You're transforming," Dr. Lipton confirmed. "The fact that your body is reacting the way it is tells me that if we try to halt the transformation, you'll end up with no viable immune system. Your best option at this point is to let us give you a rapid infusion of infected blood to speed and complete the transformation."

Richart willed her to choose the latter. The only alternative was death.

John, who Richart hadn't even realized had followed him back into the room, drew in a breath and held it.

"I'll transform."

John surged forward and hugged Jenna before Richart could embrace her again.

Richart met Dr. Lipton's gaze. "Call Roland."

Raising one eyebrow, she left the infirmary.

Jenna stared up at Richart, who smiled as John's hug went on and on and on.

"I'm sorry," John murmured.

"Why?"

"It's my fault."

She frowned.

Richart shook his head. "It's the vampire's fault."

"Right," Jenna said, not sure what her son was thinking. "Besides, I'm going to be immortal. That's not such a bad thing, right?"

John actually laughed. Straightening, he backed away. "Right."

Jenna couldn't seem to wrap her mind around it. She could potentially live forever. Forever young. Forever strong. Perhaps with Richart?

How often had he told her that he loved her? Did forever with her sound good to him?

His smile said it did.

"Does this mean Mom is going to be hunting vampires?" John asked.

Sheesh. She hadn't even thought of that.

Richart shifted uneasily. "Probably. The way things have

been going lately . . . I would be very surprised if Seth didn't
want you to train and fight alongside the rest of us."

"You don't look happy about that," she said, unable to
imagine it herself.

"Times are more dangerous than ever. I don't want you to
get hurt. I'll speak with Seth and obtain permission to train
you myself. Perhaps by the time you're ready we will have
eliminated this latest threat."

"My mom, the vampire hunter," John said with a grin.
"That. Is. *Awesome!*"

Jenna laughed.

"It pays *very* well, too," Dr. Lipton said as she returned.
"Roland is on his way."

"Good."

"You know you're going to have a fight on your hands,
right?"

"You didn't tell him why I wanted him to come?"

"No. I just said you needed him. He thinks you've been
injured."

Roland, nearly a millennium old, was a powerful healer.
And notoriously antisocial when it came to everyone but
his wife, Sarah. She alone could coax smiles and laughter
from him.

While they waited for Roland to arrive, Richart and Dr.
Lipton explained what Jenna could expect from the rest of her
transformation. Constant migraines. Intensifying nausea and
vomiting. A dangerously high fever. And "the worst freaking
toothache of your life," as Dr. Lipton put it. Richart had forgotten that part. His own transformation had taken place so
long ago, he had difficulty remembering the details.

The door slammed open and Roland Warbrook strolled in,
Sarah at his side. Both wore the standard hunting garb of
immortals and were splattered with blood.

"What happened?" Roland demanded, scowl in place, his

usual dour appearance hampered by the fact that he held
Sarah's hand and tenderly stroked the back of it with his thumb.

A foot shorter than Roland, Sarah had no difficulty keeping up with his brisk pace and eyed Richart with concern.

Roland noted Richart's pristine appearance, took in Jenna,
John, and Dr. Lipton, looked again at Jenna, and narrowed his
eyes. Drawing in a deep breath, he held it, then glared at
Richart. "Oh, hell no. You did *not* summon me here to transform your girlfriend."

"First, how did you know she's my girlfriend?" Richart
demanded.

"Almost every time I've seen you in recent weeks, you've
carried her scent."

Oh. Right. "How did you know I want you to transform her?"

"I can smell the virus on her."

"Wow," Jenna said, "you guys really know how to make a
girl feel self-conscious."

Sarah laughed. "It takes some getting used to, doesn't it?"

Richart shook his head. "Why couldn't *I* smell the virus
on her?"

Roland shrugged. "Her gift must dampen it. My senses are
sharper than yours and I'm a healer, so what may have escaped your notice, wouldn't escape mine. The point is moot
anyway. I'm not going to change her."

"You already know my arguments. Younger immortals are
always weaker than those who are older. Sarah is *far* stronger
than she should be because *you* transformed her. I don't know
if it's because you're older or a healer, but if you transform
Jenna—"

"Not in my job description."

Sarah stepped forward and offered her hand to Jenna.
"While they bicker, let me introduce myself. I'm Sarah
Bingham." She shook her head. "I'm sorry. I meant Sarah

Warbrook. I think this is the first time I've introduced myself since we married."

Jenna grinned. "I remember how weird it was. That's why I eventually went back to my maiden name. I just never got used to it."

"I guess it's going to take me a while, too. The big, gorgeous brooding guy is my husband Roland."

"Nice to meet you both. I'm Jenna McBride."

Roland turned a speculative gaze on Jenna. "Did you say McBride?"

"Yes."

"Originally from Virginia?"

"Yes."

"Are you by any chance related to Brian Tiernan McBride?"

"My paternal grandfather's name was Brian McBride, but I don't remember his middle name."

Roland studied her a long moment. "I'll do it."

Richart gaped. "You will?"

"Yes."

"Why?"

He shrugged. "She's my descendent."

Sarah's eyes widened as she turned to gaze up at him. "Sweetie! That's wonderful!"

Richart stared at him. "Jenna is related to you?"

Jenna started to smile, then noticed the no-doubt horrified expression overtaking Richart's face. "Is that not a good thing?" she asked hesitantly.

All Richart could say was, "*Chier.*"

"Exactly." Roland donned an evil smile. "Make her happy or I'll kick your arse."

He could do it, too.

"So." Roland turned to Jenna. "Are we going to do this now or what?"

She swallowed hard. "Now as in right now?"

Shaking off his dismay, Richart cupped Jenna's face in his hands. "I know you're probably nervous."

"That's an understatement."

"But I'll be right here with you the whole time. Once Roland has infused you with his blood, I'll take you and John to David's home. He's one of our elders and a very powerful healer. More powerful even than Roland, so he can help you through the transformation. Two, three days from now, you'll be healthier than you've ever been. You'll be stronger. Faster. And you'll be able to kick my ass if I ever piss you off."

"Cool," John put in.

Jenna smiled bravely. "All right. Let's do this."

Richart lifted her onto the exam table and, cupping a hand behind her neck, gently eased her back.

Roland approached the other side of the table and took her hand, raising her arm until the bend of her elbow hovered beneath his chin.

Richart took Jenna's free hand and held it to his chest.

Her nervous gaze went to Roland. "I'm not going to want to jump your bones or anything when you bite me, am I?"

Damned if the taciturn immortal didn't laugh. "No. You may want to jump Richart's though, so, John, beware."

John shifted uneasily. "Is this going to get weird? Like kinky weird? Because—"

"No," Richart assured him. "At most, Jenna will say things she ordinarily wouldn't say unless she were drunk. You might want to step outside, though, so she won't feel embarrassed later."

"Okay." He leaned over and kissed Jenna's cheek. "Love you, Mom."

She smiled. "I love you, too. Don't worry, honey. I'll be okay."

As soon as John left, Roland bent his head and sank his fangs into Jenna's arm.

* * *

Jenna panted as she slumped back against the pillows. "Immortal sex is the best sex ever," she proclaimed breathlessly.

Settling beside her, Richart grinned. "Like it, do you?"

She laughed. "Are you kidding? I could do this all day."

"We *have* been doing it all day. The sun is setting."

She glanced at the clock with surprise. "It is?"

A week had passed since her transformation, which had been pretty miserable. Fortunately, she remembered very little of it beyond Richart's being there for her through it all.

"We'd better get ready." There was no disguising her reluctance. They had spent one week of pure ecstasy together. No work for her since she quit her job. No hunting for Richart, Seth having given him a few days off to help Jenna adapt to the changes. No stress or strife. Just hours spent in bed or out of bed, making love and talking and learning even more about each other than they had already known.

She hated to see it end, but John had invited his study group over to the apartment tonight and Jenna intended to capture the vampire who had infected her.

Her stomach gave a nervous flutter.

She had never physically fought anyone before . . . aside from the night Richart had rescued her from the vampires, but she didn't remember that.

Richart seemed confident that, even with no combat training, she could easily subdue the vampire if he did as hoped and snuck into her bedroom to feed from her once more. She wouldn't have even *begun* to believe such was possible if she hadn't grown more bold than she had ever been in bed last night and overpowered Richart, holding him down and . . .

"You're blushing," Richart drawled with amusement. "What are you thinking?"

"That I've never been so . . . aggressive before," she admitted.

"Lucky me." He stole a quick kiss.

"You really don't mind?"

He laughed. "Are you kidding? Just thinking about it makes me hard again."

Smiling, she sat up and faced him. "But . . . you don't mind that I'm stronger than you now?" He had been right. She didn't know if it was because Roland was several hundred years older than Richart or because he was a healer, but his transforming her had left her stronger and faster than Richart.

He sat up beside her and stroked her hair. "No, I want you to be safe. The stronger and faster you are, the better. Your being able to overpower me would only trouble me if you made me do something I didn't want to do." He leaned in close and rubbed noses with her. "And everything you did to me, everything you *made* me do last night, I thoroughly enjoyed."

She pressed her lips to his. "I love you."

"And I adore you. Now let's go kick some vampire ass."

The biggest impediment they ran into that night ended up being John.

"I appreciate your anger," Richart told him for the dozenth time, "but you must behave as though you know nothing of the vampire's nefarious deeds."

"I don't understand why we couldn't just invite the ones I suspect and kick their asses until one confessed."

Richart sighed. John had narrowed it down to two men he thought were the likeliest candidates, but really it could be *any* of them. "John, just do as we've asked," he advised. "Behave as you normally would. No scowls or confrontations. And let your mother and me deal with this."

When John opened his mouth to object . . . again . . . Richart held up a hand. "I know your every instinct tells you to protect your mother, but she can pick you up and toss you through that wall over there with very little effort now."

John eyed his mother skeptically.

Jenna raised an eyebrow. "Want a demonstration?"

He cracked a smile. "No, ma'am."

She winked.

"I guess it's a good thing you couldn't do that back when I was in high school and broke curfew."

"I would have been seriously tempted."

At last, John laughed and relaxed a bit. "Okay. I get it. I'll stay out of it and let things play out the way you want them to."

Richart clapped him on the back. "Excellent." He motioned to the hallway. "Shall we, my love?"

The study group arrived. Jenna did her mother thing, asking if they liked their new classes, offering snacks and drinks, then said she was heading for bed.

*Good night*s trailed down the hallway after her as she entered her bedroom and swung the door until it was almost, but not quite, closed, leaving a little strip of light to illuminate her path to the bed.

Across the room, a shadow among shadows, Richart winked at her as she drew back the covers, climbed in fully clothed, then tugged them up to her neck. Quiet enfolded them, broken only by the mumbling of chemistry mumbo jumbo in the living room.

Richart's heartbeat slowed until even Jenna had difficulty detecting it. But his scent lingered.

Won't he smell you? she had asked, thinking it a dead giveaway, but Richart had shaken his head.

John has mentioned you're seeing someone. He'll just assume we slept together earlier and my scent lingers on you.

Why that had made her flush, she didn't know.

Minutes passed. An hour. Finally someone mentioned using the bathroom and strode up the hallway. A click sounded as light brightened the hallway. The bathroom door closed, darkening it once more.

Footsteps, light enough to escape mortal detection, approached. The bedroom door swung open and closed so swiftly she almost missed it. A tall form approached the bed.

Jenna concentrated on keeping her heartbeat steady, her breath even. Not an easy task. She was nervous as hell.

The vampire leaned down over the bed. His eyes acquired an emerald glow as he drew closer to her. Through her lashes, she saw his lips part, watched his fangs descend. He reached for the covers and drew them down to bare her throat.

Jenna struck. Grabbing the vampire by the throat, she cut off the yelp of surprise he tried to emit, tossed him onto his back on the floor, and held him down.

Eyes wide, he struggled to peel her fingers away and bucked to try to dislodge her as she shoved her knee in his belly and held him down.

Holy crap. It really *was* easy. The strength and power she wielded was as exhilarating as a drug, eradicating her fear.

Richart stepped up beside her.

The vamp struggled even harder.

Smiling darkly, Richart touched Jenna's shoulder and took them to a clearing not far from his home.

Jenna released her captive and rose.

The vampire scuttled backward like a crab until several yards separated them. Rising, he rubbed his neck and looked around with wild eyes.

"You've just experienced how powerful she is," Richart warned. "She'll catch you if you run."

The vampire blurred as he lunged toward the trees.

Jenna beat him there.

Skidding to a halt, he darted in another direction.

Jenna blocked his way.

"What do you want?" he blurted, expression hostile.

He couldn't be more than twenty years old, stood about five foot nine or so, and had a lean build.

"The lady has a question for you," Richart answered. "I, personally, want to draw and quarter you." He met Jenna's gaze. "He's the one who got away the night you were attacked."

"Bullshit! I didn't do anything!"

Richart's face darkened. His eyes shone like spotlights as his lips peeled back in a snarl of rage, displaying his fangs. "*You infected her!*" he roared.

Jenna's eyes widened. Richart was *pissed!*

"You knew her from John's study group and led your vampire friends to her, knowing they would kill her. When that didn't pan out, you fed from her while she slept! You preyed upon her when she was most vulnerable after she *welcomed you into her home!*"

The vampire backed away. "Fuck you!"

Jenna stepped forward. "Is that all you did?"

"What?"

"Is that all you did to me when you crept into my room and fed from me?"

Richart took a step toward him. "Answer the question. Did you touch her while you fed from her? *After* you fed from her?"

Jenna had been tormented by the knowledge that he might have.

"Fuck no!" the vamp nearly shouted. "She's old enough to be my mother!"

Well, damn. He made it sound like he was afraid she'd give him the clap or something.

Richart took another menacing step forward.

The vampire skittered to the side, farther away from him. "Wait. You're the Immortal Guardian who rescued her!" He drew a knife and settled into a crouch.

Jenna drew the pair of daggers Richart had given her earlier.

Richart drew his own. "Express a little remorse and I'll consider letting you live."

"Bullshit."

"Some of your brethren have already joined us. You can, too, if you regret harming her."

"Eat shit!" Darting to the side, the vampire swept past Richart and attacked Jenna.

Heart stopping, Jenna raised her daggers and fended off his every blow. The vampire seemed as untrained in battle as she was, swinging wildly with the desperate fury of a child taunted too many times by a bully, but hatred soon stole into his twisted features as a mad glint entered his eyes.

She deflected his blade with her own. His fist she blocked and countered with her own, fingers still curled around the hilts of her weapons, until . . .

A miscalculation.

One of her blades slid across his throat.

Warm blood slapped her in the face as the vampire stumbled backward, his gray shirt turning crimson.

Horrified, Jenna took a step toward him.

He sank to the ground.

Richart appeared at her side and took her arm to prevent her from continuing forward.

Sure enough, the vamp swung his blade again and again until he couldn't anymore.

Jenna looked up at Richart. "It was an accident."

"It was inevitable," he said softly. Withdrawing a handkerchief, he wiped her face with care. "You saw it—the madness that entered his eyes as you fought?"

She nodded.

"The brain damage was progressing more swiftly in him. Had we let him live, simply feeding from his victims would not have satisfied him much longer. He would have tortured them, killed them, and seen nothing wrong with it just as he saw nothing wrong with preying upon you or allowing his friends to kill you, as they would have had I not intervened."

Jenna's gaze went to the vampire, who stopped breathing and began to shrivel up like a mummy as the virus he housed devoured him from the inside out. "This is what it's like? This is what you do?"

"Yes. I know it seems brutal, but we save lives, Jenna. *You* saved lives. And you kept him from becoming a monster. Even good men become fiends once the madness seizes them. Most, when lucid, would much prefer the end you just delivered to harming others."

Dropping the daggers, she leaned into him. "I don't know if I can get used to this."

"I won't lie. It's difficult. But once you see what they do to their victims, it will become a little easier." He cupped her face in his hands, urging her to look up at him. "And I will be with you all the way." He smoothed his thumbs across her cheeks. "I'll be with you always, if you'll let me."

She summoned a smile. "Always sounds good."

He lowered his lips to hers for a slow kiss. "Let's go show John you're okay. You can tell the study group the vamp has become ill and is still in the bathroom, then send them home."

When she nodded, Richart wrapped his arms around her and the world dissolved.

High Stakes

Hannah Jayne

Some people were meant for big cities.

And fabulousness.

I'm one of those people.

I'm Nina LaShay and one day, my brand will be everywhere.

I stand in front of the mirror every day and say that to my reflection. Well, not so much to my reflection as to the mirrored image of my brand-new, temporary Manhattan digs as I don't have much of a reflection—or any reflection at all.

Being undead will do that to you.

Call me what you want—vampire. Bloodless one. Nightwalker; lost one; soulless, Godless aboveground hell dweller. Personally, I'm partial to Life-Backward, Fashion-Forward Temple of Awesome. How else do you explain a twenty-one-year-old (give or take 141 years) woman being one of the last three standing in the greatest fashion competition the couture world has ever seen?

I was steaming my latest Drop Dead creation—that's the name of my fashion line—Drop Dead Clothing (I know, totes adorbs, right?), when the faint scent of two-day-old patchouli oil and sweat snaked into my apartment. The whole supervamp sense of smell? Makes pastries smell a thousand times more amazing. It also makes the modern street hippie "at one with the Earth" smell like a three-day bus ride through Calcutta in June. I wrinkled my nose and did my best to breathe through my mouth before I snatched open the multi-bolted door and grimaced—then snarled—when I saw where the pungent scent was coming from.

It was her.

Emerson Hawk.

With her beady brown eyes, gaunt cheeks, and head of Supercuts-styled straw-colored locks, she looked far more drowned pigeon than hawk, but what can you do?

She gasped when she saw me, her anemic lips dropping open.

"*You're* my competition?"

I wanted to say something scathing and smart but decided to err on the side of breather-approved sportsmanlike conduct. "And I suppose that means that you're mine."

Emerson cocked her head and swooshed her ugly hair over one shoulder. "I was being facetious, sweetie. You and your welcome-to-the-dark-side designs are no kind of competition at all."

I felt myself bristle and although Emerson is shamefully, one-hundred-percent flesh-and-blood human being ("breathers" as they're known on the undead end), I desperately wanted to stake her through her patchouli-scented heart.

"Please," I said, crossing my arms in front of my chest. "Drop Dead has spanked—what is it? Tweet by Emerson Hawk?"

"Soar," she corrected with a snarl. "Soar by Emerson Hawk."

"Oh, right. Either way, Drop Dead has spanked your line often and repeatedly." I smiled sweetly, my lips pressed together—not so much in an effort to hide my always-there pointed petite incisors, but more in an effort to keep my fangs from digging into her obnoxious sallow flesh.

But I bet she'd taste like stale bread.

Emerson waved at the air like I was some gnat at her ear. "Small-town shit."

"San Francisco Fashion Week is not small-town shit."

"Emerson?" A head popped out from the door behind Emerson, and Emerson bristled.

"What do you need, Nicolette?" she asked from between gritted teeth.

Nicolette blushed a fierce red and glanced quickly at me and then directly to the stained carpet at her feet. But in that fleeting glance, I noticed that Nicolette shared Emerson's unfortunately beady eyes and sharp, defined cheekbones, though she had clearly gotten the luxe end of the stick when it came to hair. Hers was cut in a cheeky bob and glistened a pretty blond. "I have all the garments steamed if you want to take a look."

"Hi," I said casually, "who are you?"

"She's my sister," Emerson snapped. "And Nicolette, even you can't mess up steam. There are a few more things in the bathroom, though."

"Sisters?" I said. "How very *Little House on the Prairie*."

Even with her face turned toward the floor, I could see Nicolette's cheeks push up into a smile. "I'm Nina, by the way." I pushed out a hand and Nicolette shook; the female equivalent of crossing enemy lines. I could practically see the steam shooting from Emerson's ears and it gave me a happy.

"Your sister was telling me all about her cute little fashion line."

"Cute? Apparently you forgot who spanked who in Seattle?"

"It's whom. Who spanked whom. And of course I didn't forget. I generally find it hard to forget when someone steals my designs," I said.

"Steals? I prefer to call it 'borrowed inspiration.'"

"I prefer to call it a death wish."

"Um," Nicolette said, her voice soft as she addressed the floor. "Isn't there a third person in the competition?"

Emerson rested her fists on her love handles and threw back her head, looking like a stupid statue of some sort of conqueror. "There is a third person, but he's hardly part of the competition."

"He?" I hated being caught unawares, but I hadn't read my welcome packet (hello? I'm in New York. Is someone seriously expecting me to *read?*) and didn't know who was behind door number three.

Emerson jerked a thumb in the vague direction of the hallway. "Reg."

"Reginald Fairfield?" I gaped.

Reginald Fairfield was the Queen Elizabeth of the up-and-coming fashion world: regal, benign, and basically a figurehead who kept plaid walking shorts and seersucker fabrics alive and kicking. Every one of his lines was crisp and came in shades of Martha's-Vineyard-slash-old money, and the rumor around town was the man himself had never actually wielded a pair of scissors—he left the dirty work to his "traveling companion," an exceptionally well-tanned young gentleman with a heavy accent and a resumé that I am completely sure contained the words "cabana boy."

"They moved in about a week early."

I nodded. "I suppose it would take some time for Reginald to unpack his marble busts and Felipe's Speedos."

Nicolette sniggered behind her hand and Emerson went from remotely tolerable back to grade-A horrible. "Didn't you have some fabric to steam?"

Nicolette scampered away like a sad little pup and Emerson turned her eyes—and her stench—back to me.

"Look LaShay, you and I both know that this competition boils down to only two people: you and me."

I pursed my lips. "So you admit I'm competition."

Emerson just rolled her eyes and continued. "Your designs may have impressed a few lesser judges and"—she made air quotes—"spanked mine, but this time, make no mistake. I. Will. Bury. You."

I cocked an eyebrow, not the least bit bothered by Emerson's attempt at threatening me. "Don't you mean your designs will bury mine?"

She smiled this time, poking the edge of her tongue out to moisten her bottom lip as she shrugged. "Semantics."

I stood in the hallway, staring, as she slammed the door.

It was the next morning and being a vampire with no need of sleep, I spent the midnight hours checking out the town, frowning at the all beautiful clothes locked behind plate glass and CLOSED signs, and ultimately decimating two more blood bags than I needed to while watching Susan Lucci hock obscene-looking Pilates equipment and god-awful jewelry. When the sun finally began to peek through my drawn blinds, I gathered up my wares—rolls of gorgeous, plush fabric that was hand-sewn decades before the word *vintage* was coined (one of the huge benefits of having a shopping habit that spanned centuries rather than seasons), spun gold thread, bugle beads, and my absolute favorite, number-one must have: a good pair of scissors. I rolled the pair I had across my palm, enjoying their heft, the Swarovski-crusted handle, the ultrasharp blades, and the swirled-letter engraving there: *Not friend, sister. Love always, Sophie.*

It gave me a little pang when I ran my fingers over the words. Sophie Lawson is my San Francisco roommate and though so fashion-challenged it's terminal, she means the world to me. In my afterlife I tried hard to never let anything get to me, never let anything attach, but Sophie did both of those things. Besides, her constant bad body luck (the dead were constantly dropping out of the woodwork when she was around) kept me really entertained.

Good entertainment means a lot when you've been around for every movie from *The Horse in Motion* to *Spiderman* (all iterations).

My hand was hovering over the phone when I heard the *thunk-thunk-thunk* of someone beating the walls in the hallway, then a low, enraged voice echoing through the hundred-year-old architecture.

"I'm know you're in there! Get out here!"

I poked my head out into the hallway and groaned when I saw that the burly, angry voice was coming from Emerson, and the *thunk-thunk-thunk*ing from her clodhopper shoe as she kicked my next-door neighbor's door.

"What the hell is your problem, Emerson? You're going to wake up the entire borough!"

Emerson turned to me, nostrils flaring, eyes spitting fire. "It's Reginald Fairfield. I know he's in there," she said, turning her back to the still-closed door. "I know you're in there!" She gave the door another wallop—this time with her fisted hand—then a few more swift kicks before I grabbed her around the waist, yanking her back.

"Why are you beating on his door like a maniac?"

"A maniac? A maniac?" She wriggled out of my bear hold. "You were probably in on it! You probably let him into my apartment!"

"I have no idea what you're talking about."

"Reginald stole my fabric. The whole bolt! All of it!" She was flailing but hitting nothing, and sweat beaded on her upper lip and at her hairline, matting down her blunt-cut bangs. "He's a cheat! And now he's hiding out. He won't even open the door, the coward." She launched herself at the door. "You're a coward, Reginald!"

"*Dios mio!* Ladies, ladies, what is going on here?"

We both blinked at Felipe, Reginald's paramour, as he stood in the hallway, tanned legs exposed in his plaid walking shorts, muscles flexed as he carried two stuffed grocery bags against his chest.

A new rage roiled through Emerson's body, the heat coming off her in waves. I held my nose and wrapped an arm around her before she lunged at Felipe.

"Nice to see you again, Felipe," I said, doing my best to secure Emerson but avoid her stink. "Emerson is under the impression that Reginald stole some fabric from her."

"It's not an impression!" Emerson screeched.

Felipe just shook his head and clucked his tongue, unaffected. "My Reginald would do nothing of the sort," he said in his heavily accented English. "Besides," he continued, his dark eyes taking in Emerson and her cardboard-colored dress, "Reggie would not use your fabrics. They are so . . ." He let the word trail off, the disgust on his face finishing his sentence.

"He didn't steal it to use it, he stole it to fuck me up!"

"How do you know that Reginald was the one who stole your fabric?" I asked Emerson.

She gritted her teeth and spat through them. "He came over last night. Both of them did. We had a glass of wine, and Reginald was touching the fabric, admiring it."

"He was just trying to be nice," Felipe clarified, shifting his shopping bags.

"I got sleepy. They must have drugged me. I fell asleep—probably didn't even lock the door after they left. And when I woke up—gone! The *whole bolt*. And now the damn coward won't even open up the door and confront me."

"Pshhh!" Felipe let out a dismissing puff of air. "Reggie is just a hard sleeper." He handed me a bag and plugged his key into the lock. "Reggie," he sang as we trailed behind.

I heard the bag clatter to the hardwood floor first, a jar of marinated mushrooms shattering, the oil oozing toward my shoes. Then I heard Felipe, heard the air squeeze out of his lungs. I didn't have to see his face to know that it was twisted in horror, and as pearl white as mine.

"Oh! Oh!" He clutched his chest and I set my bag down, then gently pushed him aside. And if I hadn't seen it before, I would have screamed, too.

A body. Reginald.

A loop of fabric was wrapped around his neck, pinching tight as he hung from the rafter. His head lolled forward as if he had just fallen asleep. But his eyes were open, bulging. They were already clouded and dull. His skin was mottled purple and he swayed an inch this way, an inch that way, his shoes scraping across the glossy finish of the cherry-wood table underneath him. Each time his body moved, the rafter he was tied to groaned. The scrape of his feet and the groan of the rafter seemed like the only sounds in the entire world and I remembered, far before I was turned, my father sitting with me as a child while I held my grandmother's hand. She lay in bed, wilted, her body ravaged by sickness.

"She's gone now," my father said as his hand glided over her eyes.

I squeezed my grandmother's hand, unwilling to believe, even as sadness locked in my throat. "But how do you know?"

There had been no change in my grandmother from this moment to the last. Not a final word, a sigh—not even a flicker of her soul as it passed through her body.

"The silence," my father said simply, standing. "It's dead silence."

That was what surrounded us now in Reginald's apartment—dead silence, punctuated only by the scrape and groan.

And then the living came through.

"Oh, Reggie!" Felipe slapped his hands to his cheeks and

started to scream—a high-pitched, painful wail, tears welling and rolling over his manicured fingers.

"Oh, God," I whispered.

"That's my fabric!" Emerson's voice was a shrill knife cutting through Felipe's anguish and my own astonishment as I tried to tear my eyes from Reginald. Emerson shoved me aside, pointing to the ragged-edge loops around Reginald's neck. "*That's* why he stole my bolt?"

It actually was god-awful fabric, even for a suicide.

Felipe heaved and began clawing at the table, his clawed hands going for Reginald's pant legs as I tried to hold him back.

"Emerson," I snapped, "forget about the fabric and call nine-one-one."

I held on to Felipe and he crushed against me, finally giving up, crying silently. I could feel his warmth, the thud of his heart—and I couldn't look at Reginald anymore. He wasn't just a dead breather. He had been loved.

Emerson was on her cell phone; I could hear her voice, calm and rigid as she talked to the nine-one-one operator.

"Suicide . . . hanging . . . already dead." She was shielding the phone with her hand, her back toward the body. She looked over her shoulder once or twice and mumbled into the phone.

"We have to get him down!" Felipe sobbed, tearing away from me. "We can't just leave him there, hanging like that."

"No," I said, grabbing a handful of his shirt, yanking him backward. "We have to leave him, Felipe. The police will handle this." Back in San Francisco, I had tried to pull my roommate away from enough *CSI* marathons to be pretty familiar with police procedurals.

"We're going to call the police? But why?"

"They're already on their way," Emerson said, waggling her cell phone as if that explained it all.

"Holy fuck."

It could have been the slow motion of the whole situation but the two-word sentence sounded like a full monologue. My head snapped to where the deep voice was coming from. It was my direct intent to rip his throat out for interrupting this horrific moment, but when I saw him, the death scene in front of me faded into oblivion and my entire body went rigid, colder than normal, and on complete and utter I-want-to-eat-him-in-a-nonvampiric-way high alert.

He was handsome in that traffic-stopping kind of way, with brown-black hair that was just slightly shaggy and unkempt. The wave of his bangs licked over his eyebrows and framed chocolate-brown eyes that I would happily drown in. His skin was the most delicious shade of non-New York, non-vampire toasty brown, and, I happily noticed, he had the kind of body that made one think of Greek gods or jungle men in loincloths. He had a tribal tattoo running down the length of his well-muscled arm and though I had never been interested in them before, I was suddenly, wholeheartedly pro-ink.

Even from this distance, I could smell the salty, toasted coconut scent that wafted from his skin.

I was actually salivating.

Though it almost physically hurt to tear my eyes from him I did—just for a millisecond—to glance at Emerson. She had gone from open-mouthed stare to stone still, feet akimbo, hands on hips. Her eyes were hard, narrow slits spitting dagger glares toward the man I intended to spend the rest of my afterlife with.

"What the hell are you doing here, Pike?" she spat.

Pike, Pike! She knew his name! Images of harp-strumming cherubs and Vera Wang floated in my mind while his name pinged around my head like the heavenly music it was. *Pi-i-i-i-i-k-e . . .*

And then it stopped.

How did Emerson Hawk, of utter stink and stolen designs

know my new beau, Pike? Which is actually kind of a stupid name (unless you're a fish, *natch*) but still, it should never have been able to come out of Emerson's halitosis-filled mouth.

Pike held up an expensive looking camera. "Photo essay for the contest. But . . ."

Emerson pointed. "Reginald Fairfield."

"I was supposed to shoot the three finalists."

Emerson cocked out a hip, still pointing. "Meet finalist number three. A photo shoot is not going to happen." Her voice was remarkably unaffected and I cringed. Maybe I wasn't the only one without a soul.

"Is something going to be done about—"

But his deep voice was cut off by the wail of sirens and the marching band-like clatter of police officers as they thundered into the building. They spread out, corralling us as crime scene techs surrounded the body and studied the scene.

"We're going to need to clear the premises." The police officer didn't look at us as he said it, but no one dared challenge him. "But don't go far. We need to take statements."

Emerson, Felipe, Pike, and I stumbled out into the hallway, keeping our distance from the flurry of activity flowing in and out of Reginald's apartment. Felipe was quiet, nose a heady red, cheeks chapped from the constant flow of tears. I patted his shoulder awkwardly. He sniffled and shook like a wet Chihuahua.

"I'm really sorry, man," Pike said slowly.

Felipe continued to stare straight ahead, teeth chattering, but otherwise catatonic.

I heard Pike suck in a sharp breath and jam his hands in his pockets. As a dead man was hanging not thirty feet away, I shouldn't have noticed the way that motion—hands in pockets—pulled Pike's jeans just a little tighter over his ass, exposing his perfect, peach-shaped bottom, but I did.

I remembered the sweet, juicy taste of peaches and licked my lips, savoring the memory on my tongue.

Then Pike turned those mesmerizing cozy brown eyes of his on me. "I don't think we've met yet. You must be Nina, right? I'm Pike." He held a hand out—a big, wonderful hand that made me think of the old adage about big hands and feet—and I slipped my hand into his feeling dainty and demure—which was refreshing when I'm most often referred to as any variant of "soulless bloodsucker."

I brushed my long, black hair over one shoulder and pulled back my shoulders—or stuck out my breasts, depending on how you looked at it—and pasted on my most beguiling smile. I may be a little short in the soul/life department, but when it came to flirting, I was a star student and Pike warmed to my gaze.

"Yes, I'm Nina LaShay. And this," I said, touching Felipe lightly on the shoulder. "This is Felipe. He is—was . . ." I choked on the word and Felipe's eyes went round and heart-breakingly big. "He was with Reginald."

"*Dios mio!*" Felipe started again, huffing and tearing at his hair. "*Mi osito de peluche es muerte! Muerte!*"

One of the paramedics came toward us and snaked an arm around Felipe, talking in a low, soothing voice and leading him away.

Pike shook his head. "Poor guy."

There was an uncomfortable pause and I briefly thought of Googling "How to flirt at a murder scene." I decided to go with the tried and true.

"So you're—Pike?" I could feel my eyebrows scrunching together unattractively and Pike offered a small smile, his eyes completely transfixed on mine. It was like we were speaking our own incredibly sexy language.

I had every intention of making that language clothing optional.

"It's short for Paikea."

Well sure, that was better.

"It's Maori, but I'm actually Hawaiian."

I was thinking of my Pike, greased up in suntan oil and smelling like coconuts.

"You have quite a strong grip, don't you?"

I snatched my hand back, embarrassed, wishing for once that I had an ounce of blood to wash a cute crimson blush across my cheeks. Instead I just smiled demurely, glancing at my soulmate through lowered lashes.

"You could probably get out of here, Pike. There's not going to be any photo shoot. At least I'm not doing one." Emerson turned on her heel and disappeared into her apartment, slamming the door behind her.

"Ah, Emerson," Pike said. "A regular breath of vile air."

He leaned back against the wall, looking very Diesel-commercial chic. His eyes went over my head, scanning the activity in Reginald's apartment, and I took a quick moment to revel, taking in every inch of this man who should have been a calendar model.

For every month of the year.

I swallowed back the inappropriate desire to engage him in some sultry dirty talk and instead leaned against the wall across from him. I was about to open my mouth, was working up the perfect post-suicide sentence when Pike hitched his shoulder at me and silently walked away.

I fought the urge to growl and then the urge to crawl under my bed and hide. I wasn't used to people walking away from me—especially not male people. I was working up a reason to follow Pike when Emerson stopped behind me, close enough that her patchouli scent wafted off her and stuck to me. I grimaced, then immediately pasted on an appropriately demure smile.

"This is awful, isn't it?"

She actually shrugged. "Hate to speak ill of the dead, but

the coward was obviously too scared to show his face after he stole my fabric."

My voice was a hissing whisper. "Are you kidding me? A man is dead, and you're still focused on your fabric? God, even Pike," I said, jutting my chin toward him, desperate to feel his name on my tongue again. "A complete stranger feels more for Reginald than you do."

Emerson shook her head, that gnat-in-her-ear expression on her face. "Pike is no stranger." She waved her hand in his general direction. "He's an ex."

I hoped to God that Emerson meant an ex to Reginald or Felipe because even finding out that the love of my life was gay was preferable to finding out that he may have once been attracted to someone like Emerson. "He hangs around a lot. Kind of can't get the message."

I felt my mouth drop wide open. By the pleased purse on Emerson's lips, I could tell that she knew she'd hit a nerve. She looked about to say something smart but was silenced by an officer carrying a Ziploc bag stuffed with hideous fabric.

Emerson made a tiny puppy sound, then shoved me out of the way. "Where are you taking that? *That* is my fabric!" she yelled. "I told you he stole it." She snatched the whole bag out of the officer's gloved hand and gaped. "It's ruined!"

The officer snatched the bag back. "It's evidence."

"Evidence?" Emerson said. "But it's mine. I need it for the competition!"

Pike came over to us, getting in front of Emerson and letting the cop scurry away. "Reginald used that fabric to hang himself."

"Oh, my God," I whispered.

"Did he use it all? Do I have enough for my garment?"

I swung my head toward Emerson, astonished. "That's what you're worried about? Your stupid fabric?"

"We're in a competition, Nina, or have you forgotten?"

"We're at the scene of a suicide!" Part of me wanted to give Emerson's neck a little slash just to see what kind of demon *she* was. But I could hear her breath, hear the blood pumping from her heart and pulsing through her human veins. My stomach turned in on itself knowing that someone still in possession of her soul could be so callous. "A man is dead."

"Can you ask someone about the extra fabric?" she asked Pike.

"I'm just a photographer, but I can ask one of the cops. . . ." he said, though clearly uncomfortable as he stepped back.

"I cannot believe you, Emerson. I knew you were a snake but I didn't peg you for completely heartless. Reginald is dead."

"And I'm sorry for that," she said unconvincingly. "But he was still a competitor."

I thought my eyes were going to pop out of my head and for once, I couldn't think of a thing to say. That seemed to be just fine to Emerson, who shrugged again.

"And then there were two," she said before walking back toward her apartment.

I was shaking my head, still shocked, when I felt a hand on my shoulder. I turned and blinked into the slate-gray eyes of yet another police officer. This one was short and stocky, with tree-trunk legs and a little leather notebook clutched in his baseball-mitt hands. He used the tip of his Bic to scratch at his receding hairline. "Are you the one who discovered the body?"

For some reason, my voice was stuck in my throat so I nodded, dumbly.

"I just need to take a quick statement. Your name and address, please."

I must have recited everything properly because the cop seemed satisfied. He looked up from his notebook, eyes laser-focused on mine. "What was the state of the body when you first entered the premises?"

I was trying to think of a kind way to say "hanged," but nothing seemed to soften the blow. "It was, uh, deceased. Hanging. No one touched it, though."

The officer, whose name badge read Hopkins, raised his eyebrows. "It?"

"The body," I said. "Reginald. We went in with Felipe and saw him . . . there. Like that. Then . . ." I waved my hand, gesturing to the chaos.

"So, you were with the others when Felipe opened the door?"

"Yes." It was barely a whisper.

Hopkins wrote something in his little notebook and I wondered briefly why cops always seemed to repeat your answers back to you. "And the others were Felipe, Emerson, Pike, and uh, Nicolette?"

I suddenly drew a huge blank. "I think."

Hopkins raised his eyebrows.

"Yeah," I said, nodding. "I mean, yes."

Look—we have an impeccable sense of smell, super speed, and no discernible weight. Memory? Strictly breather-class. It's not good.

Hopkins cut his eyes to me, then to Felipe, who hung back in the hallway, and back to me. He chewed his bottom lip and narrowed his eyes, à la every incompetent cop I'd ever seen on TV. "What was your relationship with Mr. Fairfield?"

I swung my head. "We didn't have much of one. We were colleagues. In the fashion industry."

"So you didn't know anything about Mr. Fairfield's emotional state."

I think it is perfectly obvious that Reginald Fairfield wasn't of sound mind. No one in Easter-colored seersucker could be.

But I pegged Hopkins for more of a by-the-book kind of cop rather than a down-the-runway one. "No, I didn't."

Hopkins sucked in a long breath, then tucked his pen in his chest pocket. "It's likely we'll have some more questions for you later, okay? You'll want to stay around." He turned and disappeared into Reginald's apartment once more, and Felipe rushed toward me, a bottle of water quaking in his hands. He was no longer crying, but his body already looked ravaged from his grief. His shoulders were hunched and his eyes looked hollow and sunk into the redness around them.

"Since we're not supposed to leave, why don't you come inside, Felipe? I'm just down the hall." I looked over Felipe's shoulder and eyed Pike. "You're welcome to come inside as well, Pike." I liked the way his name sounded on my tongue and yes, I did admonish myself for thinking of Pike in my mouth while a team of police officers were cutting a dead man down next door.

I'm only vampire; so sue me.

I led Felipe into the apartment, Pike behind us. Felipe took a small sip from the water bottle and must have rehydrated. He immediately started crying again, full, body-wracking sobs while he wrung his hands and mumbled, his accent becoming thicker and more pronounced with each word. I might be without a soul but I wasn't without a heart and mine ached for him. I filled a glass of water and pushed it into Felipe's hands, then slung my arm over his shoulder and led him to the couch. He shivered under my touch.

"You're freezing."

"Circulation problem," I said automatically.

Pike took a seat on the couch and scooted over, giving Felipe room to sit. I caught Pike's hot chocolate gaze for a second and I was immediately warmed by the sweet concern in his eyes, and taken by the way his lips still looked full and tasty even when the corners turned down in a slight frown. He nodded to Felipe who crushed himself into the couch and heaved an enormous, hiccupping breath.

Through the open apartment door I could see the coroner and his assistant pushing through the crowd, could hear the squeaking wheels of the gurney as they laid Reginald out and wheeled him away. Thankfully, the din of chatter, police radios, and general city noises must have drowned out the dead sounds for Felipe because he sucked down his bottle of water and blinked repeatedly, the tears actually seeming to dry.

Officer Hopkins ambled down the hall and knocked on Emerson's door. I watched as Nicolette pulled it open, her face a yellow-hued shade of pale, her eyes small and circled by exhausted purple bags. They darted past Hopkins and took in the scene in the hall, skidded over the coroner as he pushed Reginald away. There was a slight terror in her eyes and I could see the pale edges of her lips pulled down as she murmured to Officer Hopkins. When Nicolette disappeared and Emerson took her spot, I took a step forward, my head cocked.

"Your relationship to Mr. Fairfield, miss?"

Emerson blinked quickly and even from across the hall—and by way of my super-vamp sense—I could hear her heartbeat speed up, could hear the sharpness of the shallow breath she sucked in. I crossed my arms in front of my chest, watching, as Emerson licked her lips.

"He was a designer like myself."

"And you all three live here in this complex? Is it, like, some sort of shared housing or artist co-op or something?"

I watched Emerson's head swing from side to side, her straw hair brushing her shoulders. "We're the three finalists in a design competition." She bit her bottom lip, her eyes flashing and catching mine. "Well, we were."

"So you're competitors?" Hopkins tapped the end of his pen against Emerson's doorframe, the rhythmic tap like a heartbeat. "Was there a lot of stress at this competition? Was Mr. Fairfield not doing well?"

Emerson straightened up, her hands going to the doorframe and gripping. I caught the smallest scent of sweat on the air.

Emerson was nervous.

"The competition hadn't really started yet. I don't see why Reginald would have been—would have thought he wasn't doing well. Maybe Felipe knows more." Emerson's eyes crested over Hopkins's head and she looked at me. "Or maybe Nina knows something." She glanced at her non-ironic Swatch watch and shifted her weight. "Are we through now? I've got to work on my designs."

Emerson left Hopkins standing in the doorway. He turned on his heel and we were eye to eye—me, standing in my apartment, door flung wide open, spying, and him, narrow-eyed, chewing on the end of his pen. He beckoned for me to come into the hallway.

"Can I help you?"

"Miss LaShay," he said, shifting his weight in what I was guessing he thought was some sort of imposing manner. "Is there a reason you didn't mention that you and Mr. Fairfield were direct competitors in this competition?"

I snaked my arms in front of my chest and mirrored Officer Hopkins's narrow-eyed glare. "I didn't think it was necessary information."

"Might have given someone the motive to harm Fairfield, don't you think?"

"I would think, had he not hung himself."

Hopkins shot me a slow, appraising gaze. "Just make sure you don't leave the county, all right? I might have some additional questions for you."

Something about the way Hopkins kept his watery eyes fixed on me gave me a slight chill. I had every intention of escorting him right out of my apartment until he checked his smartphone, scanned the room, and asked, "Felipe DeLaCruz?"

Felipe turned and raised a small hand. "I am Felipe."

Hopkins paused then, his flat-balloon face breaking into what passed as a smile. "Pike! Didn't expect to see you here."

Hopkins and Pike did that awkward, manly handshake-to-semi-hug kind of thing and I felt my mouth drop open. I made a beeline for them.

"You two know each other?" I hissed.

"Pike does some photography work for us on occasion." Hopkins raised his eyebrows toward Pike. "Is that why you're here now?"

"Actually, I was hired by the magazine to shoot the designers."

Hopkins's eyes showed a flash of interest. "So you knew the dec—"

I shot a glance over my shoulder and nudged Hopkins and Pike out of the living room, out of Felipe's direct line of sight.

"Can you not throw around words like *deceased* and *decedent* in front of Felipe? That man just lost the man he loved. Can't you be a little more sensitive?"

The sentence bobbed around in my head and my spine stiffened. My breather roommate was constantly telling me to "be a little more sensitive." She was usually the one inundated with dead bodies and detectives.

Guess things were starting to rub off.

Hopkins blew out a long sigh and I made a mental note to drop an inhaler off at the police station—the man obviously had breathing issues. Either that or someone along the line told him that sharp breaths were the way to throw a suspect off. I would have laughed, had I not had the sneaking suspicion that I was going to be one of his "suspects."

"Mr. DeLaCruz?" Hopkins said, edging his way back toward the living room.

I fixed him with a stare, not entirely sure what I was trying to convey. I was angry, suspicious, sad for Felipe's loss—and, strangely, a little scared.

"So you and Hopkins, huh?"

Pike broke out into a smile that looked wildly inappropriate amongst the background of crumpled tissues and crime scene techs, but it shot a bolt of fire through me just the same.

"Me and Hopkins? It's not like we were dating or anything. I just bump into him on occasion."

I nodded.

"So," Pike said as he followed me into the kitchen, inclining his head, eyes jutting to Felipe and the officer. "What do you think that's all about?"

"Probably just routine," I said, suddenly feeling the need to put space between us. "Can I get you something to eat?" I asked him, wishing to God he'd say no since the entirety of my refrigerator's contents were six O negative blood bags and sixteen varying shades of OPI nail polish.

"No, I'm cool. So what did Hopkins want with you?"

I spun, my body suddenly colder than normal. "He wanted to know what he should buy you for your birthday."

Pike scrunched his brow and I rolled my eyes.

"Hopkins didn't want anything with me."

Pike gestured toward the hall. "You guys were talking for quite a while."

I pinched my bottom lip, scanning Pike from tip to tail. He was gorgeous, there was no doubt about that. But, could I trust him?

The last time I trusted a good-looking man, he sucked away my blood and my soul. I had learned my lesson.

"It was nothing. He just had some basic questions." I shrugged, still feeling uneasy.

I peered over Pike's shoulder to see Felipe on the couch, head in his hands, index fingers pressed against his temples.

Hopkins sat across from him, that stupid pen poised over his little leather notepad.

"No one would want to hurt my Reggie," Felipe moaned. "He was such a gentle soul."

"Why is Hopkins treating Reginald's suicide like it was a murder?" I whispered.

Pike shrugged, his gaze following mine. "Maybe there is more to it than we saw."

By the time Hopkins had grilled us all and the crime scene and cop brigade had left the building, my body was humming. I could still smell Pike in my apartment, his coconut scent just hanging in the air. But there was something else, too—and having spent enough time with it I couldn't deny it: the stench of death was heavy in the air.

I leaned against my window, watching the taxicabs honking and tourists walking on the street below, watching people going about their everyday lives in the twilight. They moved in sort of an organized chaos, completely unaware that just a few hundred feet away a life had ended and another had changed completely.

I remembered the last breath of life as it seeped out of me. My body fought to hold tight to it and I felt like my insides were burning. But the handsome stranger—his arms—were tight around me and somehow I still felt safe, willing the life to drip out of me as I licked the droplets of blood on his neck. I needed them. The thirst was overwhelming. I was changing; I was becoming someone—some*thing*—else, and all around me life went on. My parents sat in the parlor; my siblings, fast asleep in their beds. And I was outside, dying, living, changing, becoming.

An immense sadness washed over me.

I flopped onto my couch and pressed my fingertips to my temples. I didn't have a headache—it's physiologically impossible for a vampire to have a headache—but I could almost swear it was on its way.

That's why I jumped a foot and a half when the goddamn black bird that had taken up residence outside my front window started squawking like the disease-infested winged rodent that it was. I rolled last week's copy of *US Weekly* into a narrow tube, flattened myself against the wall, then slammed the magazine against the glass, willing the stupid bird to exit once and for all. I didn't have the nerve to look.

It's not that I'm afraid of birds. Hello? I'm a *vampire*. I'm afraid of nothing! Except maybe sunlight, shoulder pads, and the very real idea that neon and side ponytails are coming back into fashion. But birds? No. They just disgust me. With their beady eyes and their mean, pointy beaks, and those wings. Disease is carried on those wings, I just know it. So the fact that this, this—*monster*—had the gall to pace my windowsill on a very regular basis, squawking and clawing and generally just making a nuisance of itself, bothered me to no end.

Seriously, I was considering renting a cat.

When a good minute—a silent, non–wing-beating or squawking minute—passed, I took a two-inch step forward and peered around the window molding, an indescribable relief washing over me when all I saw beyond the clear window glass were a few cabs inching along the street and a woman berating a parking meter.

My relieved sigh curdled into a scream as that stupid bird launched itself into my line of sight, squawking and flapping like a murderous maniac, the tips of its wings tapping the glass.

I was reeling backward, vaulting toward the couch when an insistent knock at my door terrified me five times more and I felt every muscle in my body instinctively stiffen. Though my fangs are always exposed, in times of true vampdom—i.e., when an artery needs ravaging or a bartender spills something on my Manolo Blahniks—the fangs extend an extra half-inch causing that frightening

scowl you see plastered all over TV. My hackles were up and
adrenaline pulsed through me; even my hair seemed to stand
on electrified end. My every thought was savagery and a hiss
of air sliced through my teeth as I snatched open the door.

I was met with pursed lips.

And a cocked eyebrow.

And an expression completely devoid of terror or shock.

"What the hell are you doing here?"

"What? A guy can't fly across country to see his favorite
aunt?" My nephew was standing in the hallway, framed by
chintzy yellow hallway light, grinning like I had just won the
Publishers Clearing House Sweepstakes. His fangs were
small but pronounced, pinching against the edges of his upturned lips.

"I'm not your favorite aunt, I'm your only aunt." I addressed
him suspiciously and the smile fell from his face.

"So can I come in or not?"

In the Hollywood sea of vampires with horrible accents,
satchels full of graveyard dirt, and the ability to turn into
bats—there was one thing they had gotten right: a vampire
can't enter private premises without first being invited. Even
if those premises were home to another vampire. I stood aside
and opened my arms. "Vlad, you are welcome to come into
my apartment."

Vlad stepped over the threshold, arms crossed in front of
his chest. Looming at just over six feet, he looked down at me
with one of those noncommittal teenage expressions. A hint
of mischief flickered in his dark eyes and I was instantly
seized with joy and sadness. Vlad looked so much like his
mother—my sister—that it warmed me. But the feeling
almost immediately fled because I knew Sonia was dead,
would never know that her son was thriving—though
undead—or that his Aunt Nina was taking good care of him.
She also would never know that Vlad headed up the West

Coast division of VERM—the Vampire Empowerment and Restoration Movement—or dressed like a fashionably suicidal cross between Bela Lugosi and Count Chocula.

Maybe it was better that she stayed in the grave.

I jumped forward anyway, enveloping Vlad in a crisp hug. "I'm sorry. I am really happy to see you! But, really, what are you doing here?"

He stepped back in true teenage fashion as though someone would catch wind of the fact that he had shown a modicum of emotion. Vlad may be one hundred and twelve, but he was forever caught in the moody, brooding, obnoxious sentience of a sixteen year old.

And he never picked up his socks.

He threw an Army duffel onto my couch and grinned again. I could tell he just fed by the deep, ruddy pink of his lips.

"I came to visit you!"

Now I crossed my arms in front of my chest and cocked a brow. "What'd you do?"

A sweet innocence flooded over Vlad's face. "What do you mean?"

I pulled my cell phone from my jeans pocket and poised a finger over the trackpad. "You know I have Sophie on speed dial." In addition to being my roommate in San Francisco, Sophie is Vlad's partial guardian by proxy, and my very best friend.

Vlad held up a silencing hand. "Okay, okay. So, there's some talk that I may have had a tiny indiscretion with a fairy."

"Fairies are awful!" Though Walt Disney painted them with big, kind eyes and pursed pink lips, anyone who's met one will tell you that fairies—and pixies, too—are awful little buggers. Mean, sassy, stuck-up.

And some of them bite.

"So you came out here to escape your fairy lover?"

"Actually, I came out here to escape Kale. You think fairies are bad? Try a jilted teenage witch." Vlad whipped off his coat, showing off a dark strip on his pale white arm. "This just happened. She made the sun rise in our damn apartment. That bitch could have killed me!"

I slung an arm over Vlad's shoulder. "Oh, she'd never kill you. Just torture you a little. I like her. And I'm glad you're here."

Vlad tugged me close in an awkward hug. "Me, too. It'll be nice to hang here for a bit. No romantic drama, no bodies dropping from the ceiling or crime scene tape." He flopped down on the couch next to his duffel and I bit my lip, before perching next to him.

"So, it's not totally drama-free around here."

"Oh, right because of your little 'fashion war' with that guy and—what's her name? Kenmore?"

"Emerson," I corrected. "Reginald and Emerson. And the war is pretty much over."

Vlad gave me an appraising smile. "You won?"

I wrinkled my nose. "Not exactly."

He quirked a brow. "Someone drop out?"

"More like dropped dead."

"Dropped on her own or . . ." Vlad waggled his eyebrows in the universal "don't-make-me-say-it" style.

"What? Are you kidding me? I had nothing to do with it. It was right next door and it looked like suicide."

"'Looked like' suicide?"

"It's a long story."

Vlad pulled a blood bag from his duffel, pierced it with a single fang, and started to suck. He emptied the thing and burped loudly before he addressed me. "So you made it look like suicide."

I turned to look at Vlad full in the face. "Are you *seriously* asking me if I had anything to do with Reginald's death? Because I follow the strictest UDA bylaws and even if I were to stray just the slightest"—I held my thumb and forefinger a smidge apart—"tiniest bit, frankly, it wouldn't be Reginald Fairfield that I'd off. It'd be Emerson Hawk. That woman is vile."

Vlad's eyes flashed.

As if on cue, there was another insistent, thundering knock on my door. "You can stay," I told Vlad as I went to answer it. "Peace and quiet, however," I said as I snatched open the door. "Died about a week ago."

Emerson was standing in the hallway, hip out, arms crossed, beady eyes even beadier though they were rimmed with coal and something hideously sparkly. She had actually brushed her hair and it was in a semi-attractive swoop pinned at the base of her skull, and her black gown had an asymmetrical hemline that was so completely last year it was laughable. But still, the dress was impeccably tailored and the ruched drop waist was understated and elegant, wondrously hiding Emerson's usual Kentucky Fried Chicken and Yoo-hoo paunch. Nicolette was behind her, back toward me as she hunched, managing two beaded purses in one hand while she struggled to lock Emerson's door.

"Hello, Emerson."

Her eyes raked over me, her sour expression not changing. "Aren't you ready yet? Or is that what you're wearing?"

"What are you talking about? What am I wearing for what?"

Nicolette, having finally gotten the door locked, rushed to Emerson's side and handed her a heavy ecru card. My stomach sunk as I recognized it.

"The cocktail reception."

Emerson nodded.

"Someone just died. Are they actually still holding that? Only the completely heartless and macabre could think of going through with any of the competition activities right now."

"Everything was already booked. They couldn't cancel

at the last minute and Mr. Forbes said that everything would go forward as planned. Except of course, with one less fashion show."

"You talked to Mr. Forbes?"

Mr. Forbes was the head of the New York Design Institute and whether or not you knew your Vera from your Versace could be overlooked if Jason Forbes was on your side.

A sly grin rolled across her face. "We may have run into each other a time or two at this quaint little coffee bar I frequent."

I was gritting my teeth so hard I imagined them starting to powder. "You've only been in New York a week."

"Anyway, Jason"—she stressed the name—"thought that the best way to honor Reginald would be to continue on as planned. So, again, are you wearing that? As far as your designs go, it is one of your better ones."

My nostrils flared and I felt myself shrink back in my fashion-fail skinny jeans, Ugg boots, and tank top.

"Is that your date?" Emerson poked a bony finger into my apartment, aiming at Vlad.

"Nephew."

Nicolette's head peeked over Emerson's shoulder. I saw her cheeks redden when her eyes met Vlad's.

"Christ," I groaned. "I'll see you at the reception."

The door had barely slammed before Vlad was at my side, smiling and licking his lips. "Who's the girl?"

"Emerson Hawk is hardly a girl. I don't even know if she's human."

"No," Vlad groaned. "The other one."

"That's Emerson's sister and A, anyone with even an ounce of Emerson Hawk blood in her is completely and totally off limits to you and your undead little friend down there," I said as my eyes skipped over his zipper, "and B, you're on the run from one woman and you're running out of safe houses. So keep it zipped. I have a party to get ready for."

The reception for the Institute for Haute Couture was at a swanky restaurant in Chelsea with low lights, polished cement, and an open bar. It was stuffed to the gills with beautiful people in one-of-a-kind dresses, white-gloved waiters wielding untouched appetizer trays, and quite possibly every hair product in the tristate area. My town car let me out in front of the restaurant at the precise time as Emerson's let her out and even though a grimace would totally throw off the incredible vibe of my gold-threaded vintage Versace, I couldn't help it when I saw her.

Emerson strode past me, her beaded clutch almost taking me out as she did. Nicolette, hurrying behind as usual, shot me a small, apologetic smile before she yanked open the door for Emerson. They walked into the restaurant and melted into the crowd; I stepped in and there was an audible gasp.

Scanning the room, I could see why.

Aside from the waiters, the place was a morbid sea of black. Black dresses, black suits, black hair décor that masqueraded as vintage. My gold dress stood out like a shiny beacon and I smiled, accepting my glory while Emerson glowered in the crowd, her drink practically evaporating from the waves of heat that rolled off her.

The energy in the restaurant was low, most people not knowing whether they should mourn or celebrate. Half a drink in, Jason Forbes took a makeshift stage and made a touching—if quick—toast to Reginald's life and career then a muted introduction of the contest, Emerson, and me. Directly afterward, the heavy appetizers—and the murmured gossip—started. I carried around a canapé and a glass of champagne and flitted from group to group, head cocked, lips in a serene yet friendly smile, ears open.

I heard that Reginald had offed himself because Felipe was going home to a mystery wife he had back in Brazil. I heard the suicide was due to a fashion line Reginald was hired for that nosedived, taking the entire company with it. I heard that it was drugs, alcohol, carbohydrates. But when I heard that Reginald hadn't committed suicide at all, I stopped walking.

A model I knew as Bea was talking, her greasy-plate lips stained a weird glossy orange as she held court.

I edged my way in, gushed appropriately, and Bea pulled me into the conversation.

"My boyfriend," she said, flapping enormous baby-girl lashes. "He is interested in so many things, so he volunteers at the city morgue."

The woman next to me nudged me in the ribs with a bony elbow and mouthed the words "community service."

Bea shot her a death glance and kept going. "Adam had to stand by and watch the coroner start the autography."

"Autopsy," I corrected, taking a burning swallow of champagne.

"Right. They started the preliminary thing and the coroner talks into a tape recorder. Adam heard him say that the . . . the," Bea said, and made a motion around her neck. "The rings on Reginald's neck were not conducted to a death by hanging."

"They weren't conducive to a hanging?"

Bea turned her enormous eyes on me and nodded. "You heard that, too?"

I had to physically control myself from rolling my eyes.

"Anyway," Bea went on, "he said that it looked like Reginald was dead before he could hang himself."

The other women in the circle shivered appropriately but I stepped forward. "How did he die, then?"

Bea's tiny bird shoulders rose. "And did he hang himself before or after?"

I handed Bea my champagne glass and beat a hasty retreat—at least I tried to, before coming face to face with Emerson.

"Someone's in a hurry," she said, her eyes raking over me. "Need to rush off and rip a few seams?"

My one-track mind went from checking out Reginald's not-suicide to wishing Emerson was the one swinging from the rafters.

I stopped there.

"Hey, Em," I said, closing the distance between us—and thankful my gag reflex had disappeared along with my soul. "What were you doing this morning?"

She cocked an anemic eyebrow that let me know she suspected something. "I was with you."

"Before that."

She whipped away from me. "Why do you ask?"

I sized Emerson up. If Bea was right—and I couldn't put much stock in that, as she was boobs over brains—and Reginald's death wasn't a suicide, could someone like Emerson be responsible?

I shrugged. "Just curious."

Emerson crossed her arms in front of her chest—or attempted to, as her horrid interpretation of sleeves swallowed her up—and flared her nostrils. "Nicolette and I were working at the apartment."

I narrowed my eyes, trying to determine if there was something in her voice, her stare that would indicate absolute guilt. I like to think my super-vampire sense would make me particularly good at reading a breather's emotions, but no.

"Stop staring at me."

"Ms. LaShay!" I felt an arm snake through mine before

I heard Jason Forbes's deep voice—but not before I saw Emerson's face tighten, her eyes sharp as naked swords.

"I was hoping to catch you. I see you and Ms. Hawk are getting acquainted."

I put on my most dazzling smile and nodded. "We certainly are."

Jason pitched his head toward mine, his lips just brushing my ear. "I'd like to talk to you about one of your designs."

I kept grinning, enjoying Emerson's pallor.

It was at the precise moment that Jason put his hand on my arm that I saw Emerson lurch forward, in the most melodramatic fall I'd seen in lifetimes. I watched the deep, red zinfandel swish from her bowl glass, up, up, up and out, and then I felt the liquid seeping through my dress, dripping over my collarbone, droplets slipping down through my décolletage.

And then all hell broke loose.

I forgot that Jason Forbes was within wetting distance and screamed, "You bitch! You did that on purpose!"

A slick grin rushed across Emerson's lips before her expression snapped into one of mock apology and horror. "Oh, dear, oh! I'm such a klutz. Please, do send me the dry-cleaning bill."

People had started to circle now, looking sadly at my spoiled dress—few things moved fashionistas like wounded couture.

"If you were worth anything as a designer, you'd know that you don't dry-clean hand-dyed, vintage Versace."

Emerson cocked her head, a hint of a smile playing on her lips. "Are you sure that's Versace? I think you may have been taken, sweetie. I did the full Versace catalog when I was there," she said, her voice rising on *Versace*. "And I really don't recall seeing that particular number in their annals."

I'm usually known for keeping my cool. But tonight, my cool was wrapped around Emerson Hawk's scraggly neck. Before I realized it we were in a full-on girl-fight, complete

with hair pulling and feline scowls. Had my entire life and
fashion career not been on the line, I would have gone full-on
Lestat on her ass and left picking subpar designer out of my
teeth.

"I swear to God I'm going to murder you!" I growled.

"With what?" Emerson wrinkled her nose. "Your polyester
excuse for couture or one of your gag-worthy designs?"

"Ladies, ladies, ladies!"

I felt strong arms snaking around my waist and suddenly I
was off the ground, being pulled backward. I craned my neck
to see who my savior/new attackee was and harrumphed
when I realized it was Pike. I had expected Jason, but found
him standing a few feet away, grinning like someone was
about to inflate the ring and fill it with mud. I was so flabber-
gasted and annoyed that I wasn't even able to take the time
to appreciate being wrapped in Pike's arms, or how devas-
tatingly handsome he looked in a slim-fitting deconstructed
tuxedo, his hair half slicked, half I-just-rolled-out-of-
bed sexy.

He yanked me a good ten feet from Emerson and her
weapon of couture destruction but I could still see the sick
smile on her face and my rage boiled again.

"Put me down!" I said between clenched teeth. "I'm going
to rip her throat out. I don't care if she's your girlfriend."

Pike dropped me with a thump. "My girlfriend?"

I waved at the air. "Ex, whatever. She *ruined* my dress. On
purpose. She's a snarky little snake in the grass."

"Shh, shh, shh. Nina, relax. She is a—what did you call
her? Snaky snark? She's that, which is why you're not going
to let her get you tossed out of this competition."

The anger in my gut was slowly, barely, starting to pull
back. I glanced at Pike's earnest expression and then back
over my shoulder at Emerson, who was being led toward
the back patio, leaning on some poor waiter as if she'd been
actually wounded.

Three more minutes and she would have been.

The tone in the restaurant went from high piano notes and polite laughter to throaty "did you see those two go at it?" whispers and averted eyes.

Pike handed me a glass of soda water and a thick cloth napkin. I dabbed at my dress delicately, each wine-soaked dab stabbing at my patience a little more. I cut my eyes out toward the patio where someone was trying to engage Emerson in conversation, but she looked up, locked my gaze, and offered a slick, ugly smile.

"Game on, bitch," I muttered under my breath.

"What was that?" Pike asked.

"Nothing."

"So, why did you think Emerson was my girlfriend?"

I tossed down my now wine-soaked napkin, something like ruined-man resignation floating over me. "Because that's what she told me."

Pike kind of grinned and crossed his arms in front of his chest, the motion pushing aside the collar of his shirt just enough for me to see a smooth, tanned length of neck and collarbone. I could see the beginnings of a thick black tattoo and I had to clench my jaws—and my knees—to keep from examining it closer. "And did that make you mad?"

His eyes sparkled with the kind of mischief that shot adrenaline and hormones throughout my body—dead or not. I licked my lips and tossed a length of slick black hair over my shoulder. "Do you want it to make me mad?"

Pike shrugged, took a long pull on the beer I didn't know he was holding. "Nah, I just didn't want you to feel bad."

I blinked my confusion. Was he just a terrible flirt . . . or really that dense?

His eyes dropped to my dress. "You should probably get out of that dress."

Another zing pinballed throughout my body. Maybe he wasn't such a bad flirt after all.

"There's a dry cleaner about a block down. Ask for Mrs. Cho; she can get out anything." Pike turned on his heel and left me standing, wet, confused, and annoyed in the center of the party.

I left shortly after, grumbling the whole cab ride home and doing that odd, legs apart, my-dress-is-soaked-and-chafing kind of walk. All I wanted was to pull on my cozy cashmere sweat suit (terry cloth is so passé) and sink my teeth into a still-warm blood bag. And that's what I would have done, if that stupid blackbird—he was taunting me, I was sure of it— hadn't been pacing on the front stoop.

I paused and glared down at the thing, waving my hands but keeping my distance. "Shooo! Shooo! You shouldn't be walking anyway. Fly you little bastard!"

The thing paused, cocked its disease-infested head and spread its wings wide as if it understood me.

Nina LaShay: bird whisperer.

Then it snapped those wings against its little bird body and glared.

I chanced a swift kick and a sprint when a damp bugle bead started to dig into my flesh. I felt the flap of the blackbird's wings and snapped the door shut on its protesting scowl.

"I warned you!" I screamed, pressing my face up against the glass in the door. The bird fluttered down to the stoop again, unharmed but, I thought, with a murderous look in its eye.

I was going to have to hire an exterminator.

The following morning I was hell-bent on restoring my reputation or, failing that, blowing everyone on the judging panel away with my incredible designs. Which was why I was at the Fashion Institute when most breathers were pulling their pillows over their heads or indulging in their last half hour of REM sleep. Though New York was truly a city

that never slept, it did seem to take the occasional doze—
apparently between four-thirty and five A.M.—because it was
decidedly, delectably calm right up until I keyed the passcode
at the Institute. I was halfway through the four-digit super-
secret code when the front door slammed open and I went
chest to chest—then butt to cement with—

"Pike?"

He was still dressed in his cocktail-hour deconstructed
tuxedo but this morning's look was for more deconstructed
than it was tuxedo. His carefully disheveled hair was actually
disheveled and he sported a spray of dark stubble over his
upper lip and chin. He brushed a hand over the would-be
beard when he glanced down at me, his eyes wild and dis-
turbingly alive.

"Oh, Nina, my God, I'm sorry. I didn't see you there." It
came out as one long string and I avoided the hand he offered,
suddenly strangely suspicious. He may have once (yesterday)
been my gorgeous future soul mate, but he was tainted by
fashion thief Emerson, and was now running out of a building where my designs were *supposed* to be safe.

I pushed myself to standing, feeling my eyes narrow as I
scrutinized him, and saw the barely imperceptible way his
head reared back from my examination. There were no telltale bulges where he might have hidden my patterns or design
notes—and I looked carefully, examining *every* bulge.

We vampires like to be incredibly thorough. *I* like to be
incredibly thorough.

I smelled beer on Pike's morning-after breath and his
whole countenance was agitated, guarded.

"Are you high?" I asked, my arms crossing in front of
my chest.

Pike actually stopped and seemed to settle, his pale
lips quirking upward. "High? May have had a few beers to
wash down my Wheaties but nothing more. What are you
doing here?"

"I have a show to prepare for. And a passcode. How did *you* get in here? *Why* did you get in here?"

Pike's sudden coolness ticked all the way through him and he patted the black camera bag that crossed his chest. "Working. I was here working."

My eyes raked over his attire and I cocked out a hip. "You were up all night shooting designs for designers who were fast asleep in their own homes? Or, you know," I said and licked my lips, trying to conjure up the best word. "Dead?"

Pike was unfazed. He actually looked cooler than before as he eyed me. "And I'm supposed to believe you were one of those fast asleep at home?"

Truth was, I'd spent my evening starring as Roxie Hart in an off-Broadway production of *Chicago*. Well, not so much an off-Broadway production as a karaoke bar with beer-stained carpet, but this grungy photog didn't need to know that.

I just raised my eyebrows until Pike rolled his eyes. "I don't only work for the Institute, you know."

He brushed past me as though that were all the explanation I needed and even though his pain-in-the-ass quotient went up to about a thousand, I couldn't help but sneak a peek and notice that his regular ass quotient still hovered somewhere between perfection and breathtaking. I watched him hail a cab with lightning speed, the yellow thing disappearing down the street.

I rode the crotchety old elevator (what is it with breathers and their need for all things retro?) up to the design studio and felt little butterfly flaps of anxiety in my belly. I have dreamed of having my own little studio since the early 1900s—you should have seen Coco's little place in Paris!—and now, because of this design opportunity, I had it.

Well, almost.

One of the enormous benefits of this competition was that both Emerson and I were awarded top-notch design studios—

outfitted with the latest and greatest of *everything*—in which to baste, steam, slice, and create the designs for each of our competing lines.

The enormous matching drawback was that each of these incredible studios shared floor space with *each other*. I had a bank of floor-to-ceiling cabinets and hanging closets at the front end of the room; Emerson had an identical setup on her side. We each had huge drafting and cutting tables, dual sewing machines, maiden forms, and steamers. As designers, all we needed to bring were our designs, our fabric bolts, and our personal tools. Where I traveled with a lucky pair of scissors, a seam ripper called Marie Antoinette, and a pin-cushion in the shape of a mushroom, I was fairly sure that Emerson only packed a tape recorder and a notebook titled "Designs I Stole."

But it was nice this morning as the sun started to break through the heavy gray fog and the entire studio was peaceful, quiet, and Emerson-free.

I went to work outlining a new design and when the spark of inspiration slipped from the page and pointed at my rack of newly designed dresses, I couldn't help but snatch one from the rack and grab my lucky scissors.

Only, they weren't there.

I tore apart my pink-rhinestoned tool kit and then went to work opening every drawer and yanking open every closet. Finally, I dropped to my knees in a desperate hope that my lucky pair had slipped from their holster. I patted and searched until my knees felt knobby and raw—and I was facing Emerson's side of the room.

I felt my hackles go up, a hot stripe of rage going from the base of my head to the end of my spine.

She did it.

Emerson Hawk stole my lucky shears.

I heard the electric lock tumbling downstairs, the *ping!* and rush of elevators coming to life as the people started to make their way into the building.

There wasn't much time.

I sprinted the fifty feet across the room and grabbed at Emerson's drawers, tearing through them like a burglar with a serious mission. In the back of my head I heard the footsteps and early-morning chatter as students and designers closed in on our room and when I grabbed the handle of Emerson's closet door—the one marked "personal"—I was in such a fury that I didn't care as the voices closed in.

I should have.

It all happened in one elongated second—my hand closing on the knob; the voices of the contest director and models breaking over the threshold. Me pulling the closet door open. Emerson line-driving me from the darkness.

"What the—?"

"Oh, my God!"

"Are they fighting again?"

Though Emerson jumped out of her closet and pummeled me—then lay there like a dead weight—she was no match for my strength so I quickly rolled her off me, but in that millisecond my nostrils twitched and my mouth started to water. It wasn't her usual noxious scent. It was something very, very different.

Heavy. Metallic.

Blood.

I felt my mouth drop open and my eyes bulge when I stared at my blood-covered hands, at the smear across my blouse.

And then I looked at Emerson.

"Oh, my—" I started to kick away, felt the inane need to put distance between me and her.

"What's wrong with her?" one of the models asked.

"Is she okay?" Jason Forbes rushed toward me and Emerson. "Are you okay? What happened? If you ladies can't—" Jason paused, looked down at Emerson, and then crouched slowly. A chalky white washed over his face. He glanced at me and I knew exactly what the hard look in his eyes meant: Emerson Hawk was dead. When I crawled over to see for myself, I wished I was, too.

Sticking out of Emerson's concave chest were my lucky scissors. And it didn't take an X-ray to figure out that their sharp double-blades were wedged firmly and deeply into her silent heart.

From the moment Emerson's lifeless body hit mine to the second she was being zipped into a slick black coroner's bag could have been five minutes or five hours. The studio was a buzz of muffled conversations and accusatory glances. I wanted nothing more than to crawl back to the cool, dark cave of an apartment and sort out what had just happened—and what it meant. I was ready to dash when a fat, round detective sidled up to me, flipping open his little leather notebook and breathing at me with his coffee breath. I had expected Officer Hopkins, but the gentleman before me was built like a fireplug and wearing his ill-fitting cotton-poly off-the-rack suit like it was an Armani.

"I'm aware of the previous case but I'm not at liberty to talk about it." He shifted his eyes as though everyone were about to pounce in an attempt to overhear us.

"It just seems odd that they'd send a detective out for this case but not Reginald's."

"You are Nina LaShay, right?" the detective said, completely ignoring my question.

I nodded silently, my arms wrapped around my chest, gripping my elbows.

"I'm Detective Moyer. You were the last to see the decedent alive, were you not?"

"Well—no, not that I know of." An image of Pike rushing

out looking disheveled and nervous flashed through my mind, the image flitting so quickly I didn't have time to dwell on it. "I saw her last night and then," I gestured to the closet door, still gaping open, its emptiness a quiet screech that Emerson Hawk was dead.

"Then you found her this morning."

"She . . . kind of . . . found me."

"Were you and the decedent friends, Ms. LaShay?"

I wanted to focus on answering the detective's questions, but every time he asked me anything, he smacked his lips in a weird kind of final gesture and it was turning my stomach. "I wouldn't say we were friends, exactly. We were colleagues. And competitors."

If I hadn't been staring at Moyer's fat, pale lips making that stupid smacking sound, I would have thought better of telling this man—who was tapping the end of his pen, looking thoughtfully at me—that I might have had motive to kill Emerson. I thought of Hopkins and his accusatory stare and then longed for it as Moyer's eyebrows went up. He poised the pen over his notepad as though he were about to take down some frantic confession, and any inch of confidence I was harboring wilted.

"Isn't it true that you two got into some kind of argument last night?"

"I wouldn't exactly call it an argument. Just a little disagreement. Emerson spilled a little wine on my dress, that's all." And by a "little wine" I meant half a bottle and by "on my dress" I meant soaked clean through until I had a faint purplish hue when I finally stripped the soaked garment off. I shrugged and tried to smile. "Crowded party and . . . accidents happen."

Accident my slightly purple ass.

Moyer cocked his head. He was a one hundred percent cardboard cutout of every other detective my San Francisco roommate DVR'd each week, right down to his bulbous red nose and the aforementioned "isn't it true."

There was an uncomfortable beat of silence as though Moyer expected me to say more.

"And, that's it," I said.

Moyer cocked a single caterpillar eyebrow and shot me one of those "prove it to me" expressions. The kind of expression that is so disconcerting it encourages perfectly innocent and well-read people to start babbling like psychopathic idiots. I was a solid four minutes into my soliloquy that contained a good selection of incriminating myself and backpedaling when my voice was drowned out by the ridiculously loud squawking of a black bird pacing the ledge of the open window.

My God, New York was infested.

Though I pathologically hate birds—not fear, *hate*—as I mentioned before, I could have run up and kissed this one on its filth-infested birdie beak for creating just the distraction that allowed me a millisecond to give myself a mental head-slap and take the vampire equivalent of a deep, calming breath.

My mouth fell open again at the precise time the bird's beak cracked wide, as though the foul thing was watching me.

"Someone shoo that bird away," Detective Moyer said, clearly annoyed.

One of the pup cops used his hat to bat at the screen and the black bird did a patronizing flap of its enormous wings, circling about six inches from the ledge, still squawking like a maniac.

Moyer blew out a disgusted sigh and raked a fat hand over his round face. "We'll need to have you come down to the station to answer some questions," he said finally. "Now."

I swallowed and glanced out the window, the sun catching the heavy leaded glass. Just the glare stung my bare shoulders and I inched away. "Can we finish the interview downstairs? Or in a non–bird-infested room? I just would like to not be here."

Moyer looked around, his eyes landing on the pattern spread on my table, edged by a heap of fabric scraps.

"What's all this about? You one of the, er, sewing students?"

I felt myself stiffen even though I knew it was not the time to throw my weight(lessness) around. "I'm a designer, actually. This"—I gestured to the tables, the dresses, the patterns—"is a contest. A competition." I swallowed, thinking of the swish-swish sound Reginald's shoes made as they scraped across the dining table, thinking of Emerson's sightless eyes, the slack in her jaw as it stayed open, forever frozen in surprise.

Moyer eyed the fabric swatches and then eyed me, skepticism written all over his face. "Like a TV thing?"

I was about to correct him, but instead bet on the draw-to-Hollywood that most breathers in this anyone-can-be-a-star decade seemed to have. "Yeah."

I pumped my head, growing more excited and happy that the majority of my never-lie-to-a-cop morals disappeared when my soul did. "Reality TV."

Detective Moyer's spider-veined cheeks reddened and pushed up into a smile. "Is that model going to be here?" He looked around as though we were storing her in a closet or a drawer. "The blonde one? The host? She's from Sweden or Switzerland. Saskatchewan or something."

"Uh, yeah, absolutely," I said.

If necessary, I'm sure I could scare up a Saskatchewan model somewhere, right?

Moyer straightened his tie and yanked his pants up over his enormous keg of a belly, his eyes scanning the studio as if he had simply overlooked an enormous camera crew.

"Are you miked?" he asked in a gruff, low murmur.

"Miked?"

He raised his bushy eyebrows and I was amused and horrified that this man of the law would be so into grabbing his fifteen minutes that he would use a homicide to get there. And to get a piece of prime Saskatchewan model ass, apparently.

"No," I said, leaning in. "This isn't part of the show."

I watched Moyer's Adam's apple bob as he considered. "I'll meet you down in the lobby."

My feet hadn't so much as touched the lobby's deco marbled floor when Pike met me at the elevator.

"What are you doing back here?" I wanted to know. "Coming back to make sure the job is done?"

Pike's eyebrows went up and I tried my best to gauge everything about him—his body heat, the thunder of his heart—but he stayed completely still and relaxed.

It's too bad the good-looking ones are always sociopaths.

"What are you—?"

I poked his chest with my index finger. "I know what you did."

"You know that I got shit-faced drunk and slept in the stairwell because I lost my keys?"

"Lost your keys?"

Pike looked sheepish. "They were in my pants."

I glanced down and realized that Pike was wearing a pair of ill-fitting pants instead of the slim pair that went with his suit. Perhaps earlier, I was too busy looking for bulges instead of the poorly stiched seams and unnatural fabrics to notice the change. But I still wasn't convinced.

"So you lost your pants and your keys."

Pike nodded then held my gaze, his eyes meltingly delicious and for the briefest of moments I considered what life with a serial killer might be like.

I shook myself from my revelry. "That's a convenient story."

The other elevator *plinged!* and Detective Moyer stepped out with another officer who was carrying two steaming cups of coffee. Moyer nodded to Pike, who raised his own paper coffee cup to the man.

I narrowed my eyes. "You know Detective Moyer?"

Pike's eyes cut to me as the steam wisped from around his deep brown eyes. "Didn't I tell you I work for a lot of people? Sometimes even the NYPD."

"Right." I felt myself grimace. "Crime scene photographer."

I glanced back at where Moyer and the pup cop were setting themselves up, then back at Pike.

"Well you'd better stay around. They want to know who saw Emerson last."

"And why do you think that was me?"

I narrowed my eyes and Pike narrowed his right back at me and stepped a little closer, his nose—his lips—barely inches from mine.

"Are you accusing me of something, Ms. LaShay?"

"Ms. LaShay?" It was Moyer's deep voice and he was looking over his shoulder at me now, those heavy brows raised expectantly.

I poked Pike in the chest. "We're not done."

And though there is no reason in this realm or the other that it should have, the second we touched, a spark shot through me like delicious wildfire. I pulled my finger back as though it burned but it was too late; Pike's eyes were low and hooded, and the half-inch of smile on his pursed lips let me know that he felt it, too.

Moyer asked me a rather routine, *CSI*-type series of questions that I answered with the practiced unease of someone who had seen her first dead body. No one needed to know that back home in San Francisco, my every day was spent with the dead. New York may be the city that never sleeps, but San Francisco was the city that never dies.

"Well," Moyer said, his pale eyes scanning his notebook as his meat hook of a hand started to close it. "I think that's pretty much all we need."

I stood up, but Moyer stopped me. "Oh, Ms. LaShay, just

one more thing. Did you recognize the scissors that were used to kill Ms. Hawk?"

My whole body stiffened and if my heart still beat, I knew it would be up in my throat, clanging like a fire bell. I swallowed slowly. "They were mine."

The buzz and hum of the active lobby was suddenly plunged into a deep, uncomfortable silence as though everyone—from the half-conscious security guard to the honking cabbies right outside the door—had heard me.

"Yours?"

I wanted to lie, to shrug it off, but those scissors would be dislodged from Emerson's chest eventually, and when they were, they would see my name engraved right across the blade.

"Ms. LaShay, I'm going to have to ask that you don't leave town until we have this all sorted out. You're free to contact your lawyer."

"My lawyer?" I felt myself blanch. "Am I—am I suspected of something?"

Moyer didn't answer me but his expression told me that his answer was nothing that I wanted to hear.

A cold stripe of fear shot down my spine and my whole body rang electric. I may have fangs, I may have walked this earth for centuries, but right now, I was in deep, deep trouble.

I handed the cabbie several crumpled bills and pushed my way into the apartment vestibule, sinking my key into the lock. It had only been a day, but I already couldn't remember not feeling like my body was covered with the stench of death (and not the good kind), or when I didn't want to slink out of my clothes, burn them—which is high holy treason with a wardrobe like mine—or slip away to parts unknown. I pulled out my cell again and hit speed dial again.

"Underworld Detection Agency, San Francisco. This is Kale. How may I direct your call?"

"Hey, Kale, it's Nina. Can you put me through to legal?"

"Nina!" Kale's voice brightened, then dropped to a low whisper. "Can you do me a favor and tell Vlad something?"

I swallowed. "Who told you he was here?"

"You just did."

Before I could respond—or backpedal—Kale had put me through to legal where my "call was very important to them and would be answered in the order it was received." I drummed my fingers on my purse while listening to an instrumental version of "(Everything I Do) I Do It For You" and told myself that I would deal with Kale's Easter egg hunt later.

I was still on hold when I made it to the fourth floor, a perky UDA employee breaking in between during "A Groovy Kind of Love" to ask me if I knew I could file most basic UDA legal documents online. I clicked my phone off, depressed at my lack of a solution and dearly missing the good, old-fashioned slam of a receiver on its base.

Sliding an icon wasn't very satisfying.

I was standing in front of Reginald's door now, one piddling strip of crime-scene tape strung across the jamb, the door sealed with a flashy red sticker warning that no one other than the police, an inspector, or the coroner was permitted entry.

"Or the resident vampire," I muttered under my breath before taking my fresh manicure to the thing.

Once the sticker was slit, I was surprised to find the door unlocked. I slipped into the apartment and winced, getting another sickly sweet hit of that new-dead smell.

I crossed the living room and cracked the kitchen window, letting the musty scent of New York summer seep in, letting the throb and bustle of the city pierce the silence.

"All right, Reginald, show me something that will help me."

But there was nothing overtly cluelike in the apartment.

The furniture, modern and standoffish, was pristine, not even bearing a telltale crease where some murderer may have taken respite after his job was done. There was nothing—except . . .

I climbed up onto the dining table, careful to skirt the dark smudges where Reginald's shoes had scraped, and rolled up onto my tiptoes. There, on the top of one of the exposed beams, was a forgotten scrap of fabric—Emerson's fabric. The fabric that Reginald's murderer had tightened around Reginald's neck until he had stopped breathing. I shuddered, pulled my barrette from my hair, and used it as a sort of makeshift, evidence-sustaining pair of tweezers and grabbed the swatch.

Other than the raggedy ends where the fabric had ripped, there was nothing significant or incriminating about it. The strip was about two inches wide, followed the print of the fabric, but was cut against the grain. No name plates, no fingerprints, no "if found please return to." I held it up to my nose, whiffing the slightest scent of tuberose and freesia locked into the stitch. Apparently it hadn't been in Emerson's apartment long enough to adopt her scent.

There was nothing and I was annoyed, but I shoved the scrap in my pocket anyway, jumping off the table and closing Reginald's door behind me.

What a waste.

I was only able to grumble for a millisecond; a feeling of stiff unease washed down the skinny hallway and my hackles went up. I spun, staring down Emerson's closed door.

My nostril flicked.

Emerson's patchouli smell still hung light on the air, but there was something else now, too, something that wasn't there earlier.

And then there was the slightest, softest sound.

A footstep.

Someone, doing their best to step lightly, to carefully avoid the creaking floorboards. A drawer slid open. Someone rifling.

I slowly wrapped my palm around Emerson's doorknob and was met with a lock. I bit my bottom lip, considering.

Then I slid a bobby pin out of my extensive updo (which was quickly falling due to my surprisingly helpful multiuse of barrettes and pins) and quietly stuck it into the lock. A single jiggle and the lock popped, the door popping open a millimeter. I pushed it open a tiny bit more and sucked in my stomach—a human habit that hadn't yet died—peering into the apartment.

It was quiet, and the heaps of clothing and crap all around could have signaled that Emerson's place had just been ransacked, or that Emerson employed the same kind of housekeeping style my roommate did back at home: slob chic.

I slid through the doorway, head cocked, still listening. Whoever was inside paused, because suddenly the room went uncomfortably still.

But the scent was still there.

I scanned the room, my footfalls silent even on the squeaky floorboard (we vamps have no discernible weight) and stopped short when I saw Emerson's sketchbook laid out on the glass-topped kitchen table. It was open to a black-draped design that was a mirror image of something I had been working on and everything in me started to boil.

Which was probably why I didn't hear him.

He clamped one leather-gloved hand around my waist and another around my mouth and dragged me backward. I tried to dig my heels into the heavy carpet to slow him down but my weightlessness worked against me and it was an easy slide. I tried kicking and punching, but with my assailant behind me, firmly clasping me against his chest, it was futile.

"Let me go," I growled against the man's hand, feeling the angle on my fangs sharpening.

He responded by tightening his grip and I opened my mouth, sinking my teeth into his palm.

He howled and pulled away from me; I lurched for the vase on the counter, swinging it hard. Water and roses shot out in a clear arc and the heavy leaded crystal made a pleasing, smacking sound when it caught my attacker square in the jaw. I thought it would stop him but the shot only angered him and his hands were on me, grabbing fistfuls of shirt. I was off my feet and face to face with eyes that spit white-hot anger.

A voice echoing in the hallway startled us both and I was tossed to the side, landing in a crumbled heap in a pile of discarded muslin sketch paper. My assailant cast one backward glance at me, cracked open the living room window, and disappeared onto the fire escape.

I sat up like a shot—vampire pride wounded, the strap on my Jimmy Choo busted, and pulsing with rage. I vaulted toward the window and followed the black-clad man out onto the fire escape for exactly forty-five seconds. He shot an upward glance at me as he climbed down the escape ladders. His eyes widened and his mouth dropped open just the tiniest bit and I knew he saw the smoke, the little burst of fire as it pierced my skin and singed my hair. I edged back as far from the single flicker of fire bringing sunlight that I could, patting my shoulder and trying to put out the flame. I slapped it out. It smoldered, smoked, and seemed to die, only to pop once again like a cobra dancing out of its basket.

"Son of a bitch!"

My entire body was rigid and the tension pulsed through me like an electric shock as Pike lunged out the window for me and dragged me inside. He pressed a dishtowel against my shoulder, holding and waiting until the flame died out. He folded up the blackened towel and tossed it on the table.

"What happened?" Pike asked me. "What are you doing here?"

I figured if I drew his attention away from my little Sterno moment, he might forget about it. "What the hell are you doing here? I live here."

He pointed. "You live there. This is Emerson's place and you were on fire."

I harrumphed. "*I* was on fire? You were seeing things, dude. I was just smoking."

Pike cocked a disbelieving eyebrow.

"I know. It's a foul habit. I'm trying to quit. Got one of those patch things, and some of that gum . . ." I was rambling.

"So you decided to come over to Emerson's house to indulge in this foul habit?"

I offered him my "duh, isn't it obvious?" shrug. "What are you doing here?"

Pike took a step toward me. "I was actually heading over to your place to check in on you." A tiny blush shot over his cheeks. "I don't have your number."

"Then how'd you end up here?"

He jerked a thumb over his shoulder. "You left Emerson's door open. And after I saw that Reginald's place had been opened, I thought I'd see what was going on."

He looked earnest enough but a girl doesn't walk the earth for centuries and (continue) to be fooled by a pair of gorgeous eyes and well-tanned swimmer's shoulders that slouched pitifully.

"How do I know you weren't coming to my place to kill me?"

Pike took another step and I backed up against the window, instinctually. I felt the singe on my back but I needed to put as much distance between him and me as possible.

He cocked a grin that would have been heartwarming, had he not been a psychopath. "Why would I kill you?"

"Because I saw you this morning. Drunk or not, you were leaving the scene of a crime. If I tell the cops . . ."

Still grinning. "Having another cigarette?"

"What are you talking about?"

"You're smoking again."

I felt my brow furrow and put my hands on my hips, feeling indignant. "I'm smoking? I'm not smoking anything, Pike. I saw you well and fine."

"No," he said, striding toward me, pointing. "You're *actually* smoking."

I glanced over my shoulder just in time to see a plume of gray-black smoke rise up from my shoulder blade and the cotton strap of my tank top engulfed by a tiny flame.

"Son of a bitch!"

Pike had me in his arms in a split second and was wrapping me in one of Emerson's discarded muslin swatches. He spun me as he wrapped and before I knew it, I was fairly well mummified.

"Thanks. I think it's out." I tried to wiggle my arms but they were clamped to my sides. "A little help?"

Pike pulled a chair out from Emerson's drafting table and plopped himself down. He kicked up his feet and crossed his own arms in front of his chest. "No."

"No?"

He wagged his head. "No. I'm not going to help you get out of that until you answer some questions for me."

I tried to take a step, but my legs were clamped too. I considered a Hulk-like show of vampire prowess, but then I'd have some explaining to do.

"What kind of girl catches on fire and doesn't know it?"

I bit down hard, feeling the edge of my fangs slicing into my gums.

Looks like I would have some explaining to do, after all.

"Why do you care?" I asked, chin hitched.

"Because I just walked in on a woman snooping around a dead woman's place, and said woman—the first one—caught *on fire.*"

I tried to shrug nonchalantly. "So?"

"So there is no fire around. And I had to tell you that you were on fire. Who does that?"

"Spontaneous combustion happens, Pike. Look it up on Wikipedia."

He cocked a disbelieving eyebrow.

"Can you help me sit down at least?"

I started to take a series of minuscule steps while Pike pulled a chair out for me. He put his large hands over my shoulder and that same spark shot through me, making every hair on my swaddled arms stand on end. But I wouldn't give him the satisfaction.

"Get off me," I said, maneuvering myself into the chair. I sat down hard, feeling Emerson's cheap chair selection ringing up my tailbone. "This is rather uncomfortable."

Pike sat across from me and narrowed his eyes into what I figured he supposed was an intimidating glare. I rubbed the tip of my tongue over one fang and felt my stomach growl when my eyes fell to the thick vein in his neck, pumping fresh blood.

"I'm here." I tried to shrug. "What the hell do you want to ask me?"

Now Pike leaned back and kicked one ankle over his knee. I told myself that the constant salivation was a result of skipping my breakfast pouch and had nothing to do with the way his jeans rode up at the thighs or the way he pursed his red, full lips.

I bit mine.

"Apart from this whole thing," he said, gesturing to the apartment. "How do you know Emerson?"

I rolled my eyes. *Why were the pretty ones always so dumb?*

"We're both fashion designers. We meet up at events and she's a two-faced design stealer." Pike's eyebrows rose and I hurriedly tacked on, "God rest her soul."

"So you and she weren't friends?"

"What gave you that impression, Colombo?"

Pike blew out a sigh. "So before you," he cleared his throat, "caught fire, what were you doing here? Stealing?"

"Stealing my own designs? Hardly. I was looking for clues."

"Clues?"

I was getting frustrated and the muslin was starting to chafe. "About who killed Emerson!"

"If you hated her, why would you care?"

"Because I'm a good fucking person, okay?" I stopped trying to hide my annoyance, and that seemed to make Pike crack a self-appreciative grin. "I'm not so sure about that. Good fucking people don't burst into flames."

"Look it up!" I snapped.

Pike popped out of his chair. "Can I take a picture of you?"

"So you can sell it to some bondage website? Hell no."

"Okay, I'll cut you free." He produced a pocketknife and flicked it open. He didn't look menacing nor did he brandish the weapon in any way other than to show me he had it, but my hackles went up.

This guy wanted something.

"What do you want?" I asked, suspicion shading my voice.

Pike leaned toward me and gingerly edged the tip of the knife into a piece of muslin, directly between my breasts. "Nothing, Nina. Just a nice, normal, honest-to-goodness photo of you."

I glanced down at the tip of the blade resting an inch from my chest. He could plunge the thing in with all his might and nothing would happen. I'd keep (not) breathing, blinking, and looking very much alive.

But the blood-free wound would be a little bit more difficult to explain than my completely plausible spontaneous combustion explanation.

"What are you?" Pike asked, his voice slow, his eyes wickedly alive with something that looked only vaguely human.

"A San Franciscan," I tried.

The blade came a hair closer, and I heard the distinctive sound of muslin starting to split. "What. Are. You." Every word was its own sentence, each punctuated by Pike's wild eyes.

I considered letting him stab me, then breaking out of my mummy costume and ripping his idiot throat out. But UDA law strictly forbade that kind of thing, even if your local breather was a nosy asshat.

Or so fiercely handsome that this completely unfortunate situation left a fire between my legs while I tried to lean into his blade. There was something sexy, something so undeniably hot about Pike's hard-set eyes, about the danger of that slick blade resting between my breasts.

I locked Pike's eyes, hoping my coal-black ones were as hard or as deep as his. I ran my tongue over my teeth and my mouth dropped open as Pike leaned into me. I could hear his heartbeat speed up. I could hear the blood as it pulsed through his veins. Could feel the hot moisture from his lips as he breathed.

"I—"

"Apartment sixty-one A, right here on the right." It was the landlord, his voice a combination of asthma and Jersey—and he wasn't alone. Another voice—low, gruff.

"Detective Moyer," I whispered to Pike.

His face paled when the doorknob rattled and before I knew it, I was staring at Emerson's ugly carpet while Pike carried me over his shoulder and shoved me—and then himself—into the bedroom closet.

"What the hell are you—" I started to hiss but he stopped me with a scathing look and a finger pressed to his lips as we heard the landlord, the detective, and, I figured, one or two of the pup cops, filing into Emerson's living room.

"Shut up or they're hauling us both off to jail," Pike said with a low hiss.

There was something about his sudden slip into alpha male that was sexy and, growing slightly more comfortable

Hannah Jayne

in my muslin shackles, I leaned back into Emerson's patchouli-scented clothes until my shoulder blades went flush with the back wall. Pike ducked and joined me in the black depths of the closet, our bodies hidden by the shapeless black clothing. I would have commented on the horror of it, but Pike had to press up against me to stay hidden. His back was to the door, his front pressed against mine, his outstretched arms essentially caging me in.

Something inside me started to flutter.

Something inside him started to harden.

"I guess we know what turns you on," I said slyly.

Pike rolled his eyes, edged over, and fished his knife from his pocket. I hoped he couldn't see my face fall in the darkness and went back to my pissed-off girl expression. "How are we supposed to—"

But Pike clapped a hand over my mouth and pressed himself against me yet again. I trained my eyes to focus on the ceiling, suddenly glad my arms were bound to my sides because they were aching to wrap around him even as I tried to ignore how perfectly our bodies seemed to fit together.

"Looks clear in here, boss," one of the pup cops was saying. I could hear him turning fabric swatches in his hands, then I chanced a glance at Pike. His eyes were hard and round, drawing me in, his lips a half-inch from mine. I watched him purse them into a small pucker and for a fleeting second I weighed the idea of mauling this man right here in a dead girl's apartment. It seemed like the wrong thing to do, but I found myself pulling toward him, a stripe of desire running like razor wire down my spine.

"Gibbs," Moyer barked, "this way."

When Pike pressed a single finger against his puckered lips, I thought my innards would explode—with embarrassment, rage, or unquenched desire, I couldn't be sure—but held myself statue-still when I heard the closet door open, a yellow orb of light penetrating the closet's darkness.

Through a drooping lapel and a circa 1982 butterflied collar I could see Detective Moyer's bloodshot eyes, his meat-hook hand directing the flashlight over Emerson's clothes. Pike held his breath but his heart kept thumping against my chest.

"I don't know," Detective Morris said to the clothes. "I'm not convinced it's the same guy."

"MO was the same. Woman, twenty-three to twenty-seven, killed in her workplace with a weapon of opportunity. I'd say that's our guy." I could see Gibbs behind the detective, shrugging, just before Moyer closed the door on us.

"That guy's a serial, and this Hawk girl isn't his type."

"So what do you think?"

I heard Moyer suck on his teeth. "You know what? I like that LaShay girl for this one."

Pike looked down at me, and my eyes widened.

"The one with the black hair who found her? She's a tiny little thing. She may have done in the second one, but you think she could have gotten Fairfield, too? She couldn't have gotten him up there," Gibbs said.

"She could have a partner. I don't know; maybe this competition was that important to her. Important enough to kill. It's supposed to be on TV, you know. That could have stressed her to the point of popping off her competitors. Between you and me, she seems a few slices short of a grilled cheese."

I bristled while Pike clapped a hand over his mouth, stifling a laugh. I glared at him, hoping to convey serial murderer seriousness, but he kept looking over my head.

Finally, I felt him let out a slow, shallow breath, as we heard the men move away from the closet.

"Yeah, a partner maybe," the cop continued. "When are we interviewing the sister? She lives here, too, right?"

"She was hysterical. Guess the two were real close."

I felt my brow furrow and Pike blinked at me. I shook my head and mouthed the word "no" as I had had the supreme displeasure of running into Emerson numerous times, but Nicolette only showed up this once.

"Medics took her to City General. Hilburn went with her, but I don't think the girl has said anything yet."

Pike started breathing again as Moyer and Gibbs left the bedroom, their footsteps getting lighter as they walked toward the door. I felt my shoulders slump and for the first time noticed sweat beading along my hairline. We started to loosen ourselves from each other but stopped when we heard Gibbs addressing the unknown cop in the living room.

"What do you think of the designer? The one who found her?"

"I don't know," the cop said slowly. "I'm not really into fashion."

"As our murderer," Moyer retorted, exasperation evident. "You saw the shears, right?"

"Heard about the engraving. And she certainly had motive."

Pike looked down at me, his expression a combination of interest and suspicion. I did my best to meet his gaze with a menacing glare.

"She's number one on the suspect list," Moyer said.

"How do we feel about the photographer? I heard he and the vic used to date."

Even in the darkness, I could see the blush washing over Pike's face, could see the fear in his eyes.

"I can't see why he'd do Fairfield in," Moyer said.

"Maybe he offed the competition for his lady friend. She didn't appreciate it so he whacked her, too."

We heard Moyer cluck his tongue and then chuckle. "Interesting theory. Remind me to make you my deputy."

Once the door clicked shut and the lock tumbled, Pike

produced his pocket knife/rock-hard member again, silently slicing me out of the muslin. I left it in a heap in the depths of the closet, stepping over Emerson's collection of thick-soled sensible shoes.

"So, you don't know when you're on fire and you're a murder suspect."

I put my hands on my hips, the heat that was roiling in my panties moving to an angry flame in my gut. "So are you."

"Yeah, but I'm not guilty."

"Neither am I."

Pike took me in from head to toe, his eyes so sharp and hard it made my own body go on high alert. Finally he turned, leaving me behind as he went for the living room. "I'm not sure I believe you," he said.

"Well, I'm not sure I believe you," I fumed. "Besides, why would I kill Emerson? I would have beaten her in the competition anyway. And it's not like she was even—hey." I clenched my hands, kicked my feet apart, and glared at Pike, who had turned to face me, slight interest on his face. "I don't have to defend myself to you."

He shrugged. "The guilty always overcompensate." He went back to work gathering his things.

"No," I said, yanking on his shoulder until he faced me. "The guilty always act nonchalant. They always point the finger of accusation."

We both looked down at my index finger, extended, my hot-pink fingernail pressed up against Pike's chest, slice of red sticker across it. I quickly withdrew, crossing my arms in front of my chest.

"Look, I don't know about you, but going to jail for a crime I didn't commit is really not on my bucket list. So if you'll excuse me, I'm going to head out."

"And do what? Hide out? Oh, no you're not. I'll tell them you were here."

Pike glared at me and cocked his head. "You were here, too."

I blinked, realizing for the first time that I had just spent the last twenty minutes tied up and trapped in a closet by and with a possible murderer. A cold shiver washed over me and I squinted, trying to pick up the slightest twitch in Pike's eyes—something that said he was hiding a secret, something that said he was guilty.

"What? You trying to read my mind?"

"That would be a short story."

"Why would I kill Emerson?" Pike huffed.

"Because she was your ex-girlfriend."

Pike opened the door. "She wasn't my ex-girlfriend and I hardly ever saw her."

"Maybe that cop was right and you killed Reginald, too. For Emerson. Or maybe you wanted her to be your girlfriend, but she scorned you—although I can't see Emerson scorning anyone, that whole beggars-can't-be-choosers thing, but whatever. That's it, huh? You loved her. It was one of those 'if-I-can't-have-her-then-nobody-can' things, huh?" I bit my lip.

"No, that's preposterous. Emerson was an awful person." A tiny niggle of guilt touched the back of my mind and I sighed. "But she didn't deserve to be shish-kabobed by a pair of designer shears."

A sympathetic look flashed over Pike's face. "You should go home, Nina. Lock your doors. Don't go anywhere alone."

I frowned. "What are you going to do?"

Pike sighed, his chest rising mightily. "I'm going to go track a killer."

The air in the room seemed to drop twenty degrees once Pike slipped out. I stood in Emerson's empty living room, listening to the silence for a full minute before I took off like a shot down the hall, nearly pummeling Pike in the apartment vestibule.

"You can't hunt down a killer," I said, my voice sounding

breathless and desperate. "You can't do it alone. You need backup."

Pike paused, listening, and I moistened my suddenly dry lips. "You need me."

A hint of exhausted smile pushed at the corner of Pike's lips. "And you're credible backup?"

I pressed my teeth together, feeling the familiar push of my razor-sharp fangs. "You'd be surprised," I muttered.

If this were a movie, our vestibule exchange would be followed by a musical montage of Pike and me with heads bent as we studied files and photo books over greasy takeout boxes of congealing Chinese food. The music would speed up as the scenes sped up to show the change of seasons, the stubble growing on Pike's chin as we grew more and more disillusioned. But this isn't a movie.

"How do we start?" I said after what seemed like an hour had passed.

Pike rested a hand on my shoulder, his eyes intense as he looked directly at me. "I meant what I said, Nina. Go upstairs. Lock your doors. Don't go anywhere alone." He spoke slowly, like a father explaining dating rules to his daughter and though I should have been offended and indignant, all I could muster up was a cold fist of fear gripping the bottom of my stomach. As Pike turned to go, I knew with every fiber of my being that he was about to fall into something grittier, dirtier, and far more dangerous than even he expected.

"Do you want to know why I couldn't feel the fire?" I said to the back of his head.

He stopped, his hand on the door, back still toward me. I swallowed heavily when I saw his hand close over the door handle, the muscles at the back of his arms flicking as he went to push it open.

"Do you want to know why you can't take my picture?"

Pike stopped. His shoulders straightened and he turned to

me, his face open, eyes soft. I saw a sliver of pink tongue dart out of his mouth, moistening his lips. "Why?"

I took a step down, unsure of how—or why—I had bartered my biggest secret to find the murderer of a woman I couldn't stand and a man I barely knew.

"Upstairs."

Vlad actually looked up from his laptop when Pike walked in. I felt my eyebrows rise and a sweet warmth spread in my stomach when Vlad's dark brows shot downward, his thin lips pulled into a menacing scowl as his eyes flickered over Pike.

Aw, Vlad. He cared.

"I'm sorry," Pike said, looking from Vlad to me. "I didn't realize you had company."

"He's not company, he's my nephew." I crossed over to Vlad. "Vlad, this is my friend"—my breath caught on the word—"Pike. Pike, my nephew, Vlad."

The two men regarded each other casually, critically, before offering each other one of those barely perceptible manly head nods.

Vlad went back to his screen and Pike followed me to the couch.

"All right," Pike said, sitting down beside me. "What's the big reveal?"

I saw Vlad stiffen in his spot at the dining table. His eyebrows shot up over the screen, his eyes, wide and accusing, following. "Can you come here for a second, Nina?"

I beelined over to Vlad and leaned my head in, certain of what he was going to say. "Please tell me your big reveal entails your tits or your ass or something else that won't potentially ruin my life or make you have to eat Pike."

"I know what I'm doing, Vlad," I hissed. And, because I felt like I should, I added, "And watch your language."

Even though I had no idea what I was doing.

Pike edged to the side of the couch. "So?"

A knock on the door stopped him and I celebrated my

good luck. I snatched open the door and was greeted by Felipe's strangled cries, his shoulders shimmying under the dead weight of his emotion.

"Nina, Nina, oh, it's awful!" He plunged himself into my arms and I was forced to hug him, to think of friend over fashion as a snot bubble popped on my dupioni silk blouse.

"Felipe, what's going on?"

"It's my Reggie," he huffed.

Pike and I shared a very déjà vu look. "What about Reginald?"

"He didn't commit the suicide. He—he—he was murdered." The admittance came out with another rash of hysterical tears and Pike rushed over.

"What do you mean he was murdered?"

I knew what I heard at the cocktail party, but Felipe's crushed face was painful confirmation.

"I just came from the police station. They did the"—sniff—"the"—sniff—"autopsy. It came back positive. Or whatever you say. My Reggie was murdered!"

Pike snaked his arms in front of his chest. "First Reginald and now Emerson," he said just under his breath. He shot me a sidelong glance and I knew exactly what he didn't say: that I was next.

We spent the next twenty minutes listening as Felipe filled us in on what the police had told him—which wasn't much. By the time he left the sun was dipping into the Hudson and I was pacing. Pike grabbed both my shoulders and I stopped my march.

"What's up?"

"What's up? There is a murderer on the loose. And you and I both know who's next on his list. Me." Being mainly immortal I wasn't all that nervous. But still, getting stabbed or hung would be nothing short of an enormous pain in my ass, not to mention the havoc it would wreak on my wardrobe.

"I'm not sure that's what you should be most concerned about," Pike said.

I raised a brow.

"Suspect." Pike mouthed the word.

I shook my head. "No, no, that's just a theory. And a flimsy one at that. You have more motive."

"Like I said, Emerson and I barely spoke. The whole boyfriend-girlfriend thing was completely in her head. Emerson and Reginald were both your competitors. With both of them gone, you've technically won the competition. That's your motive."

I yanked my shoulders away from Pike and gaped. "Are you seriously accusing me of killing off my competition? I'll have you know that I would have whipped their asses fair and square. God rest their souls."

"I'm not accusing you. I'm telling you."

"They don't think it's me. They think it's you." Pike rolled his eyes and I dropped my voice. "Or me."

"How much do you know about Emerson? You said you used to run into her all the time. I know you two weren't friends but—"

"But what? I knew nothing about her other than what I told you. I didn't even know she had a sister for God's sake until she showed up in my face." I paused. "That's it. The sister. We need to talk to her." I bit my bottom lip. "But she probably wouldn't talk to us."

"Because she was apparently so hysterical?"

"Because she might think that one of us killed Emerson."

Pike pinned me with a stare and I sighed, dropping my head in my hands. "I will be the hysterical one if I have to go to prison. They make everyone shower together. And you have to wear those stupid plastic shoes!" I frowned, my eyes skittering over the apartment and seeing bars, one of those ugly metal toilets, and a thin cot with four-thread-count sheets.

And then I saw Vlad.

Slowly, his eyes came up from behind the screen. "What?"

I felt a smile playing at the edge of my lips. "She'll talk to you."

"What?" Pike asked.

I stopped, excitement building in my chest. "She'll talk to Vlad. He's young, he's charming," I said and glanced at Pike. "He's not you. She'll open up to him."

Pike looked over at Vlad and then back at me. "No offense to your nephew, but do you really think a girl who just lost her sister to *murder* is going to suddenly go all boy crazy for him?" He jerked a thumb toward Vlad, and threw in a, "No offense, bro," for good measure.

"Well, Vlad's got—" I paused, biting my tongue before I said the word *glamours*. A glamour is almost like a vampire pheromone; it attracts humans to us like bees to honey and once they find us . . . well, humans tend to become utterly entranced and allow us to eat them. Usually.

If you don't adhere to UDA guidelines.

Glamours are strictly forbidden according to the UDA-V charter but I am almost completely sure that a glamour for solving a homicide was a way lesser charge than a glamour for *committing* a homicide. And either way, I'd rather be beheaded by the UDA than spend eternity in a prison cell and an orange jumpsuit.

"I mean Vlad's got charm." I turned toward him and threw on my best version of adorably irresistible Disney eyes. "Please, Vlad. For me?"

Vlad looked up, eyed me warily. "No."

I crossed the room in two short strides and batted my lashes again. "Pweeze?"

He shook his head.

I tossed a quick glance over my shoulder, then laid my palm flat on the table, a quarter-inch from Vlad's hand.

"Look," I said, my voice low and dripping with heat. "I made you, *Louis*." Vlad didn't regard me visually, but I could see a stiffness run through his spine as I regarded him by his real, pre-vamp, pre-Count-Chocula-obsession name. "And I will be the first one to take you out."

"Can't. UDA bylaw." There was an edge of teenage smugness in his words that made me want to kill him just a little bit more.

"Fine," I said, crossing my arms in front of my chest. "I won't kill you." I snatched my cell phone from where it rested on the counter. "But Kale will."

Vlad stood up so quickly his chair *thunk*ed to the ground behind him. "Fine!" he said, terror cutting through his eyes. "Just please," he continued, holding up both hands as if the phone were about to spit bullets. "Whatever you do, don't call Kale. Please."

Now I was smug.

Pike looped an arm over the back of the couch as he turned to stare at us. "Who's this—"

"Never mind," Vlad and I said in unison.

I pushed Vlad toward the door. "Come on. Just go over there. Ask her for coffee."

"I don't feel good about this," Vlad said, pulling on his collar.

"You're doing a good thing," I said, patting him lightly on the shoulder. "You saw the way Nicolette lit up when you introduced yourself."

Vlad glared down at me and Pike piped in, "Besides, it's just coffee." His grin was wide and genuine and I melted just a tiny bit, barely even registering the fact that he could very well be a homicidal maniac.

I had Vlad in a vice grip and the doorknob in my hand when Pike grabbed my shoulder, his hand warm and heavy. "Wait," he said, "do we have some kind of plan?"

I whirled. "Of course we do. Vlad goes out with Nicolette, asks some questions, gains some intel about whether or not Emerson has some horrid, murderous people in her immediate past—"

Vlad opened his mouth and I shot him a very loving but very deathly gaze.

"And then he relays it back to us. We find said murderous people and *voila!* Off the hook."

"Sounds awfully simple," Pike said skeptically.

"Don't worry, it won't be," Vlad answered.

Pike and I sat in an uncomfortable silence while Vlad left the apartment. When an acceptable amount of time had passed—about thirty seconds—I sprinted toward the front door and pushed my nose through the crack that Vlad had left open. He was in the hallway and had just knocked on Nicolette's door.

"What's happening?" Pike came up behind me, his chest pressing up against my back, his hands resting on my hips. I wanted to grind into him, to toss him to the couch, to experience something other than this constant edginess and suspicion.

But Nicolette opened the door.

She was red-eyed and pink-nosed, her hair pulled back in a sloppy ponytail. She immediately straightened up when she saw who her caller was.

I felt Pike lean closer to me, his lips a hairsbreadth from my ear as he leaned down, his breath warm against the marble cold of my neck. "Damn. She asked him in."

"That's a good sign, though." I tiptoed—sheerly for effect—weightless, remember?—across the hall and pressed my ear lightly to Nicolette and Emerson's apartment door.

"He's asking her to coffee," I whispered over my shoulder. "She said 'okay, how about in five minutes.' Oh, crap." I ran back across the hall, smacking chest-to-warm-carved chest into Pike and may or may not have held the stance for a longer-than-appropriate moment. I felt Pike's arms go around me, his palm on the small of my back. Then Vlad pressed through the door and we sprang apart like a negative charge.

Pike's cheeks were flushed and there was a light sheen of sweat above his upper lip.

"What were you two doing?" Vlad asked without hiding the suspicious disgust from his face.

"Waiting for you. What happened?"

Vlad patted his well-shellacked hair. "We're going for coffee. Just like he asked." He pretend-breathed on me. "How's my breath?"

"You're disgusting," I said. "Have fun. And don't forget, you tell us *everything*. And really dig, you know? Pry."

Vlad rolled his eyes. "I'll keep that in mind."

He made sure to slam the door when he left.

I waited for a beat, worrying my bottom lip. Finally, I grabbed my keys, straightened my ponytail, and gave Pike the universal sign for "come on, get off my couch."

"Where are you going?" he wanted to know.

"On a date with my nephew."

Pike and I were tucked against a back wall at a tiny round coffee table barely big enough for our elbows, let alone our drinks.

"You're sure you don't want anything? Coffee? Frap-mocha-liscious or however the hell they bastardized coffee?"

I pursed my lips together and shook my head. "I'm fine, thanks." I tapped my ever-present travel mug. "I've had about all the coffee I could take for the day."

And it wasn't a total lie. The blood bad that I had for breakfast had a distinct, burnt coffee flavor. Made my teeth curl just thinking about it.

Pike had his elbows on the table, chin in hand. "What kind of woman comes to a coffeehouse and doesn't at least order a coffee? Or . . ." He pulled a chipped white plate toward him and snatched the muffin from it, his bite leaving less than half the muffin. "A sweet?"

"The kind of girl who is on a stakeout." I nudged my chair a half-inch farther away. "Can you try to keep most of that in your mouth?"

Pike shrugged. "I can't even hear what they're talking about."

Vlad and Nicolette were seated half the shop away from us, Nicolette's light waves falling over the back of her chair while Vlad smiled kindly and nodded, all the while shooting dagger glances at us whenever Nicolette looked away.

"Nicolette is talking about Emerson. She ate a cookie—snickerdoodle, I think—and is now talking about Christmas Eve at her parents' house. Apparently, Emerson got an Easy-Bake Oven while Nicolette got the Barbie Design Studio."

Pike leaned back in his chair, clearly impressed. "You can *hear* that?"

Heat zinged through me and I felt color—whoever's it was—washing over my cheeks. "I have really, really good hearing. And I read lips. It runs in the family." I kept my eyes focused on Vlad but I knew that Pike was staring at me. "Interesting."

A good forty minutes had passed and Nicolette told Vlad about being on the cheerleading squad and her college career. Vlad looked adequately forlorn and heartbroken as he mentioned his "ex-girlfriend" and how he came out to New York to mend his broken heart. I was about to gag, Pike was about to drop dead of boredom, and we were no closer to learning anything about Emerson's private life.

"Okay, either something happens or I'm going to stab someone through the heart."

My throat tightened and my blood froze statue-still. "What did you say?"

Pike held up his hands. "Sorry—too soon? Too soon."

I felt my mouth drop open then slammed it shut again, certain that Pike was talking about stabbing in general—not staking a vampire through the heart.

And I don't know if that made me feel better or worse.

"Tell me about yourself."

"What?"

Pike let out a long sigh and leaned back in his chair, hands clasped behind his head. The motion caused his semifitted black tee to rise just the smallest bit—just enough to expose a thin, two-inch trail of jet black hair leading from his very kissable belly button and disappearing into the gathered elastic of his boxer shorts. I licked my lips.

"What do you want to know?"

"Well . . ."

I did my best to tear my eyes from that happy trail, to tear my mind from what lay beneath.

"Tell me about your family."

Nothing will pull you out of a fantasy like an incredibly sexy man asking you to talk about your family.

"Not much to tell," I said simply. "Mom, dad, sister, two brothers." I shrugged toward Vlad. "And Vlad."

"What kind of name is Vlad? I assumed you were French."

I felt my beaming grin go from ear to ear. I loved it when a man recognized my elegant French upbringing—especially now, more than a century and a half after the fact. "You did?"

"Yeah. French or Spanish—'La' Shay.'"

Well, he was pretty enough to be a little bit dumb.

"My sister married a Hungarian," I lied. "Vlad is a pretty common Hungarian name."

Pike's brows went up. "Interesting. I thought it was Russian."

It was storybook vampire cliché! I wanted to scream. Which was why *Louis* LaShay chose to adopt the annoying Dracula moniker later in his non-creative vampire life.

"Look, Vlad and Nicolette are on a date." I snaked a tongue over my bottom lip, my number one tip in my arsenal of man-without-pants-prep. "Why don't we stop talking family and start talking fantasy?"

A single eyebrow rose over Pike's dark eyes and his lips

quirked into a smile that stood halfway between innocently interested and sex god with a naughty spot. "Fantasy, huh?"

I nodded slowly, resting my chin on my hands, letting a flow of my dark hair spill over my shoulder. If I had a whipped-cream topped coffee—if I could stomach such a thing—I would trail an index finger through it. Instead I leaned just a touch closer to Pike, letting my long hair tickle his arm.

The temperature in the coffeehouse rose by ten degrees.

"Well . . ." He let his voice trail off in that half-gravelly, all-sexy way, his eyes cutting from mine to wash all over my body with an appreciative grin. "Vlad wants you."

I squelched a snarl. "That's disgusting. We're French nobles! Not Alabama hillbillies! You're into some sick—"

Pike rolled his eyes and pointed. "No, Vlad, for real, wants you."

I whipped my head toward where he pointed and this time, didn't bother toning down the snarl. Vlad stood up and walked toward the restroom; I followed at a furious pace.

"What do you want? Don't you know I was—" I paused, cleared my throat, and straightened. "Please tell me you've called this little summit because you found out something good."

Vlad shrugged, all unaffected teen. "Sorry I interrupted your attempt at a fang bang, but this is going nowhere. All Nicolette wants to talk about is Christmas in Norman Rockwellville and her stupid Barbie Design Studio."

I arched a brow. "Barbie Design Studio?"

Vlad shrugged. "I don't know. Apparently Emerson got the Easy-Bake Oven. Look, I'll give her five more minutes and then I'm taking her home."

"Five more minutes?"

Vlad whipped out his iPhone. "And this time counts."

Five minutes—to the millisecond—later, Vlad was tossing a few crumpled bills on the table and opening the door for Nicolette.

I groaned. "So, that was a waste."

"Oh, I don't know . . . we never got to talk about your fantasy . . . or your fears."

I was drained, cranky, and the sickly sweet smell of pastries going day old was making my stomach churn. As sexy as Pike was, the borrowed blood running through my veins was almost gone and all I wanted was an *US Weekly* and a vat of O Neg. "Maybe another time."

Pike sucked in a sharp breath. "There is something we haven't tried."

I was waiting for him to say sex. Or kissing. And I was cursing myself for wasting all that good blood when it could have been rushing to my—

"We need to look at the bodies."

Never mind.

"Look at the bodies? What for?" I wanted to know.

"Anything. Signs of struggle, bruises, cuts—something the police may have missed."

"I certainly don't have a whole load of faith in breathers but I figure the cops—and the coroner, or medical examiner— would probably have found, photographed, or scraped off anything of evidentiary importance."

"Did you say *breather*?"

I grabbed my purse and stood up quickly. "Sure, breather. It's what everyone calls the cops in San Francisco. You know . . ." My mind raced. "They 'breathe' justice?" I turned on my heel. "I've got to go."

I felt Pike's hand close over my forearm and the strong warmth sent a shiver of gooseflesh all over my body. He pulled me closer and my breath caught in my throat, the tight anticipation all at once amazing and uncomfortable. His lips brushed over the part in my hair, then barely touched my earlobe. "Meet me tonight."

My body felt like warm Jell-O as his command oozed

through me. I swallowed, batting my eyelashes in that slow, bedroomy way that Elizabeth Taylor created and I mastered. "Where are we going?"

"The morgue."

It's official: I've been living with Sophie Lawson for way too long.

It's never dark in the city. It's also never without a population or a pulse, which was why I was wearing a form-fitting black Shoshanna Lonstein dress (I forgive her for the Seinfeld marriage debacle; we can't always avoid the starter husband) with six-inch platform heels in blazing blue for my evening sojourn to the morgue. Besides the fact that I would never be caught dead (again) in anything velour or with a drawstring, the ensemble was a perfect cover: New Yorkers might mistake me for a socialite or a supermodel, but a morgue burglar? Not a chance.

Pike looked me up and down and despite that fact that our upcoming "date" revolved around the officially dead, his appraising grin shot a little zing down my spine. "Well you look like you're ready to catch a killer."

Vlad crossed the living room, gave me a once over, and muttered, "Or hepatitis."

The Lower Manhattan City Morgue sits like a fat, ugly beehive among other government-owned fat, ugly beehive buildings.

I suppose there isn't a lot of support of a morgue makeover.

It was easy enough to slip inside and easier still to scurry around unbidden—vampires have no scent, nor any discernible weight, which means no footsteps, no creaky floors to give us away. And also the man at the front desk was asleep.

I waved Pike through and we scurried down the dimly lit hall.

"Okay, stay out here and stand guard."

"No way," I said. "I'm going in. You stand guard."

Pike sighed. "Do you have any idea what you're looking for?"

"Look, Pike, my roommate is basically a private investigator who is dating a detective. I have inadvertently been on more stakeouts, snuck through more morgues, and flopped around with more dead bodies than all the NYPD put together."

"I don't know why, but I'm kind of aroused right now."

"You're sick." I yanked open the storage-room door. "Stand guard."

Inside, I was pleased to see the bodies were stored in an orderly fashion (did I mention we vamps are a little bit OCD?). I was able to find Reginald and stretch him out on one of the exam tables in record time, gingerly placing a file folder over his flash-frozen man bits—I could only investigate so many things at once. I checked out the red-purple bruises circling his neck—not entirely certain what I was looking for—and was walking my fingers toward a tiny red pinprick behind his left ear. "Interesting," I whispered to my dead audience. The pinprick was minuscule and could have been a broken blood vessel or a mole for all I knew, but I knew how to find out. I pulled Reginald's file and did a quick scan. The bruises were listed, as well as a hernia scar, a hair weave, and a little tattoo on Reginald's derriere. There was no mention of the pinprick.

I left Reginald laid out and went to find Emerson. She wasn't listed on any of the drawers and I gulped, staring at the heavy metal door for the "overflow" body storage. There are very few things that give me the heebie-jeebies, but walking into a room where the dead are laid out and stacked like bakery goods made my stomach lurch—and not in a good way. I sucked in a nerve-steadying breath and stepped into the walk-in freezer, jamming a Gross Anatomy book in the doorway. I had seen one too many television shows where the main characters get locked in a walk-in and end up freezing to death or eating their weight in ice cream.

All my bases covered, I went to work examining the paperwork stacked on each body. I was so engrossed—or so desperate to get Emerson and get out of there—that I didn't hear someone slyly removing the Gross Anatomy book. What I did hear was the heavy metal *thunk* of the door closing.

My heart locked in my throat, but I refused to let myself panic. I casually walked up to the door, certain that the giant refrigerator people had seen all the locked-in-the-freezer episodes as well, and had created some sort of snazzy trapdoor or inside lock pop.

Apparently, refrigerator people are not TV watchers.

I dug into my cleavage and yanked out my cell phone. I wasn't entirely sure whom I'd call to rescue me from a walkin freezer filled with people-sicles, but Vlad was usually good for the occasional rescue. I wrapped my arms around myself and hit the speed-dial button.

And nothing happened.

"No bars!" I groaned. I started to pace, staring down at my screen. Closer to the back of the fridge a few cheery bars popped up. If I held the phone above my head, I got another half. Still not enough to support a phone call.

I pressed myself as far back as I could, then eyed the stackable body shelves. If I could just get a little higher . . . I tentatively poked a foot on the edge of the lowermost platform, careful not to get anybody on my shoe. I took a step up. And then another. And then I grinned down at my phone when it decided it could make a call.

And then I heard the weird, scraping sound of the undead coming back to life. My hackles went up, hot adrenaline sparking through me.

I jumped from the cart and launched it backward. I would like to say I barrel-rolled or did something equally as theatrical but what I did was sail through the air, arms outstretched, fingers clawed and desperate for something to hold on to. When I landed on the cement floor, I had the slick, cold plastic of body bags in each hand, the contents of each bag—and several others—pummeling me from above.

I howled.

I don't think my feet hit the ground as I jumped, and tossed my body into the door, screaming bloody murder.

"Pike! PIKE! Get me out of here! Get me the fuck out of here! I'm stuck!"

It seemed to take eons for Pike to hear me and loosen the door. When he did I ran out, circling the autopsy tables, relishing the way the room-temperature air burned at my frozen skin.

I felt Pike's eyes on me, curious, as I rubbed my arms and let the adrenaline drain from my body. "Where were you?" I finally hissed, eyes narrowed.

"I was outside. Standing guard. Just like you told me to be."

I couldn't fault him for doing as I'd told him, but I wanted to. "Why did you come in here?"

"You were taking forever, I had to pee, and then I heard you huffing and thumping. I thought maybe you were getting a little frisky with ol' Reg there."

He grinned and I recoiled, disgusted. "You're a big ass."

"And you're a big ol' side of beef locking yourself in the deep freeze. Did you find anything?"

"First of all, I didn't lock myself in the freezer. I shoved a book in the doorway so I wouldn't get stuck."

Pike made a show of looking all around for a book.

"Someone filched the book and shut the door on me."

Pike raised his eyebrows, though he didn't look the least bit convinced. "Is that so? Because I've been waiting out there," he said, jerking a thumb toward the hall. "And I happen to know for a fact that no one came in here."

I gaped. "Are you calling me a liar?"

"Of course not. I might be calling you a little bit embarrassed because you locked yourself in the fridge, but definitely not a liar."

The chill from the fridge had distinctly worn off and rage burned through me. Before I could open my eyes—or my fang-filled mouth—Pike was checking the bodies piled in the fridge. "Here's our friend Emerson."

He laid her out on the slab and unzipped her. I was surprised when a stab of emotion shot through me—I'm not sure if it was seeing Emerson laid out this way, or seeing Nicolette red-eyed and torn up over the death of her sister. Either way, the body was just a shell—I knew that better than anyone. But there was something pulling me.

"So what are we looking for?"

I hugged my arms across my chest. "Look behind her left ear."

Pike did as he was told and I watched his finger slide over Emerson's marble-still flesh. "Nothing."

I peered, and pointed. "See that tiny hole? Needle prick."

"Needle prick? What does that mean?"

"Reginald has one, too. Same place. It means that neither Reg nor Emerson died the way we thought they did."

Pike was fingering Emerson's chart and I could see his lips move as he read. That should have been enough for me to shake him off but there was something charming and sweet about the way his lips moved, little bursts of breath puffing at every other word. "Well, that's something they didn't say in the papers."

"What's that?"

"Drain cleaner."

I stiffened. "What?"

"They found drain cleaner in both of them."

"Why would someone inject—"

"It would cause pain, an arrhythmia at best, death at worst."

I stepped back. "Do I want to know how you know that?"

Pike snapped the file shut and got to work putting Reginald and Emerson back. "Probably not."

We were able to sneak right back out of the morgue—a happy coincidence for us, an unsettling lack in homeland security for the rest of the country. But, I supposed, as I brushed my dress back down over my thighs, maybe terrorists going on body raids wasn't exactly at threat level red.

It was one of those nights where everything about the city hummed and moved, but the city itself stayed impossibly still. The air didn't move and the moon hung in the sky, as pale and anemic as everything else that wilted in the heat.

"Okay," I said as we walked, "two people are injected with drain cleaner, then made to look like they've either committed suicide or been murdered."

"By you."

"What?"

Pike slurped the last bit of the purple ICEE he made us stop for through his straw. "First one looked like suicide, second one looked like a murder caused by you." He grinned, his teeth tinged purple.

"Thanks for pointing that out, Colombo." I frowned. "And we have nothing in the way of leads, do we?"

"Other than you trying to kill off the competition, no."

I spun, my finger a quarter-inch from his nose. "What did I say? Look at me." I jumped back, gave him a good chance to take in my self-styled ensemble. "I would have won that competition fair and square. Someone is out to get me."

Suddenly Pike was face to face with me and I could feel his hot breath breaking over my cheeks. "Then why hasn't he gotten you yet?"

Anger bubbled in my veins. "Because I'm a—"

"A what?" His eyes flashed.

I broke his gaze. "I don't need to tell you anything." I tried to turn away but his hand was around my arm, clamping down.

His warmth shot through my whole body and I remembered things. . . .

Another ink-black night where everything hung still and quiet in the oppressing heat. A rustle in the bushes and I was on the window sill, tucking my petticoats between my legs . . . I felt the air cut open when I dropped, my boots hitting the soft earth below my window. And he was there. He was just a shadow then but he was there—I didn't need to see him to feel him over every inch of my body, to feel the air sizzle with his vibrant electricity. His fingertips brushed my arm and they were ice cold but sent fire-hot prickles and every synapse firing—and then he closed the distance between us and his lips were on mine. Wanting, tasting. And I was young and I was thirsty and I had never felt this way before . . . then his lips left mine and trailed slowly, with feather-light kisses over my jaw and down my neck. I felt my pulse throb and his tongue circled it. My heart pounded and my head was filled. There was fire roaring through me and it was at my neck. I heard the pierce before I felt it. My virgin skin popped and his teeth sunk in. And when I closed my eyes, everything was dripping in the most vibrant shade of red. . . .

"Pike." I was breathing hard and trying to push the word past my teeth. Pike had me now, tonight, in this city, and I could feel his fingers pressing at the small of my back as I crushed against him, his hand cupping my chin, my cheek. The city cracked and came alive and I was distinctly aware of every horn honking, every New Yorker talking, yelling, laughing. Waves crashed. The world crashed when Pike's lips covered mine. I tried to pull back but his fingers dug into me and my entire body was exploding with things I hadn't felt since that last night, since that last moment when my own blood shot through my veins.

I could feel.

My entire body was on high alert and I felt the hot softness of Pike's wet lips. I felt his tongue nudge my mouth open and I could taste him.

And somewhere, there was blood.

Too close.

My eyes were on the vein throbbing on Pike's neck.

"No," I said, pulling back, pushing against his chest.

"Don't go." Pike pulled me back to him and I felt the word on my earlobe as his mouth opened and he nibbled.

My body throbbed. My need deepened. I pushed away—tore myself away—from Pike and stumbled backward and then started to run.

"I know what you are." Pike's words tumbled out and hit every wall of the dismal little alley.

I stopped, turned. "What are you talking about?"

He took a slow step forward, his eyes still hard, pinning me. "I know what you are, Nina."

I licked my lips and all the energy, the heat that had surged through my body, was gone. I was hollow again, and cold. "I don't know what you think you know about me."

Pike licked his lips, bee-stung and red from our kiss. "You're a vampire."

I turned my back and left Pike standing alone in the alleyway.

I walked the rest of the way home and Pike didn't follow. I kept my thoughts focused on the murders so I wouldn't hear his voice reverberate through my head. *A vampire.* I knew it, I flaunted it—in the Underworld, *natch*—but hearing the word come out of his mouth . . .

I sunk my key into the lock and shoved into the apartment vestibule. The overhead light was buzzing and swinging lightly, illuminating the squarish, brown-paper-wrapped package on top of my mail slot. The sender had used a whole spool of tape and twine and addressed the thing simply to

"LaShay." I shoved it under my arm and carried it to my apartment.

"Hey, where've you been?" Vlad wrinkled his nose. "You smell like morgue."

I flopped down on the couch.

"What's with you?"

"Pike knows."

Vlad finished his blood bag with a mighty suck and pushed himself up to a sitting position. "Pike knows who the murderer is? That's good because all this death and dying is really ruining my vacation."

"No." I blinked, staring straight ahead. "Pike knows about me."

I didn't need to fill him in; the knowing flashed across Vlad's eyes. "He knows you're a vampire? Does he know I am?"

I swung my head. "I doubt it."

"So we have a murderer on the loose, a guy who knows you're a card-carrying member of the undead. . . . How did he find out? And, he's not going to go all Van Helsing on us, is he? Because we'd need special approval from the UDA to take him out and you know who handles that paperwork, right? Kale. She'd never approve me. Hell, she'd call Pike and leave a trail of breadcrumbs or Hostess CupCakes right to me."

I swallowed. "I don't know how he knows. He just—he just said it. 'I know what you are.'"

Vlad crushed his blood bag and tossed it onto the coffee table. "Ominous."

"Vlad, what am I supposed to do about this? A breather knows about me."

Vlad shrugged, finding the remote control and aiming at the TV. "I don't know. Kill him, I guess."

Something washed over me and it took me a good minute

to realize that it was pain. I didn't want to kill Pike. I didn't want to be what I was.

"I—I need some air."

Something was welling inside me, pressing against my chest and making my eyes sting by the time I crested the steps down to the apartment vestibule.

And then everything changed.

Two of the ancient windows were cracked open; I could see there was a gentle breeze outside but the air in the vestibule itself was staid and heavy but crackled with a weird, electric energy. I sniffed. The metallic scent was sharp and distinctive and my whole body went on high alert—my fangs sharpening and elongating, saliva rushing toward my tongue.

There was blood in the air.

It stank of injury and heat with just the slightest tinge of something fresh. I took a step. The energy-filled trail stopped dead on the bottom floor landing and so did I, spinning slowly in the darkness, and finally cussing at myself for being a scared little girl. And then I heard the whimper.

It was soft, barely a breath, but there was something in the single syllable that was anguished. I stiffened.

"Hello?"

There was a breath of pregnant silence and then two ragged, heavy breaths. "Help?"

I turned toward the voice. "Where are you? Who are you?"

"Please." The word tore at my gut and I felt my human side taking over—someone in pain, in anguish—someone reaching out. *Because she doesn't know that I'm a monster.*

I swept the thought out of my mind as quickly as it came and closed my eyes, concentrating on the breathing. Ragged breath in, ragged breath out. I took a step. Ragged breath—and suddenly the vestibule was heavy with the sweet metallic stench of blood. A drip of saliva rolled down my throat.

"Tell me where you are."

"I'm here," she said, "By the stairs. I—I don't think I can move."

I crept along the stairwell and banister. The blood scent grew stronger each step the light grew darker. I was swallowing furiously, trying not to think about how delicate the scent was, how delicious. The way it felt when fangs punctured flesh—warm, soft—like berries popping, flooding your mouth with delicious, rich juice.

My heart thudded and my stomach lurched, growled. I was ready to flee, to run back upstairs and lock myself in my apartment but then—

"Nina?"

Nicolette lay in a heap on the floor, her body impossibly bent, her face fragile and pale. Her thick, cracked lips trembled and moisture surrounded her milky eyes. "Please help me."

I swallowed and bent down to her, bending my head from the heady smell of fresh blood. I watched my own hand reach out, shakily touch Nicolette on the shoulder, my fingers barely grazing the girl's torn flesh.

"What happened?" It was my voice, but I wasn't sure that I had spoken.

"Someone attacked me," Nicolette said, her voice a low whisper. "Is he gone?"

I looked over my shoulder and rose to my full height. "I'll make sure."

I knew that her attacker wasn't there. I could smell every scent in the vestibule—layers upon layers of Clorox and urine, the cloying, salty smell of humanity coming through day after day and hour after hour—and the sinful, beckoning scent of Nicolette's fresh blood.

I pushed open the double doors and bent my head out, sucking in lungfuls of night air. Soon I was coughing—and crying. I wanted to help her. I wanted to taste her.

"Is he gone?"

I could hear Nicolette shifting on the floor and I sprang toward her, my arms reaching out, doing my best to gingerly touch her clothes, the banister, anything that wasn't soaked in her blood.

"Are you okay?"

Nicolette stood now and shakily came out of the darkness. I sucked in a breath.

Her long blond hair was matted, knotted with blood that seemed to come from nowhere and everywhere at the same time. One eye was already blooming with purple bruises and angry red scratches, her lashes disappearing in the swell. Tears rolled down her cheeks and her flesh showed underneath—a pink and delicate contrast to the smudged dirt and dried blood everywhere else.

"Who did this to you?"

Nicolette lurched toward me and crumpled in my arms. I stiffened, feeling the sticky warmth of her blood on my skin and when she started to cry—great, hiccupping sobs—I was able to hold her against me and hold my breath. When it got to be too much I chanced a tiny breath, my nose a quarter-inch above a gash that crossed the side of Nicolette's head. I recoiled just slightly, an antiseptic stench coming from her unbroken skin.

"I'm going to call nine-one-one."

I went to reach for my phone but Nicolette's arm shot out, her hand grabbing my wrist, her grip surprisingly strong. "No, please don't, Nina. I'm scared."

I patted Nicolette's shoulder awkwardly. "Don't worry, sweetie. Everything will be okay." I had no idea whether or not it would be—and betted toward the latter when I realized I had left my phone in the apartment. "I'm just going to use the emergency line down here, okay? I'm not going anywhere." I gingerly began to extricate myself from Nicolette. She whimpered lightly but shifted her weight away from me and I scurried across the tile. My hand was wrapped around the telephone receiver when I heard Nicolette's bones cracking as she stood. At the same second I turned, something heavy smashed across the side of my head. I felt my skin pucker and gash, felt the crush of my browbone and nose. The sheer force knocked me backward and I heard the clatter of the telephone receiver as it fell to the ground; I felt the cool glass of the door as I slumped against it. A horrid clanging sound reverberated through my skull. There was screaming and—squawking?

I wasn't sure which one—if either—that I was doing so I worked to pull my eyes open. I needed to protect Nicolette—frail, battered Nicolette.

Nicolette, who was vaulting directly toward me, absolute hate in her eyes, knuckles burning white as she gripped a length of metal pipe.

"Nicolette?"

She bared her teeth and let out the most heinous banshee-like scream I'd ever heard. My hands went up instinctively and I grabbed the pipe as it sliced through the air toward me. She was basically growling now, teeth clenched, chin shiny with saliva. I held the pipe but Nicolette was surprisingly strong. She lurched and caught me square in the gut with the sole of her foot; I crashed through the glass door, shards catching the moonlight and dancing like little stars. My shoulder blades slapped against the concrete and Nicolette wasted no time, dropping the pipe and clawing at my neck.

"What the hell is wrong with you?"

"Nothing is wrong with me!" she spat. "Why won't you fucking die? You were on fire—and frozen—and now—die!"

Her hands went to me again and I squirmed. She grabbed a fistful of my hair and yanked until I heard strands breaking. She pulled her arm back to show me my own hair, no longer attached to my scalp. Her grin was wide and terrifyingly maniacal.

"You bitch!"

Wallop me with a metal pipe, sure. Try and choke me? Whatever. Mess with my hair? I will *seriously* end you.

I felt my sharpening fangs and unholy rage roar through me. I was about to lunge—and finish—Nicolette when a shriek cut through the night and my winged nemesis dive-bombed. I was sure he was some sort of beaked bastion of hell answering Nicolette's beckon until he skidded over her forehead, talons extending, cutting wide gashes across her cheeks and nose.

She recoiled and swatted at the thing but it was gone instantly. I used the distraction to buck Nicolette off of me, and suddenly Pike was there and he was gripping her, dragging her away from me.

"She's crazy!" I screamed.

"You're crazy!" Nicolette's eyes were on fire.

"What happened?" Pike yelled, still holding Nicolette back.

"She attacked me!" We were both pointing fingers, but I was gaping.

I paused and stared at Pike. "Wait, where the hell did you come from?"

"Kill her!" Nicolette screamed. "She's a thief just like my damn sister!"

"You—"

"I'm the designer," she spat. "Not you, not Emerson, or Fairfield. Me!"

"Because you got the Barbie Design Studio," Pike said.

"And Emerson stole it!"

"So you killed her?" I asked.

Rage roiled through Nicolette's body. "She stole everything!"

Nicolette's screams were drowned out by the wailing of sirens and before she could finish her psychotic reasoning, police officers and paramedics were flooding out of their cars and rushing toward us.

Moyer was one of them. He jutted his chin toward Pike. "You sure about her?"

"She admitted it."

Hopkins raced in with a pair of cuffs and Nicolette was subdued and led away, though she was still squirming and screaming, doing her best to kick and bite poor Hopkins.

"Hey, you okay?" Pike touched my arm gently.

"How did you—oh, God, the drain cleaner. I smelled it all over her but I didn't put two and two together."

A sad smile played at the edges of his lips. "Why would you?"

"Well, you obviously put something together or did you just happen to—" I happened to glance down at Pike's hand, still soft on my arm. His fingernails were tinged with the slightest bit of deep red. I narrowed my eyes, unease flooding my body. "You know what I am because of what you are, huh?"

Pike's eyes grew and he led me away from the officers checking out the scene. "Yeah."

"And here I thought Emerson was the unholy one."

He looked genuinely offended. "I'm not unholy. I'm an ancient legend—my family has been shifting for hundreds of generations."

"Shifting? So what are you—?" I paused, glancing down at those nails again and then backing away. "No. Oh, no. No."

"What?"

"You're the bird. You're the fucking black bird, aren't you?"

"Crow."

"Diseased flying rodent . . ."

Pike's lip curled into a snarl. "Those are pigeons. And you should talk! Bats are, like, the most rabid animals in history."

I was suddenly more offended by Pike than I was by Nicolette's attempted thrashing. "I do not turn into a bat!"

Moyer stepped over, his bushy eyebrows curved down in confusion. "Ugh, are you guys through here? We're just about to take Nicolette downtown. Apparently, she planned to take out all three of the competitors and launch her own fashion show at the end of it."

Pike grimaced.

"Well, it does make sense. Her cuts on Emerson's fabric were impeccable—except for going against the grain."

Both Moyer and Pike gaped at me and I shrugged. "Just an observation."

"Anyway," Moyer said to me. "Good thing she didn't get her hands on you."

My hand immediately went to my smashed nose and crushed browbone that had since healed.

Love that vampire super-speed thing.

"So," Pike said after Moyer departed. "I think we make a pretty good crime-fighting team."

"What? Bird Boy and Kick Ass?"

Pike cocked a brow. "You know Bird Boy just saved your ass."

"Yeah, well." I paused, considering. "It took you long enough."

Dear Reader,

I hope you enjoyed *High Stakes*. Though famous in her own right, Nina LaShay is best known for her bloodless barbs and eternally chic wardrobe at the San Francisco branch of the Underworld Detection Agency. She's also roommate to coworker/chocolate pinwheel connoisseur Sophie Lawson. Sophie, Nina, hot fallen angel Alex Grace, sexy Guardian Will Sherman, and the ultra-stinky sex-crazed troll Steve do their best to keep above-world demons at bay while they keep the Underworld demons under wraps. Sophie may do the bulk of the crime-fighting and down-and-dirty detective work, but Nina is always by her side to lend a hand—or a fang—and as you now know, she always looks fashionably chic doing it.

Keep in touch with Nina, Sophie, and the entire Underworld gang with The Underworld Detection Agency Chronicles series. Watch for the fifth book in the series, *Under a Spell,* hitting shelves August 2013!

Hannah Jayne

GREAT BOOKS,
GREAT SAVINGS!